CONSEQUENCES

Persephone Book Nº13
Published by Persephone Books Ltd 2000

Reprinted 2006

First published by Hodder and Stoughton 1919

© 2000 The Estate of E.M. Delafield

Preface © Nicola Beauman 2000

Endpapers taken from an 1896 Silver Studio block-printed
cotton called 'Thistle' sold as a Liberty Art Fabric,
reproduced by courtesy of the Whitworth Art Gallery,
University of Manchester.

Typeset in ITC Baskerville by Keystroke,
Jacaranda Lodge, Wolverhampton

Colour by Banbury Litho

Printed and bound by Biddles Ltd,
King's Lynn

ISBN 1 903155 029

Persephone Books Ltd
59 Lamb's Conduit Street
London WC1N 3NB
0207 242 9292

www. persephonebooks.co.uk

CONSEQUENCES

by

E. M. DELAFIELD

✣✣✣✣✣✣✣✣✣✣✣

with a new preface by

NICOLA BEAUMAN

PERSEPHONE BOOKS
LONDON

DEDICATED TO M.P.P.
AND, IN SPITE OF AIR RAIDS, TO
THE PLEASANT MEMORY OF OUR
WINTER IN LONDON,
1917–18

CONTENTS

PREFACE

E.M. Delafield, best known for *The Diary of a Provincial Lady* (1930), a witty, wry, perceptive view of everyday life in the English countryside, made one theme particularly her own: the futility and emptiness of a society which envisaged no other future for young women except marriage.

The heroine of *Consequences* (1919) is twelve when the book begins in 1889 and is being brought up in true Victorian fashion in a large nursery in Bayswater – Victorian in that she is trained to be unthinkingly obedient and to conform absolutely to the precepts of her elders. And her nursery was Victorian in yet one other respect. She, like E.M. Delafield herself, was being brought up 'to believe that it was something between a minor tragedy and a major disgrace, for a girl to remain unsought in marriage after her twentieth birthday.'

Alex Clare, who is imperceptive and emotionally clumsy, endures a girlhood which in no way prepares her for the hurdles ahead; yet, with some subtlety, E.M. Delafield shows us that other young girls were equally unprepared but were nevertheless able to adapt. Her sister Barbara, for example, has roughly the same upbringing and education (although she is spared a convent because her mother never forgave the nuns for returning Alex to her with chilblains) but immediately she comes out seems already to understand the rules by which she should play society's game. Alex never understands, and has no hope of ever doing so since her education in things that really mattered was non-existent, her parents are not prepared to talk to her as an equal, and she is unlucky or clumsy enough never to make friends who will explain anything to her. However, because she knew that all life led to 'coming out', she is at first confident that the muddles would sort themselves out:

> It seemed to Alex that when she joined the mysterious ranks of grown-up people everything would be different. She never doubted that with long dresses and piled-up hair, her whole personality would change, and the meaningless chaos of life reduce itself to some comprehensible solution.

The theme of *Consequences* is that Alex is let down by everyone around her because no-one ever takes the trouble to make life comprehensible to her. It is a book that is – by implication – deeply critical both of the moral order and of religion ritual (not perhaps of God, or even the worship of God *per se*, but certainly of the ritual involved in worship). It criticises rituals ranging from the harsh rules governing the lives of girls at boarding school, to Lady Clare's not seeing her children except at proscribed times of day, to Nurse's absurd strictures and lack of loving-kindness, to the near-sadism of life in the convent.

This is an angry book, angrier, indeed, than any of E.M. Delafield's others, and for a reason: its author, who had worked as a nurse throughout the First World War, made her own friends and earned her own living, felt, at the age of twenty-eight, confident enough to express the anger she felt with her mother. The diatribe contained within *Consequences* is in essence a diatribe against the constraints of the Victorian family and was part of the anti-Victorian explosion that began to be expressed at the end of the First World War and was so famously expressed in Lytton Strachey's *Eminent Victorians* (1918); in some ways it is a scream of sheer horror against Victorianism. Hence E.M. Delafield back-dated her book to 1889, the year before she was born, moves onwards until 1898 when Alex is twenty-one and concludes in 1908, ten years later. There is a very strong sense in the novel of constraint and time-warp, but also of time moving on, of change and new freedoms for those lucky enough to be born at a time when they can benefit from them. Thus, as one of the few spots of optimism in the book (the others are the genuine warmth of Alex's sister-in-law Violet and the kindness with which the Malden Road landlady offers to light a fire), we are shown the youngest Clare child, Pamela, behaving with a late Victorian, soon-to-be Edwardian freedom that Alex, still imprisoned in mid-Victorian conventions, envies but cannot emulate.

The 1890s was an era and a way of life that E.M. Delafield knew at first hand because the ten years of her childhood had spanned it from end to end. Her life, like the fictional Alex's, had been constrained by nannies, upper middle-class social conventions, Belgravia (the Clare family, however, live north of the park, in Bayswater), the unreality of nursery life, repressive convent schools – before, suddenly, almost overnight, she was expected to display herself on the marriage market and to be married before she was twenty. As E.M. Delafield was to write in *Thank Heaven Fasting* (1932), '[Monica] could never, looking backwards, remember a time when she had not known that a woman's failure or success in life depended entirely upon whether or not she succeeded in getting a husband. It was not, even, a question of marrying well . . . any husband at all was better than none.' Nor was it possible to question this assumption, since to do this, or indeed to question anything, was disloyal. Monica, like her creator,

> belonged to a generation that was not taught to think clearly, and to a family that lived under the obsession of the word 'loyal'. It was not 'loyal' to think for oneself, to question anything said or done by one's parents, or to admit that one was not happy at home.

Monica remains loyal and yet manages to marry. But by the time E.M. Delafield herself was twenty-one, 'the only proposal of marriage that had come my way was from a youth of the type described, correctly, by my mother as "boys who don't *mean* anything."' Her failure in this regard was one of the reasons why, the moment she had come of age, and with her mother re-married and living abroad, she chose to enter a convent; the other reasons were that she really wanted to work but was denied the chance; and that as a Catholic schoolgirl she had lived in various convents and deluded herself into thinking that she felt at home within their walls. But the main reason was that, unmarried, she felt unable to lead a normal life.

It is thus true to say that the theme of the marriage market – its constraints, its absurdities, its cruelties – was the *leitmotif* that was to run throughout E.M. Delafield's thirty or so novels. Even *The Diary of a Provincial Lady*, which first appeared in the feminist weekly *Time and Tide*, was simply another way of pronouncing on the absurdity of the conventions that forced married women to undergo the various humiliations depicted within its pages. Open it at random and you will read about planting indoor bulbs, going to cocktail parties, deciding what to wear for a particular occasion, ordering meals. Yet running through it all is the unspoken assumption that none of this is necessary, that we are all participating in some ridiculous social ritual. Why have indoor bulbs? Why stand up drink in hand yabbering at someone one has never met before and will never meet again? Why have cold meat and redcurrant jelly and potatoes and salad when, if given the choice, most of us would far rather eat bread and cheese and a tomato sitting on the window seat with a book? And so on. We all participate in the ritual, for we all wish to be paid-up members of the human race and, from infancy onwards, we learn to conform to the social conventions which surround us; but unless we choose to try and destroy the entire structure of the society we have been born into, to rebel against its wisdoms, it is surely better – or at any rate E.M. Delafield thought it was better – to laugh at one's everyday life rather than to relapse into impotent, cataleptic depression.

Herein, I think, lies a clue as to why so many of the books Persephone is reprinting are, ultimately, extraordinarily sad. On one level they are merely readable, interesting, funny, thought-provoking. But when one finishes them one often feels very moved. One reason for this is, surely, that fiction which is not overtly feminist, which, in other words, describes women's lives without openly railing against their flaws and restrictions but makes the reader understand them nevertheless, this kind of fiction is almost more upsetting than straightforwardly, politically feminist fiction. Ellen in *Someone at a Distance* leads a circumscribed life about which she is, however, completely happy – then it is destroyed by the pride and stupidity of the husband who has himself circum-scribed her all her adult life; Ruth in *Fidelity* becomes a social outcast, shunned by her family and friends, because she puts (forbidden) love before conventional behaviour; Lester and Evangeline in *The Home-Maker* only find personal happiness by behaving so unconventionally that they have to keep the mechanism for so doing completely secret from their small town.

In all these novels, indeed in virtually every Persephone book, women are starved of personal freedom but choose to conform. They do so for love of their families and, just as much, from an unwillingness to tackle society head on; and they take refuge in humour, in self-deprecation, in 'keeping busy', in 'mustn't grumble'. Yet, and this is a very important yet, these books are still deeply feminist. Each and every one of them is asking – does it have to be like this?

In the preface I wrote to the 1984 edition of *The Diary of a Provincial Lady* I made this point, mentioned that 'when convention precludes [E.M. Delafield's heroines] from widening their horizons, they can at least be powerful at home', and then rather naively remarked, having described the Provincial Lady's endless attempts to find – and keep – a cook: 'We may wonder why provincial ladies did not simply do the cooking and the housework themselves: their daughters have, after all, managed.' The naivety was my failure of historical perspective, my lack of empathy with the complete impossibility of this happening unless and until there was absolutely no choice bar starving. (Hence the radical, and almost political, quality of a book Persephone will publish soon after *Consequences* – *House-Bound* (1942) by Winifred Peck, in which a middle-class Edinburgh housewife decides to manage without a cook. Her decision was infinitely more radical – and is shown as such – than I could possibly have imagined when I glibly suggested that the Provincial Lady should have considered doing the same thing.)

The concept of putting up with things, of staunchness, of remaining patient and good-humoured, is one that most women share and that runs through so much twentieth century English women's fiction. It is not a feminist attitude, however. This is brought home to us in a recently published feminist dictionary, in which E.M. Delafield is at least allowed an entry and *Consequences* approved for being one of its author's favourite among her books. The writer of the entry observes that:

> Her principal characters are all drawn from the narrow world in which she herself moved, and though she consistently excoriates the emptiness and futility in contemporary women's lives, bound as they invariably were by husbands, children and domestic responsibilities, she stops short of advocating any drastic solutions. However much her heroines may bewail their lack of freedom or intellectual stimulation, Delafield herself seems ultimately to advocate stoical endurance.

I never understand how feminist critics who 'excoriate' writers for being class-bound, reconcile this with the mantra of creative writing classes – write about what you know. Does this mean the conforming middle classes should never write books? E.M. Delafield happened to be a middle-class wife and she loved her children too much to run away from the restrictions of life as she knew it. (Many 'feminist' critics seem to forget that, until as late as the 1970s, a freedom-seeking wife who left her husband was not at all certain to be given custody of her children.) So E.M. Delafield wrote about her life, laughed at it, whinged about it in an always understated way. And so, it is true, she stopped short of 'advocating any drastic solutions.' This does not, however, undervalue her work – or make it less tragic.

Because, underlying the superficial humour of so many of E.M. Delafield's books, there is indeed a layer of tragedy – if one can accept that tragedy happens to the comfortable middle classes, and if one cannot accept this one can simply call it sadness. It is sad, to say the least, that the Provincial Lady and her husband only communicate on the most superficial of levels. It is sad that the women in *The War Workers* (1918) are so needlessly cruel to each other. It is sad that Monica in *Thank Heaven Fasting* can see no possible life for herself unless she finds a man, any man. It is sad that the couple in *Nothing is Safe* (1937) carelessly divorce and thereby destroy their children's lives. It is not perhaps tragic. But it is certainly sad.

Thus *Consequences*: the complete lack of comprehension and sensitivity and indeed love, with which Alex, the heroine, is treated by those around her is, if not tragic, in any case deeply sad. Indeed, the miseries of her life may be seen in a worse light than ever when the reader of this Persephone edition has finished the novel and read the two contemporary book reviews in the Appendix. (They are printed at the end because, unforgivably, they give away the plot.) Then she or he will realise, even more forcibly, that contemporary readers themselves had apparently little empathy with Alex, that they thought E.M. Delafield was exaggerating and that no-one can possibly get it as consistently and persistently wrong as Alex does.

They can of course, and they do. But if the modern age can congratulate itself on one thing it is that misfits are – often, if not always – handled better than this. Alex would, quite possibly, have had some psychiatric help; she would have had it explained to her that the fault was not entirely in her but in the unyieldingness of Nurse, Lady Clare and the nuns at her school; in essence, she would have been helped to understand herself and thus to value herself. Even more importantly, she would have been directed towards a career – because it would be recognised that Alex was not the marrying type – why should she have been? – and she might perhaps have looked after horses, or worked in a library or in an orphanage, anywhere indeed where her deep need to be of service could be channelled into something more useful than futile adoration of some chosen person.

Thus, for me, and – I hope – for Persephone readers, *Consequences* is a deeply feminist book. E.M. Delafield may be stopping short of 'advocating any drastic solution' – but only because she was a realist through and through. What she is saying is: this is how it was; empathise, sigh, groan, but accept that, with only a few exaggerations, my heroine's life was like that and that nothing, absolutely nothing, could then be done about it – unless by some miracle a disciple of Sigmund Freud had arrived from Vienna, or, equally miraculously, Alex had happened to meet somebody constructive and humane like a nurse or a market gardener or a suffragist (for, as the reviewer in the *New York Times* remarked shrewdly: 'One feels that it was largely from such neurotic, defeated womanhood, chafing against its uselessness, as is represented in Alex Clare, that the militant suffragists recruited their explosive forces in the years before the war.')

Despite its tragic overtones, *Consequences* shares many characteristics with E.M. Delafield's other books. It is funny, sardonic, perceptive, mostly written in readably short paragraphs rather than in the dense verbosity of the three-decker Victorian novels. It explores the theme that runs through so many of her novels of children being confined to the nursery and kept in ignorance of the ways of the worlds before being suddenly catapulted into adulthood. Where *Consequences* is different is that it describes a girl who cannot understand grown-up rituals, fails to conform to them, is shunned by the little world in which she is confined and is forced to find another. It is a novel that has a lot to teach us about ourselves as people (for there can be few who do not see *something* of themselves in Alex), about the struggle of the young to reach contented maturity, and above all about the constraints imposed in the name of social convention and order. The questions running throughout the book are, why were young women reared for no other purpose than to be kept by someone else and give birth to the next generation? And have we made things any better for ourselves now? E.M. Delafield, who wrote in a white heat of anger and compassion about the waste of women's lives, may not have had the answer to these questions, and nor may we – but the novel gives us a great deal to think about.

Nicola Beauman

CONSEQUENCES

BOOK I

CHAPTER ONE

THE GAME OF CONSEQUENCES

The firelight flickered on the nursery wall, and the children sat round the table, learning the new game, which the nursery- maid said they would like ever so, directly they understood it.

'I understand it already,' said Alex, the eldest, tossing her head proudly. 'Look, Barbara, you fold the piece of paper like this, and then give it to Cedric, because he's next to you, and I give mine to you, and Emily gives hers to me. That's right, isn't it, Emily?'

'Quite right, Miss Alex; what a clever girl, to be sure. Here, Master Baby, you can play with me. You're too little to do it all by yourself.'

'He isn't Baby any more. We've got to call him Archie now. The new little sister is Baby,' said Alex dictatorially.

She liked always to be the one to give information, and Emily had only been with them a little while. The children's own nurse would have told her to mind her own business, or to wait till she was asked, before teaching her grandmother, but Emily said complacently:

3

'To be sure, Miss Alex! and such a big boy as Master Archie is, too. Now you all write down a name of a gentleman.'

'What gentleman?' asked Cedric judicially. He was a little boy of eight, with serious grey eyes and a good deal of dignity.

'Why, any gentleman. Someone you all know.'

'I know, I know.'

Alex, always the most easily excited of them all, scribbled on her piece of paper and began to bounce up and down on her chair.

'Hurry up, Barbara. You're so slow.'

'I don't know who to put.'

Alex began to whisper, and Barbara at once said:

'Nurse doesn't allow us to whisper. It's bad manners.'

'You horrid little prig!'

Alex was furious. Barbara's priggishness always put her into a temper, because she felt it, unconsciously, to be a reflection on her own infallibility as the eldest.

'Miss Barbara,' said Emily angrily, 'it's not for you to say what Nurse allows or doesn't allow; *I'm* looking after you now. The idea, indeed!'

Barbara's pale, pointed little face grew very red, but she did not cry as Alex, in spite of her twelve years, would almost certainly have cried at such a snub.

She set her mouth vindictively and shot a very angry look at Alex out of her blue eyes. Then she wrote something on the slip of paper, shielding it with her hand so that her sister could not read it.

Cedric was printing in large capitals, easily legible, but no one was interested in what Cedric wrote.

There was a good deal of whispering between Emily and little Archie, and then the papers were folded up once more and passed round the table again.

'But when do we see what we've written?' asked Alex impatiently.

'Not till the end of the game, then we read them out. That's where the fun comes in,' said Emily.

It was a long while before the papers were done, and most of the children found it very difficult to decide what *he* said to *her*, what she replied, and what the world said. But at last even Barbara, always lag-last, folded her slip, very grimy and thumb-marked, and put it with the others into Emily's apron.

'Now then,' giggled the nursery-maid, 'pull one out, Master Archie, and I'll see what it says.'

Archie snatched at a paper and they opened it.

'Listen!' said Emily.

'The Queen met Master Archie – whoever of you put the Queen?'

'Cedric!' cried the other children.

Cedric's loyalty to his Sovereign was a by-word in the nursery.

'Well, the Queen met Master Archie in the Park. She said to him, "No," and he answered her, "You dirty little boy, go 'ome and wash your face." Well, if that didn't ought to be the other way round!'

'I wish it was me she'd met in the Park,' said Cedric sombrely. 'I might have gone back to Buckingham Palace with her and –'

'Go on, Emily, go on!' cried Alex impatiently. 'Don't listen to Cedric. What comes next?'

'The consequences was – whatever's here?' said Emily, pretending an inability to decipher her own writing.

'Well, I never! The consequences was, a wedding-ring. Whoever went and thought of that now? And the world said –'

The nursery door opened, and Alex shrieked, 'Oh, finish it – quick!'

She knew instinctively that it was Nurse, and that Nurse would be certain to disapprove of the new game.

'Don't you make that noise, Alex,' said Nurse sharply. 'You'll disturb the baby with your screaming.'

For a moment Alex wondered if the game was to be allowed to proceed, but Barbara, well known to be Nurse's favourite, must needs say to her in an amiable little voice, such as she never used to her brothers and sister:

'Emily's been teaching us such a funny new game, Nurse. Come and play with us.'

'I've no time to play, as you very well know, with all your clothes wanting looking over the way they do,' Nurse told her complacently. 'What's the game?'

Alex kicked Barbara under the table, but without much hope, and at the same moment Cedric remarked very distinctly:

'It is called Consequences, and Archie met the Queen in the Park. I wish it had been me instead.'

'Well!' exclaimed Nurse. 'That's the way you do when my back's turned, Miss Emily, teaching them such vulgar, nonsensical games as that. Never did I hear – now give me those papers this minute.'

She did not wait to be given anything, but snatched the little slips out of Emily's apron and threw them on to the fire.

'I'm not going to have no Consequences in *my* nursery, and don't you believe it!' remarked Nurse.

But omnipotent though Nurse was, in the eyes of the Clare children, she could not altogether compass this feat.

There were consequences of all sorts.

Cedric, who was obstinate, and Barbara, also obstinate and rather sly as well, continued to play at the new game in corners by themselves, refusing to admit Alex to their society because she told them that they were playing it all wrong. She knew that they were not playing it as Emily had taught them, and was prepared to set them right, although she felt uncertain, in the depths of her heart, as to whether she herself could remember it all. But at least she knew more than Barbara, who was silly and a copy-cat, or than Cedric, who had concentrated on the possibilities the game presented to him of a hypothetical encounter between himself and his Sovereign. The game for Cedric consisted in the ever-lengthening conversation which took place under the headings of what he said to her, and what she replied. When Her Majesty proceeded, under Cedric's laborious pencil, to invite him to drive her in her own carriage-and-pair to Buckingham Palace, Alex said scornfully that Cedric was a silly little boy, and of course the Queen wouldn't say *that*. To which Cedric turned a perfectly deaf ear, and continued slowly to evolve amenities eminently satisfactory to his admiration for Her

Majesty. Alex went away, shrugging her shoulders, but secretly she knew that Cedric's indifference had got the better of her. However much she might laugh, with the other children, or sometimes even, in a superior way, with the grown-ups, when the children went into the drawing-room, at Cedric's slowness, and his curious fashion of harping upon one idea at a time, Alex was subconsciously aware of Cedric as a force, and one which could, ultimately, always defeat her own diffused, unbalanced energies. If anyone laughed at Alex, or despised one of her many enthusiasms, she would quickly grow ashamed of it, and try to pretend that she had never really been in earnest. In the same way, she would affect qualities and instincts which did not belong to her, with the hope of attracting, and of gaining affection.

But Cedric went his own way, as genuinely undisturbed by Nurse's scoldings and hustlings as by his elder sister's mockery, which had its origin in her secret longing to prove to herself, in spite of her own inmost convictions, that she was the dominant spirit in her little world.

It always made her angry when Cedric left her gibes unanswered, not from a desire to provoke her further, but simply from his complete absorption in the matter in hand, and his utter indifference to Alex' comments.

'Don't you hear what I say?' Alex asked sharply.

'No,' said Cedric baldly. 'I'm not listening. Don't interrupt me, Alex.'

'You're playing it all wrong – you and Barbara. Two silly little babies,' she cried angrily and incoherently. 'And it's a stupid, vulgar game. Nurse said so.'

Although Alex had been the most enthusiastic of them all when Emily had first taught her the game, she had at once begun to think it vulgar when Nurse condemned it.

She would have nothing more to do with 'Consequences.' It was quite likely that in a few days Barbara would get into one of her priggish, perverse moods, and in a fit of temper with Cedric go and tell Nurse that he was still indulging in the forbidden pastime. Alex thought she might as well be out of it.

She was in trouble often enough in the nursery. Nurse always took Barbara's part against her, and accused her of being violent and over-bearing, and then Lady Isabel, the children's mother, would send for her to her room while she dressed for dinner, and say complainingly:

'Alex, why do you quarrel so with the others? I shall send you to school, if you can't be happy with Barbara at home.'

'Oh, don't send me to school, mummy.'

'Not if you're good.'

'I will be good, really, I will.'

'Very well, my child. Now ring for Hawkins, or I shall be late.'

'May I stay and watch you put on your diamond things, mummy? Do let me.'

And Lady Isabel always laughed, and let her stay, so that Alex eventually went back to the nursery with an elated sense of having been very good, and accorded privileges which never fell to the lot of self-righteous Barbara.

She knew she was her mother's favourite, because she was the eldest, and was often sent for to the drawing-room when there were people there. Barbara, of course, was too ugly to go much to the drawing-room. Alex would toss her own mane of silky brown curls, and draw herself up conceitedly, as she thought of Barbara's pale face, and thin, attenuated ringlets. Besides, Lady Isabel had said that Barbara really mustn't come down again when 'people' were there until her second teeth had put in their tardy appearance. Even Cedric, though acclaimed as 'quaint' and 'solemn' by his mother's friends, was too apt to make disconcerting comments on their sparkling conversation, and would return to the nursery in disgrace. Alex' only rival for downstairs favour was little Archie, who was only four, and at present a very pretty little boy. But he was too small for Alex ever to feel jealous of him. The new baby, christened with pomp in the big Catholic Church at the end of the Square, Pamela Isabel, was, so far, a negligible quantity in the nursery world.

She slept in the little room called the inner nursery, most of the day, and was only with the others when they were taken into the Park or to play in the Square garden. Then Emily pushed the big pram that contained the slumbering Pamela, and Nurse grasped the hands of Barbara and Archie and dragged them over the crossings.

Cedric, by Nurse's express orders, always walked just in front of her with Alex, and unwillingly submitted to having his hand held by his sister.

'Not that I trust Alex for common-sense,' Nurse was careful to explain, 'not a yard, but so long as they're together I can keep an eye on both, and see they don't get under no hansom's feet. That boy's spectacles are too downright uncanny for me to let him cross the road alone.'

For Cedric was obliged to wear a large pair of round spectacles, without which he could only see things that were very close to his eyes. He even had another, different, pair for reading, which seemed to Alex an exaggerated precaution, likely to increase Cedric's sense of his own importance.

'Well,' said Cedric. 'You have a plate, and I haven't.'

Alex' plate was an instrument of torture designed to push back two prominent front teeth. It not only hurt her and kept her awake at night, but was very disfiguring besides, and she passionately envied Barbara, who at nine years old still had only gaps where her front teeth should have been.

'Of course,' Alex would sometimes declare grandly, repeating what she had heard Lady Isabel say, 'Barbara is dreadfully backward. She's such a baby for her age. *I'm* very old for my age.'

But she only said this in the drawing-room, where it would provoke kindly laughter or perhaps interested comment. In the nursery, Nurse never suffered any airs and graces, as she called them, and would pounce on Alex and shake her at the least hint of any such nonsense.

'Just you wait till you're sent to a good strict school, my lady, and see what you'll get then,' she told her threateningly.

'I'm not going to school. Mummy said I shouldn't go if I was good.'

'We shall see what we shall see. Children as think themselves everybody at home, gets whipped when they go to school,' Nurse told her severely.

Alex was used to these prognostications. They did not alarm her very much, because she did not think that she would be sent to school. She knew instinctively that her father disapproved of ordinary girls' schools, and that her mother disliked convents, and indeed most things that had to do with religion.

Alex supposed that this was because Lady Isabel was a Protestant. She thought that it was much the nicest religion to belong to, on the whole, since it evidently imposed no obligations in the nature of church-going, and she often wondered why her mother had let all her children be Catholics, instead of Protestants like herself. It certainly couldn't be because father cared which church the children went to, or whether they went at all.

The only person in the house who did seem to care was Nurse, who took Alex and Barbara and Cedric to High Mass at the Oratory every Sunday, where there was a front bench reserved for them, with little cards in brass frames planted at intervals along the ledge in front of them, bearing the name of Sir Francis Clare.

Nurse put Barbara on one side of her and Alex on the other, and Cedric on the outside, and was very particular about their kneeling down and standing up at the right moment, and keeping their prayer-books open in front of them. Alex and Barbara each had a *Garden of the Soul*, but Cedric was only allowed *Holy Childhood*, which had pictures and anecdotes illustrative of Vice and Virtue at the end.

Alex knew all the anecdotes by heart, and preferred her own grown-up-looking book with its small, close print. She had long since discovered that the one matter over which Nurse could be hoodwinked was print, and that she might quite safely indulge herself in the perusal of the pages devoted to the Sacrament of Holy Matrimony, or to a mysterious ceremony called Churching after Child-birth, during the many dull portions of the long service.

The only part of Church that held possibilities was when the little bell rang at the Elevation, and everyone bent his or her head as far down as it would go over the bench. Alex always looked up surreptitiously, then, to see if by any chance a miracle was taking place, or to watch Cedric's invariable manœuvre of hanging on to the ledge by his teeth and hands and trying to raise his feet from the floor at the same time.

Nurse was always piously bent double, her face hidden in her cotton gloves, breathing stertorously, with Barbara on the other side devotedly imitating her, even to the production of strange sounds through her own tightly-compressed lips.

After that, Alex always knew that the end of Church was near, and that as soon as the priest had taken up his little square headgear and faced the congregation for the last time, Nurse would begin to poke her violently, as a sign that she was to get up and to make Cedric pick up his cap and his gloves.

Then came the genuflection as they filed out between the benches, and Nurse was always very particular that this should be done properly, frequently pressing a heavy hand on Alex' shoulder until her knee bumped painfully against the stone floor. The final ceremony connected with the children's religion took place at the door, when Cedric had to make his way through rustling skirts and an occasional pair of black trousers to the big stone basin of holy water. Into this, standing

13

on tiptoe with immense difficulty, he plunged as much of his hand as was necessary to satisfy the sharp inspection of Nurse when he returned, proffering dripping fingers to her and to his sisters.

The last perfunctory sign of the cross made, then the worst of Sunday, in Alex' opinion, was over.

Roast beef and Yorkshire pudding for dinner was pleasant. Mademoiselle did not come in the afternoon, and Nurse generally went out and left Emily in charge. In the summer she took the children to sit in the Square garden – the Park on Sundays was not allowed – and in the winter they always walked as far as the Albert Memorial, for which Cedric entertained a great admiration.

Sunday was Lady Isabel's At Home day and the children, except during the season, always went down to the drawing-room after tea, Alex and Barbara in pale, rose-coloured frocks with innumerable frills at throat and wrists, and a small pad fastened under each skirt so that it might stand well out at the back. Cedric, like most other little boys of his age and standing, was forced to wear a Lord Fauntleroy suit, from which his cropped bullet head and spectacles emerged incongruously.

The half-hour in the drawing-room was not enjoyed by the others as it was by Alex, especially if there were many visitors. She would lean against Lady Isabel confidently, and hear people say how like she was to her mother, which always delighted her. Her mother looked so pretty, sitting on the sofa with her fringe beautifully curled and a lovely dress that was half a teagown, the tight bodice coming down into a sharp point in front and behind, and the skirt falling into long folds, with a train sweeping the ground, and huge loops and bows of soft ribbon draping it cross-wise.

Barbara was incurably shy, and poked her head when she was spoken to, but very few people took as much notice of her as of talkative Alex or pretty little Archie, who was all blue ribbons and fearless smiles. And before very long Lady Isabel was sure to say:

'Now you'd better run back to the nursery, hadn't you, darlings? or Nurse will be comin' down in search of you. I've got the most invaluable old dragon for them,' she generally added to her friends. 'She's been with us since Alex was a baby, and rules the whole house.'

'Oh, don't send them away!' one of the visiting ladies would exclaim politely. '*Such* darlings!'

'Oh, but I must! Their father won't *hear* of my spoilin' them. Now run along, infants.'

Cedric and Barbara were only too ready to obey, though it was understood that Lady Isabel's 'run along' only meant a very ceremonious departure from the room, Barbara taking little Archie by the hand and leading him to the door, where they both dropped the obeisance considered 'picturesque', and Cedric making an unwilling progress to execute his carefully practised bow before each one of the ladies scattered about the big room.

If Alex, however, was enjoying herself, and getting the notice that her soul loved, she always said in a pleading whisper, loud enough to be heard by two or three people besides her mother:

'Oh, do let me stay with you a little longer, mummy. Don't send me upstairs yet!'

'How sweet! Do let her stay, dear Lady Isabel.'

'You mustn't encourage me to spoil her. She ought to go up with the others.'

'Just for this once, mummy.'

'Well, just for this once, perhaps. After all,' said Lady Isabel apologetically, 'she *is* the eldest. She'll be comin' out before I know where I am!'

And Alex would enjoy the privilege of being the eldest, and sit beside her mother, listening to the conversation, and sometimes joining in with remarks that she thought might be acclaimed as amusing or original, or even merely precocious. No wonder that the nursery greeted her return with disdain. Even Emily called her 'drawing-room child,' and by her contempt brought Alex' ready tears of mortified vanity to the surface. But it was much worse on the rare Sunday afternoons when Nurse was in, when she would greatly resent the slight to Barbara if she was sent up from the drawing-room before her sister.

'Working on your mamma to spoil you like that, just because you're a couple of years older!' Nurse would say, pulling the comb fiercely through Alex' hair as she went to bed.

'I'm three whole years older.'

'Don't you contradict me like that, Alex. I'm not going to have any showing-off up here, I can tell you. You can keep those airs and graces for your mamma's friends in the drawing-room.'

Alex generally went to bed in tears.

If Nurse had not been scolding her, then Barbara had been quarrelling with her. They always quarrelled whenever Barbara ventured to differ from Alex and take up an attitude of her own, or still more when Barbara and Cedric made an alliance together and excluded Alex' autocratic ruling of their games.

'But it is for your good,' she would tell them passionately. 'I want to show you a better way. It'll be much more fun if you do it my way – you'll see.'

But they did not want to see.

Their obstinacy always brought to Alex the same sense of incredulous, resentful fury. How *could* they not want to be shown the best way of doing things, when she knew it and they didn't? And, of course, she always did know it. Was she not the eldest?

It was not till Alex was almost thirteen that her belief in her own infallibility as eldest received a rude shock.

She nearly killed Barbara.

It was the first week of August, and Sir Francis and Lady Isabel had gone to Scotland. The children were going to the sea with Nurse on the following day, and took advantage of her state of excitement over the packing, and the emptiness of the downstairs rooms, to play at circus on the stairs. Emily only said, 'Now don't go hurting yourselves, whatever you do, or there'll be no seaside tomorrow' and then went back to amuse Pamela, who was crying and restless from the heat.

'I'll tell you what!' said Alex. 'We'll have tight-rope dancing. I'm tired of learned pigs and things like that –' This last impersonation having been perseveringly rendered by Cedric with much snuffling and snorting over a pack of cards.

'Give me the skipping-rope, Barbara.'

'Why?' said Barbara, whining.

'Because I say so,' replied her sister, stamping her foot. 'I've got an idea.'

'It's my skipping-rope.'

'But if you don't give it to me we can't have the tight-rope dancing,' said Alex in despair.

'I don't care. Why should you do tight-rope dancing with my skipping-rope?'

'You shall do it first – you shall do it all yourself, if you'll only let me show you,' Alex cried in an agony of impatience.

On this inducement Barbara slowly parted with her skipping-rope, and let Alex knot it hastily and insecurely to the newel post on the first landing above the hall.

'Now just get up on to the post, Barbara, and I'll hold the other end of the rope like this, and you'll see –'

'But I can't, I should fall off.'

'Don't be such a little muff; I'll hold you on.'

'No, no – I'm frightened. Let Cedric do it.'

'No,' said Cedric. 'I'm being a learned pig.' He went down the short flight of stairs and sat firmly down upon the tiled floor with the pack of cards out-spread before him.

'Now come on, Barbara,' Alex commanded her; 'I'll hold you.'

Between hoisting and pulling and Barbara's own dread of disobeying her, Alex got her sister into a kneeling position on the broad flat top of the newel post.

'Now stand up, and then I'll hold out the rope. You'll be the famous tight-rope dancer crossing the Falls of Niagara.'

'Alex, I'm frightened.'

'What of, silly? If you did fall it's only a little way on to the stairs, and I'll catch you. Besides, you'll feel much safer when you're standing up.'

Barbara, facing the stairs, and with her back to the alarming void between her perch and the hall-floor, rose trembling to her feet.

'You look splendid,' said Alex. 'Now then!' She jerked at the rope, and at the same instant Barbara screamed and tried to clutch at her.

Alex caught hold of her sister's ankles, felt Barbara's weight slip suddenly, and screamed aloud as a shriek and crash that seemed simultaneous proclaimed Barbara's fall backwards into the hall.

Cedric and Barbara in a confused struggling heap on the floor – doors opening upstairs and in the basement – the flying feet of the servants – all was an agonized nightmare to Alex until Barbara, limp and inert on Nurse's lap, suddenly began to scream and cry, calling out, 'My back! my back!'

They hushed her at last, and Nurse carried her into the boudoir, which was the nearest room, and laid her down on the broad sofa. Then Alex became aware of a monotonous sound that had struck on her ear without penetrating to her senses ever since the accident happened.

'My spectacles are broken. You've broken my spectacles,' reiterated a lamentable voice.

'You horrid, heartless little boy, Cedric! When poor Barbara –' Sobs choked her.

'I like that!' said Cedric. 'When it was all you that made her fall at all – and break my spectacles.'

'What's that?' said Nurse, miraculously reappearing. 'All you, was it? I might have known it, you mischievous wicked child. Tell me what happened this minute.'

But Alex was screaming and writhing on the floor, feeling as though she must die of such misery, and it was Cedric who gave the assembled household a judicial version of the accident.

The doctor came and telegrams were sent to Scotland, which brought back Lady Isabel, white-faced and tearful, and Sir Francis, very stern and monosyllabic.

'Father, my spectacles are broken,' cried Cedric earnestly, running to meet them, but they did not seem to hear him.

'Where is she, Nurse?' said Lady Isabel.

'In the boudoir, my lady, and better, thank Heaven. The doctor says her back 'll get right again in time.'

Alex, hanging shaking over the balustrade, saw that Nurse was making faces as though she were crying. But when she came upstairs, after a long time spent with Lady Isabel in the boudoir, and saw Alex, her face was quite hard again, and she gave her a push and said, 'It's no use crying those crocodile tears now. You should have thought of that before trying to kill Barbara the way you did.'

'I didn't, I didn't,' sobbed Alex.

But nobody paid any attention to her.

Good-natured Emily was sent away, because Nurse said

she wasn't fit to be trusted, and Cook, who was Emily's aunt, and very angry about it all, told Alex that it was all her fault if poor Emily never got another place at all. Everything was Alex' fault.

There was no going to the seaside, even after Barbara was pronounced better. But Lady Isabel, who, Nurse said, had been given a dreadful shock by Alex' wickedness, was going into the country, and would take Archie and the baby with her, if they could get a new nursery-maid at once.

'And me and Cedric?' asked Alex, trembling.

'Cedric doesn't give me no trouble, as you very well know, and he'll stay here and help me amuse poor little Barbara, as has always got on with him so nicely.'

'Shall I stay and play with Barbara too?'

'She's a long way from playing yet,' Nurse returned grimly. 'And I should think the sight of you would throw her into a fit, after what's passed.'

'But what will happen to me, Nurse?' sobbed Alex.

'Your papa will talk to you,' said Nurse.

Such a thing had never happened to any of the children before, but Alex, trembling and sick from crying, found herself confronting Sir Francis in the dining-room.

'I am going to send you to school, Alex,' he told her. 'How old are you?

'Twelve.'

'Then I hope,' said Sir Francis gravely, 'that you are old enough to understand what a terrible thing it is to be sent from home in disgrace for such a reason. I am told that you have the deplorable reputation of originating quarrels with your brothers and sister, who, but for you, would lead the normal existence of happily-circumstanced children.'

Alex was terrified. She could not answer the terrible imputations, and began to cry convulsively.

'I see,' said Sir Francis, 'that you are sensible of the appalling lengths to which this tendency has led you. Even now, I can scarcely believe it – a harmless, gentle child like your little sister, who, I am assured, has never done you wilful injury in her life – that you should deliberately endanger her life and her reason in such a fashion.'

He paused, as though he were waiting for Alex to speak, but she could not say anything.

'If your repentance is sincere, as I willingly assume it to be, your future behaviour must be such as to lead us all, particularly your poor little sister, to forget this terrible beginning.'

'Will Barbara get well?'

'By the great mercy of Heaven, and owing to her extreme youth, we are assured by the doctor that a year or two will entirely correct the injury to the spine. Had it been otherwise, Alex –' Sir Francis looked at his daughter in silence. 'When thanking Heaven for the mercy which has, preserved your sister's life,' he said gently, 'I hope you will reflect seriously upon redeeming this action by your future conduct.'

'Oh, I'm sorry – oh, shall you ever forgive me?' gasped Alex, amongst her sobs.

'I do forgive you, my child, as does your mother, and as I am convinced that little Barbara will do. But I cannot, nor would I if I could, avert from you the consequence of your own act!' said her father.

Barbara did forgive Alex, in a little, plaintive, superior voice, as she lay very white and straight in bed. She was to stay quite flat on her back for at least a year, the doctor said, and she need do no lessons, and later she would be taken out in a long flat carriage that could be pushed from behind, then she would be able to walk again, and her back would be quite straight.

'If she'd been a hunchback, we might have played circus again, and I could have been the learned pig,' said Cedric reflectively.

Alex went to school at the end of September.

And that was her first practical experience of the game of Consequences, as played by the freakish hand of fate.

CHAPTER TWO

✦✦✦✦✦✦✦✦✦✦✦

SCHOOL

Alex' schooldays were marked by a series of emotional episodes.

In her scale of values, only the personal element counted for anything. She was intelligent and industrious at her classes when she wished to gain the approbation of an attractive class-mistress, and idle and inattentive when she wanted to please the pretty girl with yellow hair, who sat next to her and read a storybook under cover of a French grammar.

Alex did not read; she wanted to make the yellow-haired girl look at her and smile at her. She thought Queenie Torrance beautiful, though her beauty did not strike Alex until after she had fallen a helpless victim to one of those violent, irrational attractions for one of her own sex, that are apt to assail feminine adolescence.

'I hope that you will find some nice little companions at Liège,' Sir Francis had gravely told his daughter in vale-diction, 'but remember that exclusive friendships are not to be desired. Friendly with all, familiar with none,' said Sir Francis, voicing the ideal of his class and of his period.

As well tell a stream not to flow downhill. Nothing but the most exclusive and inordinate of attachments lay within the scope of Alex' emotional capacities. She was incapable alike of asking or of bestowing in moderation.

Theoretically she would tell herself that she would give all, trust, confidence, love, friendship, and ask for nothing in return. Practically she suffered tortures of jealousy if the loved one addressed a word or smile to any but herself, and cried herself to sleep night after night in the certainty of loving infinitely more than she was loved.

The material side of her life as a *pensionnaire* at the Liège convent made very little impression upon her, excepting in relation to the emotional aspect, of which she was never unaware.

To the end of her days, the clean, pungent smell of a certain polish used upon the immense spaces of bare *parquet ciré* all over the building, would serve to recall the vivid presentment of the tall Belgian *postulante* whose duty it was to apply it with a huge mop, and whom, from a distance only to be appreciated by those who know the immensity of the gulf that in the convent world separates the novice from the pupils, Alex had worshipped blindly.

And the acrid, yet not unpleasant taste of *confiture* thinly spread over thick slices of brown bread, would remind her with equal vividness of the daily three o'clock interval for *goûter*, with Queenie Torrance pacing beside her in the garden quadrangle, one hand of each rolled into her black-stuff apron to try and keep warm, and the other grasping the enormous double *tartine* that formed the afternoon's refection.

Even the slight, steady sound of hissing escaping from a gas jet of which the flame is turned as high as it will go, stood to Alex for the noisy evening recreation, spent in the enforced and detested amusement of *la ronde*, when her only preoccupation was to place herself by the object of her adoration, for the grasp of her hand in its regulation cotton glove, as the circle of girls moved drearily round and round singing perfunctorily.

The tuneless tune of those *rondes* remained with Alex long after the words had lost the savour of irony with which novelty had once invested them.

'Quelle horrible attente
D'être postulante . . .
Quel supplice
D'être une novice
Ah! quel comble d'horreur
Devenir sœur de chœur. . . .'

Alex' symbols were not romantic ones, but there was no romance in the life of the Liège convent, save what she brought to it herself. Even the memory of the great square *verger*, in the middle of gravelled alleys, brought to her mind for sole token of summer only her horror of the immense pale-red slugs that crawled slowly and interminably out and across the paths in the eternal rains of the Belgian climate. Nothing mattered but people.

And of all the people in the world, only those whom one loved.

Thus Alex' sweeping, unformulated conviction, holding in it all the misapplication of an essential force, squandered for lack of a sense of proportion.

She despised herself secretly, both for her intense craving for affection and for her prodigality in bestowing it. She was like a child endeavouring to pour a great pailful of water into a very little cup.

Waste and disaster were the inevitable results.

The real love of Alex' young enthusiasm, fair-haired Queenie Torrance, was preceded by her inarticulate, un-reasoned adoration for the Belgian *postulante*. But the Belgian *postulante* was never visible, save at a distance, so that even Alex' unreasonable affections found nothing to feed upon.

There was a French girl, much older than herself, for whom Alex then conceived an enthusiasm. Marie-Angèle smiled on her and encouraged the infatuation of the curiously un-English little English girl. But she gave her nothing in return. Alex knew it, and recklessly spent all her weekly pocket-money on flowers and sweets for Marie-Angèle, thinking that the gifts would touch her and awaken in her an affection that it was not her nature to bestow, least of all on an ardent and ungainly child, six years her junior. Alex shed many tears for Marie-Angèle, and years later read some words that suddenly and swiftly recalled the girl who passed in and out of her life in less than a year.

'I love you for your few caresses,
I love you for my many tears.'

The lines, indeed, were curiously typical of the one-sided relations into which Alex entered so rashly and so inevitably throughout her schooldays.

She was fifteen, and had been nearly three years at Liège, when Queenie Torrance came. She was Alex' senior by a year, and the only other English girl in the school at that time. Alex was told to look after her, and went to the task with a certain naïve eagerness, that she always brought to bear upon any personal equation. In an hour, she was secretly combating an enraptured certainty, of which she felt nevertheless ashamed, that she had found at last the ideal object on whom to expend the vehement powers of affection for which she was always seeking an outlet.

Queenie was slight, very fair, with a full, serious oval face, innocent grey eyes set very far apart, and the high, rounded forehead and small, full-lipped mouth, of a type much in vogue in England at the time of the Regency. This was the more marked by the thick flaxen hair which fell back from her face, and over her shoulders into natural heavy ringlets. She was not very pretty, although she was often thought so, but she was charged with a certain animal magnetism, almost inseparable from her type. Half the girls in the school adored her. Queenie, already attractive to men, and sent to the convent in Belgium in reality on that account, nominally for a year's finishing, before her début in London society, was for the most part scornful of these girlish admirers, but Alex she admitted to her friendship.

She was precociously aware that intimacy with Lady Isabel Clare's daughter was likely to accrue to her own advantage later on in London.

The genius for sympathy which led Alex to innumerable small sacrifices and tender smoothings of difficulties for her idol, Queenie at first received with a graceful gratitude which yet held in it something of suspicion, as though she wondered what return would presently be exacted of her.

But it became obvious that Alex expected nothing, and received with eager thankfulness the slightest recognition of her devotion.

Queenie despised her, but was lavish of gentle thanks and caressing exclamations. Hers was not a nature ever to make the mistake of killing the goose that laid the golden eggs.

Finding to her concealed astonishment that Alex only asked toleration, or at the most acceptance of her ardent devotion, and was transported at the slightest occasional token of affection in return, Queenie stinted her of neither. It would have seemed to her the most irrational folly to discourage a love, however one-sided, that found its expression in tireless sympathy, endless championship, and unlimited material gifts and help of any or every description. Alex did all that she could of Queenie's lessons, made her bed and mended her clothes for her whenever she could do so undetected by the authorities, spent her pocket-money on gratifying Queenie's shameless and inordinate passion for sweet things, and once or twice told lies, badly and unsuccessfully, to shield Queenie from the effects of her own laziness and constant evasions of regulations.

Alex had been taught, in common with every other child of her upbringing and nationality, that to tell a lie was the worst crime to which a self-respecting human being can stoop. She also believed that a person who has told a lie is a liar, and that all liars go to Hell. Yet by some utterly illogical perversity of which she was hardly even aware, it did not shock or very much distress her, to find that Queenie Torrance told lies, and told them, moreover, with an air of quiet and convincing candour that placed them in a very different category to Alex' own halting, improbable fibs, delivered with a scarlet face and a manifest air of hunting for further corroboration as she spoke.

In the extraordinary scale of moral values unconsciously held by Alex, there were apparently no abstract standards of right and wrong. Where she loved, though she might, against her own will, see defects, she was incapable of condemning.

Queenie took a curious, detached interest in coldly gratifying her vanity by seeking to test the lengths of extravagance to which Alex' admiration would go.

'Supposing I quarrelled with everyone here, and they all sent me to Coventry – whose part would you take?'

'Yours, of course.'

'But if I were in the wrong?'

'That wouldn't make any difference. In fact, you'd need it more if you were in the wrong.'

'I don't see that!' Queenie exclaimed. 'If I were in the wrong I should have deserved it.'

'But that would make it all the worse for you. It's always the people who are in the wrong who need most to have their part taken,' Alex explained confusedly, yet voicing an intimate conviction.

'I don't think you have much idea of justice, Alex,' said Queenie drily.

The conversation made Alex very miserable. It was characteristic of her want of logic that while she reproached herself secretly for her own impiety in setting the objects of her affection far above what she conceived to be the abstract standard of right and wrong, yet she never questioned but that any love bestowed upon herself would be measured out in direct proportion to her merits.

And despairingly did Alex sometimes review the smallness of her deserts.

She was disobedient, untruthful, quarrelsome, irreligious. It seemed to Alex that there was no fault to which she could not lay claim. Her lack of elementary religious teaching put her at a disadvantage in the convent atmosphere, and made its frequent religious services and instructions so tedious to her, that she was in constant disgrace for her weary, inattentive attitudes, not unjustly designated as irreverent, in the chapel.

She was not at all popular with the nuns. The 'influence' which her class-mistress wielded over so many of the pupils, or the 'interest' which the English Assistant Superior would so willingly have extended to her youthful compatriot were alike without effect upon Alex. She was not drawn to any of these holy, black-clad women, to one or other of whom almost all her French and Belgian and American contemporaries devoted a rather stereotyped enthusiasm.

Had the vagrant fancy of Alex lighted upon anyone of the elder nuns charged with the direction of the school, the attraction would have been discreetly permitted, if not admittedly sanctioned, by the authorities. It would almost inevitably have led Alex to an awakening of religious

31

sensibilities and the desirability of this result would have outweighed, even if it did not absolutely obscure in the eyes of the nuns, the excessive danger of obtaining such a result by such means.

But the stars in their courses had designed that Alex should regard the Mesdames Marie Baptiste and Marie Evangeliste of her convent days with indifference, and devote her ardent temperament and precocious sensibilities to the worship of Queenie Torrance.

The enthusiasm was smiled upon by no one, and thereby became the more inflamed.

'Je n'aime pas ces amitiés particulières,' said the class-mistress of Queenie Torrance severely, to which Miss Torrance replied with polite distress that she was powerless in the matter. It made her ridiculous, she disliked the constant infringement of rules to which Alex' pursuit exposed her, but – one could not be unkind. She did not know why Alex Clare showed her especial affection – she herself had done nothing to encourage these indiscreet displays. Of course, it was pleasant to be liked, but one wished only to do right about it. Queenie mingled candour with perplexity, and succeeded in convincing everyone with perfect completeness of her entire innocence of anything but a too potent attraction.

'Ce n'est donc même pas une amitié? C'est Alex qui vous recherche malgré vous!' exclaimed the class-mistress.

Under this aspect the question soon presented itself alike to the *pensionnat* and its authorities, rendering Alex ridiculous. In a system of *surveillance* which admitted of no loophole for open defiance or outspoken rebuke, Alex' evasions of that law of detachment which is the primary one in convent legislation, became the mark of every blue-ribboned *enfant de Marie* who wished to obtain a reputation for zeal by reporting the defection of a companion to her class-mistress.

It was always Alex who was reported. Queenie never sought opportunities to snatch a hurried colloquy during recreation, or manœuvred to obtain Alex as companion at *la ronde*, or when they played games in the garden. She never infringed one of the strictest rules of the establishment, by giving presents unpermitted or purchasing forbidden sweets and chocolate to be given away at the afternoon *goûter*.

Queenie accepted the presents, wrote tiny notes to Alex and skilfully gave them to her unperceived, and cut Alex to the heart by telling her sometimes that she made it very hard for one to try and be good and keep all the rules and perhaps get one's blue ribbon next term.

These speeches were to Queenie's credit, and made Alex cry and worship her more admiringly than ever, but they did not tend to lower the transparent, dog-like devotion with which Alex would gaze at Queenie's bent profile in the chapel, utterly unconscious of the scandal which her manifest idolatry was creating for the severe nun in the carved stall opposite. She was scolded, placed under strict observation, and every obstacle placed in the way of her exchanging any word with Queenie, until she grew to see herself as a martyr to an affection which every fresh prohibition increased almost to frenzy.

One day she was made the victim of a form of rebuke much dreaded by the *pensionnaires*. A monthly convocation of the school and mistresses, officially known as *la réclame du mois*, and nicknamed by the children 'the Last Judgment,' was held in the *Grande Salle* downstairs, with the Superior making her state entry after the children had been decorously seated in rows at the end of the long room, and all the other nuns who had anything to do with the school had placed themselves gravely and with folded hands against the walls.

They all stood when the Superior came in, followed by the First Mistress, carrying a sheaf of notes and a great book, which each pupil firmly believed to be devoted principally to the record of her own progress through the school.

Then the Superior, with inclined head and low, distinct voice, spoke a few words of prayer, and settled herself in the large chair behind which the nuns clustered in orderly rows.

The children sat down at the signal given, and listened, at first with smiles as the record of the baby class were read aloud and each mite stood up in her place for all the universe to gaze at her, while the analysis of her month's work, mental and moral, sounded with appalling distinctness through the silence.

'Bébée de Lalonde! première en catéchisme, première en géographie . . . calcul, beaucoup mieux . . . elle y met beaucoup de bonne volonté!'

'A la bonne heure!'

The Superior is smiling, everyone is smiling, Bébée de Lalonde, her brown curls bobbing over her face, is pink with gratification. Her young class-mistress leans forward, the white veil of a novice falling over her black habit.

'Ma Mère Supérieure, pour le mois de S. Joseph, elle se corrige de cette vilaine habitude de mordre ses ongles. Elle a fait de vrais efforts. . . .'

'C'est bien. Faites voir . . . Venez, ma petite.'

Up the long room marches Bébée, two freshly washed tiny pink hands thrust out proudly for the Superior's inspection.

'Très bien, très bien. Vous ferez bien attention au pouce droit, n'est pas?'

The Superior is quite grave, however, everyone laughs, and then the serious part of the proceedings begins.

The very little ones are not nervous. Most of them are good, even the naughty ones only get a very gentle homily from the Superior. Then their class-mistress claps her hands smartly and they get up and file out of the room, it not being considered politic to let *les petites* hear the record of that pen of black sheep, *les moyennes*.

The indictments become more serious. Marie Thérèse, twice impertinent to a mistress, taking no trouble over her lessons, worst of all, taking no trouble to cure that trick of which we have complained so often – sitting with her knees crossed.

'Even in the chapel, ma Mère Supérieure.'

This is very bad! It is unladylike, it is against all rules, it is extremely immodest. . . . And what an example!

Marie Thérèse, says the Superior decisively, can abandon all hope of obtaining the green ribbon of an *aspirante enfant de Marie* until she has reformed her ways. The mention of a première in literature gains no approving smile from anyone, and Marie Thérèse sits down in tears.

Gabrielle, Marthe, Sadie – all through the three classes of the *moyenne* division of the school, with very few stainless reports and two or three disastrous ones.

Then *les grandes*. The first of these, in the lowest section, is a name to which the reader, a French woman, always takes exception. She finally compresses her lips and renders it as: 'Kevinnie!'

Queenie is always cool and unmoved as she stands up, and Alex always looks at her. At this particular *séance*, the April one, she took her glances more or less surreptitiously, miserably aware that she had not enough self-control to refrain from them and so avoid risking a rebuke later on.

Queenie held no première. She was always last in her form, undistinguished at music, drawing, needlework, anything requiring application or talent alike.

But her perfectly serene complacency was more or less justified by the exaggerated applause of her companions at her faultless conduct marks and the assurance of her class-mistress, always given readily, that she was 'très docile, très appliquée.'

Queenie's popularity was independent of anything extraneous to herself.

The Superior leant forward and asked a question in a low voice.

'Non, ma Mère Supérieure, non.'

The denial of a possible accusation, of which Alex guessed the purport, was emphatic. She felt glad and relieved, but had no suspicions as to the indictment following on her own name.

'Alexandra Clare,' said Mère Alphonsine sonorously, and Alex stood up.

She no longer felt self-conscious over the ordeal, and was indifferent to the habitual litany of complaints as to her unlearnt lessons, disregard of the rule of silence, and frequent bad marks, for disorder and unpunctuality. But to the accusations which she knew by heart, and shared with the majority of the *moyenne classe*, came a quite unexpected addition, hissed out with a sort of dramatic horror by Mère Alphonsine.

'Alex recherche Kevinnie sans cesse, ma Mère Supérieure.'

Only those familiar with the code of *pensionnaire* discipline in Belgium during the years when Alex Clare and her contemporaries were at school, can gauge the full heinousness of the offence, gravest in the conventual decalogue.

Even Alex, although she had been scolded and punished and made the subject of innumerable homilies, some of them pityingly reproachful, and others explanatorily so, on the same question, felt as though she had never before realized the extent of her own perversion.

She stood up, her hands in the regulation position, pushed under the hideous black-stuff pelerine that fell from her stiff, hard, white collar to the shapeless waist-band of her skirt, the whole uniform carefully designed to conceal and obscure the lines of the figure beneath it.

Overwhelmed with uncomprehending misery and acute shame, she heard two or three of the mistresses add each her quota, for the most part regretfully and with an evident sense of duty overcoming reluctance, to the evidence against her.

'She seeks opportunity to place herself next to Queenie at almost every recreation, ma Mère Supérieure.'

'I am afraid that even in the chapel she lets this folly get the better of her – one can see how she lets herself go to distractions all the time. . . .'

So the charges went on.

The summing up of ma Mère Supérieure was icily condemnatory. She had tried every means with Alex, had spoken to her with kindness and tenderness; in private, had reasoned with her and finally threatened her, and now a public denouncement must be tried, since all these means had proved to be without effect.

Alex was principally conscious of the single, lightning-swift flash of reproach that had shot from the eyes of Queenie Torrance into hers.

How silently and viciously Queenie would resent this public coupling of her immaculate reputation with Alex' idiotic infatuation, only Alex knew.

With the frantic finality of youth, she wondered whether she could go on living. Oh, if only she might die at once, without hearing further blame or reproach, without encountering the ridicule of her companions or the cold withdrawal of Queenie's precariously-held friendship. Alex cried herself sick with terror and shame and utterly ineffectual remorse.

The despair that invades an undeveloped being is the blackest in the world, because of its utter want of perspective.

Alex could see nothing beyond the present. She felt all the weight of an inexpressible guilt upon her, and all the utter isolation of spirit which surrounds the sinner who stands exposed and condemned.

She knew that nobody would take her part. She was young enough to reflect forlornly that an accusation mattered nothing if unjust, since the consciousness of innocence would sustain one, serene and unfaltering, through any ordeal.

But she had no consciousness of innocence. She saw herself eternally different from her companions, eternally destined to lose her way, wickedly and shamefully she supposed, without volition of her own she knew, amongst those standards to which the right thinking conformed, and which she, only, failed to recognize. With sick wistfulness Alex sought Queenie's glance as they came one by one into the refectory, after the *réclame* was over.

Queenie's fair, opaque face was as colourless as ever, her eyes were cast down.

Frantically, Alex willed her to cast one look of pity or forgiveness in her direction, but Queenie passed on to the refectory where the children's mid-day meal was waiting for them without a sign.

Amidst all the blur of emotions, passionate remorse and hopeless loneliness, which made up Alex' schooldays, that Saturday mid-day meal stood out in its black despair.

The choking attempts to swallow a mass of vegetable cooking, made salt and sodden with her own streaming tears, the sobs that strangled her and broke in spite of all her efforts into the decorous silence of the refectory, even the awed and scandalized glances that the younger children cast at her distorted face, remained saliently before her memory for years.

At last the nun in charge rose from her place at the end of the room and came down and told Alex that she might leave the table. The long progress down the endless length of the refectory destroyed the last remnants of Alex' self-control.

The tide of emotional agony that swept over her was to ebb and flow again, and many times again.

But only once or twice was that high-water mark to be reached, that bitter wave to engulf her, and each time add to the undermining of that small stability of spirit with which Alex had been endowed.

She left the misery of that black Saturday behind her, and was left with her childish nerves a little shattered, her childish confidence of outlook rather more overshadowed, her childish strength less steady, and, above all, set fast in her childish mind the ineradicable, unexplained conviction that because she had loved Queenie Torrance and had been punished and rebuked for it, therefore to love was wrong.

CHAPTER THREE

QUEENIE TORRANCE

Schooldays in Belgium went on, through the steamy, rain-sodden days of spring to the end of term and the *grandes vacances* looked forward to with such frantic eagerness even by the children who liked the convent best. Alex was again bitterly conscious of an utter want of conformity setting her apart from her fellow-creatures.

The misery of parting for eight weeks from Queenie Torrance overwhelmed her. Casually, Queenie said:

'I may not come back, next term. I shall be seventeen by then, and I don't see why I should be at school any longer if I can get round father.'

'What would you do?'

'Why, come out, of course,' said Queenie. 'I am quite old enough, and everyone says I look older than I am.'

She moved her head about slightly so as to get sidelong views of her own reflection in the big windowpane. There were no looking-glasses at the convent.

It was true that, in spite of a skin smooth and unlined as a baby's and the childish, semicircular comb that gathered back the short flaxen ringlets from her rounded, innocent brow, Queenie's slender, but very well-developed figure and the unvarying opaque pallor of her complexion, made her look infinitely nearer maturity than the slim, long-legged American girls, or over-plump, giggling French and Belgian ones. Alex gazed at her with mute, exaggerated despair on her face.

'Your parents will permit that you make your début at once, yes?' queried Martha Poupard, as one resigned to the incredible folly and weakness of British and American parents.

'I can manage my father,' said Queenie gently, and with the perfect conviction of experience in her voice.

As the day of the breaking-up drew nearer, discipline insensibly relaxed, and Queenie suddenly became less averse from responding in some degree to Alex' wistful advances.

On the last day, one of broiling heat, the two spent the afternoon alone together unrebuked, in a corner of the great *verger* where the pupils were scattered in groups, feeling as though the holidays had already begun.

'I shall have the journey with you,' said Alex piteously.

'Madame Hippolyte is taking us over, with one of the lay-sisters,' said Queenie, naming the most vigilant of the older French nuns. 'So it will be much better if we don't talk together on the boat. You know there will be the three Munroe girls as well, because they are going to spend their holidays in Devonshire or somewhere.'

'How do you know it will be Madame Hippolyte?' said Alex disconsolately.

The authority deputed to conduct pupils on the journey to and from Liège was one of the many items in the convent curriculum always shrouded in impenetrable mystery until the actual moment of departure.

'I overheard two of them talking about it, in the linen-room this morning,' placidly said Queenie. 'I kept behind the door.'

Part of her curious attractiveness was that she never attempted to disguise or deny certain practices which Alex had been taught to consider as dishonourable.

Alex counted this as but one more stone in the edifice erected for the worship of her idol. It was not until she saw Queenie Torrance long after, in other relations and other surroundings, that she dimly realized how much of that streak of extraordinary candour was the direct product of a magnificently justified self-confidence in the potency of her own attraction, needing no enhancement from moral or mental attributes.

'Do you always live in London, Alex?'

'Yes, in Clevedon Square. You know, I told you about it, Queenie.'

'Yes, I know, but I only wondered if perhaps you had a house in the country as well.'

'No. Father and mother go to Scotland in the summer, and generally they send us to the seaside with Nurse and a governess or someone.'

'I see,' said Queenie reflectively. She had wondered if perhaps the Clares had a country house to which she, as a favourite school friend, would be asked to stay.

'Father hates the country,' said Alex. 'We are sure to be in London for a little while in September, before I come back here. Would you – would you –' She gulped and clasped her hands nervously. Certain of Lady Isabel's rules and recommendations rushed to her mind, but she desperately tried to ignore them.

'I suppose you would not come to tea with me one day, if I were allowed to ask you? Oh, if *only* your mother knew my mother!'

Smoothly Queenie took her cue. 'Of course, mother won't let me go to tea with anyone – unless she knows them herself – but I don't know . . . What Club does your father belong to?'

'Two or three, I think,' said Alex, surprised. 'He often goes to Arthur's or the Turf Club.'

'So does father. Perhaps we could manage it that way,' said Queenie reflectively.

She had every intention of cultivating her friendship with Alex Clare in London.

'Then you'd like to come, Queenie?' breathed Alex ecstatically.

'Of course I would,' Queenie told her affectionately.

'My dear, you know I have hated all the, fuss here, and our never being allowed to speak a word to one another. But what could I do?' She shrugged her shoulders.

Then Queenie had really cared all the time!

Alex in that moment was compensated for all the tears and storms and disgraces of the year. That afternoon spent under the thick, leafy boughs of the old apple-trees with Queenie, enabled Alex to face with some degree of courage the prospect of their approaching separation. She knew that any sign of unhappiness for such a reason would be imputed to her as wrong-doing by the authorities, and as unnatural and heartless indifference to home on the part of her companions.

So Alex, who had no trust in any standards of her own, was ashamed of the tears which she nightly stifled in her hard pillow, and felt them to be one more of those degrading weaknesses with which her Creator had malignantly endowed her in order that she might be as a pariah among her fellows.

She felt no resentment, only blind wonder and fatalistic apathy. Nevertheless, all through Alex' childhood and early girlhood, unhappy though she was, there dwelt within her a curious certainty that, somewhere, happiness awaited her, which she, and she alone, would have full capacity to appreciate.

Side by side with that, was her intense capacity for suffering, but that she was learning to think of as only a cruel, tearing affliction despised alike by God and man.

Of the immense force latent in the power of intense feeling Alex knew nothing, nor did any of the teaching which she received vouchsafe to her any illumination.

She and Queenie and the three Munroe girls made the journey to England with Madame Hippolyte, who showed Alex a marked kindness not usual with her.

At fifteen, wakeful nights and storms of crying leave their traces, and Alex, pale-faced and with encircled eyes, was pitiful in her propitiatory attempts to join in the eager anticipations of holiday enjoyment exchanged between her companions.

Perhaps, thought the French nun, the little black sheep had not a very happy home. A bad report would follow Alex to England she well knew, and it might be that the poor child was dreading its results.

Her manner to Alex grew gentle and compassionate, and Alex noticed it with a relieved, uncomprehending gratitude that held something abject in its surprised, almost incredulous acceptance of any kindness.

Madame Hippolyte, though she sternly rebuked herself for the uncharitable impulse, felt a certain contempt of the way in which her advances were received.

She knew nothing of the self-assertive, arrogant manner that would presently revive, in the childish sense of security in home surroundings, and would yet be merely another manifestation of the unbalanced complexity that was Alex Clare.

But as the crossing came to an end and they found themselves in the train speeding towards London, Alex was silent, her small face white and her eyes tragical.

The American girls made delighted use of the strip of looking-glass in the carriage, and exchanged predictions as to the pleased amazement that would be caused by Sadie's growth, the length of Marie's plait of red hair, and Diana's added inches of skirt.

Queenie Torrance only glanced at her reflection once or twice, though an acute observer might have seen that she was not indifferent to the advantage of facing a looking-glass, after the many weeks in which none had been available. But she was merely completely serene in the immutability of her own attractiveness. Queenie did not need to depend upon her looks, which seldom or never varied from soft, colourless opacity and opulence of contour. The pale, heavy rings of her fair hair always fell back in the same way from her open, rounded forehead, her well-modelled hands, with fingers broad at the base, and pointed, gleaming nails, were always cool and white.

The Americans were all three pretty girls, and something of race that showed in Alex' bearing and gestures made her remarkable amongst any assembly of children, but it was at Queenie that every man who passed the little group in the railway carriage glanced a second time.

Good Madame Hippolyte, as serenely unaware of this as only a woman whose life had been passed in a religious Order could be, regarded Queenie as by far the least of the responsibilities on her hands, and did not conceal her satisfaction when Marie and Sadie and Diana were immediately claimed at the terminus by a group of excited, noisy cousins, and hurried away to an enormous waiting carriage-and-pair.

'Et vous?' she demanded, turning to the other two.

'Dad 'll come for me,' said Queenie confidently, inadvertently uttering a nickname that would not have been permitted to the Clare children, and was, in fact, never in those days heard in the class of society to which they belonged.

Queenie shot an imperceptible glance of confusion at Alex, who was clinging speechlessly to her hand.

Next moment she had recovered herself.

'There's my father!' she cried.

Colonel Torrance was making his way rapidly towards them, a tall, soldierly-looking man, a trifle too conspicuously well groomed, a trifle too upright in his bearing, a trifle too remarkable altogether, with very black moustache and eyebrows and very white hair.

He raised his tall white hat with its black band at the sight of his daughter, expanded his white waistcoat and grey frock-coat with the *malmaison* buttonhole yet further, and whipped off his pale grey glove to take the limp hand extended to him by Alex, as Queenie self-possessedly introduced her.

Alex hardly heard Colonel Torrance's elaborately courteous allusion to Sir Francis Clare, whom he had had the pleasure of seeing several times at the Club, but she wondered eagerly if that introduction would be considered sufficient to allow of her inviting Queenie to Clevedon Square.

She felt as though her spirit were being torn from her body when Queenie said, 'Good-bye, Alex, dear. Mind you write. *Au revoir, ma mère.*'

Compliments were exchanged between Madame Hippolyte and Queenie's father, the gentleman flourished his top hat again, and then said to his daughter:

'My dear, I have a hansom waiting; the impudent fellow says his horse won't stand. I trust you have no large amount of luggage.'

Queenie shook her head, smiling slightly, and in a moment, the brevity of which seemed incredible to Alex, and left her with an instant's absolute suspension of physical faculties, they disappeared among the crowd.

Madame Hippolyte grasped the arm of her distraught-looking pupil.

'But rouse yourself, Alex!' she said vigorously. 'Who is to come for you?'

'The carriage,' muttered Alex automatically, well aware that neither would Lady Isabel sacrifice an hour of her afternoon to waiting at a crowded London station in July, nor old Nurse permit the other children to do so, had they wished it.

'And where is it, this carriage?' sceptically demanded Madame Hippolyte, harassed and exhausted, and aware that she had yet to find a four-wheeled cab of sufficiently cleanly and sober appearance to satisfy her, in which she might proceed herself to the convent branch-house in the east of London. But presently Alex came partially out of her dream and pointed out the brougham and bay horse and the footman in buff livery at the door.

'But you will not drive alone – in this *quartier*?' cried the nun, in horrified protest at this exhibition of English want of propriety.

Her fears proved groundless.

The neat, black-bonneted head of a maid appeared at the brougham window, and with a sigh of infinite relief Madame Hippolyte bade farewell to the last and most anxiously regarded of her charges.

'How you've grown, Miss Alex!' cried the maid, but her tone was scarcely one of admiration, as she gazed at the stooping shoulders and pale, travel-stained face under the ugly sailor hat of dark blue straw. 'We shall have to make you look like yourself, with some of your own clothes, before your mamma sees you,' she added kindly.

Alex scarcely answered, and sat squeezing her hands together.

She knew she must come out of this dream of misery that seemed to envelop her, and which was so naughty and undutiful. Of course, it was unnatural not to be glad to come home again, and it wasn't as though she had been so very happy at Liège.

It was only Queenie.

No one must know, or she would certainly be blamed and ridiculed for her foolish and headlong fancy.

Alex wondered dimly why she was so constituted as to differ from everyone else.

The cab turned into Clevedon Square. Alex looked out of the window.

The big square bore already the look of desertion most associated in her mind with summer in London. Shutters and blinds obscured the windows of the first and second floors of many houses, and against one of the corner houses a ladder was propped and an unwontedly dazzling cream-colour proclaimed fresh paint.

Some of the houses showed striped sun-blinds, and window-boxes of scarlet geraniums. Alex saw that there were flowers in their own balcony as well as an awning.

When the carriage drew up at the front door, she jumped out and replied hastily to the man-servant's respectful greeting, a slight feeling of excitement possessing her for the first time at the prospect of seeing Barbara, and impressing her with her added inches of height.

She ran quickly up the stairs, hoping that Lady Isabel would not chance to come out of the drawing-room as she went past. On the second landing, safely past the double door of the drawing-room, she paused a moment to take breath, and heard a subdued call from overhead.

Barbara was hanging over the banisters with Archie,

'Hallo, Alex!'

Alex went up to the schoolroom landing, and she and Barbara looked curiously at one another, before exchanging a perfunctory kiss.

Alex suddenly felt grubby and rather shabby in her old last year's serge frock, which had been considered good enough for the journey, when she saw Barbara in her clean white muslin, with a very pale blue sash, and her hair tied up with a big pale blue bow.

Barbara's hair had grown, which annoyed Alex. It fell into one long, pale curl down her back, and no longer provoked a contrast with Alex' superior length of shining wave. Deprived of the supervision of Nurse, with her iron insistence on 'fifty strokes of the brush every night, and Rowland's Macassar on Saturdays,' Alex' hair had somehow lost its shine, and hung limply in a tangled, uneven pigtail.

Alex thought that Barbara eyed her in a rather superior way.

She felt much more enthusiastic in greeting little Archie. He was prettier and pinker and more engaging than ever, and Alex felt glad that he had not yet been sent to school, to have his fair curls cropped, and his little velvet suit exchanged for cricketing flannels.

He pulled Alex into the schoolroom, with the enthusiasm

for a new face characteristic of a child to whom shyness is unknown, and Alex received the curt, all-observant greeting which she had learnt to know would always await her from old Nurse.

'So you are back from your foreign parts, are you, Miss Alex?'

Nurse always said 'Miss Alex' when addressing her returned charge at first, and as invariably relapsed into her old peremptory form of address before the end of the evening.

'My sakes, child, what have they been doing to you? You look like a scarecrow.'

'Has she grown?' asked Barbara jealously. She knew that grown-up people were always, for some mysterious reason, pleased when one had 'grown'.

'Grown! Yes, and got her back bent like a bow,' said Nurse vigorously. 'An hour on the backboard's what you'll do every day, and bed at seven o'clock tonight. Have they been giving you enough to eat?'

'Of course,' said Alex, tossing her head.

She did not like the convent when she was there, but a contradictory instinct always made her when at home uphold it violently, as a privileged spot to which she alone had access.

'You look half-starved, to me,' Nurse said unbelievingly.

Nothing would ever have persuaded her of what was, in fact, the truth, that Alex received more abundant, more wholesome, and infinitely better cooked food in Belgium than in London.

Barbara sat on the end of the sofa, swinging her legs and fidgeting with the tassel of the blind-cord.

'Have you brought back any prizes, Alex?' she inquired negligently.

And Alex replied with an equal air of indifference:

'One for composition, and I've got a certificate of proficiency for music.'

This was not at all the way in which she had planned to make her announcements. She had thought that her prizes would impress Barbara very much, and she had foreseen a sort of small ceremony of display when she would bring out the big red-and-gilt book. But Barbara only nodded, and presently said:

'Cedric has got quantities of prizes: the headmaster wrote and told father that he was a "boy of marked abilities and remarkable power of concentration," and father is going to give him a whole sovereign, but that's because he made his century.'

'When will he be here?'

'Next week. His holidays begin on Tuesday, and he's got a whole fortnight longer than we have.'

'We?' asked Alex coldly. 'How can *you* have holidays? You're not at school.'

'I have lessons,' cried Barbara angrily. 'You know I have, and Ma'moiselle is going to give me a prize for writing, and a prize for history, and a prize for application. So there!'

'Prizes!' said Alex scornfully. 'When you're all by yourself! I never heard such nonsense.'

She no longer felt wretched and subdued, but full of irritation at Barbara's conceit and absorption in herself.

'It's not nonsense!'

'It is. If you'd been at school you'd know it was.'

'One word more of this and you'll go to bed, the pair of you,' declared old Nurse, the autocrat whom Alex had for the moment forgotten. 'It's argle-bargle the minute you set foot in the place, Miss Alex. Now you just come along and be made fit to be seen before your poor mamma and papa set eyes on you looking like a charity-school child, as hasn't seen a brush or a bit of soap for a month of Sundays.'

Useless to protest even at this trenchant description of herself. Useless to attempt resistance during the long process of undressing, dressing again, brushing and combing, inspection of finger-nails and general, dissatisfied scrutiny that ensued. Alex, in a stiff, clean frock, the counterpart, to her secret vexation, of Barbara's, open-work stockings, and new shoes that hurt her feet, was enjoined 'to hold back her shoulders and not poke,' and dispatched to the drawing-room with Barbara and Archie as soon as the schoolroom tea was over.

She felt as though she had never been away.

No one had asked her anything about the convent, and all through tea Barbara and Archie had talked about the coming holidays, or had made allusions to events of which Alex knew nothing, but which had evidently been absorbing their attention for the last few weeks.

They seemed to Alex futile in the extreme.

Downstairs, Lady Isabel kissed her, and said, 'Well, my darling, I'm very glad to have you at home again. Have you been a good girl this term, and brought back a report that will please papa?' and then had turned to speak to someone without waiting for an answer.

Alex sat beside her mother while she talked to the one remaining visitor, and felt discontented and awkward.

Barbara and Archie were looking at pictures together in the corner of the room, very quiet and well behaved. The caller stayed late, and just as she had gone Sir Francis came in from his Club, the faint, familiar smell of tobacco, and Russia leather, and expensive eau-de-Cologne that seemed to pervade him striking Alex with a fresh sense of recognition as she rose to receive his kiss. He greeted her very kindly, but Alex was quite aware of a dissatisfaction as intense as, though less outspoken than, that of old Nurse as he put up his double eye-glasses and gazed at his eldest daughter.

'We must see if the country or the seaside will bring back some roses to your cheeks,' he said in characteristic phraseology.

But when the children were dismissed from the drawing-room, Sir Francis straightened his own broad back, and tapped Alex' rounded shoulder-blades.

'Hold yourself up, my child,' he said very decidedly. 'I want to see a nice flat, straight back.'

He made no other criticism, and none was needed.

Alex had gauged the extent of his dismay.

CHAPTER FOUR

✺✺✺✺✺✺✺✺✺

HOLIDAYS

'Mother, may I ask Queenie Torrance to tea?'

Alex had rehearsed the words so often to herself that they had almost become meaningless.

Her heart beat thickly with the anticipation of a refusal, when at last she found courage and opportunity to utter the little stilted phrase, with a tongue that felt dry and in a voice that broke nervously in her throat.

'What do you say, darling?' absently inquired Lady Isabel; and Alex had to say it again.

'Queenie Torrance?' said Lady Isabel, still vaguely.

'Mother, you remember – I told you about her. She is the only other English girl besides me at the convent, and she knows all about father and you and everything, and her father belongs to the same Club –'

Snobbishness was not in Alex' composition, but she adopted her mother's standards eagerly and instinctively, in the hope of gaining her point.

'But, my darling, what are you talkin' about? You know mother doesn't let you have little girls here unless she knows somethin' about them. Give me the little diamond brooch, Alex; the one in the silver box there.'

Lady Isabel, absorbed in the completion of her evening toilette, remained unconscious of the havoc she had wrought.

Alex felt rather sick. The intensity of feeling to which she was a victim, for the most part reacted on her physically, though she was as unconscious of this as was her mother.

But with the cunning born of urgent desire, Alex knew that persistence, which with Sir Francis would invariably win a courteous rebuke and an immutable refusal, could sometimes bring forth rather querulous concession from Lady Isabel's weakness.

'But, mummy, darling, I do want Queenie to come here and see Barbara and Cedric.'

It was not true, but Alex was using the arguments which she felt would be most likely to appeal to her mother.

'She wants to know them so much, and – and I saw her father at the station when we arrived, and he was very polite.'

'Who was with you? I don't like your speakin' like that to people whom father and I don't know.'

'Oh, it was only a second,' said Alex hastily. 'Madame Hippolyte was there, and Colonel Torrance just came up to take Queenie away.'

'Torrance – Torrance?' said Lady Isabel reflectively. 'Who's Torrance?'

The question made Alex' heart sink afresh. It was one which, coming from her parents, she heard applied to new acquaintances, or occasionally to protégés for whom some intimate friends might crave the favour of an invitation to one of the big Clare 'crushes' during the season, and the inquiry was seldom one which boded well for the regard in which the newcomer would be held.

'Mother, you'd like her, I think, really and truly you would. She's awfully pretty.'

'Alex!'

Lady Isabel for once sounded really angry.

'I'm so sorry; it slipped out – I didn't mean it – I never really say it. I never *do*, mother.'

Alex became agitated, trying to fend off the accusation which she foresaw was coming.

'I suppose you learn those horrid slang words from this girl you've taken such a violent fancy to?'

'No, no.'

'Well, darling, both father and I are very much disgusted with some of the tricks you've picked up at the convent, and you'll have to find some way of curin' yourself before you put up your hair and come out. As for the way you're holdin' yourself, I'm simply shocked at it, and so is your father; I shall see about sendin' you to MacPherson's gymnasium for proper exercises as soon as you get back from the country.'

Lady Isabel gazed with dissatisfaction at her daughter.

'You mustn't be a disappointment to us, darling,' she said. 'You know you'll be coming out in another two years' time, and it's so important –'

She broke off, eyeing Alex anxiously. Already she had forgotten the question of the invitation to Queenie Torrance. Alex, in an agony, rushed recklessly at her point.

'But, mother, you haven't said yet – may I ask Queenie

on Saturday? You know we shan't be here after Saturday. May I?'

Lady Isabel moved to the door with more annoyance than she often displayed.

'My dear child, you're old enough to know that these things aren't done, and besides, I've already said no. Father and I dislike these sudden, violent friendships, in any case. Run along upstairs, my darling, and if you and Barbara want a little tea-party on Saturday, you may ask those nice Fitzgerald children. Tell Nurse that I said you might.'

Lady Isabel kissed Alex, and went downstairs, the trailing folds of her evening dress carefully held up in one hand as she descended the broad, curving stairs.

From the upper landing Alex watched her for a few moments, her face burning with mortification and the effort to restrain her tears. Then she broke into sobs and ran away upstairs.

Mother had not understood in the very least. She never understood, never would understand.

No one understood.

Alex felt, as so often, that she would barter everything she possessed for the finding of someone who would understand.

In her craving for self-expression, she talked to Barbara about Queenie Torrance, but represented their intercourse as that of an equal friendship, with unbounded affection and confidence on both sides.

Barbara listened believingly enough, and even exhibited signs of a faint jealousy, and gradually Alex' inventions brought her a slight feeling of comfort, as though the ideal friendship which she so readily described to her little sister must have some real existence.

The old sense of supremacy began to assert itself again, and Barbara fell into the old ways of following Alex' lead in everything.

Alex lost her shrinking convent manner, born of the sense of helpless insecurity, and when Cedric's return brought Barbara back to her earliest allegiance – the league which she and Cedric had always formed against Alex' overbearing ways in the nursery – her defection was resented by her sister with no lack of spirit.

'Idiotic little copy-cat! Just because Cedric's come, you pretend you only care for cricket and nonsense like that – as though he wanted to play cricket with a little girl like you.'

'He doesn't mind playing cricket with me; he says I can bowl very well for a girl, and it gives him practice. Anyway,' said Barbara shrewdly, 'he likes talking about it, and how am I to be his pal unless I understand what he means?'

'You're not to say that horrid, vulgar word. You know mother would be very angry.'

'I shall say what I like. It's not your business. You're a prig, ever since you went to that hateful convent!'

'You're not to speak to me like that, you're not!' shouted Alex, stamping her foot.

The dispute degenerated into one of the furious quarrels of their nursery days, and Alex, completely mastered by her temper, flew at Barbara, as she had not done since they were seven and ten years old respectively, and hit her and pulled her long curl viciously.

Barbara stood stock-still on the instant. She had infinitely more self-control than Alex, and a strong instinct for being invariably in the right.

But she uttered shriek upon piercing shriek that brought old Nurse, heavy-footed but astonishingly swift, upon the scene, and reduced Alex to dire disgrace for the rest of the day.

She cried again, suffering remorse and shame that seemed almost unbearable, and told herself hopelessly that she could never be good anywhere.

'Such an example to your little sister, who's never given me a moment's trouble all the while you've been away,' Nurse declared, at the end of a long monologue during which Alex learnt and implicitly believed that a temper like hers, unbridled at the age of fifteen, must have irrevocably passed beyond one's own control into that of the Devil himself.

'When you remember,' Nurse wound up, 'how you nearly killed her with your naughty ways and had her on her back for a year, and she with never a word of complaint against you, poor lamb, one would think you'd want to make it up to her, instead of hitting one as never even hits you back. But you've no heart, Alex, as I've always said and always shall say about you.'

Heart or no heart, old Nurse thoroughly succeeded in working upon Alex' feelings, and in sobbing abjection she begged Barbara's forgiveness.

Barbara, agreeably conscious of martyrdom, found it easy to grant, with a gentleness that redoubled Alex' shame, and the incident, except for Alex' swollen eyes and subdued tones next day, was closed. Cedric, characteristically, remained oblivious of it throughout.

He had grown into a good-looking boy, not tall for his eleven years, but sturdy and well set up, with steady, straight-gazing eyes behind the spectacles that his short sight still necessitated, to the grief of Lady Isabel. His mind was obsessed by cricket, and from his conversation one might have deduced that no other occupation had filled the summer term. Nevertheless, he brought home a large pile of prizes, and a report that caused Sir Francis to smile his excessively rare smile and utter two words that Cedric never forgot, and never mentioned to anyone else: 'Well done!'

Two days after Cedric's return, Sir Francis and Lady Isabel went away for their annual round of country visits, and old Nurse, with the new, young nurse who devoted her services exclusively to Pamela, and a nursery-maid to wait upon them, went with the children to stay at Fiveapples Farm in Devonshire.

The farm was glorious.

The girls might run about the hay-fields, and in the lanes, though Nurse, mindful of Lady Isabel's injunction as to complexion and the danger of freckles, always insisted on hats and gloves; and Cedric, followed everywhere like a little shadow by Archie, rode the farm horses and even went into Exeter to market with Farmer Young on Fridays.

Alex insensibly began to cease her preoccupied outlook for letters from Queenie, and the convent life began to relax its hold on her memory and imagination, as older influences resumed their sway.

Correspondence with Queenie had never been satisfactory.

Although not forbidden, Alex knew that it was considered a foolish and undesirable practice, and that her letters, although, as a matter of fact, generally given to her unopened, were always liable to supervision by the authorities as a matter of course.

Old Nurse might be unable to read, although no one had ever heard her admit as much, but she always slit open any letter that came for Alex or Barbara and made a feint of perusing it; unless the envelope, as rarely happened, bore Lady Isabel's superscription.

'In the absence of your mamma,' said old Nurse severely, and she never failed to refuse unhesitatingly any request from Alex to be allowed to go to the post office for the purpose of buying stamps.

Queenie had only written twice. The second letter reached Alex at Fiveapples Farm, when she had nearly given up hope for it.

'Dear Alex,

'Thank you very much for your letters. It is nice of you to write to me so often. Please forgive me for not writing oftener to you, but I haven't got much time. It's so hot in London now. You are very lucky to be in the country. I think we shall go soon, but I don't know yet where we shall go.

'Do you know that you are quite near where the Munroes are staying? Diana wrote to me the other day. Perhaps you will see them. Please give them my love. Do you remember how funny Diana was at her singing lessons? I often think of the convent, don't you? Now I must end, Alex, with fond love from your affectionate school friend,

'Queenie.

'P.S. – I am not going back next term. I am very glad, except for not seeing you. I hope we shall see each other in London.'

Alex read and re-read the postscript, and tried not to think that the rest of the letter was disappointing.

'Your great friend doesn't write you nearly such long letters as you write her,' observed Barbara, eyeing the four small sheets which Queenie's unformed, curiously immature-looking writing had barely succeeded in covering.

'She hasn't got time,' said Alex quickly and defensively.

'More like she's got a sensible governess who doesn't let her waste good pen and paper on such rubbish,' old Nurse severely pointed the moral.

'What do girls want to write to one another for?' said Cedric. 'They can't have anything to say.'

Barbara, who was secretly curious, seized the opportunity.

'What does she write about, Alex?'

Alex would have liked to tell them to mind their own business, but she knew that any accusation of making mysteries would bring down Nurse's wrath upon her, and as likely as not the confiscation of the letter.

She read it aloud hastily, with a pretence of skipping here and there, leaving out the 'dear Alex' at the beginning, and the whole of the last sentence and the postscript.

'I suppose you've left out all the darlings and the loves and kisses,' Cedric remarked scornfully, more from conventionality than anything else.

Alex was not averse to having it supposed that Queenie had been more lavish with endearments than she had in reality shown herself.

'Who are the Munroes?' asked Barbara. 'Are they nice?'

'The American girls who crossed from Liège with me. I remember now, they were going to spend their holidays with an aunt somewhere in Devonshire.'

'Perhaps we shall see them. How old are they?'

'Sadie and Diana are much older than you,' Alex told her crushingly. 'In fact, they're older than I am. But the little one, Marie, is only twelve.'

'Where does the aunt live?'

'How should I know?' said Alex. She reflected bitterly that even if her schoolmates should ever meet her in Devonshire, it would be impossible for her to make any advance to them, with old Nurse even more strictly mindful of the conventions than Lady Isabel.

But for once it seemed as though fate were on Alex' side.

'I hear,' wrote Lady Isabel, in one of her hasty, collective letters, addressed impartially to 'My darling Children,' 'that Mrs. Alfred Cardew, who lives at a very pretty house called Trevose, not more than a few miles from where you are, has her three little nieces with her for the holidays, and that they are at the same convent as Alex. So if you like, darlings, as I know Mrs. Alfred Cardew quite well, you may ask Nurse to let you arrange some little picnic or other and invite the three children.'

Alex, taken by surprise, felt doubtful. She did not know whether she wanted to expose herself to the criticisms which she thought, disparagingly gazing round at her brothers and sisters and their autocratic guardian, they would inevitably call forth from strangers. Suppose they came, and Barbara was shy and foolish, and Cedric doggedly bored, and then the Munroes went back to Liège next term and laughed at Alex, and told the other girls what queer relations she had. And again, thought Alex, Nurse would probably think the Americanisms, which had amused Queenie and Alex at the convent, merely vulgar, and Barbara and Cedric would wonder.

'You *are* extraordinary, Alex!' said Barbara petulantly. 'You're always talking about your friends at the convent and saying how nice they are, and then when there's a chance of our seeing them too, you don't seem to want to have them.'

'Yes, I do,' said Alex hastily, and consoled herself with the reflection that very likely the plan would never materialize.

But as luck would have it, Alex, the very next day, saw Sadie Munroe waving to her excitedly from the carriage where she was driving with a very gaily-dressed lady, obviously the aunt.

The following week, a charming note invited Alex, Barbara, Cedric and Archie to lunch and spend the afternoon at Trevose. They should be fetched in the pony-cart, and driven back after tea.

At least, Alex reflected thankfully, old Nurse would not be there to put her to shame.

About Archie, with his clean sailor suit and shining curls, she felt no anxiety. He was always a success.

But she inspected Cedric, and especially Barbara, with anxiety.

The day was a very hot one, and Cedric in cricketing flannels looked sufficiently like every other boy of his age and standing to reassure his critical sister.

But Barbara!

Surely the three pretty, sharp-eyed Americans would despise little, pale, plain Barbara, with her one ridiculous curl of pale hair, and the big, babyish bow of blue ribbon against which Alex had protested so vigorously in her own case that Nurse had finally substituted black.

No amount of protest, however, even had Alex dared to offer it, would have induced Nurse to depart from the rule which decreed that the sisters should be dressed alike, and Barbara's clean cotton frock was the counterpart of Alex'.

Alex thought the similarity ridiculous, and hated the twin Leghorn hats, each with a precisely similar wreath round the crown, of thick, pale blue forget-me-nots, of which the clusters were unrelieved by any blade or hint of green.

Even their brown shoes and stockings and brown gauntlet gloves were alike.

Alex felt disgusted at the aspect which she thought they must present, and was unable to enjoy the four-mile drive in the pony-cart Mrs. Cardew had sent over for them. She could not have told whether she was more apprehensive of the effect

Barbara and Cedric might have on the Munroes, or the Munroes on Barbara and Cedric.

'What do you suppose we shall do all the afternoon?' asked Barbara. She was in one of her rare moods of excitement, and her futile chattering and unceasing questions filled Alex with impatience.

The two were on the verge of a quarrel by the time the last hill was reached.

Then came a long, shady avenue, with two pretty little lodges and a wide stone gate, and the groom drove the pony smartly round a triangular gravel sweep which lay before the arched entrance to the big Georgian house.

Sadie, Marie and Diana were sitting on the low stone wall that divided the drive from what looked like a wilderness of pink and red roses, and Alex noticed with relief that they were all three dressed exactly alike in white muslin frocks, although she also saw that in spite of the blazing sun they were without hats or gloves.

They jumped off the wall as the pony-cart drew up before the door and greeted the Clare children eagerly, and with no trace of shyness.

CHAPTER FIVE

❖❖❖❖❖❖❖❖❖

OTHER PEOPLE

It seemed to Alex that the day was going to be a success, and her spirits rose.

She was rather surprised to see that Diana Munroe, who was seventeen, wore her hair in a thick plait twisted round the crown of her head, and asked her almost at once:

'Have you put your hair up, Diana? Are you going to "come out"?'

'Oh no. It'll come down again at the end of the holidays, for my last term. Only Aunt Esther likes to see it that way. There's Aunt Esther, at the bottom of the rose garden.'

Looking over the terrace wall they saw half-a-dozen grown-up people, men in white flannels, and youthful-looking ladies in thin summer dresses. Alex was rather pleased. She had always been more of a success with her mother's grown-up friends than with her own contemporaries, from the time of her nursery days, when she had been sent for to the drawing-room on the 'At Home' afternoons.

But though Mrs. Cardew looked up and waved her hand to the group of children on the terrace, she did not appear to expect them to join the party, and the interval before lunch was spent in the display of white rabbits and guinea-pigs.

At first Alex watched Barbara rather nervously, wondering if she would be shy and foolish, and disgrace her, but Barbara, no longer over-shadowed by an elder sister who outshone her in every way, had acquired a surprising amount of self-assurance. Alex was not even certain that she approved of the ease with which her little sister talked and exclaimed over the pet animals, asking Diana whether she might pick up the guinea-pigs and hold them, without so much as waiting or a lead from Alex.

'Of course you may!' Diana exclaimed. 'Here you are.'

She distributed guinea-pigs impartially, and earnestly consulted Cedric as to the bald patch on the Angora rabbit's head.

As they went back towards the house, Sadie Munroe said to him:

'Do you mind not having any other boys here – only girls? I'm afraid it's dull for you, but Aunt Esther's boys will be here after lunch, only they had to go over and play tennis with some people this morning; it was all settled before we knew you were coming.'

But Cedric did not seem to mind at all.

At lunch Archie, as Alex had known he would be, was an immediate success.

Even Mr. Cardew, who was bald and looked through Alex and Barbara and Cedric without seeing them when he shook hands with them, patted Archie's curls and said:

'Hullo, Bubbles!'

'Come and sit next to me, you darling,' said Mrs. Cardew, 'and you shall have two helpings of everything.'

It was a very long luncheon-table, and Alex found herself placed between Sadie and a grey-headed gentleman, to whom she talked in a manner which seemed to herself to be very grown-up and efficient.

Barbara was on the same side of the table and invisible to her, but she saw Cedric opposite, quite eagerly talking to Marie Munroe, which rather surprised Alex, who thought that her brother would despise all little girls of twelve.

Quite a number of people whose names Alex did not know asked her about Lady Isabel, and she answered their inquiries readily, pleased to show off her self-possession, and the gulf separating her from the childishness of Barbara, who was giggling almost all through luncheon in a manner that would unhesitatingly have been qualified by her parents as ill-bred.

The meal was nearly over when the two schoolboy sons of the house came rushing in, hot and excited, and demanding a share of dessert and coffee.

'Barbarians,' tranquilly said Mrs. Cardew. 'Sit down quietly now, Eric and Noel. I hope you said "How d' you do" to every-one.'

They had not done so, but both made a sort of circular salutation, and the elder boy dropped into a chair next to Alex, while Eric went to sit beside his mother.

Noel Cardew was fifteen, a straight-featured, good-looking English boy, his fairness burned almost to brick-red, and with a very noticeable cast in one of his light-brown eyes.

71

Alex looked at him furtively, and wondered what she could talk about.

Noel spared her all trouble.

'Do you ever take photographs?' he inquired earnestly. 'I've just got a camera, one of those bran-new sorts, and a tripod, quarter-plate size. I want to do some groups after lunch. I've got a dark-room for developing, the tool-house, you know.'

He talked rapidly and eagerly, half turning round in his chair so as almost to face Alex, and she tried to feel flattered by the exclusive monologue.

She knew nothing about photography, but uttered little sympathetic ejaculations, and put one or two timid questions which Noel for the most part hardly seemed to hear.

When Mrs. Cardew at length rose from her place, he turned from Alex at once, in the midst of what he was saying, and demanded vehemently:

'Can't we have a group on the terrace now? Do let me do a group on the terrace – the light will be just right now.'

'Dear boy, you really mustn't become a nuisance with that camera of yours – though he's really extraordinarily clever at it,' said his mother, in a perfectly audible aside. 'Would it bore you all very much to be victimized? You won't keep us sitting in the glare too long, will you, dear boy?'

Almost everyone protested at the suggestion of being photographed, but while a good many of the gentlemen of the party disappeared noiselessly and rapidly before the group could be formed, all the ladies began to straighten their hats, and pull or push at their fringes. Noel kept them waiting in the hot sun for what seemed a long while, and Alex reflected rather gloomily that Mrs. Cardew showed a tolerance of his inconvenient passion for photography that would certainly not have been approved by her own parents.

At last it was over, and Sadie jumped up crying, 'Now we can have some proper games! What shall we play at?'

'Don't get over-heated,' her aunt said, smiling and nodding as she moved away.

'Do you like croquet?' Diana asked, and to Alex' disappointment they embarked upon a long, wearisome game. She was not a good player, nor was Barbara, but Cedric surprised them all by the brilliant ease with which he piloted Marie Munroe and himself to victory.

'I say, that's jolly good!' Eric and Noel said, and gazed at their junior with respect.

Alex felt pleased, but rather impatient too, and wished that it were she who was distinguishing herself.

When they played hide-and-seek, however, her opportunity came. She could run faster than any of the other girls at Liège, and when Diana suggested picking up sides she added good-naturedly:

'Alex runs much faster than any of us – she'd better be captain for one side, and Noel the other.'

Noel looked as though his own headship were a matter of course, but Alex felt constrained to say:

'Oh no, not me – You, Diana.'

'Would you rather not? Very well. Cedric, then. Hurry up and choose your sides, boys. You start, Cedric.'

'I'll have Marie,' said Cedric unhesitatingly, and the little red-haired girl skipped over beside him with undisguised alacrity.

'Noel?'

Noel jerked his head in the direction of Alex.

'You,' he said.

She was immensely surprised and flattered, connecting his choice with the same attraction that had made him sit beside her at lunch, and not with her own reported prowess as a runner.

Cedric's reputation for gallantry suffered somewhat in his next selections, which fell with characteristic common-sense on Noel's brother Eric, and upon Barbara. Noel took Sadie and Diana, and they drew lots for Archie.

The game proved long and exciting, played all over the terrace and shrubbery.

Alex screamed and laughed with the others, and enjoyed herself, although she found time to wish that Barbara were not so stupid and priggish about keeping on her gloves, because old Nurse had said she must, and to wonder very much why Cedric appeared so pleased with the society of red-haired, chattering Marie, whose side he never left.

Presently, as she was looking for somewhere to hide, Noel Cardew joined her.

'Come on with me – I know a place where they'll never find us,' he told her, and led her on tip-toe to where a very small, disused ice-house was half-hidden in a clump of flowering shrubs.

Noel pushed open the door with very little effort, and they crept into the semi-darkness and sat on the floor, pulling the door to behind them. Noel whispered softly:

'Isn't it cool in here? I *am* hot.'

'So am I.'

Alex was wondering nervously what she could talk about to interest him, and to make him go on liking her. Evidently he did like her, or he would not have sat next to her at lunch and told her about his photography, and afterwards have chosen her for his partner at hide-and-seek.

Alex, though she did not know it, possessed a combination that is utterly fatal to any charm: she was unfeignedly astonished that anyone should be attracted by her, and at the same time agonizedly anxious to be liked.

She wanted now, wildly and nervously, to maintain the interest which she thought she had excited in her companion.

She found the silence unbearable. Noel would think her dull, or imagine that she was bored.

'Is this where you do your developing? ' she asked in an interested voice, although she remembered perfectly that he had said he used a tool-house for his dark-room.

'No – we've got the tool-house for that. Why, there wouldn't be room to stand up in here. Sometimes I get my things developed and printed for me at a shop, you know. Chemists will generally do it for one – though, of course, I prefer doing my own. But there isn't time, except in the holidays, and then one's always running short of some stuff or other. The other day I ruined a simply splendid group – awfully good, it would have been: mother and a whole lot of people out on the steps – like we were today, you know –' He paused for sheer lack of breath.

'I hope the one you took today will be good,' said Alex, her heart beating quickly.

'Oh yes, sure to be, with a day like this. Some fellows say you can get just as much effect on a dull day, using a larger stop, but, of course, that's all nonsense really. I say, I'm not boring you, am I?'

He hardly waited to hear her impassioned negative before going on, still discussing photographic methods.

It was quite true that Alex was not bored, although she was hardly listening to what he said. But his voice went on and on, and it flattered her that he should want to talk to her so exclusively, as though secure of her sympathy.

'. . . And they say colour-photography will be the next thing. I believe one could get some jolly good effects down here. Young Eric is all for messing about with beastly paints and stuff, but I don't agree with that.'

'Oh no!'

'My plan is to get hold of a real outfit, as soon as they get the thing perfected, and then be one of the pioneers, you know. I say, I hope you don't think this is awful cheek –'

'Oh no!'

'This isn't a bad place for experiments, I will say. You see, you can get the sea, and quite decent scenery, and any amount of view and stuff. I say, what ages they are finding us,' he broke off suddenly.

Alex felt deeply mortified. Evidently Noel was bored, after all. But in another minute he began to talk again.

'I shouldn't be surprised if one of these days I tried my hand at doing sort of book stuff. You know, photographs for illustrations. I believe it's going to pay no end.'

'What sort of things?'

'Oh, scenery, you know, and perhaps houses and things. Sure I'm not boring you?'

'No, indeed, I'm very interested.'

'It is rather interesting,' Noel agreed simply.

'Another thing I'm keen on is swimming. Rather different, you'll say; but then one can't do one thing all the time, and, of course, the swimming is first class at school. I went in for some competition and stuff last term; high diving, you know.'

'Oh, did you win?'

'Can't say I did. Young Eric got a cup of sorts, racing, but I just missed the diving. Some day I shall have another try, I daresay. You know, I've got rather a funny theory about swimming. I don't know whether you'll see what I mean at all – in fact, I daresay it'll sound more or less mad, to you – but *I* believe we do it the wrong way.'

'Oh,' said Alex, wishing at the same time that she could divest herself of the eternal monosyllable. 'Do tell me about it.'

'Well, it's a bit difficult to explain, but I think we're all taught the wrong way to begin with. It doesn't seem to have occurred to anyone to look at the way *fishes* swim.'

Alex thought that Noel must really be very original and clever, and tried to feel more flattered than ever at being selected as the recipient of his theories.

'I believe the whole thing could be revolutionized and done much better – but I'm afraid I'm always simply chock-full of ideas of that kind.'

'But that's so interesting,' Alex said, not consciously insincere.

'Don't you have all sorts of ideas like that yourself?' he

asked eagerly, filling her with a moment's anticipation that he was about to give the conversation a personal turn. '*I* think it makes life so much more interesting if one goes into things; not just stay on the surface, you know, but go into the *way* things are done.'

Alex thought she heard someone coming towards their hiding-place, and wanted to tell Noel to stop talking, or they would be found, but she checked the impulse, fearful lest he should think her unsympathetic.

The dogmatic schoolboy voice went on and on – swimming, photography, cricket, and then photography again. Alex, determined to feel pleased and interested, could only contribute an occasional monosyllable, sometimes only an inarticulate sound, expressive of sympathy.

And at the end of it all, when she was half proud and half irritated at the thought that they must have been sitting there in the semi-darkness for at least an hour, Noel exclaimed:

'I say, they *are* slow finding us. I should think it must be quite tea-time, shouldn't you? How would it be if we came out now?'

'Yes, let's,' said Alex, trying to keep the mortification out of her voice.

They emerged into the sunlight again, and Noel pulled out his watch.

'It's only a quarter past four. I thought it would be much later,' he remarked candidly. 'I wonder where they all are. I expect they'll want to know where we've been hiding, but you won't give it away, will you? It's a jolly good place, and the others don't know about it.'

'I won't tell.'

Alex revived a little at the idea of being entrusted with a secret.

'Do you often play hide-and-seek?'

'Oh, just to amuse the girls, in the summer holidays. They've spent the last three summers with us, you know. Next year I suppose they'll go to America, lucky kids!'

'I'd love to go to America, wouldn't you?' Alex asked, with considerable over-emphasis.

'Pretty well. I tell you what I'd really like to do – I shall do it one day, too – make a regular tour of England, with a camera. I don't know whether you'll think it's nonsense, of course, but my idea has always been that people go rushing abroad to see other countries before they really know their own. Now, my plan would be that I'd simply start at Land's End, in Cornwall, just taking each principal town as it came on my way, you know, and exploring thoroughly. I shouldn't mind going off the main track, you know, if I heard of any little place that had an old church or castle or something worth looking at. I don't know whether you're at all keen on old buildings?'

'Oh yes,' Alex said doubtfully; 'I've seen Liège and Louvain, in Belgium –'

'Ah, but I'm talking about English places,' Noel interrupted her inexorably. 'Of course the foreign ones are splendid too, and I mean to run over and have a look at them some day, but my theory is that one ought to see something of one's own land first. Now take Devonshire. There are simply millions of old churches in Devonshire, and what I should do, would be to have a note-book with me, and simply jot down impressions. Then with photographs one might get out quite a sort of record, if you know what I mean –'

Alex was rather glad that her companion should be talking to her so eagerly as they came in sight of a group of people on the terrace.

'Here are the truants,' said Mrs. Cardew, laughing, and Diana Munroe exclaimed that Aunt Esther had called them all to tea, and they had given up further hunt for them.

'Noel always finds extraordinary places to hide in,' she added rather disparagingly.

It was evident that Noel was not very popular with the American cousins.

'That boy would be very good looking if he had not that terrible cast,' Alex overheard one lady say to another, as the visitors were waiting on the steps for the pony-carriage to take them away. The grey-haired man next to whom Alex had sat at lunch, and who evidently did not know any one of the group of children apart, nodded in the direction of little Archie, flushed and excited, trying to climb the terrace wall, surrounded by adoring ladies.

'That's the little chap for my money.'

'Isn't he a darling? That's one of Isabel Clare's children – so are the two girls in blue. I couldn't believe anything so tall was really hers.'

'Oh yes – I noticed one of them – rather like her mother.'

Alex felt sure that she ought not to listen, and at the same time kept motionless lest they should notice her and lower their voices.

She felt eagerly anxious to overhear what the grey-haired gentleman might have to say after the very grown-up way in which she had made conversation with him at lunch, and having been a very pretty and much-admired drawing-room child in her nursery days, could not altogether divest herself of the expectation that she must still be found pretty and entertaining.

But the grey-haired gentleman said impartially:

'They are neither of them a patch on Lady Isabel, are they?'

'They are at the awkward age,' laughed the lady to whom he was talking. 'One of them sat next to you at lunch, didn't she?'

'Yes. Not quite so natural as the other children. That little, red-haired American girl, now – a regular child –'

Alex, with a face grown suddenly scarlet, left Barbara, shyly, and Cedric briefly, to thank their hostess for the pleasant day they had spent.

A new, and far more painful self-consciousness than any she had yet known, hampered her tongue and her movements, until they were safely in the pony-carriage half-way down the drive.

'They are nice, aren't they?' said Barbara. 'I'm sure they are nicer than Queenie.'

'No, they aren't,' Alex contradicted mechanically.

'Well, Marie and Diana are, anyway.' She looked slyly at Cedric. 'Don't you think so, Cedric?'

'How can I tell whether they are any nicer, as you call it, than another kid whom I've never seen?' inquired Cedric reasonably.

'But didn't you like Marie?'

'She's all right.'

Barbara giggled in the way most disliked by her family, the authorities of whom stigmatized the habit as 'vulgar,' and Cedric said severely:

'I shouldn't think decent girls would want to play with you at all, if you don't leave off that idiotic trick of cackling.'

But Barbara, who was not at all easily crushed, continued to giggle silently at intervals.

'Why are you so silly?' Alex asked her crossly, as they were going to bed that night.

She and Barbara shared a room at Fiveapples Farm.

Barbara whined the inevitable contradiction, 'I'm not silly,' but added immediately, 'you wouldn't be so cross, if you knew what I know. I expect you'd laugh too.'

'Well, what is it?'

'I shan't tell you.'

Alex was not particularly curious, but she had been the nursery autocrat too long to be able to endure resistance to her command.

'Tell me at once, Barbara.'

'No, I won't.'

'Yes, you will. Well, what is it about?' said Alex, changing her tactics.

'It's about Cedric.'

'Is he in a scrape?'

'No, it's just something he did.'

'*What*? Did he tell you about it?'

'Oh no. He doesn't know I know. He'd be furious if he did, I expect.'

'Who told you? Does anyone else know?'

'Nobody told me. One other person knows,' giggled Barbara, jumping up and down in her petticoat.

'Keep still, you'll have the candle over. Who's the other person who knows?'

'Guess.'

'Oh, I can't; don't be so silly. I am not going to ask you any more.'

'Well,' said Barbara in a great hurry, 'it's Marie Munroe then; it's about her.'

'What about her? She didn't take any notice of anyone except Cedric, and I think it was very rude and stupid of her.'

'It was Cedric's doing much more than hers,' Barbara said shrewdly. 'I think he thinks he is in love with her. I saw them in the shrubbery when we were playing hide-and-seek; and – what do you think, Alex?'

'Well, what?'

'Cedric kissed her – I saw him.'

'Then,' said Alex, 'it was perfectly hateful of him and of Marie and of you.'

'Why of *me*?' shrieked Barbara in a high key of indignation. 'What have I done, I should like to know?'

'You'd no business to say anything about it. Put out the candle, Barbara, I'm going to get into bed.'

In the darkness Alex lay with her mind in a tumult. It seemed to her incredible that her brother, whom she had always supposed to despise every form of sentimentality, as he did any display of feeling on the part of his family, should have wanted to kiss little, red-haired Marie, whom he had only known for one day, and who was by far the least pretty of any of the three Munroe sisters. 'And to kiss her in the shrubbery like that!'

Alex felt disgusted and indignant. She thought about it for a long while before she went to sleep, although she would gladly have dismissed the incident from her mind. Most of all, perhaps, she was filled with astonishment. Why should anyone want to kiss Marie Munroe?

In the depths of her heart was another wonder which she never formulated even to herself, and of which she would, for very shame, have strenuously denied the existence.

Why had she not the same mysterious attraction as unbeautiful little Marie? Alex knew instinctively that it would never have occurred, say, to Noel Cardew – to ask if he might kiss her. She did not want him to – would have been shocked and indignant at the mere idea – but, unconsciously, she wished that he had wanted to.

CHAPTER SIX

THE END OF AN ERA

No salient landmarks ever seemed to Alex to render eventful the two and a half years that elapsed between those summer holidays at Fiveapples Farm and her final departure from the Liège convent to begin her grown-up life at home.

The re-arrangement of the day's routine consequent on the beginning of the winter half-year caused her to miss Queenie less acutely than she had done when she first came home for the holidays, and with Queenie's absence there were fewer revolts against convent law, and less disfavour from the authorities.

She made no other great friends. Marie Munroe showed her a marked friendliness at first, but Alex could not forget that giggling revelation of Barbara's, and shrank from her advances unmistakably. She had very little in common with her French contemporaries, and knew that they thought her English accent and absence of proficiency in needlework, marks of eccentricity and of bad form, so that she became self-conscious and aggressive before them.

She was hardly aware of her own intense loneliness – the

poignant realization of it was to come later – but the want of any channel of self-expression for her over-developed emotional capabilities produced in her a species of permanent discontent that reacted on her health and on her spirits, so that she got the reputation, least enviable of any in schoolgirl circles, of being 'a tragedy queen.'

Her morose pallor, partly the result of an under-vitalized system, and partly of her total lack of any interest in her surroundings, was considered fair game.

'Voyez, Alex! Elle a son air bête aujourd'hui.'

'A qui l'enterrement, Alex?'

They were quite good-humoured, and did not mean to hurt her. It was not their fault that such pin-pricks stabbed her and sent her away to cry over her own friendlessness until she felt sick and exhausted.

She did not expend on anyone else the extravagant worship bestowed upon Queenie Torrance. For a year she wrote to Queenie throughout the holidays, and received meagre and unsatisfactory replies, and then gradually the correspondence ceased altogether, and Alex only looked forward with an occasional vague curiosity to the possibility of meeting Queenie again in London, on the terms of equality symbolized by their both being 'grown-up.'

During her last year at school, lack of intimate intercourse with anyone, and the languid sentimentality of adolescence, made her take for the first time some interest in religion as understood at the convent. She prolonged her weekly confession, which had hitherto been a matter of routine to be got through as rapidly as possible, in order to obtain the solace of talking about herself, and derived a certain tepid pleasure in minutely following and applying to herself the more anecdotal portions of the New Testament.

For a time, it seemed to her that she had found a refuge.

Then came the affair of the examination. Alex, in her last term, and taking part in the final midsummer *concours*, could not bear the penalty of failure which it seemed to her would be displayed in the mediocrity which had all along been her portion. She had never been admitted to the virtuous society of the *enfants de Marie*, had never taken more than one of the less distinguished prizes at the end of any term, and had no warmly-worded report to display her popularity and the sense of loss that her departure would leave.

Her place in the half-yearly examination was not a good one. She had none of Cedric's power of concentration, and her abilities were not such as to win her any regard in the continental and Catholic system of education of the middle nineties.

She cheated over the examination.

It was quite easy to copy from the girl next to her, who happened to be one of the best vehicles for carefully-tabulated and quite unconnected facts in the school. Alex could read the dates, and the proper names, and all the principal words on her history paper, and transferred them to her own, clothing the dry bones in the imaginative fabric of her own words, for the English girls were allowed to do most of the papers in their own language.

At the end of the morning she was oddly elated, at the sight of her well-filled paper, and felt no qualms at all. In the afternoon she was again next to Marie-Louise, and congratulated herself that the paper should be the literature one. Arithmetic, she knew, was not the strong point of Marie-Louise, and besides, it would be almost impossible to copy the working of problems figure for figure without ultimate detection.

That night, however, when Alex knelt down to say her prayers, she was suddenly overwhelmed by remorse and terror.

Her crime came between her and God.

The vaguely comforting belief that because she was lonely and miserable, He would vouchsafe to her an especial pity, was destroyed. Between God and a sinner, so Alex had been told, lay an impassable gulf that only repentance, confession, atonement and punishment could bridge – and even then, an indelible entry against one's name testified to eventual exposure and shame at some dreadful, inevitable assizes, when sins hidden and forgotten, large and small, of commission and omission alike, would be made known to all the world, assembled together for the Last Judgment. Faced with this inevitable retribution, Alex felt that no present success was worth it, and wondered whether she could not repair her wickedness as far as possible on the morrow by confession.

But when the morrow had come, the Day of Judgment seemed far removed from the hot July morning, and the breaking-up, when the result of the examinations would be heard, a very present reality indeed.

It was a relief to the hot, tossing sensation of balancing values in her mind, to remember that it was the day of the Catechism examination, which would be viva voce.

She acquitted herself very badly, and the temptation to retrieve her failure in the afternoon was irresistible, when she again found herself placed next to the prodigy Marie-Louise.

The paper was headed 'Histoire de l'Église,' and immense value was attached to proficiency in the subject, strenuously taught to the convent pupils out of enormous old-fashioned volumes containing much loyal fiction with a modicum of distorted historical fact.

Alex fell.

She could overlook her neighbour's papers so easily, hardly even turning her head, that it only struck her as inconvenient, and did not awake in her any fear of detection, when presently Marie-Louise pulled a piece of blotting-paper towards her so that it covered the page on which she was working.

Alex finished the question to which Marie-Louise had unwittingly supplied her with material for the answer, and looked about her, subconsciously waiting for the removal of the blotting-paper. Her eyes met those of a younger child, seated exactly opposite to her, whose sharp, dark gaze was fixed upon her with a sort of eager, contemptuous horror. In that instant, when it seemed as though her heart had stopped beating, Alex knew herself detected.

The colour rushed from her face and she felt cold and giddy.

Lacking the instinctive guard against self-betrayal which is the hall-mark of the habitual deceiver, her terrified gaze turned straight to Marie-Louise.

The smooth, dark head was bent low, one hand still

clutched at the covering blotting-paper, and the ear and piece of cheek which were all that Alex could see, were scarlet.

Marie-Louise knew.

The sharp-eyed child opposite had seen Alex cheat, and had no doubt conveyed a silent telegraphic warning.

It seemed to Alex that the world had stopped. Accusation, disgrace, expulsion, all whirled through her mind and left no permanent image there. Her imagination stopped utterly dead at the horror of it.

She sat perfectly motionless for the remaining hours of the morning, unconscious of the passage of time, only conscious of an increasing sense of physical sickness.

It was an absolute relief to her when the bell rang and she found herself obliged to get up and move across the long class-room with the others to give up her papers.

'Vous êtes malade, Alexandra?'

'J'ai mal-au-cœur,' said Alex faintly.

She was sent to the infirmary to lie down, and the old lay-sister in charge of it was so kind to her, and commiserated her wan, forlorn appearance so pityingly, that Alex burst into a flood of tears that relieved the tension of her body, and sent her, quivering, but uncomprehendingly sensible of relief, to rest exhaustedly upon the narrow infirmary bed with little white curtains drawn all round it.

No doubt everyone would soon know of her disgrace, and she would be expelled, to the shame and anger of her father and mother, and the downfall of all her boastings to Barbara. No doubt God had abandoned one so unworthy of His forgiveness – but Sœur Clementine was kind, and it seemed, in the incredible comfort of a little human tenderness, that nothing else mattered.

And, after all, that hour's anticipation proved to be the worst that happened to her. She went downstairs for the evening preparation, and Marie-Louise, a trusted *enfant de Marie*, obtained permission to speak to her alone, and solemnly conducted her to the lavatory, as the most private place in the school.

Standing over the sink, with its stiff and solitary tap of cold water, Marie-Louise conducted her inquiry with business-like, passionless directness.

Alex made no attempt either to deny her sin or to palliate it. She was mentally and emotionally far too much exhausted for any effort, and it did not even occur to her that any excuse could avail her anything.

Marie-Louise was not at all unkind.

She knew all about *la charité*, and was agreeably conscious of exercising this reputable virtue to the full, when she informed Alex that no one should ever know of the lapse from her, provided that Alex, making her own explanation to the class-mistress, should withdraw her papers from the examination.

'But what can I say to her?' asked Alex.

'Quant à ça,' said Marie-Louise, in the detached tones of one who had accomplished her duty and felt no further interest on the point at issue, 'quant à ça, débrouillez-vous avec votre conscience.'

To this task she left Alex.

And Alex ended by doing nothing at all. Partly from

inertia, partly because she knew that Marie-Louise would never ask her what she had done, she shirked the shame and trouble of confession to her class-mistress, and let her papers go in with the others. She knew that she would not get a high place, for her work all through the term had been bad, and would have to be taken into consideration, and over all the remaining papers she muddled hopelessly. Besides, she was leaving for good, and no one would know.

She had lost her self-respect when she first realized that she was cheating, and it was then, as she neared the completion of her seventeenth year, that the belief was ineradicably planted in Alex' soul that she had been born with a natural love of evil, and that goodness was an abstract attitude of mind to which she could never do more than aspire fruitlessly, with no slightest expectation of attainment. She was further conscious of an intense determination to hide the knowledge of her own innate badness from everyone.

If she were ever seen in her true colours, no one would love her, and Alex already knew dimly, and with a further sense of having strange, low standards of her own, that she wanted to be loved more than anything in the world.

Far more than she wanted to be good.

The affair of the examinations passed, and although Alex did not forget it, she mostly remembered it as merely the culminating scandal of a succession of petty evasions and cowardly deceptions.

She left Liège without regret.

She had hated the physical discomfort of the conventual system, the insufficient hours of sleep, the bitter cold of the

Belgian winters and the streaming rain that defiled the summers; she had hated the endless restrictions and the minute system of *surveillance* that was never relaxed; above all, she had hated the sense of her own isolation in a crowd, her own utter absence of attraction for her kind.

It seemed to Alex that when she joined the mysterious ranks of grown-up people everything would be different. She never doubted that with long dresses and piled-up hair, her whole personality would change, and the meaningless chaos of life reduce itself to some comprehensible solution.

Everything all her life had been tending towards the business of 'growing up.' Everything that she was taught at home impressed the theory that her 'coming out' would usher in the realities of life, and nothing impressed her more with a sense of the tremendous importance of the approaching change than Lady Isabel's greeting, when she came back to Clevedon Square after her final term at Liège.

'We've put off Scotland for a week, darling – your father's been so good about it – so that I may see about your clothes. I've made appointments with Marguerite and the other places for you, so there'll be nothin' to do but try on, but, of course, I shall have to see the things myself before they finish them, and tell them about the colours; they're sure to want to touch everything up with pink or blue, and white is so much prettier for a young girl. White with a tiny little *diamanté* edging, I thought, for one of your evenin' dresses . . .

'The first thing, of course, is your hair. Louise must go with you to Hugo's, and watch them very carefully while they do it in two or three different styles, then she'll be able to do it for you every evening. I expect she'll have to do it every day to begin with, but you must try and learn. I should like you to be *able* to be independent of a maid in that sort of way – one never knows quite that some time one mightn't find oneself stranded for a day or two. . . .

'I don't think your hair will need waving, Alex, which is such a comfort. So many women have to wear their fringe in curlers every night – thank Heaven, I've never had to. As a matter of fact, they say fringes are goin' out now, but I'm certainly not goin' to let yours grow until we're quite certain about it . . . and a bald forehead is always so unbecomin'.'

Alex listened with a sense of importance and excitement, but she was also rather bewildered. The contrast between all this preoccupation with her clothes and her appearance, and the austere mental striving after spiritual or moral results which had permeated the convent atmosphere, was too violent.

'You'll be interested in it all, my darling, won't you?' asked Lady Isabel disappointedly. 'I couldn't bear to have a daughter who didn't care about her things. Some girls are like that – so disappointin'; after one's had all the trouble of their upbringin' and is lookin' forward to a little reward.'

Alex could find no words in which to explain what she knew quite well, that she was as full of eager anticipations as Lady Isabel could wish, but was too much bewildered by the novelty of it all, as yet, to give any expression to them.

She became rather boisterous and unconvincing in her endeavours to express, by means which were not spontaneous, the pleasure and excitement expected of her.

'You'll learn to move prettily and quietly, darling, and we must see about some dancin' lessons before next year. Dancin' fashions alter so quickly now-a-days,' said Lady Isabel, her low, gentle tones a shade lower and more gentle than usual.

'But I shan't go to balls – yet,' stammered Alex.

She and Barbara had only been allowed a very few children's parties, and for the last few years she had been considered too old for these. She thought of a ball as a prolonged, glorified party.

'Not until after your presentation, of course, and that won't be till the spring. But there may be one or two affairs in the country at Christmas, if I take you to stay about, as I hope. You see, darling, my plan is to let you have the next two months in the country with little Barbara, just as usual – only you must take great care not to let yourself get freckled in the sun – and then, when you come back to town in October, you can have your hair properly put up, and come about with me, so as to get to know people and make a little beginnin' before there's any question of really doing the season properly next summer.'

Alex began to feel vastly important. She had never been the centre of so much attention before.

Evidently this affair of coming out was the culminating point to which all life had hitherto been tending.

Even Barbara treated her with a rather envious respect now.

Only Cedric remained unimpressed, and treated his eldest sister's marked tendency to assume airs of extreme maturity with silent indifference.

His school career was proceeding more triumphantly than ever, and his 'removes' succeeded one another with a rapidity only less startling than his increasing reputation as a cricketer.

He spent most of his holidays with a schoolfellow, and showed himself rather scornful of girls in general and of his sisters in particular, although he played willingly enough with little Pamela, who had grown to an attractive and talkative age.

Barbara asked him once, with the touch of slyness characteristic of her in certain moods, whether he remembered Marie Munroe.

'Red-haired American kid? Oh yes,' said Cedric loftily. 'Didn't she have a sister who was bosom friends with Alex at Liège, or some rot of that kind?'

And Alex had felt unaccountably relieved at the implication of the evanescent character of Cedric's whilom admiration.

They spent August and September at the seaside on the Cornish coast.

Alex enjoyed the daily bathing, and scrambling over the rocks barefooted, and the picnic teas in any sheltered cove that old Nurse judged sufficiently protected from the profane gaze of possible trippers. But she had all the time the sense that these hot, leisurely days were only a time of waiting, and even when she enjoyed herself most she was conscious of a gnawing impatience for the next step.

The week in London before Lady Isabel and Sir Francis started for Scotland had rather disappointed Alex, although she did not own it, even to herself.

Perpetual 'tryings on' in hot weather had proved a tiring performance, and her feet ached from standing and from the hot pavement, so that she dragged herself rather than walked, or stood on one foot so as to save the other, which had vexed Lady Isabel, and led to a long admonition as to the importance of moving properly and always holding oneself upright.

Moreover, Alex, although she did not give very much thought to her own looks as a rule, had always expected that as soon as she grew up she would almost automatically become very beautiful, and it vexed and surprised her to find that her new frocks, still in a very incompleted stage, did not at once produce any startling change in her appearance. It was also disappointing that her mother and her mother's dress-maker should so often seem to find in her hitherto unsuspected deficiencies.

'Mam'selle won't be able to wear elbow-sleeves just at present, Mòddam, I'm afraid – at least, not until we've got rid of that redness.'

'Dear me, no! I suppose that comes from keepin' her elbows on a school desk – how very vexin'. Really, the nuns must have been very careless to let you get into the way of it, Alex. And it's made your shoulders round, too.'

'Mam'selle *must* keep her shoulders well back if that white chiffon is to look like anything at all,' chimed in Madame Marguerite most impressively. 'It will simply be ruination to let it drop like that in the front . . . takes away all the smartness from it.'

Alex straightened herself uneasily.

'It's such a simple little frock, the whole thing is how it's worn . . .'

Which made Alex feel miserably unequal to the responsibility laid upon her.

'Her neck is very thin,' sighed Lady Isabel, and Madame Marguerite, her large head with its weight of elaborate yellow waves well on one side as she gazed at Alex, had looked very disparaging indeed as she said, in tones more consolatory than hopeful:

'Of course, Mam'selle may fill out a bit before next year.'

Alex, in her heart, had been thankful when it was all over, and she had gone back to the old blue cotton frocks that were to be worn out at the seaside.

Her only responsibility there was the daily struggle of putting up her hair.

To her disgust, and to Barbara's derision, the hairdresser had insisted upon a large, bun-like frame, which made her head ache, and, pinned on by her unskilful hands, displayed a strong tendency to slip down the back of her neck. And however much she might brush and pull her hair over it, there always appeared a hiatus sooner or later, through which a large patch of what Barbara jeeringly called 'false horsehair' might plainly be seen.

In spite of it all, however, Alex enjoyed those last school-room days of hers more than any she had yet known.

Real life was going to begin, and though Alex had no idea as to how the transformation would be effected, she was convinced that everything which she had longed for, and utterly missed, throughout her schooldays would now be hers.

CHAPTER SEVEN

✼✼✼✼✼✼✼✼✼✼✼✼

LONDON SEASON

Alex' first London season, from the very extravagance of her expectations, was a disappointment to her.

Her own appearance, indeed, in her first ball-dress, surprised and delighted her, and she stood before the great pier glass in the drawing-room, under the chandelier which had been specially lit for the occasion, and gazed at her reflection with incredulous admiration.

Her dress, in the height of the prevailing fashion, had been the subject of Lady Isabel's minute and careful consultations with Madame Marguerite of New Bond Street. Of stiff white satin, the neck was cut into a hard square, and the bodice, as it was still called, unsoftened except for a small draping of pleated white chiffon held on the left shoulder with a cluster of dead-white roses, which were repeated at the side of the broad, white-ribbon belt. The most prominent feature of the dress was the immensity of the sleeves, stiffened within by strips of petersham, and standing well up from the shoulders. Thence, the monstrous, balloon-shaped things narrowed imperceptibly, and were gathered in just below the elbow, leaving no hiatus visible between them and the *mousquetaire* white-kid gloves.

The skirt had no train, but fell into plain, heavy folds, sweeping the ground, and with a slight additional length of 'tail,' and a considerable additional fullness behind. A white ostrich-feather fan hung by white satin ribbon from her waist.

'It looks charming,' said Lady Isabel delightedly. 'Better than your presentation frock.'

The servants, who had respectfully petitioned through Lady Isabel's maid to be allowed to see Miss Clare in her ball-dress before she started, were grouped in the doorway, the long white streamers of the maids' caps contrasting sharply with their neat black dresses.

Old Nurse, a privileged personage, was right inside the drawing-room, inspecting critically.

'I never thought you'd look so well, Miss Alex,' she observed candidly. 'They've hid your failings something wonderful, and your hair and complexion was always good, thanks to the care I've took of them – that I will say.'

'Don't those shoes pinch, Alex?' asked Barbara, looking on enviously in her plain schoolroom frock and strapped shoes, with her hair still hanging down her back.

Alex did not care whether her pointed, white satin shoes pinched her feet or not. She was too happy in her first triumph.

It was not quite a solitary triumph, for Sir Francis, after a prolonged gazing through his double eye-glasses that made her flush more than ever from nervousness, gave one of his rare smiles of gratification and said:

'Very pretty indeed. I congratulate you on your appearance, my dear child.'

But it was to Lady Isabel that he turned next moment, with that sudden softened glance that he never bestowed elsewhere.

'How beautifully you've dressed her, my dear. You will be taken for sisters, now that she is in long dresses.'

The compliment was not ill-deserved, and Alex, watching her mother's exquisite flush, felt a vague dissatisfaction with her own immaturity.

She might be pretty, with youthful colouring and smooth skin, but she lacked the poise that added charm to her mother's beauty, and a struggling consciousness of that lack disturbed and vexed her.

'I think she's better without any ornament, don't you, Francis?' asked her mother critically. 'Some girls wear pearls, I know, but I never quite like it – not the first year, anyway.'

Her opera cloak over her shoulders, its cape-like outline and heavy, turned-back collar of swansdown adding to the already disproportionate width of the upper part of her person, Alex followed Lady Isabel into the carriage.

She wore nothing over her head, for fear of disarranging the light Princess-of-Wales' fringe curling on her forehead.

That first ball remained in her mind as a medley of valse tunes, quadrilles and jigging polkas, blazing lights and red and white flowers everywhere, and a sequence of strange young men brought up in rapid succession by the daughters of her hostess and introduced in an unvarying formula, to which each responded by a bow and a polite request for the pleasure of a dance with her. Alex danced readily enough, but found conversation strangely difficult, expecting she knew not what profundities of intercourse which were never forthcoming. Her chief gratification was that of seeing Lady Isabel's pretty, pleased smile at the sight of her daughter dancing.

'Are you enjoyin' yourself, darling?' she asked several times, as Alex returned between each dance to the row of gilt chairs against the wall.

Alex said 'Yes' sincerely enough, but she was all the time reminded of that strange, disconcerting experience that had been hers a year or two earlier, when she had sought to persuade herself of a great success with the boy Noel Cardew.

She boasted of her enjoyment of the ball to Barbara next day, and said that she had been so busy dancing that she had never gone down to supper at all.

'But that must never happen again,' Lady Isabel said, horrified. 'Girls do that sort of thing at first, when they're foolish, and then they get over-tired and lose all their looks and have no more good times.'

It seemed the omega of disaster.

Nevertheless, there were other balls when Alex did not go down to supper, sometimes because no one had asked her to do so.

She nearly always had partners, for she danced reasonably, though not superlatively, well, and introductions were still the fashion. But the number of her partners depended very largely upon the attentiveness of her hostess or of her hostess's daughters. Young men did not always claim dances from her, although they had been amongst her partners at the ball of the week before. Nor did many of them ask for two or three dances in one evening.

Lady Isabel had said, 'Never more than three dances with the same man, Alex, at the very *outside*. It's such bad form to make yourself conspicuous with anyone – your father would dislike it very much.'

Alex bore the warning carefully in mind, and was naïvely surprised that no occasion for making practical application of it should occur. She was intensely anxious to be liked and admired, and she strangely confounded the two issues in her own mind. Attributes such as her clear skin, her exquisitely-kept hair, or her expensive frocks, she thought would promote interest in her amongst her fellow-creatures, and to the same end she simulated an enthusiasm – which was so entirely foreign to her real feelings that it lacked any semblance of body – for the crazes of her immediate generation, centred in Planchette and in the publication of *Barabbas*. She was full of preconceived ideas as to that which constituted attractiveness, and in her very ardour to realize the conventional ideal of the day failed entirely to attract. In intercourse with other girls, still in their first or second season, she slowly began to suspect the deficiencies in herself.

'I'm engaged for nearly every single valse at the Duchess's ball on Tuesday already!' a very young childish-looking little creature exclaimed in Alex' hearing.

Alex was astounded. What could the little thing mean?

'Nearly all my last night's partners will be there, and they've all asked me for dances, and some for two or three,' said the child with ingenuous pride.

Alex was frankly amazed. Lady Mollie was not particularly pretty, and her conversation was the veriest stream of prattle. Yet she was asked to reserve the favour of her dances three days or four days in advance, and the experience was evidently no new one to her, although she had only come out a few weeks earlier than Alex!

It was the same little Lady Mollie who gave Alex a further shock by demanding of her very seriously:

'Do you know a girl called Miss Torrance, a girl with very fair hair? She says she was at school with you.'

'Queenie Torrance? Oh *yes!*' said Alex, the old fervour rushing to her voice at the sudden memory of Queenie, who had left her letters unanswered – of whom she had heard nothing for two years.

'She's tremendously admired by *some* people,' said Lady Mollie, shaking her head with a quaint air of sapience. 'I know two or three who rave about her. Mother says she's rather inclined to be fast. I think people don't like her father very much, and he generally takes her about. You don't know them very well, do you?'

Alex hastily disclaimed any intimacy with Queenie's unpopular parent. She felt disloyal to Queenie for the eagerness with which she did so.

Two nights later, at one of the big evening receptions that Alex enjoyed least of any form of entertainment, Miss Torrance's name was again mentioned to her.

She was listening to the conversation of a brilliantly-good-looking young German Jew, whose name of Goldstein, already spoken with bated breath in financial circles, conveyed less to her inexperience than did the dark, glowing eyes, swarthy skin and the Semitic curve of his handsome nose. His voice was very slightly guttural, and he slurred his r's all but imperceptibly as he spoke.

She found that conversation with him was exceedingly easy, and translated the faint hint of servility in his deference, as did most women not of his own race, into sympathy with her utterances.

'You think so, you really think so . . .?' he inquired gently, when she expressed a *banale* admiration for the prettiness of some girl whose entry, preceded by that of an insignificant couple, had made a slight stir round the huge open doorway of the reception-room.

'Yes,' said Alex, emboldened by the interested look in the dark eyes which he kept upon her face, as though finding it more worthwhile to gaze upon her than upon the entering beauty.

'I have seen more beautiful faces than hers, nevertheless,' he responded.

The eloquence of his look made Alex feel as though she had received a compliment, and she blushed. As though to cover her shyness, the young Jew went on speaking. 'I wonder if you know Miss Torrance – Miss Queenie Torrance?'

She noticed that his throaty voice lingered over the syllables a little.

'She was my great friend at school.'

'Indeed! What a delightful friendship for both, if I may say so. I think I may say that I, also, have the privilege of counting myself amongst the friends of Miss Torrance.'

'I haven't seen her since she left school,' said Alex wistfully. 'I should like to see her.'

'You spoke of beauty just now,' said the young Jew deliberately. 'To my mind Miss Torrance was the beauty of the season, when she came out last year.'

She felt faintly surprised, but spoke hastily lest he should think her jealous, although he had carefully emphasized the date of Queenie's appearance into society.

'I heard only the other day how much she was admired.'

Goldstein's dark face grew darker. 'She is very much admired indeed,' he said emphatically.

'Perhaps she will be here tonight,' Alex suggested, thinking that she would like to see Queenie grown-up.

'She is not coming tonight,' said Goldstein with calm assurance. 'Are you going to the Duchess's ball on Tuesday? But I need not ask.'

Alex felt unreasonably flattered at the homage implied, rather than expressed, in the tone, and replied in the affirmative.

'Then you will see Miss Torrance.'

'Oh, I'm glad,' said Alex. She felt rather elated at the success which her friend must have undoubtedly met with, to be so much admired, and she remembered with added resentment Lady Isabel's old inquiry: 'Torrance – Torrance – who is Torrance?'

'Did you know that the girl I was at Liège with, Queenie Torrance, came out last year, and everyone says she's lovely?' she demanded of her mother.

'I'd forgotten you were at school with her. I remember now,' said Lady Isabel thoughtfully. 'Who says she is lovely?'

'Oh, Lady Mollie and everyone. That Mr. Goldstein I was talking to.'

'Goldstein!' exclaimed her mother with infinite contempt. She was silent for a little while and then said, 'I've heard about the Torrance girl. Men – of a sort – admire her very much indeed, but I should be sorry if you copied her style, Alex.'

Alex felt more curious than ever. Blindly though she had adored Queenie, it had not occurred to her that she would be considered very pretty, and she wondered greatly concerning the development of her old playmate.

When she did see Queenie, at the Duchess's ball, as Goldstein had predicted, Lady Isabel was not with her. Excess of fatigue had unwillingly constrained her to stay at home, while Sir Francis, bored but courteous, escorted his eldest daughter in her stead.

They arrived late, and stood for a few minutes in the doorway, watching the kaleidoscopic scene of colour and movement in the great illuminated ballroom.

Alex' attention was attracted by a group of men all gathered near the door, and prominent among them Goldstein, his eager, searching gaze fixed upon the broad stairway without, up and down which innumerable figures passed and re-passed. From the sudden lightning flash in his ardent black gaze, not less than from a sort of movement instantly communicated to the whole group, Alex guessed that he had focussed the object of his quest.

The announcement made at the head of the stairs was inaudible amid the crashing of dance music, but Alex recognized the entering couple in a flash.

Colonel Torrance, white-haired, with black moustache and eyebrows, upright and soldierly still, had changed less than Queenie. She looked much taller than Alex had imagined her, and her graceful outline was fuller, but she moved exquisitely.

Her very fair hair, at a time when every woman wore a curled fringe, was combed straight back from her rounded brow, leaving only the merest escaping curls at either temple, and gathered into the ultra-fashionable 'jug-handle' knot on the top of her head. She wore a wreath of tiny blue forget-me-nots that deepened the tint of her grey-blue eyes, and the colour was repeated freely in the deep frills and ruchings of her white, *décolletée* dress, of an elaboration that Alex instinctively knew her mother would not have countenanced. Turquoises were twisted round the white, full column of her throat, and clasped her rounded arms.

Alex watched her eagerly.

Every man in the little waiting group was pressing round her, claiming first possession of her attention.

The faint, remotely smiling sweetness of Queenie's heart-shaped mouth recalled to Alex with extraordinary vividness the schoolgirl at the Liège convent.

Goldstein, his eyes flaming, stood demonstratively waiting, with insolent security in his bearing, while she dispensed her favours right and left, always with the same chilly, composed sweetness.

The music, which had ceased, broke into the lilt of the *Blue Danube*, and on the instant Goldstein imperiously approached Queenie. She swayed towards him, still smiling slightly, and they drifted into the throng of dancers. Alex turned round with a sort of gasp.

What must it feel like to be the heroine of a ballroom triumph, to know that a dozen men would count the evening worthwhile for the privilege of dancing once with her, that they would throng in the doorway to watch and wait for her coming?

Some of them remained in the doorway still, watching her dance, the folds of her dress and her great white fan gathered into one hand, her white, heavy eyelids cast down under her pure, open forehead, and Goldstein's arm encircling her waist as he guided her steps skilfully round the crowded room. Alex saw that Sir Francis, his double eyeglass raised, was also watching the couple.

'I wonder who that remarkably pretty woman is, of whom young Goldstein is very obviously enamoured?'

Alex felt oddly that Sir Francis supposed Queenie to be of maturer years than she in reality was.

'It's Queenie Torrance, father. She was at school with me,' Alex repeated. 'I've not seen her since she grew up – but she's only about a year older than I am.'

'Indeed!'

Curiosity as to the unanimity of masculine judgment made Alex appeal to him with a question.

'Do you think she's pretty, father?'

'Exceedingly striking – beautiful, in fact,' said Sir Francis.

Queenie was not beautiful, and Alex knew it, but the glamour of her magnetic personality was evidently as potent

with older men as with young Goldstein and his contemporaries. Alex felt a curious pang, half of envy and half of
wonder.

Sir Francis put down his glasses. 'A pity,' he said deliberately,
'that she is not – altogether –' and raised his grizzled
eyebrows.

CHAPTER EIGHT

GOLDSTEIN AND QUEENIE

Queenie Torrance spoke to Alex that night with characteristic suavity, and showed pleasure at meeting her again.

'Those old convent days seem a long way off, don't they?' she asked, smiling a little.

Her glance, sweeping the big ball-room, seemed to appraise its glories and claim them for her own.

It was the glance, rather than the words, to which Alex replied.

'You're having a splendid time, aren't you, Queenie? You like being grown-up?'

'I adore it,' said Miss Torrance, her eyes gleaming like stars.

Alex did not wonder at it.

Night after night she watched Queenie Torrance accepting as her right the homage of innumerable men, halving the favour of her dances at crowded balls where 'wall-flowers' were too numerous to be rescued from oblivion by the most determined of hostesses, going down to supper on the arm of young Goldstein and lingering with him in prolonged *tête-à-tête* – Goldstein, at the little round table across which he leant,

111

recklessly oblivious of comment, endeavouring, sometimes fruitlessly throughout a whole evening, to obtain one direct look from those widely-set, downcast eyes under their flaxen lashes.

It was not easy, Alex found, to talk to Queenie. They often met at entertainments, and once or twice in the Park, but Queenie never rode in the mornings, as Alex sometimes did, and Lady Isabel did not allow her daughter to take up the fashionable practice of bicycling in Battersea Park, at which Queenie Torrance, in the neatest and most daring of rational costumes, was reported to excel. Once Alex, as she had said before in her childish days, asked Lady Isabel:

'Mother, may I ask Queenie Torrance to tea here? We meet everywhere, and it will be so odd if I never ask her to come here. Besides, I should like to have her.'

'I'm sorry, Alex, but I'd rather you contented yourself with meetin' her in society – if you do.'

'Why?' said Alex unwisely, urged by some mysterious unreason to provoke the answer which she already anticipated with resentment.

'She's not the sort of girl I should care about your bein' friends with very much,' said Lady Isabel without heat. 'I hear she's already bein' talked about.'

Alex knew what the words meant, uttered by her mother and her mother's circle of intimates.

'Why is she being talked about?' Alex asked rebelliously.

'Any girl who goes in for bein' fast gets talked about,' said Lady Isabel severely. 'And it does them no good in the long run either. Men may flirt with girls of that sort, and like to dance with them and pay them attention, but they don't marry them. A man likes his wife to be simple and well-bred and dignified.'

'I'm sure heaps of people would like to marry Queenie.'

'How do you know?' Lady Isabel asked quickly.

Alex did not reply. She only knew that men looked at Queenie Torrance as they did not look at other women, and, true to the traditions of youth and of the race to which she belonged, the admiration of a man for a woman, to her inexperience spelt a proposal of marriage.

'I don't want to be hard on a girl who is, after all, very young,' said Lady Isabel. 'And, of course, her father doesn't look after her. She is allowed to go to restaurants with him and every sort of thing . . . It's not the girl's fault exactly, though I don't like the way she dresses, and a wreath of artificial flowers, or whatever it is she wears in her hair, is thoroughly bad form. But one can't be too particular, Alex, and I *do* want you to make a success of things, and have the right friends and not the wrong ones.'

The wistful anxiety in her mother's voice, no less than in her glance at her daughter, made Alex wonder sensitively if, perhaps, she were secretly somewhat disappointed.

Certainly no overwhelming triumph had attended Alex' social career. She was merely the newly-come-out daughter of a charming and popular mother, less pretty than many of the season's débutantes, alternately embarrassingly self-conscious, or else, when she found herself at her ease, with an unbecomingly dictatorial manner. She had been led to expect, from constant veiled references to the subject, that as soon as she grew up, opportunity would be afforded her to attain the goal of every well-born girl's destiny – that of matrimony. Girls who became engaged to be married in their first season were a success, those who had already twice, or perhaps thrice, been the round of London gaiety with no tangible result of the sort, had almost invariably to give way to a younger sister, in order that she, in her turn, might have 'the chances' of which they had failed to profit.

Of young women of twenty-two or twenty-three years old, still going yearly through the season, Lady Isabel merely said matter-of-factly:

'What a pity!'

For the first time, a disquieting twinge seized Alex, lest the same words should apply to her. No one had shown the faintest inclination to ask her in marriage, or even expressed any particular admiration for her.

She could not imagine any of the men whom she knew falling in love with her.

At balls or dinner-parties, she made conversation with her partners. They never grew to know one another more intimately. Sometimes she had heard girls talk of looking forward to some forthcoming entertainment because they knew that their particular friends would be there.

She herself did not care. She was on the same terms with all of them – polite, impersonal, mutually rather bored and boring.

The nearest approach to intercourse other than merely surface that she attained to, was with Queenie's most openly declared worshipper, Maurice Goldstein. His manner to all women verged upon the effusive, and Alex was secretly faintly ashamed of feeling slightly, but perceptibly, flattered at the deference which he showed her, and even at his favourite mannerism of gazing straight into her eyes as he shook hands with her on meeting or parting.

Although Lady Isabel never invited him to Clevedon Square, and sometimes spoke of him as 'that dreadful young Jew who seems to get himself asked everywhere,' she did not forbid Alex to dance with him, and he was the only young man of her acquaintance who invariably asked her to keep a second dance for him later in the evening.

She felt greatly curious as to his sentiment for Queenie, partly from youth's love of romance, partly from a desire to find out, if she could, both the cause and the effect of the process known as 'falling in love'.

If she knew more about it, she felt dimly, perhaps it might happen also to her.

One night, towards the end of the season, at the last big ball she was to attend that year, Alex was taken down to supper by Maurice Goldstein.

She was surprised, and for a moment flattered, for Queenie was also present, although she had apparently vouchsafed him neither word nor look.

Goldstein gave Alex his arm and conducted her ceremoniously downstairs to the supper-room.

It was late in the evening, only four or five couples, or an occasional group of three or four, lingered at the small, round, flower-decked tables.

'Shall we come here?' said Goldstein rather morosely.

He selected a table in a remote corner, and as she took her seat, Alex perceived that they were within sight of the alcove where sat Queenie Torrance with her partner, a young Danish diplomat whom Alex knew only by sight.

'Who is that?' she asked almost involuntarily, as Goldstein's lowering gaze followed the direction of her own.

The young man beside her needed no more to make him launch out into emphatic speech.

Alex was half frightened, as she watched the glow in his eyes and the rapid gesticulations of his hands, as though emotion had startled him into a display of the racial characteristics that he habitually concealed so carefully.

He told her crudely that he adored Queenie, and that it drove him nearly mad to see her in the company of other men.

'But why don't you ask her to marry you?' exclaimed Alex innocently.

Goldstein stared at her.

'I have asked her fourteen times,' he said at last with a slight gasp.

'Fourteen times!' Alex was astounded.

According to her preconceived notions a proposal was carefully led up to, uttered at some propitious moment, preferably by moonlight, and then and there either definitely accepted or rejected.

'But I shouldn't have thought you'd even seen her fourteen times,' she remarked naïvely.

'I see her every day,' Goldstein said gloomily. 'It's playing the deuce with my business. You won't give me away, I know –

you're her friend, aren't you? – and people are so stupid and conventional, they might talk.'

Alex remembered Lady Isabel. Was this what she had meant?

'I can always manage to see her. I know her movements, and when I can meet her, and when I may take her out to lunch or tea – some quiet place, of course.'

Alex was puzzled.

'But are you engaged?'

'Yes, a thousand times!' he answered in low, vehement tones, and then appeared to recollect himself. 'She has never said no, although I can't induce her to say yes,' he admitted; 'and I have to see her surrounded and admired everywhere she goes, and have no hold on her whatever. If she would only marry me!' He made a gesture of rather theatrical despair, indicating the far corner where the young Dane still sat, oblivious of everything but Queenie, drooping over the small round table that separated them.

'Cad! he's going to smoke,' Goldstein muttered furiously below his breath.

The room had emptied, and Alex saw Queenie deliberately glance over her shoulder, as though to make sure of being unobserved. Her eyes moved unseeingly across Alex and Maurice Goldstein. The rest of the room was empty. With a little half-shrug of her white shoulders she delicately took a cigarette from the case that the diplomat was eagerly proffering.

It was the first time that Alex had seen a woman with a cigarette between her lips. She felt herself colouring hotly, as she watched, with involuntary fascination, Queenie's partner carefully lighting the cigarette for her, his hand very close to her face.

She dared not look at Goldstein. The cheap vulgarity of Queenie's display of modern freedom shocked her sincerely, nor could even her inexperience blind her to the underlying motive governing Queenie's every gesture.

She fumbled hastily for her fan and gloves.

'Shall we come upstairs again?' she asked in a stifled voice.

Goldstein rose without a word.

Alex, venturing to cast one glance at him, saw that his face had grown white.

As he took her back to Lady Isabel, he spoke in a quick, low, dramatic voice between clenched teeth:

'You saw? She knows she is driving me frantic; but after this – it's all over.'

Alex was frightened, and yet exultant at playing even a secondary rôle in what seemed to her to be a drama of reality.

An hour later, sitting, for the time being partnerless, beside her mother, she saw Queenie re-enter the ballroom, followed by the Dane.

Queenie's widely-set eyes were throwing a glance, innocent, appealing, the length of the long room. At once her eyelids dropped again. But in that instant Maurice Goldstein had left the wall against which he had been leaning, listless and sulky-looking, and was making his way through the lessening crowd.

Alex, wondering, saw him reach the side of the tall, white-clad figure, and claim her from the young diplomat.

He gravely offered Queenie his arm, and Alex saw them no more that night. She herself drove home to Clevedon Square beside Lady Isabel with her mind in a tumult.

She felt that for the first time she had seen love at close quarters, and although a faint but bitter regret that the experience had not been a personal one underlay all her sensations, she was full of excitement.

'No more late nights after this week,' said Lady Isabel, her voice sleepy. 'A rest will do you good, Alex. You are losing your freshness.'

Alex scarcely listened. She stood impatiently while the weary maid, whose duty it was to sit up for her mistress's return, undid the complicated fastenings of her frock, and took the pins out of her hair.

'I'll brush it myself,' said Alex hastily. 'Goodnight, mother.'

'Good-night; don't come down till lunch-time, Alex – we are not doing anything.'

Alex carried her ball dress carefully over her arm and went up one more flight of stairs to her own room, wrapped in her pink dressing-gown, and with her hair loose on her shoulders.

Sitting on the edge of her bed, and gazing at her own reflection in the big, swinging mirror, she made personal application of the small fragments of human drama that she had just witnessed.

What man would speak and think of her as Maurice Goldstein spoke and thought of Queenie Torrance?

When would any man's ardent glance answer hers; any man make his way to her through a crowd in response to the silent summons of her eyes?

119

She fell into one of the idle, romantic dreams evoked by a highly-strung imagination, untempered by any light of experience. But the hero of the dream was a nebulous, shadowy figure of fiction. No man of flesh and blood held any place in the slender fabric of her fancies.

It occurred to her, more with a sense of disconcertment than of that panic which was to come later, that she did not possess the power of drawing any reality from her communion with others, and that no intimacy other than one of the surface had as yet ever resulted from any intercourse of hers with her fellow-creatures. Her nearest approach to reality had been that one-sided, irrational adoration of her schooldays for Queenie Torrance, that had met with no return, and with so much and such universal condemnation.

Alex did not doubt that the condemnation was justified. The impression left upon her adolescent mind remained ineradicable: it was wrong to attach so much importance to loving; it was *different*, in some mysterious, culpable way, to feel as she did – that nothing mattered except the people one loved, that nothing was so much worthwhile as the affection and understanding which one knew so well, from oneself, must exist, and for the bestowal of which on one's own lonely, ardent spirit one prayed so passionately; and all these desires, being wrong and unlike other people, must at all costs be concealed and denied. Thus Alex, putting the perverted and yet unescapable interpretation of her disconsolate youth upon such experience of life as had been vouchsafed to her.

Still sitting on the side of the bed and facing the looking-glass, she sought in her own reflection for traces of the spell wielded by Queenie Torrance. She had not yet outgrown the belief that beauty and the power to attract should be synonymous.

Was she as pretty as Queenie?

Her colour was bright and pure, and her hazel eyes reflected the brown lights gleaming in her soft, tumbled hair, that fell no lower than her shoulders. She reflected disconsolately on the undue prominence of the two, white front teeth that the plate which had tormented her childhood had just failed to render level with the others.

Straight brows added to the regularity of her features, only the corners of her mouth habitually drooping very slightly. The angularity which Lady Isabel so regretted was sharply manifested in the exposed collar-bones just above the open dressing-gown, and in the childishly thin arms and wrists. With an odd, detached shrewdness, she appraised the prominent attributes of her own appearance, its ungraceful immaturity.

As she got slowly into bed, she passed other, moral, attributes, in fleeting review.

Alex believed that one might be loved for one's goodness, if not for one's beauty. But she could not suppose herself to be good. The tradition of the nursery black sheep still clung to her.

Should love come to her, she had nothing but the force of the answer within her to bring to it, and that force she had been taught to think of in the light of an affliction to be overcome.

Yet Alex Clare fell asleep smiling a little, nursing the

foolish, romantic fancies that usurped the place of realities, and unaware that the temperament which craves to give all, is often that of which least will ever be asked.

CHAPTER NINE

❉❉❉❉❉❉❉❉❉❉❉

SCOTLAND

Queenie's engagement to young Goldstein was formally announced at the beginning of the year following that one in which Alex made her début.

'A most suitable match, I should imagine,' was Lady Isabel's emphasized comment.

Alex was romantically delighted, and hoped for an opportunity of obtaining first-hand impressions.

Queenie, however, sent only the most conventional of notes in reply to Alex' eagerly written congratulation, and Alex had only a glimpse of her at the crowded wedding, exquisitely pale and pure under her veil, with Goldstein, his swarthy face radiant and illuminated, at her side.

Remembering the night when the young Jew had spoken to her freely of his adoration for her friend, Alex, with awkward fervour, addressed a few words of ardent congratulation to him.

He showed his remarkably white teeth in a quick smile, brilliant with triumph and happiness, and wrung her hand warmly; but alas! his eyes failed to answer her gaze, and it was obvious that no deeper issues between them held any place in his recollections.

Alex went away vaguely disappointed and humiliated.

She, who so longed for a first place, seemed doomed to relegation to the ranks. Even at home there was no longer any excitement such as that which had surrounded her launch into the great world, and Lady Isabel occasionally betrayed a hint of disappointment that no family council had as yet been required on the subject of Alex' future, such as those which had punctuated the epoch of her own brief girlhood.

Indeed, it was rather Barbara who was the centre of attention.

She still suffered from backache and general languor, consequent upon over-rapid growth during the year she had spent on the flat of her back. Old Nurse pitied and was much inclined to spoil her, dosed her religiously with a glass of port at eleven o'clock every morning, and supported her whining assertions that lessons with Mademoiselle made her ill.

'I want to go to school,' said Barbara inconsistently. 'Alex went to school, so why shouldn't I?'

'Darlin' child, you know very well that your father won't hear of girls goin' to school. A convent is quite different – but I certainly shan't send you to that sort of establishment, after the trick they played me with Alex, sendin' her back round-shouldered, and with her hands all clapped and red and covered with chilblains. *Never* again,' said Lady Isabel.

Barbara sulked.

She sulked so long and so effectively that the unfortunate Mademoiselle came of her own accord to implore that

Barbara might be released from the schoolroom. She was not learning anything, and her example was making little Pamela naughty and defiant.

'What a plague children are!' Lady Isabel said helplessly.

She consulted her friends, drawing a plaintively humorous picture of the recalcitrant young person, which, to the annoyance of Alex, caused a certain amount of amused sympathy to be expressed in Barbara's favour.

At last someone suggested that she should be sent abroad. Not to a school or a convent, certainly not – everyone was unanimous on that point excepting one or two ultra-Catholic old aunts of Sir Francis – but to a charming Marquise, living at Neuilly, and desirous of companionship for her only child, a girl of about the same age as Barbara.

'She will learn to speak French like a native, and have dancing and singing lessons with the Hélène child, and go to all the art galleries and places . . . That girl of the Duchess went there to be finished just before she came out, and *loved* it, and she came back so much improved – knowing how to put on her clothes, you know . . . just the sort of thing that makes all the difference.'

So spoke Lady Isabel's enthusiastic friends.

Barbara was not consulted, but when the plans had been finally settled upon and everything arranged, she was told, in accordance with the usage of her day, that as she was so discontented and troublesome at home, her parents felt obliged, for the sake of the younger children, to send her away from them. Barbara, following her wont, said nothing at all, and did not relax her pouting expression, but once back in the schoolroom again, she jumped up and down on the sofa in a manner denoting extravagant glee.

'I knew they'd have to give in,' she chanted. 'I knew they would, I knew they would.'

For a long while she teased Archie and Pamela by refusing to give them any explanation, and at the same time exciting their curiosity by her continual reference to an approaching triumphant emancipation for her, until Cedric, home for the Easter holidays, and expert in the administration of school-boy tortures, ruthlessly made use of them to reduce his sister to her proper position of inferiority.

Barbara was sent to Neuilly early in April, and Alex proceeded to enter upon the second phase of her social career.

It was less of a success than her first season had been.

It was assumed that she had by this time made her own friends, and her mother's contemporaries accordingly took less pains in the matter of introductions on her behalf.

If it be true that nothing succeeds like success, it is truer still that nothing fails so completely as a failure.

When Alex had sat out four or five dances at a ball, partnerless, her conviction of her own social degradation was absolutely overwhelming. Her surroundings only interested her as a background to her own personality, and as she derived no pleasure, but only disappointment and mortification, from the majority of the functions at which she was present, her young, expressive face unconsciously advertised both her vexation and the cause of it.

Her youth and her vanity alike were in rebellion against

the truth; which she more than half divined, that she, who so longed to please and to attract, was as utterly devoid of that magnetic charm possessed by other girls in a lesser, and by Queenie Goldstein in supreme, degree, as it was possible for a reasonably pretty and healthy young girl to be.

Neither her health nor her beauty improved, moreover.

Late hours, in her case uncounteracted by the vivid sparkle of enjoyment, drew unbecoming dark circles beneath her eyes, and the physical fatigue always engendered in her by boredom was most unmistakably manifested in her slouching shoulders and mournful pallor.

'Alex a son air bête aujourd'hui.'

Memory mercilessly recalled to her the old gibe of her schoolmates sometimes, as she felt, against her own will, her features stiffening into the stupid 'tragedy-queen' look which had met with the mockery of her companions.

'Do try and cheer up, darlin',' Lady Isabel sometimes said, with more impatience than compassion in her voice, as she glanced at her daughter; and the implication that her looks were betraying her feelings made Alex more wretched and self-conscious than ever.

She often saw Queenie Goldstein, as much surrounded as in the days before her marriage, and her excessive *décolletage* now enhanced by the jewels showered upon her by her husband.

Queenie once invited her to a dinner-party at her new house in Curzon Street, but Alex knew that she would not be allowed to go, and showed the invitation with great trepidation to her mother.

'Very impertinent of her! Why, she's never been introduced to me. I shouldn't dream of allowin' any daughter of mine to go and dine with people whom I didn't know personally, even if they were *absolutely* all right.'

Lady Isabel, so easy-going and tepidly affectionate towards her children, was adamant where her social creed was concerned.

'In any case, Alex, I've told you before that I don't want you to go on with the acquaintance. That Goldstein woman is gettin' herself talked about, unless I'm very much mistaken.'

Again that mysterious accusation! Alex said no more, but wondered naïvely how the phrase that had been used in connection with Queenie Torrance could still be applicable to Maurice Goldstein's wife.

Surely married women did not flirt! The term, to Alex, symbolized she knew not what of offensive coquetry and of general 'bad form'.

This belief had been inculcated into her as a precept, but, nevertheless, she could not divest herself of a secret suspicion that, although Lady Isabel might have rebuked, she would not have been altogether averse from a lapse or two in that direction on the part of her daughter.

But Alex embarked upon no flirtation. The men who danced with her or took her in to dinner never seemed desirous of talking personalities. They made perfunctory remarks about the decorations of the tables, the quality of the floor and the music, and the revival of the Gilbert and Sullivan operas.

The sense that the intercourse between them must be sustained by conversation never left her for an instant.

There had been one occasion when she had actually forgotten to think of herself and of the effect she might be producing, and had joined with real interest in a discussion about books with a man a great deal older than herself, who happened to be placed next to her at a big dinner-party. Lady Isabel, opposite, had glanced once or twice at her daughter's unusually animated expression.

'You seemed to be gettin' on very well with the man on your other side – not the one who took you down, but the oldish one,' she said afterwards in a pleased voice.

'I never found out his name,' said Alex. 'He told me he wrote books. It was so interesting; we were talking about poetry a lot of the time.'

Her mother's face lost something of its smile.

'Oh, my darling!' she exclaimed in sudden flattened tones, 'don't go and get a reputation for being *clever*, whatever you do. People do dislike that sort of thing so much in a girl.'

Alex, her solitary triumph killed, knew that here was yet another item to be added to that invisible score of reasons for which one was loved or disliked by one's fellow-creatures.

Without formulating the conviction to herself, she believed implicitly that in the careful simulation of those attributes which she had been told would provoke admiration or affection, lay her only chance of obtaining something of that which she craved.

Dismayed, wearied, and uncheered by success, she continued to act out her little feeble comedies.

At the end of her second season she felt very old and very much disillusioned. This was not real life as she had thought to find it on leaving schooldays behind her.

There must be something beyond – some happy reality that should reveal the wherefore of all existence, but Alex knew not where to find it.

Morbidity was a word which had no place in the vocabulary of her surroundings, but Lady Isabel said to her rather plaintively, 'You must try and look more cheerful, Alex, dear, when I take you about. Your father is quite vexed when he sees such a gloomy face. You enjoy things, don't you?'

And Alex, in her complicated disappointment at disappointing her mother and father, answered hastily in the affirmative.

In the autumn, in Scotland, she met Noel Cardew again.

They were staying at the same house. Alex felt childishly proud of saying, when her hostess brought the young man to her side with a word of introduction:

'Oh, but we've met before! I know him *quite* well.'

She wished that she had spoken less emphatically, at the sight of Noel's politely non-committal smile. It was evident that he had not the faintest recollection of the meeting at his mother's house in Devonshire. She reminded him of it rather shyly.

'Oh yes, of course. You were at school with my young cousins. I remember you coming over to see us quite well, with your brothers. We all played hunt the slipper or something, didn't we?'

'Hide-and-seek,' said Alex literally. She wondered why

encounters which remained quite vividly in her own memory should always appear to present themselves so indistinctly and trivially to other people.

'I haven't heard from your cousins for a long while. Are they in America?'

'Diana is in India, of course. She married, you know – a fellow in the Indian Police.'

'I remember,' said Alex, determined to ignore the tiny prick of jealousy that now habitually assailed her almost every time that she heard of the marriage of another girl.

'Are the other two married?' she made resolute inquiry.

'Oh no. Why, Marie isn't properly grown-up yet. They are both in America. I've some idea of going over to New York myself next year, and I suppose I shall stay with their people. My uncle's at the Embassy, you know.'

'It would be splendid to see New York,' said Alex, with the old imitation of enthusiasm.

'I should like the journey as well,' young Cardew remarked. 'Board ship is an awfully good way of studying human nature, I fancy, and I'm rather keen on that sort of thing. In fact, I've a mad idea of perhaps writing a book one of these days, probably in the form of a novel, because it's only by gilding the pill that you can get the great B.P. to swallow it – but it'll really be a kind of philosophy of life, you know, with a good deal about the different sides of human nature. It may sound rather ambitious, perhaps, but I believe it could be done.'

Alex assented eagerly, and wondered what the initials that he had used – 'the great B.P.' – represented. She glanced at him sideways.

He was even better-looking than he had been as a boy, his sunburn of a deeper tan, and the still noticeable cast in one eye adding a certain character to the straightness of his features. He had grown a little, fair moustache, contrasting pleasantly with his light brown eyes. The boyish immaturity of the loosely knit figure was obscured to her eyes by the excellence of his carriage and his five foot eleven inches of height.

She was inwardly almost incredulously pleased when he chose the place next to hers at breakfast on the following morning, and asked whether she was going out to join the guns at lunch on the moors.

'I think so,' said Alex. She would have liked to say, 'I hope so,' but something within her attached such an exaggerated importance to the words that she found herself unable to utter them.

'Well,' said Noel, 'I shall look out for you, so mind you come.'

Alex' gratification was transparently evident. She was the only girl of the party, which was a small one; and Lady Isabel, declaring herself obliged to write letters, sent her out at lunch-time under the care of her hostess.

They lunched on the moors with the five men, two of whom had only come over for the day.

Noel Cardew at once established himself at Alex' side and began to expatiate upon the day's sport. He talked a great deal, and was as full of theories as in their schoolroom days, and Alex, on her side, listened with the same intense hope that her sympathy might continue to retain him beside her.

She answered him with eager monosyllables and ejaculations expressive of interest. Without analyzing her own motives, it seemed to her to be so important that Noel Cardew should continue to address his attention exclusively to her, that she was content entirely to sink her own individuality into that of a sympathetic listener.

When she dressed for dinner that evening and looked at herself in the big mirror, it seemed to her that for the first time her own appearance was entirely satisfactory. She felt self-confident and happy, and after dinner, when the elders of the party sat down to play cards, she declared boldly that she wanted to look at the garden by moonlight.

'Rather,' said Noel Cardew.

They went out together through the open French window.

Alex held up her long-tailed white satin in one hand, and walked up and down with him under the glowing red globe of the full moon. Noel talked about his book, taking her interest for granted in a manner that flattered and delighted her.

'I think psychology is simply the most absorbing thing in the world,' he declared earnestly. 'I hope you don't fight shy of long words, do you?'

Alex uttered a breathless disclaimer.

'I'm glad. So many people seem to think that if anyone says anything in words of more than two syllables it's affectation. Oxford and that sort of thing. But, of course, you're not like that, are you?'

He did not wait for an answer this time, but went on talking very eagerly about the scheme that he entertained for obtaining material for his book.

'It might revolutionize the whole standard of moral values in the country,' he said very simply. 'You know, just put things in a light that hasn't struck home in England yet at all. Of course, on the Continent they're far more advanced than we are, on those sort of points. That's why I want to travel, before I start serious work. Of course, I've got a mass of notes already. Just ideas, that have struck me as I go along. I'm afraid I'm fearfully observant, and I generally size up the people I meet, and then make notes about them – or else simply dismiss them from my mind altogether. My idea is rather to classify human nature into various *types*, so that the book can be divided up under different headings, and then have a sort of general summing up at the end. Of course, that's only a rough sketch of the whole plan, but you see what I mean?'

'Yes I do,' said Alex with conviction. 'I've always, all my life, thought that *people* mattered much more than anything else, only I've never found anybody else who felt like that too.'

'It's rather interesting to look at things the same way, don't you think?' Noel inquired.

'Oh yes,' Alex answered with shy fervour, her heart beating very fast.

She was only anxious to prolong the *tête-à-tête*, and had no idea of suggesting a return to the drawing-room, in spite of the damage that she subconsciously felt the damp ground to be doing to her satin slippers. But presently Lady Isabel called to her from the window, and she came into the lighted room, conscious both of her own glowing face and of a certain kindly, interested look bent upon her by her seniors.

CHAPTER TEN

NOEL

In the ensuing days, Alex met that look very often – a look of pleased, speculative approval, pregnant with unspoken meanings.

Noel sought her company incessantly, and every opportunity was given them of spending time in one another's society. For five glowing, heather-surrounded days and five breathless, moonlit evenings, they became the centre of their tiny world.

Then Lady Isabel said one night to her daughter:

'You've enjoyed this visit, haven't you, darlin'? I'm sorry we're movin' on.'

'Oh,' said Alex faintly, 'are we really leaving tomorrow?'

'Tomorrow morning by the early train,' her mother assented cheerfully.

The true instinct of the feeble, to clutch at an unripe prize lest it be taken from them, made Alex wonder desperately if she could not postpone her departure.

But she dared not make any such suggestion, and Lady Isabel, looking at her dismayed face, laughed a little as though at the unreason of a child. Alex blushed with shame as she thought that her mother might have guessed what was in her mind. That evening, however, Lady Isabel came into her room as she was dressing for dinner.

'I thought you'd like to put *this* over your shoulders, Alex,' she said negligently. 'It will improve that cream-coloured frock of yours.'

It was a painted scarf that she held out, and she stood gazing critically while the maid laid it across Alex' shoulders.

'You look so nice, darling child. Are you ready?'

'Yes, mother.'

They went downstairs together. Alex was acutely conscious of a certain maternal pride and tenderness, such as she had not experienced from Lady Isabel since the first days of her return from Liège, when she had finally left school. She did not let herself speculate as to what such unusual emotion might portend.

But at the sight of Noel Cardew, better-looking than ever in evening clothes, a chaotic excitement surged up within her in anticipation of their last evening together.

Almost as she sat down beside him at the dinner-table, she said piteously, 'I wish we weren't going away tomorrow.'

'You're *not*?'

'Oh yes. Didn't you know?'

'I hadn't realized it,' said Noel, and although she avoided looking at him, she noted with a feeling of triumph the dismay in his voice.

'Oh, I say! What a shame! Must you really go?'

'We're going to pay two more visits and then leave Scotland altogether.'

'I shan't stay much longer myself,' observed Noel nonchalantly.

Alex was conscious of keeping the words as it were at the back of her mind, with the implication which she attached to them, while the conversation at the small table became general.

As she followed her hostess and Lady Isabel from the room, Noel, holding open the door, said to her in a rapid, anxious tone, very low:

'You'll come out into the garden afterwards, won't you?'

An enigmatic 'perhaps' was not in Alex' vocabulary.

She gave him a quick, radiant smile, and nodded emphatically.

It never occurred to her eager prodigality that she ran any risk of cheapening the favours that so few had ever coveted.

In the garden she moved along the gravelled walk beside him, actually breathless from inward excitement.

'There was heaps more I wanted to say to you about the book,' Noel remarked disconsolately. 'I shan't have anyone to exchange ideas with now. They're all so old – and besides, I don't think English people, as a rule, care much about psychology and that sort of thing. They're so keen on games. So am I, in a way, but I must say it seems to me that the study of human nature is a good deal more worth one's while.'

'People are so interesting,' said Alex. She was perfectly aware of the futility of her remark as she made it, but in some undercurrent of her consciousness there floated the conviction that one need not put forth any great powers of originality in order to obtain response from Noel Cardew.

137

'I can be perfectly *natural* with him – we think alike.' She defended herself against her own unformulated accusation with inexplicable anger.

'I think they're frightfully interesting,' said Noel with conviction. 'Of course, men are far more interesting than women, if you don't mind me saying so, simply from the psychological point of view. I hope you don't think I'm being rude?'

'Oh *no*.'

'You see, women, as a general rule, are rather shallow, though, of course, there are a great many exceptions. But you know what I mean – as a rule they're rather shallow. That's what I feel about women, they're shallow.'

'Perhaps you're right,' said Alex rather discouraged. She would not admit to herself that his sweeping assertion awoke no echo whatever within her.

To her immaturity, the essence of sympathy lay in complete agreement, and abstract questions meant nothing to her when weighed in the balance against her desire to establish, to her own satisfaction at least, the existence of such sympathy between herself and Noel Cardew.

'I've got another mad plan,' said Noel slowly. 'You'll think I'm always getting insane ideas, and this one rather depends on you.'

'Oh, what?'

'I hope you won't mind my suggesting such a thing –' He paused so long that Alex' imagination had time for a hundred foolish, ecstatic promptings, such as her reason knew could not be forthcoming, but for which her whole undisciplined sense of romance was crying.

'Well, look here: what should you think of collaborating with me over the book? I'm sure you could write if you tried, and anyway, you could probably give me sidelights on the feminine part of it. It would be most awfully helpful to me if you would.'

'Oh,' said Alex uncertainly. She was invaded by unreasoning disappointment. 'But how could we do it?'

'Oh, well, notes, you know – just keep notes of anything that struck us particularly, and then put it in together later. We should have to do a good deal of it by correspondence, of course . . . I say, are you a conventional person?'

'Not in the least,' said Alex hastily.

'I'm glad of that. I'm afraid I'm rather desperately unconventional myself. Of course, in a way it might be rather unconventional, you and me corresponding – but would that matter?'

'Not to me,' said Alex resolutely.

'That's splendid. We could do a lot that way and then I hope, of course, that you'll let me come and see you in London.'

'Of course,' Alex cried eagerly. 'I don't know the exact date when we shall be back, but I could let you know. Have you got the address?'

'Clevedon Square –'

She hastily supplied the number of the house.

'Oh, that's all right. I'm sure to forget it,' said Noel easily; 'but I shall find you in the books, I suppose.'

'Yes,' said Alex, feeling suddenly damped.

She herself would have been in no danger of forgetting the number of a house wherein dwelt anyone whom she wished to see, but with disastrous and quite unconscious humility, she told herself that it was, of course, not to be expected that anyone else should go to lengths equal to her own. In her one-sided experience, Alex had always found herself to be unique.

That Noel Cardew was not in despair at the idea of her departure was evident. But he repeated several times that he wished she were not going so soon, and even asked whether she would stay on if invited to do so.

'I'm sure they'd all love you to,' he assured her. 'Then Lady Isabel could pay the other visits and call for you on her way back.'

'I'm sure I shouldn't be allowed to stay on by myself,' said Alex dolefully.

'There you are! Conventionality again. *My* daughters,' said Noel instructively, 'if I ever have any, shall be brought up quite differently. I've made up my mind to that. I daresay you'll laugh at all these theories of mine, but I've always been keen on ideas, if you remember.'

But for once Noel did not receive the habitual ready disclaimer called for by his speech.

His easy allusion to his hypothetical daughters had reduced Alex to utter silence.

Afterwards, alone in the darkness of her own room, she wondered why such a startling sense of protest had revolted within her at his words, but her mind shied away instinctively from the question, and she found herself unable to pursue it.

The next morning, in the unromantic atmosphere induced by an early breakfast, and Sir Francis' anxiety to make sure of catching the connection, politely concealed, but quite evident to the perceptions of his wife and daughter, Noel Cardew and Alex exchanged their brief and entirely public farewell.

'I'll write about the book,' was his cheerful parting assurance.

'Don't forget,' said Alex.

Lady Isabel was rather humorous on the subject of *fin de siècle* emancipation, amongst the house party in the midst of which she and her daughter found themselves that evening.

'What are boys and girls coming to? I hear young men gaily promisin' to write to Alex on all sorts of subjects, and making private assignations with her,' she declared amusedly. 'Aren't you and that nice-looking Cardew boy writin' a book in collaboration, or something, darling?'

The slight jest was made popular amongst her seniors, and Alex was kindly rallied about her modern freedom and assumption of privileges undreamed of by the older generation. The inference obviously placed upon her friendship with Noel Cardew was evident, and pleased her starved vanity even more than the agreeable amount of flattery and attention which at last was being bestowed upon her.

It was her first hint of success achieved amid standards which she had been taught to believe were all-prevalent. Brushed lightly by the passing wing of triumph she became eager and self-confident, even rather over-clamorous in the assertion of her own individuality, as had been the child Alex in the nursery at Clevedon Square.

Lady Isabel did not check her. She made subtle

141

exploitation of Alex' youth and sudden, rather boisterous gaiety, and occasionally laughed a little, and alluded to the collaboration scheme between her and Noel Cardew. 'But all the same, darlin' child,' she observed to Alex in private, 'I can't have you correspondin' with young men all over the country unbeknown to me. Once in a way is all very well, perhaps, but you'll have to let me see the letters, I think.'

Alex was only mildly resentful of the injunction. She surmised shrewdly enough that her mother was more anxious to establish the authentic existence of a correspondence between Noel Cardew and herself than to supervise the details of it. She herself waited with frantic, furtive eagerness for his first letter. It did not reach her until after her return to London. Secretly bitterly disappointed, she read the short, conventional phrases and the subscription:

> 'I never know how to end up a letter, but hope this will be all right – Yours very sincerely,
>
>   'Noel E. Cardew.'

Across the top of the front page was a postscript:

> 'Next month I shall be in town. Don't forget that I am coming to call upon you. I hope you won't be "out"!'

Alex, to whom nothing was trivial, saw the proposed call looming enormous upon the horizon of her days.

Every afternoon she either sat beside Lady Isabel in the carriage in an agony, with only one thought in her mind – the expectation of finding Noel's card upon the hall table on their return – or else took her part disjointedly and with obvious absent-mindedness in the entertainment of her mother's visitors.

When, during a crowded At Home afternoon, in the course of which she had necessarily ceased to listen for the sound of the front-door bell, 'Mr. Cardew' was at length announced, Alex felt almost unable to turn round and face the entering visitor.

Her own imagination, untempered either by humour or by experience, had led her to picture the next encounter between herself and Noel so frequently, and with such a prodigal folly of romantic detail, that it seemed incredible to her that the reality should take place within a few instants, amidst brief, conventional words and gestures.

Noel did not talk about the book that they were to write together, although he remained beside Alex most of the afternoon. Only, just as he was leaving, he asked cheerfully:

'You've not forgotten our collaboration, have you, partner? I've heaps of things to discuss with you, only you were so busy this afternoon, looking after all those people.'

'We shall be in on Sunday,' Alex told him eagerly. 'and there won't be such a crowd.'

'Oh, good,' said Noel. 'Perhaps we'll meet in the Park before that, though.'

'I hope so,' said Alex.

They met in the Park and elsewhere, and Noel, all through the ensuing weeks before Christmas, called often at the house in Clevedon Square.

Lady Isabel twice asked him to dinner, but although he was once placed next to her, on neither occasion, to

Alex' astonished resentment, was he assigned to her as a partner.

Alex, for the first time conscious of being sought after, and receiving with avidity the fragments that fell to her share, forced herself to believe that they would eventually constitute that impossible whole of which she had dreamed wildly and extravagantly all her life.

Into the eager assents which she gave to all Noel's many theories, she read a similarity of outlook, into her almost trembling readiness to fall in with his every suggestion, a community of tastes, and into his interminable expositions of his own views, an appeal to her deeper sympathies that surely denoted the consciousness of affinity between them.

She was happy, although principally in a nervous anticipation of happiness to come. She was able, when alone, to imagine that from absolutely impersonal good comradeship, Noel would suddenly plunge into the impassioned declarations of her own fancy, but when she was actually with him, his cool, pleasant, boyish voice dispelled the folly, and her fundamental shyness, that never deserted her save in the realm of her own thoughts, was relieved with an intense and involuntary relief, that it should be so.

She saw Noel's father and mother again, and was greeted by the latter with a bright and conditional affectionateness that inspected even while it acclaimed.

It was after this that the trend of Noel's thoughts appeared suddenly to change, and he spoke to Alex of the place in Devonshire.

'One's first duty is to the place, of course,' he said

reflectively, 'and I'm not at all sure that I oughtn't to look into the management of an estate, and all that sort of thing very thoroughly. Some day – a long, long time hence, of course – I shall have to run our own place, and I'm rather keen about the duties of a landlord, and improving the condition of the people. I used to be a Socialist, as you know, but I must say one's ideas alter a bit as one goes on through life, and I've had some talks with the pater lately.'

He broke off, and looked rather oddly at Alex for a moment.

'They want me to think of settling down, I believe,' he said, almost shyly.

Alex spent that night in feverishly placing possible and impossible interpretations on the words, and on the look he had given her.

The sense of an approaching crisis terrified her so much that she felt she would have given worlds to avoid it.

The following evening it came.

Most conventionally, she met Noel Cardew at an evening reception, and he conducted her rather solemnly to a small conservatory where two chairs were placed, conspicuously enough, beneath a solitary palm.

An orchestra was just audible above the hum and buzz of conversation.

'It's luck getting in here,' said Noel. 'I wanted to see you very particularly tonight. I must say I never thought I should find myself particularly wanting to see *any* girl – in fact, I'd practically made up my mind never to have anything to do with women – but I see now that two people who had very much the same sort of ideas about life in general could do a tremendous lot for a place, and for the country generally; don't you agree? – and, of course –' He became hopelessly incoherent '. . . knowing one another's people – it all makes such a difference . . . I could never understand fellows running after Gaiety girls and marrying them, myself!! After all, one's duty to the estate is . . . and then, later on, perhaps, if one thought of Parliament –'

Alex felt that the pounding of her heart was making her physically faint, and she raised her head desperately, in the hope of stopping him. Noel met her eyes courageously.

'I wish you'd let me tell our people that you – that we – we're engaged,' he said hoarsely.

His words struck on Alex' ear almost meaninglessly. Irrationally in love as she was, with Love, she knew only that he was asking something of her – that she had at last an outlet for that which no one had ever yet desired.

Unable to speak, and unconscious of bathos, she vehemently nodded her head.

Noel immediately took both her hands and shook them wildly up and down. 'Thank Heaven, it's over,' he cried boyishly. 'You can't imagine how I've been funking asking you – I thought you'd say yes, but one feels such an awful fool – and I've never done it before. I say, Alex – I can call you Alex now, can't I – you're like me, aren't you? You don't want sentimentality. If there's one thing I bar,' said the newly-accepted lover, 'it's sentimentality.'

CHAPTER ELEVEN

※※※※※※※※※※

ENGAGEMENT OF MARRIAGE

'I am engaged to be married,' Alex repeated to herself, in a vain endeavour to realize the height to which she must have now attained. But that realization, by which she meant tangible certainty, for which she craved, continually eluded her.

The preliminary formalities, indeed, duly took place, from her own avowal before a graciously-maternal Lady Isabel, to Noel's formal interview with Sir Francis in the traditional setting of the library.

After that, however, a freakish fate seemed to take control of all the circumstances connected with Alex' engagement.

Noel Cardew's father became ill, and in the uncertainty consequent upon a state of health which his doctor declared might be almost indefinitely prolonged, there could be no question of immediately announcing the engagement.

'Just as well, perhaps. We're all delighted about it, but they're both young enough to wait a little while.' Lady Isabel smilingly made the best of it. 'Next year will be quite time enough to settle anything.'

Her serenity was the obvious outcome of an extreme contentment.

Alex found herself better able to regard herself in the light of one betrothed in her mother's company than in that of Noel. He treated her almost exactly as he had always done, with cheerful good-fellowship, and only at the very outset of the engagement with any tinge of shyness in his bearing.

'Of course, I ought to have got a ring,' he said very seriously, 'but I don't believe in taking any chances, and so, just in case there was any hitch, I waited. Besides, I don't know what you like best – you'll have to choose.'

Alex smiled at the words. There was a glamour about such a choice, even beyond that with which her own sense of the romantic perforce enveloped it.

She wondered whether she would be allowed to go with Noel to a jeweller's, or whether he would, after all, choose his token alone, and bring it to her, and place it on her finger with one of those low, ardently-spoken sentences which she could hear so clearly in her own mind, and which seemed so strangely and utterly impossible in Noel's real presence.

But the arrival of Noel's ring, after all, took her by surprise.

He had been lunching with them in Clevedon Square, when the jeweller's assistant was announced, just as Lady Isabel was rising from the luncheon-table.

She turned inquiringly.

'Noel?'

'I told him to come here. I thought you wouldn't mind. You see, I want Alex to choose her ring.'

'Oh, my dear boy! how very exciting! But may we see too?'
Mrs. Cardew was also present.

'Oh, rather,' said Noel heartily. 'We shall want your advice.'

They all trooped hastily into the library, where the man was waiting, with the very large assortment of gleaming rings ordered for inspection by Noel.

'What beauties!' said Lady Isabel. 'But, really, I don t know if I ought to let him.'

She glanced at Mrs. Cardew, who said in a very audible voice:

'Of course. He's so happy. It's quite delightful to watch them both.'

She was looking hard and appraisingly at the rings as she spoke.

Alex looked at them too, quite unseeing of their glittering magnificence, but acutely conscious that everyone was waiting for her first word.

'Oh, how lovely!' she exclaimed faintly.

She chid herself violently for the sick disappointment that invaded her, not, indeed, at the matter, but at the manner of the gift.

And yet she realized dimly that it was impossible that it should have happened in any other way – that any other way, indeed, would have been as utterly uncharacteristic of Noel Cardew as this was typical.

'Which do you like?' he asked her. 'I chose all the most original ones I could see. I always like unconventional designs better than conventional ones, I'm afraid. Where's that lone one you showed me this morning?'

'The diamond marquise, sir?' The assistant deferentially produced it, glancing the while at Alex.

'That's it,' said Noel eagerly. 'Try it on, Alex, won't you?'

He used her name quite freely and without any shyness.

Alex felt more of genuine excitement, and less of wistful bewilderment, than at any moment since Noel had first asked her to marry him, as she shyly held out her left hand and the jeweller slipped the heavy, beautiful ring on to her third finger.

She had long, slim hands, the fingers rather too thin and the knuckles, though small, too prominent for beauty. But, thanks to the tyranny of old Nurse, and to Lady Isabel's insistence upon the use of nightly glycerine-and-honey, they were exquisitely soft and white.

The diamonds gleamed and flashed at her as she moved the ring up and down her finger.

'We can easily make it smaller, to fit your finger,' said the jeweller's assistant.

'It really is beautiful. Look, Francis,' said Lady Isabel.

Alex' father put up his glasses, and after inspection he also exclaimed:

'Beautiful!'

'You've such little fingers, dear, it'll have to be made smaller,' said Mrs. Cardew graciously.

'Is it to be that one, then?' Lady Isabel asked.

Alex saw that her mother's pretty, youthful-looking flush of pleasurable excitement had mounted to her face. She herself, conscious of an inexplicable oppression, felt tongue-tied, and unable to do more than repeat foolishly and lifelessly:

'Oh, it's lovely, it's perfectly lovely. It's *too* beautiful.'

Noel, however, looked gratified at the words of admiration.

'That's the one *I* like,' he said with emphasis. 'I knew when I saw them this morning that I liked that one much the best. We'll settle on that one then, shall we?'

'You silly boy,' laughed his mother, 'that's for Alex to decide. Perhaps she likes something else better. Try the emerald, Alex.'

'Oh, this is lovely,' repeated Alex again, shrinking back a little. Furious with herself, she was yet only desirous that the scene should not be prolonged any longer.

'Come and look at it in the light.' The urgent pressure of Lady Isabel's hand on her arm drew her into the embrasure of the window.

'Alex,' said her mother low and swiftly, all the time holding up her hand against the light as though studying the ring, 'Alex, you *must* be more gracious. What *is* the matter with you?'

'Nothing,' said Alex childishly, feeling inclined to burst into tears.

'Then for Heaven's sake do try and smile and show a *little* enthusiasm,' said her mother with unwonted sharpness.

Alex, scarlet, and most visibly discomposed, returned to the group round the library table.

Forcing herself to make some attempt at obeying her mother's behest, she picked up the nearest jewel, two pearls in a prettily-twisted setting, and began to examine it.

'I like that design, too. It's original,' said Mrs. Cardew.

'Oh, but pearls are unlucky – she couldn't have pearls,' protested Lady Isabel.

'They mean tears, don't they?' Alex contributed to the discussion, for the sake of making her mother see that she was willing to do her best.

'Are you superstitious?' Noel asked rather reproachfully. 'I can't say I believe in all that sort of thing myself, you know. In fact, I make rather a principle of doing things on a 13th, or walking under ladders, and all the rest of it, just to prove there's nothing in it.'

Sir Francis fixed the young man benevolently through his monocle.

'I presume, however, that in this instance you prefer not to tempt the gods,' he remarked affably, and Noel, always obviously in awe of his betrothed's father, hastily agreed with him.

'Then it's diamonds, is it? – unless Alex prefers the emerald.'

'I like the diamond one best,' Noel reiterated. 'I really pitched on that one the minute I saw it. I like originality.'

'Well, it couldn't be lovelier,' said Lady Isabel contentedly.

The jeweller was shown out, leaving the diamond marquise ring, in its little white-velvet case, on the table in front of Alex.

Sir Francis opened the door for his wife and Mrs. Cardew.

'Oh,' said Noel urgently. 'You *must* stay and see her put it on.'

Both ladies laughed at the boyish exclamation, and Alex flushed scarlet once more.

Noel opened the case and looked proudly at his gift.

'You must put it on for her,' said his mother, 'when it's been made smaller.'

The hint was unmistakable.

Noel held out the ring.

'Let's see it on now at once, Alex. It can go back to the shop later.'

Alex, in a sort of utter desperation, thrust out her hand, and Noel, politely and carefully avoiding touching it with his own, slipped the heavy hoop over her finger.

'Thank you,' she stammered.

There was another laugh.

'Poor dears! Let's leave them in peace,' cried Mrs. Cardew mockingly, and rustled to the door again.

'Did you ever see anything so young as they both are?' she murmured sweetly to Lady Isabel, audibly enough for Alex to guess at the words, if she did not actually hear them.

She was thankful that they should no longer be watching her, and turned with something like relief to Noel's gratified, uncritical looks.

It became suddenly much easier to speak unconstrainedly.

Perhaps she was subconsciously aware that of all of them, it was Noel himself who would expect least of her, because his demands upon her were so infinitesimal.

'It's a beautiful ring; thank you very, very much. I –' She stopped and gulped, then said bravely, 'I *love* it.'

She emphasized the word almost without knowing it, as though to force from him some response.

Although she had never actually realized it, it was a word which, in point of fact, had never yet passed between them. Noel's fair face coloured at last, as his light eyes met her unconsciously tragical gaze.

'Alex a son air bête aujourd'hui.'

With horrid inappropriateness, the hated gibe of her schooldays flashed into Alex' thoughts, stiffening her face into the old lines of morbid, self-conscious misery.

Part of her mind, in unwilling detachment, contemplated ruefully the oddly inadequate spectacle which they must present, staring shamefacedly at one another across the glittering token of their troth.

Frenziedly desirous of breaking the silence, heavy with awkwardness, that hung between them, she began to speak hastily and almost at random.

'Thank you so very much – I've never had such a lovely present – it's lovely; thank you so much.'

'I thought you'd like it,' muttered Noel, more overcome with confusion, if possible, than was Alex.

'Oh yes, yes. It's lovely.'

'I thought you'd like something rather original, you know, not a conventional one.'

'Oh yes!'

'You're sure you wouldn't rather have one of the others – that emerald one that mother liked?'

'Oh no.'

'I dare say they'd let me change it, the man knows us very well.'

'Oh no, no.'

'Well, I, I – I'm awfully glad you like it.'

'Yes, I *do* like it. I – I think it's lovely.'

'I – I thought you'd like it.'

Alex began to feel as though she was in a nightmare, but

she was mysteriously unable to put an end to their sorry dialogue.

'It's perfectly lovely, I think. I don't know how to thank you.'

Noel swallowed two or three times, visibly and audibly, and then took a couple of determined steps towards her.

'I think you – you'd better let me kiss you,' he said hoarsely. 'You haven't yet, you know.'

Something deep down within Alex was surging up in angry bewilderment, and she was sufficiently aware of a sense of protest to rebut it indignantly and with lightning-swift determination.

It was the humility of love that had prompted her lover to crave that permission which should never have been asked.

So she told herself in the flash of a moment, while she waited for Noel's kiss to lift her once and for all into some far realm of romance where trivial details of manifestation should no longer obscure the true values of life.

Unconsciously, she had shut her eyes, but at an unaccountable pause in the proceedings, she opened them again.

Noel was carefully removing his pince-nez.

'I say,' he stammered, 'you're – you're sure you don't mind?'

If Alex had followed the impulse of her own feelings, she must have cried out at this juncture:

'Not if you're quick and get it over!'

But instead, she heard herself murmuring feebly:

'Oh no, not at all.'

She hastily raised her face, turning it sideways to Noel,

and felt his lips gingerly touching the middle of her cheek. Then she opened her eyes again, and, scrupulously avoiding Noel's embarrassed gaze, saw him diligently polishing his pince-nez before replacing them.

It was the apotheosis of their anti-climax.

Alex possessed neither the light-heartedness which is – mistakenly – generally ascribed to youth, nor the philosophy, to face facts with any determination.

She continued to cram her unwilling mind with illusions which her innermost self perfectly recognized as such.

It was, on the whole, easier to place her own interpretation, upon Noel's every act of commission or omission when the shyness subsequent to their first ill-conducted embrace had left him, which it speedily did. Easier still, when inter-course between them was renewed upon much the same terms of impersonal enthusiasm in discussion as in Scotland, and easiest of all when Alex herself, in retrospect, wrenched a sentimental significance out of words or looks that had been meaningless at the time of their occurrence.

When Noel went to Devonshire, whither his father by slow, invalid degrees had at last been allowed to move, he said to Alex in farewell:

'I shall expect to hear from you very often, mind. I always like getting letters, though I'm afraid I'm not much good at writing them. You know what I mean: I can write simply pages if I'm in the mood – just as though I were talking to someone – and other days I can't put pen to paper.'

'I don't think I write very good letters myself' said Alex wistfully, in the hope of eliciting reassurance.

'Oh, never mind,' said Noel consolingly. 'Just write when you feel like it.'

Alex, who had composed a score of imaginary love-letters, both on his behalf and her own, tried to compensate herself the following evening for the vague misery that was encompassing her spirit, by writing.

She was alone in her own room, the fire had fallen into red embers, and her surroundings were sufficiently appropriate to render attainable the state of mind which she desired to achieve.

As she involuntarily rehearsed to herself the elements of her own situation, she lulled herself into a species of happiness.

His ring on her finger, his letter on its way to her – she was going to write to the man who had asked her to become his wife.

There was really someone at last, Alex told herself, to whom she had become the centre of the universe, to whom her letters would matter, to whom everything that she might think or feel would be of importance.

She remembered Maurice Goldstein, his knowledge of Queenie's every movement, his triumphant rapture at being allowed to take her out to luncheon or tea. Even now, Alex had seen him follow his wife with his ardent, glowing gaze, as she moved, serene and graceful, round a crowded room on the arm of some other man – and the look had made her heart throb sympathetically, and perhaps not altogether unenviously.

Almost fiercely she told herself that she had Noel's love. She was to him what Queenie was to young Goldstein.

To every rebellious doubt that rose within her, she opposed the soundless, vehement assertion, that the indelible proof of Noel's love lay in the fact that he had asked her to marry him.

Gradually she persuaded herself that only her own self-consciousness, of which she was never more aware than when with Noel, was responsible for that strange lack, which she dared not attempt to define, lest in so doing she should shatter the feeble structure built out of sentimentality and resolute self-blinding.

Partly because she instinctively craved a relief to her own feelings, and partly because she had really almost made herself believe in the truth of her own imaginings, Alex wrote her first love-letter, the shy, yet passionately-worded self-expression of a young and intensely romantic girl, in love with the thought of Love, too ignorant for reserve, and yet too conscious of the novelty of her own experience for absolute spontaneity.

Alex did not sleep after she had written her letter, but she lay in bed in the warm, soft glow of the firelight, and saw the square, white envelope within which she had sealed her letter, leaning against the silver inkstand on her writing-table.

When the maid came to her in the morning, she brought a letter addressed in Noel's unformed hand.

It was quite short, and began:

'Dearest Alex (is that right?)'

It told her of the journey to Devonshire of an improvement in the invalid's state of health, and of Noel's own projected tour of inspection round the estate, which he thought had been neglected by the agent of late.

'But I shall be able to put all that right, I hope, as I'm rather keen about the housing of the poor, and questions of that sort. You might look out for any decent book on social economy, will you, Alex?'

The letter did not extend beyond the bottom of the second page, but Noel was going to write again in a day or two, when there was more to tell her, and with love to everyone, he was hers for ever and a day, Noel.

Alex' reply went to Trevose the same day, but the letter she had written in the firelight, she burnt.

CHAPTER TWELVE

CHRISTMAS PANTOMIME

The engagement was not announced, but a good many people knew about it.

Their congratulations pleased Alex, as did her mother's obvious pride and satisfaction.

She liked wearing her diamond ring although she only did so at home, and she even found pleasure in writing of her new dignities to Barbara at Neuilly.

In such trivial anodynes did Alex seek oblivion for the ever-increasing terror that was gaining upon her.

Noel came back from Devonshire after Christmas – and Lady Isabel sometimes spoke tentatively to Alex of a wedding early in the season.

'Jubilee year would be so charmin' for your wedding, my darling,' she said effusively.

Alex thought of a white satin dress and long train, of orange blossom and a lace veil, of brides-maids, presents, the exciting music of Mendelssohn's Wedding March, and the glory of a wedding-ring. On any other aspects of the case her mind refused to dwell.

Nevertheless, she made little or no response to her mother's hinted suggestions. Neither Noel nor Alex ever exchanged the slightest reference to their marriage, although Noel often discoursed freely of a Utopian future for the tenantry at Trevose, the basis of which, by implication, was his suzerainty and that of Alex.

'I rather believe in the old-fashioned feudal system, personally. You may say that's just the contrary of my old socialistic ideas, Alex, but then I always think it's a mistake to be absolutely cast-iron in one's convictions. One ought to assimilate new ideas as one goes through life, and, of course, sometimes they're bound to displace preconceived notions. I'm a tremendous believer in *experience*; it teaches one better than anything else. Besides, Emerson says, "Dare to be inconsistent." I'm keen on Emerson, you know. Are you?'

'Oh yes,' said Alex enthusiastically, wishing to be sympathetic. 'But I only read Emerson a long while ago, when I was at school. Noel, were you happy at school?'

'Oh yes,' said Noel unemotionally. 'The great thing at school is to be keen, and get on with the other fellows. They were always very decent to me.'

'*I* wasn't very happy,' said Alex. She was passionately desirous of sympathy, and was full of youth's mistaken conviction, that unhappiness is provocative of interest.

Noel cheerfully and unconsciously disabused her of the idea.

'Of course, girls don't have nearly such a good time as boys do at school. But don't let's talk about rotten things like being unhappy. I always believe in taking things as they come, don't you? I never look back, personally. I think it's morbid. One ought always to be looking ahead. I tell you what I'll do, Alex – I'll give you a copy of Emerson's *Essays*. You ought to read them.'

Noel was very generous, and often made her presents. Alex was disproportionately grateful, but to her extreme, though unavowed, relief, he never again claimed such a recognition as that which had followed the bestowal of her engagement-ring.

She drifted on from day to day, scarcely aware of her own unhappiness, but wondering bitterly why this, the supreme initiation, should seem to fail her so utterly, and still hoping against hope that the personal element for which she looked so avidly, might yet enter into her relation with Noel.

One day she told herself, with a shock of discovery, that Noel was curiously obtuse. He had taken her with Lady Isabel and his brother Eric to Prince's skating-rink. Alex did not skate, but she enjoyed hearing the band and watching the skaters. Eric Cardew was among the latter, and Alex recognized Queenie Goldstein, in magnificent furs.

'Noel, do you see that very fair girl – the one in white? She was my great friend at school.'

Alex at the same instant saw a look of fleeting, but unmistakable vexation on her mother's face at the description.

'Why, that's Mrs. Goldstein, isn't it?' said Noel, screwing up his eyes in an interested look.

'Yes. I wish I could catch her eye.' Alex was reckless of her mother. 'I haven't talked to her for such a long while. Do you know her?'

'I've met her once or twice.'

'Couldn't you go and speak to her, and bring her over here?' asked Alex wistfully.

Noel looked at her, surprised.

'I don't think I can do that. She wants to skate.'

'Of course not,' broke in Lady Isabel. 'Don't be a little goose, Alex. What do you want her for?'

'Oh nothing,' Alex replied dejectedly, and also very crossly.

She was in the frame of mind that seeks a grievance, and her nerves were far more overstrained than she realized.

She felt a sudden, absolute anger when Noel said didactically:

'I don't think it would be very good manners for me to go and force myself on Mrs. Goldstein's notice. I don't know her at all well, and there are heaps of people who want to talk to her – just look at all those fellows!'

'You might do it just to please me,' muttered Alex, less from coquetry than from injured pride.

Noel became rather red, and after a minute he remarked in a severe voice:

'I must say, Alex, I think that's rather a ridiculous thing to say.'

Alex was silent, but from that day the spirit of resentment had at last awakened within her.

She became irritable, and although she still strove to persuade herself that her engagement meant the ultimate realization of happiness, she often spoke impatiently to Noel, and no longer sought to conform herself to the type of womanhood which he obviously desired and expected to find her.

The old sense of 'waiting for the next thing' was strong upon her, and she spent her days in desultory idleness, since Lady Isabel made fewer engagements for her, and Noel's calls upon her time were far from excessive.

She made the discovery then, less illuminating at the time than when viewed afterwards in retrospect, that she could not bear to read novels.

All of them, sooner or later, seemed to deal with the relations between a man and a woman in love, and Alex found herself reading of emotions and experiences of which her own seemed so feeble a mockery, that she was conscious of a physical pang of sick disappointment.

Was all fiction utterly untrue to life? or was hers the counterfeit, while the printed pages but reproduced something of a reality which was denied to her?

She dared not face the question, and was further perplexed by the axiom, mechanically passed on by successive authorities in rebuke of her childhood's passion for reading:

'You can't learn anything about Real Life from story-books.'

At all events, Alex found the story-books of no solace to her mental sickness, and turned away from their perusal with a sinking heart.

She seldom quarrelled with Noel, because, although he was sometimes unmistakably offended at her petulance, he never lost his temper. On the contrary, he argued with her at such length that Alex, although the arguments left her quite unconvinced of the rightness of his point of view, often gave in from sheer weariness and the sense of hopeless, exhausting muddle.

She could visualize no possible eventual solution of the intangible problem that somewhere lay heavy, undefined and undefinable, at the back of all her thoughts.

It seemed to her that such a state of affairs had endured for a lifetime, and must extend into eternity, when her relations with Noel entered into the inevitable crisis to which a fortnight's mutual fret and dissatisfaction had been only the prelude.

Sir Francis, graciously benevolent, invited Noel Cardew to make one of an annual gathering that, for the Clare children, amounted to an institution – to view the Christmas pantomime at Drury Lane. For more years than any of them, except Alex, could remember, a box at the pantomime had been the yearly, almost the solitary, expression of Sir Francis Clare's recognition of his younger children's existence as beings other than merely ornamental adjuncts to their mother.

Lady Isabel, who detested pantomimes, never joined the party, and Alex could remember still – had, indeed, never altogether lost – the feeling of extreme awe that rendered unnecessary old Nurse's severe injunctions to the children as to the behaviour suitable to so great an occasion.

This year, Barbara was at Neuilly, and it was considered inadvisable to 'unsettle' her by a return to London for the Christmas holidays. But Cedric was at home, and Archie and Pamela, as clamorous as they dared to be for their father's treat.

Sir Francis did not sacrifice himself to the extent of foregoing late dinner altogether, but he dined at seven o'clock, and issued what more nearly approached to a royal mandate than an invitation, to Alex, Cedric and Noel to bear him company.

The big cuckoo clock in the hall still showed the hour as short of eight o'clock when Pamela and Archie, the former muffled in a large pink shawl, and both of them prancing with ill-restrained impatience, were at last permitted to dispatch the footman in search of a cab.

The carriage, in the opinion of Sir Francis, would be amply filled by himself, his two daughters and Noel Cardew, and it was part of the procedure that the boys should be allowed to journey to the theatre by themselves in a hansom-cab.

The streets were snowy, and as shafts of light from the street-lamps fell across the crowded pavements and brilliant shop windows, still displaying the Christmas decorations put up a month ago, something of the old childish glamour surrounding the yearly festival came upon Alex.

Pamela, already a modern child in the lack of that self-conscious awe of their father that had kept Alex and Barbara tongue-tied in his presence, nevertheless, had none of the modern child's *blasé* satiety of parties and entertainments of all kinds.

The Drury Lane pantomime was her solitary annual experience of the theatre, and she was proportionately prepared to enjoy herself to the full. When Sir Francis, with kind, unhumorous smile, made time-honoured pretence of having forgotten the tickets, Pamela gave Alex a shock by her cheerful and unhesitating refusal to carry on the dutiful tradition of her elder sisters and conform tacitly to the jest by a display of pretended consternation.

'Oh no, I know you haven't forgotten them,' Pamela cried shrilly. 'I saw you look at them just before we started. Besides, you said last year you'd forgotten them, and you had them in your pocket all the time. I remember quite well.'

She began to bounce up and down on the seat of the carriage, the accordion-pleated skirts of her new pink frock billowing round her.

'Sit still,' said Alex repressively. She reflected that she herself as a little girl, and even Barbara, had been very much nicer than was Pamela.

She wondered what Noel had been like as a little boy, and looked at him almost involuntarily.

His glance met hers, and he smiled slightly. The response touched Alex suddenly and acutely, and she felt a pang of remorse for the intense irritation that his presence had often caused her lately.

When the carriage stopped and he sprang out to offer her his hand in descending, she gave hers to him with a tiny thrill, and her fingers lingered for an instant in his, as though awaiting, almost in spite of herself, an all-but-imperceptible pressure that was not forthcoming.

'It's begun,' gasped Pamela in an agony of impatience in the *foyer*.

Sir Francis, always punctilious, placed Alex in the right-hand corner of the box, the two children in the centre, and then, with a slight smile, offered Noel his choice of the remaining chairs.

Alex was conscious of a throb of gratification, perhaps more attributable to vanity than to anything else, when the young man placed himself just behind her own chair.

Sir Francis, the comparative isolation of the engaged couple sufficiently sanctioned by the family party surrounding them, immediately disposed himself behind Cedric at the extreme left of the box.

The curtain went down to the sound of applause almost as they took their places, and the lights were turned up. Alex looked round her.

The huge house was everywhere sprinkled with groups of children – Eton boys in broad, white collars such as Archie wore, little girls in white frocks with wide pink or blue sashes and hair-ribbons.

When the orchestra began a medley of old-fashioned popular airs, *Home, sweet Home, 'Way down upon the Swanee River, Bluebells of Scotland*, and the like, Alex, overwrought, fell an easy victim to the cheap appeal to emotionalism.

In the irrational passionate desire for reassurance that fell upon her, she leant back until her shoulder almost touched Noel's.

'Look at all those children!' she whispered, hardly knowing what she said.

Noel gazed at the stalls through his pince-nez.

'The place is crammed,' he said. 'They say it's the best show they've ever had. Of course, I haven't seen it yet, but my own idea about these pantomimes is that they don't stick enough to the original story. Take "Cinderella" now, or "The Babes in the Wood." The whole thing is simply a mass of interpolations – they never really follow the thread of one idea all the way through. I can't help thinking it would be much better if they did, you know. After all, a pantomime is supposed to be for children, isn't it?'

'Yes.'

Alex wondered what reply she had expected from him to her sudden ejaculation, that the actuality should bring such a sense of ironical disappointment.

She leant forward again as the curtain went up.

She was still child enough to enjoy a pantomime for its own sake, but the swing of catchy tunes and sentimental ballads brought with them something more than the easy heartache to which youth falls so ready a victim.

As the crash of the orchestra heralded a big scenic effect of dance and colour, Noel leant a little towards her and began to speak.

'Of course, it's a good show in its way. Look, Alex, you can see the man manipulating the coloured lights, up there. If you lean right back into this corner – there, up there.'

His voice was full of interest and almost of eagerness. Alex leant back as he suggested and gazed obediently up at the lime-light operator, although she felt no interest, but rather a faint distaste.

'It's the ingenuity of these things I like,' Noel's voice in her ear was explaining. 'Of course, the dancing's good, and the comic bits, though I don't know that I care tremendously about that. They're always apt to be rather vulgar, even in front of a lot of ladies and children. Pity, that is. But take the songs, now, Alex; wouldn't you think it would pay someone to write really *good* libretto, and get it taken on at a place like this and set to decent music? The tunes are good enough, but it's the words that are so poor, I always think.'

Alex listened almost without hearing. The time had gone by when she could tell herself, with vehement attempt at self-deception, that such assertions indicated a fundamental resemblance between her tastes and those of Noel Cardew.

She was now only unreasonably angry and disappointed because of her baffled desire for the introduction, however belated, of a personal element into their intercourse.

She actually felt the tears rising to her throat as the evening wore on, and an intolerable fatigue overcame her.

Sitting upright became more and more of an effort, and the box seemed narrow and over-full.

The instinct of self-pity made her attempt to draw Noel's sympathy indirectly.

'Could you move back a little?' she half whispered. 'I am getting rather cramped.'

'Are you?' returned Noel with surprise, as he pushed his chair back.

But he did not appear to be in the least concerned about the matter. She looked at him once or twice, and he met her glance absently. She knew that her face must show signs of the fatigue that she felt, but she knew also that they would not be perceptible to Noel.

For a moment, one of the rebellious gusts of misery of her stormy childhood shook Alex.

Why – why should there be no one to care, no one to whom it mattered that she be weary or out of spirits, no one to perceive, unprompted, when she was tired? She realized what such instinctive protection and care would mean to her, and the almost passionate gratitude with which she could welcome and return such solicitude.

But with Noel, she need not even exercise it. Had she loved him as she had endeavoured to persuade herself that she did, instead of only the figure of Love called by his name, Alex knew that Noel would have passed by all the smaller manifestations of her love unheeding and uncomprehending.

Her gods were mocking her with counterfeit indeed.

'You look tired, Alex,' said her father's courteously-displeased voice.

Alex knew that on the rare occasion when he personally supervised a party of pleasure, Sir Francis liked the occasion to be met with due appreciation. She gave a forced smile and sat rather more upright.

'To be sure,' her father said seriously, 'it is a prolonged entertainment.'

But Alex knew that neither Cedric, Archie nor Pamela would hear of any curtailment of their enjoyment, and Pamela was already urgently whispering that they *must* stay for the clown – they always did.

Sir Francis yielded graciously, evidently well-pleased, and they remained in the theatre for the final humours of the harlequinade.

Snow was actually falling when at length Sir Francis Clare's carriage was discovered, and Alex, her always low vitality at its lowest, was shivering with mingled cold and fatigue.

'Get in, children,' commanded their father. 'Noel, my dear boy, we can give you a lift, but pray get in – we must not keep the horses standing. What a terrible night!'

Crouched into a corner of the carriage, with Pamela half asleep on her lap, Alex was conscious of the relief of the darkness and the swift motion of the wheels.

Noel was next to her, and in the sudden sense of almost childish terror and loneliness that possessed her, Alex sought instinctive comfort and reassurance in the unavoidable contact. She leant against his shoulder in the shelter of the dark, closely-packed carriage, and was sorry when Clevedon Square was reached at last, and she found herself obliged to descend.

'Good-night – thanks most awfully,' said Noel at the door. 'Good-night, Alex. I say, I'm afraid you were frightfully jammed up in the corner there – I'm so sorry, but I simply couldn't move.'

CHAPTER THIRTEEN

DECISION

On making up her mind that she must break off her engagement, Alex, unaware, took the bravest decision of her life.

She was being true to an instinctive standard, in which she herself only believed with part of her mind, and which was absolutely unknown to any of those who made up her surroundings.

She hardly knew, however, that she had taken any resolution in her many wakeful nights and discontented days, until the moment when she actually put it into execution. She wrote no eloquent letter, entered into no elaborate explanation such as would have seemed to her, after the manner of her generation, theoretically indispensable to the situation.

She blurted out three bald words which struck upon her own hearing with a sense of extreme shock the moment they were uttered.

'It's no use.'

Noel looked hard at her for a moment, and then did not pretend to misunderstand her meaning.

'What, us being engaged?'

His intuitive comprehension, of which Alex had received so little proof ever before, might be unflattering, but it struck her with immense relief.

'Yes.'

They gazed at each other in silence for a few moments, and Alex was furious with herself for a phrase sprung from nowhere that reiterated itself in her brain as she looked at Noel's handsome, inexpressive face.

'*Fish-like flaccidity.* . . .'

And again and again, '*Fish-like flaccidity.*'

They were in the drawing-room at Clevedon Square, and Noel, as though seeking to relieve his obvious embarrassment by moving, got up and walked across the room to the window.

'Of course, I've felt for some time that you weren't very happy about it all, and naturally – if you feel like that . . .'

All the seething disappointment and wounded vanity and aching loneliness that had tortured her since the very first moments of her engagement to Noel Cardew, rushed back on Alex, but she sought vainly for words in which to convey any part of her feelings to him.

It would be like trying to explain some abstruse principle of science to a little child. The sense of the utter uselessness of any attempt at making clear to him the reasons which were chaotic even to herself, paralysed Alex' utterance.

'I don't think it's any use going on,' she repeated feebly.

'You're perfectly free,' Noel assured her scrupulously; 'and though, of course, I – I – I – you – we – it would be – ' He broke off, very red.

Alex wished vaguely that it was possible for them to talk it all out quite frankly and dispassionately with one another, but the hard, crystalline detachment of the generation that was to follow theirs, had as yet no place in the scheme of things known to Noel and Alex.

They made awkward, conventional phrases to one another.

'Naturally,' the boy said with an effort, 'the whole blame must rest with me.'

'Oh no, I'll tell father and mother that I wanted to – to – break it off.'

Alex stopped, conscious that she could not think of anything else to say.

But, rather to her surprise, it appeared that Noel had something else to say.

He faced her with hands thrust into his pockets, his hair and little, fair moustache and his brown eyes looking very light indeed contrasted with his flushed face.

'Of course, you're absolutely free, as I said, only I must say, Alex, that you're making rather a mistake. Everyone was awfully pleased about it, and we've known each other, since we were kids – since *you* were a kid, at any rate – and a broken engagement – well, of course, I don't want to say anything, naturally, but it *does* put a girl in a – a – well, in what's called rather an invidious position. Especially when it isn't as though there was any particular reason for it.'

'The principal reason – ' Alex began faintly, not altogether certain of what it was that she was about to say.

'You see, I always thought we should hit it off together so

well. We always did as kids – when you were a kid, I mean,' Noel explained. 'We always seemed to like the same things, and have a good deal in common.'

'I don't think that you liked any of the things *I* cared about especially,' Alex said, with a flash of spirit.

'What does that matter,' Noel demanded naïvely, 'so long as one of us likes the things that the other does? It comes to exactly the same thing.'

Alex had never told herself, and was therefore quite unable to tell Noel, that she had never liked anything particularly, except his liking for her, which she had striven almost frenziedly to gain and retain by means of an artificially-stimulated display of sympathetic interest in his enthusiasms.

'There's another thing – I don't know whether I ought to say it to you, quite – but, of course, after one's – well, married – there's a lot more one has in common, naturally.'

'Yes,' said Alex forlornly. She quite believed it.

There was an awkward silence.

'Are you angry, Noel?'

She did not think he was at all angry, or very violently moved in any way, but she asked the question from an instinctive desire to hear from him any expression of his real feelings.

He replied stiffly, 'Not at all. Of course, it's much better that you should say all this in time . . . as I say, I've felt for some time that you weren't particularly cheerful. But I must say, Alex, I'm dashed if I know why.'

'I don't know why, exactly – except that I – I don't feel as if we – really – cared – enough for one another – '

Alex spoke with a pause between each word, blushing scarlet, as though it really cost her a physical effort to break through the barrier of reserve that she had been taught so relentlessly should always be erected between her own soul and the naked truth of her own sensations and intimate convictions.

Noel blushed too and Alex felt that he was shocked, which increased her own self-contempt almost unbearably.

'Naturally, if I hadn't – ' he left a blank to supply the words, 'I shouldn't have asked you to – be engaged to me. I must say, Alex, I think you're rather exacting, you know.'

Alex quivered from head to foot, as though he had insulted her most brutally. She, who had shrunk, with a genuine dread that had surprised herself, from Noel's few, shyly-uttered endearments, and had found so entire a lack of response in herself to his occasionally-attempted displays of tenderness, to be accused of having been exacting!

She did not for an instant realize, what even Noel faintly surmised, that she had indeed been exacting, of a romantic fervour which she was as incapable of inspiring as he of bestowing; from which, had it existed, the outward expressions of love would have leapt spontaneously, supremely appropriate, and necessary to them both.

In the mental chaos and muddle of their extreme youth, they looked at one another confused and bewildered, almost like two children suddenly conscious of the magnitude of their own naughtiness.

Noel said, rather proudly, as though one of the children suddenly tried to appear grown-up:

'You must allow me to undertake the distressing task of – breaking it to – *them*.'

Alex almost shuddered, so acute was her own apprehension of the disclosure to her father and mother.

'I shall tell mother at once,' she said, lacking the courage even to mention Sir Francis.

It was typical of the whole time and circumstances of their brief engagement that both Noel, and, in a lesser degree, Alex, had looked upon the relation into which they had entered as one in which their parents held the stakes and were of primary concern. They themselves were only puppets for whom strings were pulled, so as to cause certain vibrations and reactions over which they had no personal control.

This belief, unformulated by either, and entirely charac-teristic of a late Victorian generation, was, perhaps, that which they held most in common.

Alex even wondered whether she ought to wait and speak to Lady Isabel before taking the next step which she had in mind, but her desire to try and raise their trivial, shame-faced parting to a higher level by one dramatic touch, was too strong for her.

She slowly pulled the diamond engagement-ring off her finger, and handed it to him.

'Oh, I say,' stammered Noel. He looked miserably undecided, and she knew that he was wondering whether he could not ask her to keep it just the same.

But in the end he slipped it into his pocket, after balancing it undecidedly for a moment in the palm of his hand.

She sat on the sofa, her left hand feeling strangely bare,

unweighted by the heavy, glittering hoop, and Noel looked out of the window.

'I think I shall go abroad,' he announced suddenly, and with mingled relief and mortification, Alex detected the sound of satisfaction, latent in his voice. She felt that he thought himself to be doing the proper thing in the circumstances, and the sting inflicted on her pride by his acquiescence in their parting, though she had expected nothing else, gave her the sudden impulse necessary to rise and cross the room until she stood beside him at the window.

'Please forgive me, Noel.'

'Oh, there's nothing to forgive,' he returned hastily. 'Of course, if you feel like that, it's all over.'

He looked at her steadily, and Alex felt the suspicion rush over her that he was trying obliquely to convey a warning to her that if she dismissed him now, it would be of no use to recall him later.

Alex felt passionately that in the depths of his stubborn vanity lay the truest presentment of himself that Noel would ever show her. If there was another side to his personality – and she was dimly willing to believe it for all her utter ignorance of him – the power to call it forth did not dwell in her.

Her momentary feeling of anger gave way to humiliation, and she half held out her hand.

'Good-bye, Noel' she said humbly.

As though to atone for the lack of feeling in his tone, Noel wrung her hand until it hurt her, as he replied automatically:

'Good-bye, Alex.'

'I suppose we shall never meet again,' thought Alex, with all the finality of youth, and felt dazed as she saw him open the door.

Mechanically, she rang the bell, in order that the servants downstairs might know that he was leaving, and come into the hall to find his hat and stick and to open the door for him.

Lady Isabel had instilled into Alex that it was part of her responsibility in grown-up life to ring the bell for departing guests, as unostentatiously as possible, at just the right moment, and every time that she remembered to do it, she always felt rather proud of herself.

This time she thought:

'It's the last time Noel will ever be in this room with me. He is going right out of my life.'

She was quite unconsciously trying to awaken in herself an anguish of regret that might yet justify her to herself in recalling her lover.

If he turns round at the door and says, 'Alex!' She tried to cheat herself with a hope that was yet not a hope.

Noel turned at the door.

In a solemn, magnanimous voice he said:

'Alex! I don't want you to feel – ever – that you need reproach yourself, whatever anyone may say. Remember that, if ' – he suddenly looked like a rather frightened little boy – 'if there's a great fuss.'

Then the door closed very quietly behind him, and Alex heard him go downstairs slowly.

It seemed to her that Noel's farewell had plumbed the final depth of his inadequacy.

Presently she sank into an armchair before the fire, and tried to visualize the effects of her own action.

She was principally conscious of a certain amazement, that a step which seemed likely to have such far-reaching consequences should have been so largely the result of sudden impulse. She had not thought the night before of breaking off her engagement. It had all happened very quickly in a few minutes, when the sense of tension which had hung round her intercourse with Noel had suddenly seemed to reach an unbearable pitch, so that something had snapped. Was this how Important Things happened to one through life?

Alex felt that she could not believe it.

But a broken engagement – could there be anything more important, more desperate? Alex felt with melancholy satisfaction that at least it was real life, as she had always imagined it, full of drama and tragedy. With, of course, a glory of happiness as final climax, that would make up for everything. . . . More physically tired than she knew, Alex abandoned herself dreamily to the old, idle visions of the wonderful, perfect love that should come to crown her life. There was no faint, latent sense of disloyalty to Noel now, in returning to her old dreams, that had been hers in one form or another ever since her childish ideal of a perfect friend who would always understand, and yet love one just the same.

It was with a violent start that Alex came back to reality again. She had dismissed Noel Cardew, had given him back his beautiful diamond engagement-ring, and now she would have to tell her father and mother, with no better reason to adduce than her own caprice.

She felt sick with fright.

She remembered Sir Francis' silent but unmistakable pride and pleasure in his engaged daughter, and Lady Isabel's additional display of affection, and even of deference to Alex' taste in choosing her frocks and hats, and her own sense of having at last atoned to them both for her unsatisfactory childhood and lack of any conspicuous social success, such as they had coveted for her.

Alex, cowering in her chair now, wondered how she could face them. Her only shred of comfort lay in the remembrance that Lady Isabel had said to her:

'My darlin', I'm so thankful to know you are marrying for love.'

Alex, in bitter bewilderment, remembered those words again and again in the days which followed.

No one reproached her, she heard hardly a word of blame, and the most severe censure spoken to her was in her mother's soft voice, far more distressed than angry.

'But, Alex, do you know what people say, about a girl who's behaved as you have? That she's a vulgar *jilt*, neither more nor less. To throw over a young man after bein' engaged to him for four weeks, with no reason except a capricious fit. . . . Oh, my darling, *why* couldn't you have asked me first? To go and give him back that lovely ring, and hurt and insult him. . . . Of course, he'll never come back. Your father says how well he's behaved, poor boy. . . . Alex, Alex, what shall I do with you?'

Tears were running down her pretty face, so slightly lined even now.

Alex cried too, from pity for her mother and wretched, undefined remorse, and a growing conviction that in acting on her own distorted impulse she had once more involved herself, and, far worse, others, in far-reaching and disastrous consequences.

'Thank Heaven, we hadn't announced the engagement but, of course, it will all get about – things always do. And there's nothin' worse for a girl than to get that sort of reputation, especially when she's not – not tremendously sought after, or pretty or anythin'.'

Lady Isabel had never before come so near to an avowal that her eldest daughter's career had proved a disappointment to her, and Alex, in the admission, rightly gauged the extent of her mother's dismay.

'Why did you do it, Alex?'

Alex tried haltingly to explain, but she could only say:

'I – I felt I didn't care for him enough.'

'But you hadn't had time to find out! You accepted him when he proposed, so you must have been quite ready to like him then, and you'd only been engaged for four weeks. How could you tell – a little thing like you?' wailed Lady Isabel.

'Oh, Alex, if you'd only come to me about it first – I could have explained it all to you – girls often get fancies about being in love.'

'I thought you wanted me to marry for love. You said so,' sobbed Alex.

'Of course, I don't want you to marry without it. But it's the love that comes *after* marriage that really counts – and a boy you'd known all your life, practically – that we all liked – you could have been ideally happy, Alex.' Lady Isabel looked at her almost resentfully.

'I don't know what will happen to you, my darling, I don't indeed. I sometimes think you are just as headstrong and exaggerated as when you were a little girl. And, Alex, I don't like even to say such a thing to you – but – there's never been anyone *but* Noel, and I'm afraid this isn't the sort of thing that makes any man. . . . Nothin' puts them off more – and no wonder.'

Alex thought momentarily of Queenie, but she knew that was different. In the supreme object of woman, to attract, Queenie stood in a class apart. Nothing that Queenie could ever do would rob her of the devotion that was hers, wherever she chose to claim it, by mysterious right of attraction.

From her father, Alex heard very little. She was left, in her abnormal sensitiveness, to measure his disappointment and mortification by his very silence.

Feeling again like the naughty little girl who had been responsible for Barbara's fall from the balusters, and had been sent to Sir Francis for sentence, she listened, in a silence that was broken only by the sobs that she could hardly control, to his few, measured utterances.

'You are old enough to know your own mind.' Sir Francis paused, swinging his glasses lightly to and fro in his hand. Then he deliberately put them across his nose and looked at her.

'At least,' he added carefully, 'I suppose you are. Your mother tells me that you appear to have been – er – rather suddenly overwhelmed by a fear of marrying without love. I don't wish to say, Alex, that such a sentiment was not more or less proper and natural, but to act upon it so hastily, and with such a heartless lack of consideration, appears to me to be the action, my dear child' – Sir Francis paused, and then added calmly – 'of a fool. The word is not a pretty one, but I prefer it to the only other alternative that I can see, for describing your conduct.'

'Have you anything to say, my dear?'

Alex had nothing to say, and would, in any case, have been rendered by this time powerless of saying it. Sir Francis looked at her with the same grief and mortification on his handsome, severe face that had been there eight years before when the nursery termagant, sobbing and terrified, had stood before him in her short frock and pinafore.

'You could have asked advice,' he said gently. 'You have parents whose only wish is to see you happy. Why did you not go to your mother?'

Alex tried to say, 'Because – ' but found that the only reason which presented itself to her mind was her own conviction that Lady Isabel would not have understood, and she dared not speak it aloud.

The Clare axiom, as that of thousands of their class and generation, was that parents by Divine right knew more than their children could ever hope to learn, and that nothing within the ken of these could ever prove beyond their comprehension.

Sir Francis shook his head sadly.

'I will tell you, my poor child, since you will not answer me, why you did not seek your mother's advice. It was because you are weakly impulsive, and by one act of impetuous folly will lay up for yourself years of unavailing remorse and regret.'

Alex recognized with something like terror the truth of his description.

Weakly impulsive. She had blindly followed an instinct and, as usual, all her world had blamed her, and she had found herself faced by consequences that appalled her.

Why must one always involve others?

She ceased to see clearly that marriage with Noel Cardew would have meant misery, and blindly accepted the vision thrust upon her by her surroundings. She had hurt and disappointed and shamed them, and they could only see her action as a cruel, capricious impulse.

Alex, weakly impulsive, as Sir Francis had said, and sick with misery at their unspoken blame and silent disappointment, presently lost her always feeble hold of her own convictions, and saw with their eyes.

CHAPTER FOURTEEN

BARBARA

Alex became more and more unhappy.

It was evident that Lady Isabel felt hardly any pleasure now in taking her daughter about with her, and the consciousness of not being approved rendered Alex more self-conscious and less sure of herself than ever.

It was inevitable that one or two of her mother's more intimate friends should know of her affair with Noel Cardew, and it did not need Lady Isabel's occasional sorrowful comments to persuade Alex that they took the same view of her conduct as did her parents. The sense of being despised overwhelmed her, and she fretted secretly and lost some of her colour, and held herself worse than ever from the lassitude that overwhelmed her physically whenever she was bored or unhappy.

Towards Easter Lady Isabel sent for Barbara to come home from Neuilly.

Alex revived a little at the idea of having Barbara at Clevedon Square again.

She thought it would impress her younger, still schoolgirl

sister to see her as a fully-emancipated grown-up person, and she could not help hoping that Barbara, promoted to being a confidante, would thrill at the first-hand story of a real love affair and a broken engagement. Alex was prepared to attribute to Noel a romantic despair that had not been his, at her ruthless dismissal of him, in order to overawe little, seventeen-year-old Barbara.

But behold Barbara, after those months spent in the household of the Marquise de Métrancourt de la Hautefeuille!

No need to tell *her* to keep her shoulders back. She was not quite so tall as Alex, but her slim figure was exquisitely upright. Encased in French stays that made even Lady Isabel gasp, she wore, with an air, astonishing French clothes that swung gracefully round her as she moved, and her hair, which had developed a surprising ripple, was gathered up at the back of her head with a huge, outstanding bow of smartly-tied ribbon that seemed to form a background for the pale, pointed little face, that was still Barbara's, but had somehow acquired an elusive charm that actually seemed more distinguished than ordinary, healthy English prettiness.

And the self-assurance of the child!

Alex was disgusted at the ease with which Barbara, hitherto shy and tongue-tied in the presence of her parents, chattered lightly to them on the evening of her return, and offered – actually offered unasked! – to sing them some of her new songs. 'New songs' indeed, when it was only a year ago that she had written to ask whether she might have a few singing lessons with the Marquise's daughter! But neither Sir

Francis nor Lady Isabel rebuked her temerity, and they even exchanged amused, approving glances when the slim, upright figure moved lightly across the room to the big grand piano.

Alex, in her pink evening dress, with her elaborately-coiled hair, felt infinitely childish and awkward as she watched Barbara slip off a new gold bangle from her little white, rounded wrist, and strike a couple of chords with perfect self-assurance.

She was going to play without music! It was absurd; Barbara had never been musical.

Certainly the voice in which she sang a couple of little French *ballades* was a very tiny one, but there was a tunefulness, above all a vivacity, about her whole performance, which caused even Sir Francis to break into unwonted applause at the finish. Alex applauded too, principally from the desire to prove to herself that it would be impossible for *her* ever to feel jealous of little Barbara.

When they had sent her to bed, Lady Isabel laughed with more animation than she often displayed.

'How the child has developed!'

'Charming, charming!' said Sir Francis. 'We must show her something of the world, I think, even if she is rather young.'

But it soon became evident, to Alex, at least, that Barbara had not been without glimpses of the world, even at Neuilly. She listened with interest, but very coolly, to Alex' attempted confidences, and finally said, 'Well, I can't imagine how you could have borne to give up the diamond ring, and it would have been fun to get married and have a trousseau and a house of your own. But I don't think Noel would make much of a husband.'

The calm disparagement of her tone annoyed Alex. It seemed to rob her solitary conquest of any lingering trace of glory.

'I don't think you know very much about it,' she said rather scathingly. 'You haven't met any men at all, naturally, so how can you judge?'

Barbara laughed.

Something of security that would not even take the trouble to dispute the point pierced through that cool, self-confident little laugh of hers.

Later on, she told Alex, with rather overdone matter-of-factness, that a young Frenchman, a cousin of Hélène de la Hautefeuille, had fallen very much in love with her at Neuilly.

Alex at first pretended not to believe her, although she felt an uncomfortable inward certainty that Barbara would never waste words on an idle boast that could not be substantiated.

'You need not believe me if you don't want to,' said Barbara indifferently.

'But how could you *know*? I thought the Marquise was so particular?'

'So she was. They all are, in France, with *jeunes filles*. It's ridiculous. But, of course, as Hélène was his cousin, they weren't quite so strict, and he used to give her notes and things for me.'

'Barbara!'

'You needn't be so shocked, Alex. Of course, *I* never wrote to *him* – that would have been too stupid; but he's very nice,

190

and simply madly in love with me. Hélène said he always admired *le type Anglais*, and that I was his ideal.'

Alex was thoroughly angered at the complacency in Barbara's voice.

'You and Hélène are two silly, vulgar little schoolgirls. I didn't think you could be so – so common, Barbara. What on earth would father and mother say?'

'I daresay they wouldn't mind so very much,' said Barbara calmly, 'so long as they didn't know about the notes and our having met once or twice in the garden.'

'I don't believe it!' exclaimed Alex. 'You think it sounds grown-up, and so – you're exaggerating the whole thing.'

Barbara looked at her sister, with her eyebrows cocked in a provoking, conceited sort of way, not angrily, but rather contemptuously.

'Really, Alex, to hear you make such a fuss about it, anyone would think that you'd never set eyes on a man. Of course, that sort of thing happens as soon as one begins to get grown-up. It's part of the fun.'

'You know mother would say it was vulgar.'

It was almost a relief to see one of Barbara's rare blushes at the word.

'I don't see why it should be more vulgar than you and Noel.'

'How can you be so ridiculous! Of course, that was quite different. We were both grown-up, and properly engaged and everything.'

'Alex,' said Barbara suddenly, 'when you were engaged, did he ever kiss you?'

Alex turned nearly as scarlet as her sister had been a moment before.

'Shut up!' she said savagely. A thought struck her. 'You don't mean to say you ever let that beastly French boy try to do anything like that?' she demanded.

'No, no,' said Barbara hastily; 'of course not. But he's not such a boy as all that, you know. He has a moustache, and he's doing his *service militaire* now. Otherwise,' said Barbara calmly, 'I daresay he would have followed me to England.'

'You conceited little idiot! He must have been laughing at you.'

Barbara shrugged her shoulders, with a gesture that had certainly not been acquired in Clevedon Square.

'You'll see for yourself presently,' she remarked. 'He's going to get his *permission* next month, and he's coming to London.'

'You don't suppose you'll be able to go sneaking about writing notes and meeting him in corners *here*, do you?' cried Alex, horrified.

Barbara looked at her disdainfully, and gave deft little pulls and pats to the bow on her hair, so that it stood out more than ever.

'What on earth do you take me for, Alex? Of course, I know as well as you do that that sort of thing can't be done in London. It will all be perfectly proper,' said Barbara superbly. 'I have given him permission to call here.'

Alex remained speechless.

She was quite unable to share in the tolerant amusement with which her parents apparently viewed the astonishing emancipation of Barbara, although it was true that Barbara still retained a sufficient sense of decorum to describe M. Achille de Villefranche to them merely as 'a cousin of Hélène's, who would like to come and call when he is in London.'

Lady Isabel acceded to the proposed visit with gracious amusement, and Alex wondered jealously why her own attempts to prove grown-up and like other girls never seemed to succeed as did Barbara's preposterous, demurely-spoken pretensions – until she remembered with a pang that, after all, *she* had never had to ask whether admiring strangers might call upon her. She knew instinctively that however much Lady Isabel might exact in the way of elaborate chaperonage, she would secretly have welcomed any such proof of her daughter's attraction for members of the opposite sex.

One day Barbara, more boastful or less secretive than usual, showed Alex one of Achille's notes, written to her on the day that she had left Neuilly.

Alex deciphered the pointed writing with some difficulty, and then turned first hot and then cold, as she remembered the few letters she had ever received from Noel Cardew, written during the period of their lawful, sanctioned engagement, when she had so fiercely told herself that, of course, a man was never romantic on paper, and that his very reticence only proved the depth of his feeling.

And all that time Barbara, utterly cold and merely superciliously amused, had been the recipient of this Latin hyperbole, these impassioned poetical flights:

'Ma petite rose blanche anglaise, ma douce Sainte Barbe.'

(Good heavens! he had never seen Barbara in one of her cold furies, when she would sulk in perfect silence for three days on end!) And finally, with humble pleadings that he might be forgiven for such a *débordement*, Achille apostrophized her as *'ma mignonne adorée'*.

Alex could hardly believe that it was really Barbara who had inspired these romantic ebullitions.

'How did you answer him?' she asked breathlessly.

'I didn't answer at all,' Barbara coolly replied. 'You don't suppose I was so silly as that, do you? Why, girls get into the most awful difficulties by writing letters and signing their names, and then the man won't let them have the letters back afterwards. Achille has never had one single scrap of writing from me.'

Alex felt as much rebuked as angered by this display of worldly wisdom. She knew, and was sure that Barbara, pluming herself over her own shrewdness, knew also, that had she herself been able to provoke similar protestations, no considerations of prudence or discretion would have restrained the ardour of her response.

During the Easter holidays Barbara remained in the schoolroom, sometimes playing with Archie and Pamela, but generally engaged on one of the many forms of embroidery which she appeared to have learned at Neuilly, or diligently practising her French songs at the schoolroom piano.

She did not appear to be at all envious of Alex' grown-up privileges, for which Alex felt rather wonderingly grateful to her, until one day when she was out driving with Lady Isabel, when a sudden enlightenment fell upon her.

'What do you think of this ambition of little Barbara's?' her mother asked her, with a trace of hesitation.

'What?' asked Alex stupidly.

'Why, this frantic wish of hers to be presented next May and allowed to make her début. She will be seventeen, after all, and she seems to have set her heart on it.'

'Barbara! She wants to be presented and come out in May! Why, it's nearly April now, mother! That would mean in another six weeks.'

Alex was stupefied.

'Hasn't she said anything to you?' said Lady Isabel, with a sort of vague, unperceiving wonder. 'Funny little thing! I thought she would have been sure to have talked it all over with you. She's been beggin' and implorin' us ever since she got back from Neuilly, and your father is half inclined to say she may.'

How like Barbara! Begging and imploring them to let her be presented next May, and all the time saying nothing at all to Alex, and slyly pretending to care nothing for coming out, and listening with deceptive quiet to Alex' little occasional speeches made to mark the difference between twenty and seventeen. No doubt Barbara knew very well that she would get her own way by dint of ardent pleading, and did not want the effect of her arguments and reasonable-sounding representations to be spoilt by Alex' vigorous protests.

For, of course, Alex was indignant. Why should Barbara

come out when she was barely seventeen, when her sister had had to wait until the orthodox eighteen?

Alex might not value her privileges highly, but she was far from wishing Barbara to share them.

In the depths of her soul was a lurking consciousness that neither did she want sharp-eyed, critical Barbara to see how poor and dull a figure her sister cut, after the imaginary triumphs of which she had so often boasted.

Lady Isabel might be disappointed, but she never voiced her disappointment or hinted at it, and Alex thought she tried to conceal it from herself. But Barbara would not be disappointed. She might be rather pleased, and make the small, veiled, spiteful comments by which she occasionally, and always unexpectedly, paid one back for past slights or unkindnesses.

Alex felt that she could not bear any further mortifications.

The question of Barbara's coming out was still undecided, principally owing to Alex' strenuous efforts to persuade her mother not to allow it, when M. Achille de Villefranche made the ceremonious visit to Clevedon Square which Barbara had announced.

He came on a Sunday, so soon after three o'clock that Lady Isabel's luncheon guests had barely departed, and sat on the extreme edge of his chair, a slim, beautifully-rolled umbrella between his knees, and his silk hat balanced on the top of it. His tie was tied into an astonishing bow with outspread ends that irresistibly reminded Alex of Barbara's hair-ribbon.

He spoke excellent English, very rapidly, but occasionally lapsed into still more rapid French, in which he poured forth his enthusiasm for 'cette chère île des brouillards,' which description of her native land was fortunately uncomprehended by Lady Isabel.

Altogether Achille was so like a Frenchman on the stage that Alex almost expected to see him fall upon his knees in the drawing-room when Barbara demurely obeyed the summons sent up to the schoolroom by her mother, and appeared in her prim, dark blue schoolroom frock. He certainly sprang to his feet with a sort of bound, but any further intentions were frustrated by his elegant umbrella, which got between his feet and nearly tripped him up, and sent his beautiful top-hat rolling into the furthest corner of the drawing-room.

Alex had to recognize that Achille behaved with great presence of mind, even taken at such a disadvantage. He bowed over Barbara's hand, at the same time kicking his umbrella carelessly aside. He waved a contemptuous hand which made the behaviour of his hat a thing of no account, and he did not even trouble himself to retrieve it until Barbara was seated, when he strolled away to pick it up in a nonchalant manner, talking all the time of other things.

But in spite of the high-handedness of Achille, Alex felt that the whole affair was of the nature of a farce, and was ashamed of herself for deriving unmistakable satisfaction from the conviction that no one could take Barbara's conquest seriously.

Even Sir Francis, who found Achille still discoursing in the drawing-room on his return from the Club at seven o'clock, indulged in a little mild chaffing of his younger daughter when M. de Villefranche, amid many bows, had finally taken his leave.

Barbara responded with a sprightly amiability that she had never displayed in her pre-Neuilly days, and which Alex angrily and uncomprehendingly perceived both pleased and amused Sir Francis.

'But I am not sure that I approve of your taste in the selection of your admirers, my dear,' he said humorously, his right hand lightly swinging his glasses against his left.

'I have never met any Englishmen, you know, father,' said Barbara piteously, opening her eyes very wide. 'If mother would only let me come out this year and see a few people!'

Alex was aghast at Barbara's duplicity, recognizing perfectly her manœuvre of implying that only her mother's consent was still required for her début.

'Well, well, well,' said Sir Francis, wearing the expression of an indulgent parent; 'but surely young ladies are expected to wait till their eighteenth birthday?'

'Oh, but I *should* so like a long frock,' sighed Barbara, her head on one side – an admirable rendering of the typical 'young lady' known and admired of her father's generation.

Sir Francis laughed, unmistakable yielding foreshadowed in his tone, and in the glance he directed towards his wife.

''Gad! Isabel, we shall have a regular little society butterfly on our hands; what do you think?'

Lady Isabel, also smiling, nevertheless said almost reluctantly, as though to imply that assent would be in defiance of her better judgment:

'Of course, this year will be exceptionally gay because

of the Jubilee. I should rather like her to come out when there is so much going on, but I don't quite know about taking two of them everywhere.' She glanced at Alex and sighed almost involuntarily. It was impossible not to remember the tentative plans that they had discussed so short a while ago for a brilliant wedding that should take place just when all London was busy with festivals in honour of the Queen's Diamond Jubilee. The same recollection shot like a pang through Alex, feeling the pain of her mother's disappointment far more acutely than her own humiliation, and making her speak sharply, and almost unaware of what she said, sooner than endure a moment's silence:

'You can take Barbara instead of me. I hate balls and I'm sick of going to things.'

She was horrified at the sound of the words as she spoke them, and at her own roughened, mortified voice.

There was a moment's silence.

'That,' said Sir Francis gently and gravely, 'is neither a very gracious nor a very dutiful speech, Alex. Your mother has spared herself neither trouble nor fatigue in conducting you to those entertainments organized for your pleasure and advantage, and it is a poor reward for her many sacrifices to be told with a scowling face that you are "sick of going about." If those are your sentiments, I shall strongly advise her to consult her own convenience in the future, instead of making everything give way to your pleasures, as she has done for the last two years.'

Lady Isabel looked distressed, and said, 'It is very difficult to know what you want, Alex. If you'd only say!'

'I don't want anything; I'm quite happy,' began Alex, overwhelmed with the sense of her own ingratitude; and by way of proving her words she began to cry hopelessly, although she knew that Sir Francis could not bear tears, and that anything in the nature of a scene made Lady Isabel feel ill.

'Control yourself,' said her father.

They all looked at her in silence, and her nervousness made her give a loud sob.

'If you are hysterical, Alex, you had better go to your room.'

Alex was only too thankful to obey. Still sobbing, she received the conventional good-night kiss which neither she nor her parents would have dreamed of omitting, however deep their displeasure with her, and left the room reproaching herself bitterly.

They had all been so cheerful before she spoilt it all, Sir Francis in unwontedly good spirits, and both of them pleased at the harmless amusement caused by Barbara's visitor.

'I spoil *everything*,' Alex told herself passionately, and longed for some retreat where she might be the solitary victim of her own temperament, and need not bear the double pang of the vexation and grief which she inflicted upon others.

She did not go downstairs to dinner, and soon after eight o'clock Barbara came in and told her that there was supper in the schoolroom for both of them.

'Though after this,' said Barbara importantly, 'I shall be having dinner properly in the dining-room quite soon. They are going to let me put up my hair, and I *think* they will let me be presented at a late Drawing-room, though they won't promise. It was settled after you went upstairs.'

'Are they vexed with me?' asked Alex dejectedly.

'Not particularly. Only disappointed.'

Alex would rather have been told that they were angry.

She had not spirit enough left to snub Barbara, discoursing untiringly of all that she meant to do and to wear, until at last her younger sister remarked patronizingly:

'Cheer up, Alex! I believe you're afraid of my cutting you out. But we shall be quite different styles, you know. I can't hope to be a beauty, so I shall go in for being *chic*. Hélène always says it pays in the long run. By the bye, Achille thought you were very pretty.'

'How do you know?'

'He told me so.'

'Nonsense! How could he? I was in the room the whole time.'

'Oh, there are ways and means,' retorted Barbara, tossing her head.

Alex would not gratify her by asking further questions. To her habitual fashion of ignoring slights until it became convenient to repay them, however, Barbara added now an impervious armour of self-satisfaction at the prospect of her approaching entry into the world.

She even, three months later, received with no other display of feeling than a rather contemptuous little laugh, the elaborately-worded *lettre de faire part* which announced the approaching marriage of Hélène de Métrancourt de la Hautefeuille to her cousin, Achille Marie de Villefranche.

CHAPTER FIFTEEN

※※※※※※※※※※

DIAMOND JUBILEE

All that summer everyone spoke of 'Jubilee weather', and London grew hotter and sunnier and more crowded day by day.

Alex found herself wishing, fretfully and almost angrily, that she could enjoy it all. But the sensation of loneliness that had always oppressed her, although she did not analyze it, was always most poignant amongst a great number of people, and her listlessness and self-absorption in society, at last caused Lady Isabel to ask her gently, but with unmistakable vexation, whether she had rather 'leave most of the gaieties to little Barbara, to whom it's all new and amusing.'

'Why?' asked Alex, startled.

'My darling, I can see you're not very happy, and I quite understand that, of course, one doesn't get over these things in a minute,' said Lady Isabel, with a sigh for the memory of Noel Cardew. 'This will be your third season, and I had hoped it would be the best of them all, what with the Jubilee celebrations and everythin' – but if you're rather out of heart with the gaieties just now, I don't want to force you into them, poor child.'

Lady Isabel gazed with wistful, puzzled eyes that held nothing but uncomprehending perplexity at her disappointing eldest daughter. Alex knew that she was wondering silently why that daughter, expensively educated and still more expensively dressed, admittedly pretty and well-bred, should still lack any semblance of attractiveness, should still fail to achieve any semblance of popularity.

Alex herself wondered drearily if she was always destined to find herself out of all harmony with her surroundings. She never questioned but that the fault lay entirely in herself, and a sort of fatalism made her accept it all with apathetic matter-of-factness.

She gave inert acquiescence to Lady Isabel's tentative suggestion that most of the invitations pouring in daily should be accepted on Barbara's behalf only, partly because she hated being taken out with her sister, who was always critical and observant, and partly from sheer desire that Lady Isabel should no longer have the mortification of watching a social progress, the indifference of which Alex regarded with morbid exaggeration.

Barbara, rather to Alex' surprise, although enjoying herself with a sort of quiet determination, proved to be exceedingly shy, but in two months she had achieved several gushing, intimate friendships with girls rather older than herself, which led to her receiving innumerable invitations to tea-parties, a form of entertainment always abhorred by Alex, but from which Barbara generally returned with one or two new acquaintances, who were sure to claim dances from her on meeting her at subsequent balls.

She was not very pretty, and evening dresses, displaying her thin arms and shoulders, detracted from the effect of smartness that she had acquired in France, but she danced exceptionally well, and was seldom left partnerless.

Alex often wondered what Barbara, who was notoriously silent and awkward with strangers, could find to talk about to her partners.

It did not occur to her that Barbara made an art of listening to them.

The climax of the season's festivities was reached on the blazing day towards the end of June, when the Jubilee procession wound its way through the flagged and decorated streets, with the small, stout, black-clad figure in the midst of it all, bowing indefatigably to the crowds that thronged streets and windows and balconies and even, when practicable, roofs.

A window of Sir Francis' Club was placed by him, with some ceremony, at the disposal of his wife, his eldest son up from Eton, and one daughter, but it was evident that he would regard any further display of family as rather excessive, and Alex herself suggested that she should see it all from a window in Grosvenor Place which had been procured for Pamela and Archie, under the care of old Nurse, and various minor members of the household.

'But that would be so dull!' protested Lady Isabel, shocked.

'Alex can do as she pleases, my dear,' said Sir Francis stiffly.

He was not pleased with his oldest daughter, and imagined that her evident shrinking from society arose, not from her acute perception of this fact, but from shame at the recollection of her behaviour towards Noel Cardew, which Sir Francis in his own mind stigmatized as both dishonourable and unladylike. The further reflection he gave to the matter – and reflection with Sir Francis was never anything but deliberate – the more seriously he resented his daughter's lapse from the code of 'good form', and the harassed look which she was gradually causing to mar his wife's placid beauty.

He would have liked Alex to be prettily eager for pleasure, as were the young ladies of his day and ideal, and he regarded her obvious discontent and unhappiness as a slur on Lady Isabel's exertions on her behalf.

Very slowly, with the dull implacability of a man slow to assimilate a grievance, and slower still to forgive what he does not understand, Sir Francis was becoming angry with Alex.

'Let her do as she likes, Isabel,' he repeated. 'If the society we can provide is less amusing than that of children and servants, by all means let her join them.'

Lady Isabel did not repeat his words to Alex. She only said: 'Your father says, do as you like, darlin'. We shan't have over-much room, of course, especially as we have asked so many people for lunch afterwards, but if you really cared about comin' with us, I could arrange it in a minute – '

She paused, as though for Alex' eager acclamation, but Barbara broke in quickly:

'There won't be much room, with all those people coming, will there? And father always says that *one* grown-up daughter at a time is enough, so if Alex really doesn't want to come it seems a pity . . .'

So Alex, with an unreasonable sense of injury, that yet was in some distorted way a relief to her, as showing her not to be alone in fault, watched the procession from Grosvenor Place, with Archie flushed and shouting with excitement, and Pamela, with curly, cropped hair and Liberty silk picture frock, such as was just coming into fashion, breaking into shrill cheers of rather spasmodic loyalty, as she fidgeted up and down the length of the bunting-hung balcony.

Alex, on the whole, was sorry when it was all over, and the two children ordered into the carriage by Nurse for the return to Clevedon Square.

She declared that she was going to walk home across the Park, partly because the crowds interested her, partly to assert her independence of old Nurse.

'Then you'll take James with you, in a crowd like this,' the old autocrat declared.

'Nonsense, I don't want James. You'll come with me, won't you, Holland?'

'Yes, Miss,' said the maid submissively.

Since Barbara's coming out, the sisters had shared a maid of their own, and Holland very much preferred Alex, who cared nothing what happened to her clothes, and read a book all the time that her hair was being dressed, to the exacting and sometimes rather querulous Barbara.

They found the Park comparatively free from people. Everyone had gone to find some place of refreshment, or had made a rush to secure places for the return route of the procession from St. Paul's Cathedral.

Flags streamed and waved in the sunshine, and swinging

rows of little electric globes hung everywhere, in readiness for the evening's display of illuminations.

Alex suddenly felt very tired and hot, and longed to escape from the glare and the noise.

She wondered whether, if Noel had been with her, she could have taken part in the general sense of holiday and rejoicing, sharing it with him, and whilst her aching loneliness cried 'Yes,' some profounder instinct warned her that a companionship rooted only in proximity brings with it a deeper sense of isolation than any solitude.

Her steps began to flag, and she wished that the way through the Park did not seem so interminable.

'Couldn't we find a cab, Holland? I'm tired.'

'It won't be easy, Miss, today,' said the maid, a disquieted eye roving over the Park railings to the dusty streets where pedestrians, indeed, thronged endlessly, but few vehicles of any sort were to be discerned.

Alex would have liked to sit down, but none of the benches were unoccupied, and, in any case, she knew that Lady Isabel would be shocked at her doing such a thing, under no better chaperonage than that of a maid.

Quite conscious of her own unreason, she yet said fretfully:

'I really can't get all the way home, unless I can sit down and rest somewhere.'

She had only said it to relieve her own sense of fatigue and irritability, and was surprised when Holland replied in a tone of reasonable suggestion:

'There's the convent just close to Bryanston Square, Miss. You can always go in there – it's always open.'

'What convent?'

Holland named the Order of the house at Liège where Alex had been at school.

She exclaimed at the coincidence.

'I thought their London house was in the East End.'

'Yes, Miss,' Holland explained, becoming suddenly voluble. 'But the Sisters opened a new house last year. I went to the consecration of the chapel. It was a beautiful ceremony, Miss.'

'Of course, you're a Catholic, aren't you? I forgot.'

'Yes, Miss,' said Holland, stiffening. It was evident that the fact to which Alex referred so lightly was of supreme importance to her.

'Well, a church is better than nowhere in this heat,' said Miss Clare disconsolately.

Lady Isabel had decreed nearly two years ago that churchgoing, at all events during the season, was incompatible with late nights, and Alex had acquiesced without much difficulty.

Religion did not interest her, and she had kept up no intercourse with the nuns at Liège since leaving school.

Holland, looking at once shocked and rather excited, pointed out the tall, narrow building, wedged into a line of similar buildings, with a high flight of steps leading to the open door.

'It's always open like that,' Holland said. 'Anyone can go into the chapel.'

The open door, indeed, gave straight on to the oak door of the chapel across a narrow entrance lobby.

Alex was instantly conscious of the sharply-defined contrast between the hot glare and incessant roar of multifarious noises outside in the brilliant streets, and the dark, cool hush that pervaded the silent convent chapel.

The sudden sensation of physical relief almost brought tears to her eyes, as she sank thankfully on to a little cushioned *prie-dieu* drawn up close to the high, carved rood-screen before the chancel steps.

Holland had slid noiselessly to her knees behind one of the humble wooden benches close to the entrance.

There was absolute silence.

As her eyes grew accustomed to the soft gloom, Alex saw that the chapel was a very small one, of an odd oblong shape, with high, carved stalls on either side of it that recalled the big convent chapel at Liège to her mind. The wax candles shed a peculiarly mild glow over the High Altar, which was decked with a mass of white blossom and feathery green, but the rest of the chapel was unlit except by the warm, softened shaft of sunshine that struck through the painted oval windows behind the altar, and lay in deep splashes of colour over the white-embroidered altar-cloth and the red-carpeted altar steps

The peace and harmony of her surroundings fell on Alex' wearied spirit with an almost poignant realization of their beauty. The impression thus made upon her, striking with utter unexpectedness, struck deep, and to the end of her life the remembrance was to remain with her, of the sudden sense which had come upon her of entering into another world, when she stepped straight from the streets of London into the convent chapel, on Diamond Jubilee Day.

It seemed to her that she had been sitting still there for

some time, scarcely conscious of thought or feeling, when the remembrance gradually began to filter through her mind, as it were, of teachings, unheeded at the time, from her schooldays at Liège.

What if the solution to all her troubles lay here, before the small gilt door of the tabernacle?

Alex had never prayed in her life. The mechanical formula extorted from the Clare children by old Nurse had held no meaning for them, least of all for Alex, who was not temperamentally religious, and instinctively disliked anything which was presented to her in the light of an obligation.

Her lack of fundamental religious instruction had remained undiscovered, and consequently unrectified, throughout her schooldays, and she had unconsciously adopted since then the standard typified no less in Sir Francis' courteously blank attitude towards the faith of his fathers, than in Lady Isabel's conventional adherence to the minimum of church-going permitted by the social code.

What if comfort had been waiting for her all the time?

'Come unto Me, all ye that labour and are heavy burdened, and I will refresh you.'

Alex did not know that she was crying until she found herself wiping away the tears that were blinding her.

The loneliness that encompassed her seemed to her to be suddenly lightened, and she formulated the first vague, stammering prayer of her life.

'Help me . . . make me good . . . and let there be someone soon who will understand . . . someone who will understand and still love me . . . who will want me to care too . . . If only there was someone for whose sake everything really mattered, I believe I could be good. . . . Please help me. . . .'

She felt certain that her prayer would be heard and granted.

There was the slightest possible movement beside her, and turning sharply, she saw the tall figure of a woman wearing the habit of the Order, standing over her.

She had not known that this nun was in the chapel.

The tall, commanding presence bent and knelt down on the ground beside her, with a deep inclination of her head towards the High Altar.

'Forgive me for disturbing you, but when you are quite ready to come away, will you come and speak to me for a moment or two before you go?' She paused for a second, but Alex was too much surprised to reply.

'Don't hurry. I shall wait for you outside.'

The nun rose slowly, laying her hand for an instant on Alex' shoulder, and moved soundlessly away.

Alex looked at her watch, and was surprised by the lateness of the hour.

She drew down her veil, and gathered up the long, fashionable skirt of her dress, preparatory to leaving the chapel.

In the little lobby outside she looked round curiously. On the instant, someone moved forward out of a shadowy corner.

'Come in here for a moment, won't you? I think it is Miss Clare?'

'Yes.'

Alex, faintly uneasy, although she could not have explained why, looked round for her maid.

Holland came forward at once.

'Good afternoon, Mary,' said the nun, addressing her calmly. 'How are you?'

'Very well, thank you, Mother Gertrude. I hadn't hoped to be here again so soon, but Miss Clare was tired, and we were just going past, on the way back after the procession.'

'Ah yes, to be sure,' said the nun with the air of recalling an unimportant fact, 'the Jubilee procession takes place today. That must make the streets unpleasantly crowded. Won't you rest a little while in the parlour, Miss Clare? Perhaps your maid might find a cab to take you home.'

'Will you try, Holland?' said Alex eagerly. She felt unable to walk any more.

This time Holland made no demur at the suggestion, and only glanced a respectful farewell, at the nun, who said, with a smile that seemed somehow full of authority, 'Good-bye, then, Mary, for the present. I will take care of your young lady whilst you are away. It may take a little while to find a cab on a day like this.'

As the maid went out, Mother Gertrude motioned to Alex to precede her down the small, uneven steps leading out of the lobby into a better-lighted passage beyond.

'There are two steps down, that's all. These old houses are dark, and inconveniently built – but we were lucky to get anything so central. . . . Come into the parlour, we shall not be disturbed, and your maid will know where to find us when she returns.'

'I had no idea that Holland came here, and – and knew you,' said Alex, rather confused.

In the stiff, ugly parlour, furnished with cane-seated chairs and a round table, it was easy to see Mother Gertrude, as she seated herself opposite to Alex in the window.

She was an exceptionally tall, upright woman, a natural dignity of carriage emphasized by the sweeping black folds of veil and habit, her hands demurely hidden under the wide-falling sleeves as she sat with arms lightly crossed. Her strong, handsome face, of a uniform light reddish colour, showed one or two hard lines, noticeably round the closed, determined mouth, and her strongly-marked eyebrows almost met over straight-gazing, very light grey eyes. Even her religious habit could not conceal the lines and contour of a magnificent figure, belonging to a woman in the full maturity of life.

'Are you surprised to find that your maid comes to the convent?' she asked, smiling.

Her voice was deep and of a commanding quality that seemed to match her personality, but her smile was her least attractive feature. It was only a slow widening of her mouth, showing a set of patently porcelain teeth, and deepening the creases on either side of her face. Her eyes remained watchful and unchanged.

'Mary Holland was one of our children when she was quite a little thing, at our Poor-school at Bermondsey. She has always been a good girl, and we take a great interest in her.'

'Was that why you knew who I was?' Alex inquired, remembering how the nun had addressed her by name.

'Yes. I knew that Mary Holland had taken a place with Lady Isabel Clare, and was much interested to hear from her of her "young lady". Tell me, were you not at school at our Mother-house in Belgium?'

Alex, unversed in the infinitely far-reaching ramifications of inter-conventual communication, was again surprised.

'Yes, I was there for about five years, but I don't remember – ' She hesitated.

'Oh no, I was never there. I have been Superior at one or other House in London for more than ten years, but I have heard your name several times, though not since you left school. We like to keep in touch with our children, but you have probably been busy going about with your mother?'

'I didn't even know there was a house of the Order here,' Alex admitted.

'It has not been established very long. Our chapel was only consecrated a few months ago. It is very tiny, but perhaps some day you will pay another visit here.'

Mother Gertrude was not looking at Alex as she spoke, but down at her own long rosary beads; and the fact somehow made it easier for Alex to reply without embarrassment:

'Yes, I should like to come, if I may – and if I can. It felt so – so peaceful.'

'Yes,' returned the nun, without any show of surprise or, indeed, any emotion at all, in her carefully colourless voice. 'Yes, it is very peaceful here – a great contrast to the hurry and unrest of the world. And for anyone who is tired, or troubled, or perhaps unhappy, and conscious of wrongdoing, there is always comfort to be found here. No one asks any questions, and if, perhaps, a poor soul is too much worn-out with conflict for prayer, why, even that is not necessary.'

Alex gazed at her, surprised.

'Do you think that God wants things put into words?' said the nun, with her slow smile.

Alex did not know what to reply. She looked silently at the Superior, and felt that those light, penetrating, grey eyes had probed to the depths of her confusion and beyond it, to the sense of loneliness and bewilderment that had made her weep in the chapel.

'Do a lot of people come here?' she asked involuntarily, from the sense that a wide experience of humanity must have gone to the making of those keen perceptions.

'Yes. Many of them I know, and see here, and anything that passes in this little room is held in sacred confidence. But very often, of course, there are visitors to the chapel of whom we know nothing – just passers-by.'

'That was what I was.'

The nun looked at her for a moment. 'And yet,' she said slowly, 'something made me want to come and speak to you, even before I caught sight of your maid, and guessed you must be Miss Clare. It is curious that you should have turned out to be one of our children.'

Alex thought so too, but the term with its sense of shelter touched her strangely. She was shaken both by physical fatigue and her recent violent crying, and moreover, the forceful, magnetic personality of the Superior was already making its sure impression upon her young, unbalanced susceptibilities.

'May I see you again, next time I come?' she asked rather tremulously.

Mother Gertrude stood up.

'Whenever you like,' she said emphatically, her direct gaze adding weight to the deliberately-spoken words. 'Come whenever you like. You have been brought here by what looks like a strange chance. Don't neglect the way now that you know it.'

She held Alex' hand in hers for a moment, and then took her back to the little lobby.

'Mary has actually got a four-wheeled cab! That is very clever of her. I hope they will not have been anxious about you at home. You must tell them that you were with *friends*, quite safe.'

She laid a slight emphasis on the words, smiling a little.

'Good-bye,' said Alex; 'thank you very much.'

'Good-bye,' repeated the nun. 'And God bless you, my child.'

CHAPTER SIXTEEN

※※※※※※※※※

MOTHER GERTRUDE

Alex felt strangely comforted for some time after that visit to the convent. It seemed to her that in appealing to the God who dwelt in the chapel shrine, she had found a human friend. Secretly she thought very often of the Superior, wondering if Mother Gertrude remembered her and thought of her too. Once or twice when she was out with Holland, or even with her mother, she manœuvred a little in order to go past the tall, undistinguished-looking building, and look up curiously at its shrouded windows. But she did not actually enter the convent again until three weeks later, after she had said rather defiantly to Lady Isabel:

'Do you mind my going to see the Superior of the convent near Bryanston Square, mother? It's the new house they've opened – a branch of the Liège house, you know.'

'If you like,' said Lady Isabel indifferently. 'What's put it into your head?'

'Holland told me about it. She went there for some ceremony or other when they opened the chapel, and – and she knew I'd been at school at Liège,' Alex answered.

She was conscious that the reply was evasive, but she was afraid of admitting that she had already made acquaintance with the Superior, with that innate sense, peculiar to the period in which she lived, that anything undertaken upon the initiative of a child would *ipso facto* be regarded as wrong or dangerous by its parents.

'But mind,' added Lady Isabel suspiciously, 'I won't have your name used by them. I mean that you are not to promise that you'll patronize all sorts of dowdy, impossible charities.'

'Very well, I won't.'

Alex was glad to have permission to visit the convent under any conditions, and she secretly resolved that she would make an elastic use of the sanction given her, during the short time that remained before the usual exodus from London.

She felt half afraid that Mother Gertrude might have forgotten her, but the nun greeted her with a warmth that fanned to instant flame the spark of Alex' ready infatuation. She quickly fell into one of the old, enamoured enthusiasms that had cost her so much in her childish days.

Mother Gertrude did not speak of religion to her, or touch upon any religious teaching, but she encouraged Alex to speak much about herself, and to admit that she was very unhappy.

'Have you no one at home?'

'They don't understand me,' Alex said with conviction.

'That is hard to bear. And you are very sensitive – and with very great capabilities for either good or evil.'

Alex thrilled to the echo of a conviction which she had hardly dared to admit to herself.

'My dear child – do you mind my calling you so?'

'Oh no – no! I wish you would call me by my name – Alex.'

'What,' the Superior said, smiling, 'as though you were one of my own children, in spite of being a young lady of the world?'

'Oh yes – if you'll let me,' breathed Alex, looking up at the woman who had fascinated her, with all the fervour of her ardent, unbalanced temperament in her gaze.

'My poor, lonely little Alex! You shall be my child then.' The grave, lingering kiss on her forehead came like a consecration.

Alex went home that day in ecstasy. The whole force of her nature was once more directed into one channel, and she was happy.

One day she told Mother Gertrude, with the complete luxury of unreserve always characteristic of her reckless attachments, the story of her brief engagement to Noel Cardew.

The nun looked strangely at her. 'So you had the courage to go against the wishes of your family and break it all off, little Alex?'

It seemed wonderful to Alex that the action which had been so condemned, and which she had long ceased to regard as anything but folly, should be praised as courageous.

'I wasn't happy,' she faltered. 'I used always to think that love, which one read about, made everything perfect when it came – but from the first moment of our engagement I knew it was all wrong somehow.'

'So you knew that?' the Superior said, smilingly. 'You have been given very great gifts.'

'Me – how?' faltered Alex.

'It is not everyone who would have had the courage to withdraw before it was too late.'

'You mean, it would have been much worse if I'd actually married him?'

'Much, much worse. A finite human love will never satisfy that restless heart of yours, Alex. Tell me, have you ever found full satisfaction in the love of any creature yet? Hasn't there always been something lacking – something to grieve and disappoint you?'

Alex looked back. She thought of the stormy loves of her childhood; of Queenie, on whom she had lavished such a passion of devotion; of her vain, thwarted longing to bestow all where the merest modicum would have sufficed; lastly, she thought of Noel Cardew.

'Noel did not want all that I could have given him,' she faltered. 'He never knew the reallest part of me at all.'

'And yet he loved you, Alex – he wanted you for his wife. But the closest of human intercourse, the warmest and dearest of human sympathy, will never be enough for a temperament like yours.' She spoke with such authority in her voice that Alex was almost frightened.

'Shall I always be lonely, then?' she asked, feeling that whatever the answer she must accept it unquestioningly for truth.

'Until you have learnt the lesson which I think is before you,' said the nun slowly.

'I am not lonely now that I have you,' Alex asserted, clinging passionately to her hand.

Mother Gertrude did not answer – she never contradicted such assertions – but her steady, light eyes gazed outward with a strange pale flame, as though at some unseen bourne destined both to be her goal and that of Alex.

'No one has ever understood me like you do.'

'Poor little child, I think I understand you. You have told me a great deal, and your confidence has meant very much to me. Besides – ' The Superior paused. 'A nun does not often tell her own story, but I am going to tell you a little of mine. It is not so very unlike your own.

'When I was seventeen I wanted to be a nun. I told my parents so, and they refused their permission. They loved me very, very dearly, and I was the only child. My father told me that it would break his heart if I left them, and my mother was delicate – almost an invalid. I held out for a little time, but their grief nearly broke my heart, and I persuaded myself that it was my duty to listen to them, and to stay at home. So I stifled the voice of God in my heart, and when I was two-and-twenty, a man much older than I was, whom I had known all my life, asked me to marry him.' The nun spoke with difficulty. 'I have not spoken of this to any human being for over twenty years, but I believe that I am right in telling you a little of what I went through. I will gladly bring myself to speak of it, if it is going to be of any help to you. I hesitated for a long while. He told me that he loved me dearly, and I knew it was true. I knew that his wife would have the happiest of homes and the most faithful and devoted of husbands. A hundred times, Alex, I was on the verge of telling him that I would marry him. It would have been the greatest happiness to my father and mother, and it would have done away, once and for all, with that lurking dread of a convent which I knew was always at the back of their minds. They were growing old, too – they had neither of them been young people when I was born – and I knew that a time would come when I should find myself all alone. I had no very great friends, and very few relations – none with whom I could have found a home; and in those days a woman left by herself had very little freedom, very few outlets indeed. I had given up the thought of being a nun altogether. I thought that God had taken away the gift of my vocation because I had wilfully neglected it. Even at my blindest I could never persuade myself that it had never existed – that vocation which I had tried so long to ignore. And then, Alex, God in His great love again took pity on me, and showed me where my treasure really was. I had tried hard to cling to human love and happiness, to find my comfort there, but – just think of it, Alex – a Divine Love was waiting for me . . . It was a very hard struggle, Alex. I knew that he wanted *all* of me, unworthy as I was. And I was so weak and so cowardly and so selfish – that I shrank from giving all. I knew that no half measures would be possible. Like you, I knew that it would have to be, with me, all or none – to whom much is given, from him will much be asked, Alex – and one night I could hold out no longer. I resolved that it should be all. After that, there was no drawing back. I wrote and said that I should never marry – that my mind was made up. Less than a year afterwards I was in the convent. But it was a terrible year. It was not for a long, long while that God let me feel any consolation. Time after time, I felt that He had forsaken me, and I could only cling to the remembrance of the certainty that I had felt at the time, of following His will for me. But He spared me the greatest sacrifice of all, knowing, perhaps, that I should have failed again in courage. My father and mother died within three months of one another that same year, and when my father lay dying, he gave me his blessing and consent, and after he died I went straight to the Mother-house in Paris, where it was then, and a few months after I became an orphan they received me into the novitiate there.'

The Superior had flushed very deeply, and her voice was shaken, but there were no tears in her steady eyes. Alex, trembling with passionate sympathy, and with a gratitude so intense as to be almost painful, for the confidence bestowed upon her, asked the inevitable question of youth:

'Have you been happy? – haven't you ever regretted it? Oh, tell me if you are really and truly *happy*.'

'Absolutely,' said Mother Gertrude unhesitatingly. 'But not with happiness such as the world knows. The word has acquired a different meaning. I hardly know how to convey what I mean. 'Grief' and 'Joy' mean something so utterly different to the soul in religious life, and to the soul still in the world. But this much I can say – that I have never known one instant of regret – never anything but the deepest, most intense gratitude that I was given strength to follow my vocation.'

There was a long, silence, Alex watching the nun's fervent, flame-like gaze, in which her young idolatry detected none of the resolute fanaticism built up in instinctive self-protection from a temperament no less ardent than her own.

'So you have the story of God's great mercy to one poor soul,' said the nun at last. 'And the story of every vocation is equally wonderful. The more I see of souls, Alex – and a Superior hears many things – the more I marvel at the ways of God's love. As for the paths by which He led me to the shelter of His own house, I shall only know the full wonder of it all when I see Him face to face. I have only given you the barest outlines, but you understand a little?'

'Yes,' breathed Alex, her whole being shaken by an emotion to the real danger of which she was entirely blind.

She went home that day in a state of exaltation, and could not have told, had she been obliged to analyze it, how far her uplifted condition was due to the awakening of religious perceptions hitherto undreamed of, to her increasing worship of the woman who had roused those perceptions, or to her exultant sense of having been made the repository of a confidence shared with no other human being. It was small wonder that Lady Isabel traced the rapt look on Alex' face to its source.

'But most girls go through this sort of thing at school,' she said hopelessly. 'Of course, I know it is only a phase, Alex, whatever you may think now. But *why* can't you be more like other people? Why insist all of a sudden on makin' poor Holland get up early and go out to church with you on Sunday, when I always like the maids to have a rest?'

'Holland doesn't mind,' said Alex sulkily. She could not explain to her mother that the Superior had asked a promise of her that she would not again willingly miss going to Mass on Sundays.

'If it was a reasonable hour I shouldn't object so much – I know heaps of very devout Catholics who always do go to Farm Street or somewhere every Sunday, and I wouldn't forbid that, Alex – though *why* you should suddenly get frantic about religion I can t imagine. I suppose it is the influence of that woman you have been seein' at the convent.'

Alex grew scarlet, to her own dismay.

'I thought so,' said Lady Isabel, looking annoyed. 'I don't want to prevent your doing anything that *does* give you pleasure – Heaven knows it's difficult enough to find anything you seem to care about in the very least – but I am not goin' to let you infect Barbara.'

'Oh no!' said Alex, with sincere horror in her voice. The last thing she wanted was to take Barbara to the convent. She instinctively dreaded both her sister's shrewd, cynical judgment, and the misrepresentations that she always somehow contrived to make of all Alex' motives and actions. Alex clung to the thought of her exclusive, claim on Mother Gertrude's interest and sympathy as she had never yet clung to any other possession.

'Well, we shall be leavin' town next week, and there'll be an end of it. When I said you might go to the convent, Alex, I never meant you to rush off there three or four times a week, as you know. But if you have taken a fancy to this nun, I suppose nothing will stop you.'

Lady Isabel sighed, and Alex, from the glow of contentment that possessed her, felt able to speak more warmly and naturally than usual.

'I don't want to do anything to vex you, mother, truly, I

don't, but the Superior is very kind to me, and I do like going to see her. You know you always say you want me to do whatever makes me happiest. She spoke urgently and coaxingly, like the impulsive, impetuous child Alex, who had been used to beg for favours and privileges with all the confidence of a favourite.

Lady Isabel sighed again, but her face wore a touched, softened look, and she said resignedly, 'So long as you cheer up, and don't vex your father by seemin' doleful and uninterested in things . . . Of course, girls nowadays do take up good works and slummin' and all that sort of thing – but not till they are older than you are, darling, and then it's generally because they haven't married – at least,' added Lady Isabel hurriedly, 'people are sure to say it is that.'

'I don't mind if they do,' said Alex proudly, her mind full of Mother Gertrude's story.

'Well, I suppose you must do as you like – girls do, nowadays.'

Alex almost instinctively uttered the cry that, with successive generations, has passed from appeal to rebellion, then to assertion, and from the defiance of that assertion to a calm statement of facts. '*It is my life*. Can't I live my own life?'

'A woman who doesn't marry and who has eccentric tastes doesn't have much of a life. I could never bear to think of it for any of you.'

Alex was rather startled at the sadness in her mother's voice.

'But, mother, why? Lots of girls don't marry, and just live at home.'

'As long as there is a home. But things alter, Alex. Your father and I, in the nature of things, can't go on livin' for ever, and then this house goes to Cedric. There is no country place, as you know – your great-grandfather sold everything he could lay his hands on, and we none of us have ever had enough ready money to think of buyin' even a small place in the country.'

'But I thought we were quite rich.'

Lady Isabel flushed delicately.

'We are not exactly poor, but such money as there is mostly came from my father, and there will not be much after my death,' she confessed. 'Most of it will be money tied up for Archie, poor little boy, because he is the younger son, and your grandfather thought that was the proper way to arrange it. It was all settled when you were quite little children – in fact, before Pamela was born or thought of – and your father naturally wanted all he could hope to leave to go to Cedric, so that he might be able to live on here, whatever happened.'

'But what about Barbara and me? Wasn't it rather unfair to want the boys to have everything?'

'Your father said, "The girls will marry, of course." There will be a certain sum for each of you on your wedding-day, but there's no question of either of you bein' able to afford to remain unmarried, and live decently. You won't have enough to make it possible,' said Lady Isabel very simply.

'But one of us might want to marry a very poor man.'

'A man in your own rank of life, my dear child, could hardly propose to you unless he had enough to support you. Of course, we don't wish either of you to feel that you must marry for money, ever, but at the same time I think you ought to be warned. Girls very often go gaily on, thinkin' it will be time enough to settle later, and then something happens, and they find they have no money of their own, and perhaps no home left. For a few years, perhaps, it's possible to go on paying visits, and staying with other people, but it's never very pleasant to feel one has no alternative, and the sort of environment where a man looks for his wife is in her own sheltered home,' said Lady Isabel with emphasis.

Alex felt rather dismayed, though less so than she would have done before her intimacy at the convent had given her glimpses of another possible standard.

She paid one more visit to Mother Gertrude before leaving London.

This time she was kept waiting for a while in the parlour, so that she began to wish that she had not told Holland to call for her in an hour's time. She never dared stay any longer, partly from a vague impression that Mother Gertrude had a good deal to do, and partly from a very distinct certainty that Lady Isabel always noted the length of her visits to the convent, no less than their frequency.

She looked round the ugly room rather disconsolately and fingered the books on the table. They seemed very uninteresting, and were mostly in French. One slim volume, more attractively bound than the others, drew her attention for a moment, and she turned idly to the title-page.

'Notre Mère Fondatrice, Esquisse de piété filiale.'

Alex smiled at the wording, which she read in the imperfect, literal translation of an indifferent French scholar, and turned to the next leaf.

Two photographs facing one another were reproduced, one on either page.

The first portrait was of a young woman standing by a table in a stiffly artificial attitude, with enormously wide skirts billowing round her, decked with elaborate, and, to Alex' eyes meaningless, trimmings of some dark, narrow ribbon that might have been velvet. She wore long, dangling ear-rings, and her abundant plaits of dark hair were gathered into the nape of her neck, confined by a coarse-fibred net. The face, turned over one shoulder, was heavy rather than handsome, with strongly marked features and big, sombre, dark eyes.

It was with a little thrill approaching to awe that Alex recognized her again on the next page in the veil and habit of the Order.

The girth of the figure had increased, and the face showed traces of having being heavily scored by the passing of some twenty or thirty years, but this time the strong mouth was smiling frankly, and the eyes had lost their brooding look and were directed upwards with an ardent and animated expression. The hands, so plump as to show mere indents in place of knuckles across their remarkable breadth, grasped a small crucifix.

Under the first portrait Alex read the inscription: 'Angèle Prédoux a dixhuit ans.'

Beneath the picture of the nun, Angèle's not very distinguished patronymic had been replaced by the title of 'Mère Candide du Sacré Cœur,' and still further supplemented by the announcement:

'Fondatrice et Supérieure de son Ordre.'

Old-fashioned though the dress in the photograph looked

to Alex' eyes, she was yet astonished that any woman so nearly of her own time should have founded a religious Order. She had always supposed vaguely that the educational variety of religious Orders which she knew flourished in Europe had taken their existence from the old-established Dominican or Benedictine communities.

But it seemed now that a new foundation might come into being under the auspice of so youthful and plebeian-seeming a pioneer as Angèle Prédoux.

Alex wondered how she had set about it. A grotesque fancy flitted through her mind as to the fashion in which Sir Francis and Lady Isabel might be expected to receive an announcement that Alex or Barbara felt called upon to found a new religious Order.

Alex could not help dismissing the imaginary situation thus conjured up with a slight shudder, and the conviction that Angèle Prédoux, if her position had been in any degree tenable, must have been an orphan.

Wishing all the time that Mother Gertrude would come to her, she glanced through the first few pages of the book.

It somehow slightly amazed her to read of the Foundress of a religious Order as a little girl, who had, like herself, passed through the successive phases of babyhood, school-days and the society of her compeers in the world.

'And to what end,' inquired the author of the *esquisse*, when Angèle Prédoux had celebrated her twenty-first birthday at a ball given on her behalf by an adoring grandfather – 'to what end?'

Alex repeated the question to herself, and marvelled rather vaguely as various replies floated through her mind.

Life all led to something, she supposed, and for the first time it occurred to her that she herself had never aimed at anything save the possession of that which she called happiness. What had been Angèle Prédoux's aim? – what was that of Mother Gertrude? Certainly not human happiness.

Life was disappointing enough, Alex reflected drearily. One was always waiting, always looking forward to the next stage, as though it must reveal the secret solution to the great question of *why*. Alex' thoughts turned to Noel Cardew and the sick misery and disappointment engendered by her engagement.

The door opened and she sprang up.

'Oh, I am so glad you have come at last.'

'Were you getting impatient? I'm sorry, but you know our time is not our own.'

The nun sat down, and Alex flung, rather than sat herself in her favourite position on the floor, her arms resting on the Superior's knee.

'What is the matter?' asked Mother Gertrude. 'What was troubling you just before I came in, Alex?'

'You always know,' said Alex, in quick, passionate recognition of an intuition that it had hitherto been her share to exercise on behalf of another, never to receive.

'Your face is not so very difficult to read, and I think I know you pretty well by this time.'

'Better than anyone,' said Alex, in all good faith, and unaware that certain aspects of herself, such as she showed to Barbara, or to her father and mother when they angered or frightened her, had never yet been called forth in the Superior's presence, and probably never would be.

'Well, what was it? Was it our Mother Foundress?'

'How did you know?' gasped Alex, unseeing of the still open book lying on the table.

Mother Gertrude did not refer to it. She passed her hand slowly over the upturned head. Alex had thrown off her hat.

'I was looking at the picture of her. It seemed so difficult to realize that anyone who actually formed a new religious Order could live almost nowadays and be a girl just like myself.'

'God bestows His gifts where He pleases! Sometimes the call sounds where one might least expect to hear it – in the midst of the world, and worldly pleasure, sometimes in the midst of the disappointment and grief of the world.'

Alex did not speak, but continued to gaze up at the nun. Mother Gertrude went on speaking slowly:

'You see, Alex, sometimes it is necessary for a soul, a loving and undisciplined one especially, to learn the utter worthlessness of human love, in order that it may turn and see the Divine Love waiting for it.'

'But all human love isn't worthless,' said Alex almost pleadingly, her eyes dilating.

'Surely a finite love is worthless compared to an Infinite,' said the nun gently. 'We can hardly imagine it, Alex, with our little, limited understanding, but there is a love that satisfies the most exacting of us – asking, indeed, *all*, and yet willing to accept so little, and, above all, giving with a completeness to which no human sympathy, however deep and tender, can ever attain.'

Alex heard only the ring of utter conviction permeating every word uttered in that deep, ardent voice, and listening to the mystic, heard nothing of the fanatic.

'But not everyone,' she stammered.

The nun did not pretend to misunderstand her.

'Many are called,' she said, 'but few are chosen. Do you want me to tell you a little of all that is promised to those who leave all things for His sake?'

'Yes,' said Alex, her heart throbbing strangely.

CHAPTER SEVENTEEN

LAWN-TENNIS

Looking back long afterwards, to that last week of the brilliant Jubilee season in London and to the two months that followed, spent in a house near Windsor, taken principally to gratify Cedric's passion for tennis, Alex could never remember whether the first definite suggestion of her entering the religious life had come from herself or from Mother Gertrude.

Neither she nor Barbara had been taken to Cowes that year, and the first fortnight spent at the Windsor house, which stood in a large, rambling garden, full of roses, close to the river, reminded her strangely of the summer holidays they had spent together as children.

Cedric, very sunburnt and sturdy, played tennis with a sort of concentrated, cumulative enthusiasm, took part in innumerable cricket matches – possessing already a very real reputation in Eton circles as a promising slow bowler and a very reliable bat – and occasionally took his sisters on the river. Barbara, on whom late nights in London had told, slept half the morning, and then practised 'serves' at tennis assiduously under her brother's coaching, while Pamela, already a hoyden, romped screaming over the lawn, in a fashion that in Alex' and Barbara's nursery days would have met with instant and drastic punishment. But old Nurse was lenient with the last and youngest of her charges, and nowadays her guardianship was almost a nominal one only.

Alex was preoccupied, aimlessly brooding over one absorbing interest, as in the summer holidays that the Clare children had spent at Fiveapples Farm.

Just as then she had waited and looked and longed for Queenie's letters, so now she waited for those of Mother Gertrude.

Day after sunlit day, she stood at the bottom of the straggling, over-grown paddock that gave on to the dusty high-road, and waited for the afternoon post to be delivered.

She was often disappointed, but never with the sick intensity of dismay that had marked every fresh stage in her realization of Queenie Torrance's indifference to friendship.

Mother Gertrude only wrote when she could find a little spare time, and left by far the greater number of Alex' daily outpourings to her unanswered, but she read them all – she understood, Alex told herself in a passion of pure gratitude – and she thought of her child and prayed daily for her.

Her letters began, 'My dearest child,' and Alex treasured the words, and the few earnest counsels and exhortations that the letters contained.

It was much easier to carry out those exhortations at Windsor than it had been in London. Alex went almost every day to a small Catholic church, of which Holland had discovered the vicinity, and sometimes spent the whole afternoon in the drowsy heat of the little building, that was almost always empty.

Her thoughts dwelt vaguely on her own future, and on the craving necessity for self-expression, of which Mother Gertrude had made her more intensely aware than she knew. Could it be that her many failures were to prove only the preliminary to an immense success, predestined for her out of Eternity? The allurement of the thought soothed Alex with an infinite sweetness.

When Sir Francis and his wife joined the Windsor party, Lady Isabel exclaimed with satisfaction at her daughters' looks. 'Only a fortnight, and it's done such wonders for you both! Barbara was like a little, washed-out rag, and now she's quite blooming. You've got more colour too, Alex, darling, and I'm so thankful to see that you're holdin' yourself rather better. Evidently country air and quiet was what you both needed.'

Nevertheless, Lady Isabel lost no time in issuing and accepting various invitations that led to luncheons, tennis-parties and occasional dinners with the innumerable acquaintances whom she immediately discovered to be within walking or driving distance.

It annoyed Alex unreasonably that her liberty should be interfered with thus by entertainments which afforded her no pleasure. She ungraciously conceded her place to Barbara as often as possible, and went off to seek the solitude of the chapel with an inward conviction of her own great unworldliness and spirituality.

Barbara showed plenty of eagerness to avail herself of the opportunities thus passed on to her. She had sedulously cultivated a great enthusiasm for tennis, and by dint of sheer hard practice had actually acquired a certain forceful skill, making up for a natural lack of suppleness that deprived her play of any grace.

Her rather manufactured displays of enjoyment, which had none of the spontaneous vitality of little Pamela's noisy, bounding high spirits, were always in sufficient contrast to Alex' supine self-absorption to render them doubly agreeable to Sir Francis and Lady Isabel.

'I like to take my little daughter about and see her enjoying herself,' Sir Francis would say, with more wistfulness than pleasure in his voice sometimes, as though wishing that Barbara's gaiety could have been allied to Alex' prettier face and position as his eldest daughter.

It was only in his two sons – Cedric, with his sort of steady brilliance, and idle, happy-go-lucky Archie, by far the best-looking of the Clare children – that Sir Francis found unalloyed satisfaction.

Pamela was the modern child in embryo, and disconcerted more than she pleased him.

It was principally to gratify Cedric that Lady Isabel arranged a tennis tournament for the end of the summer, on a hot day of late September that was to remain in Alex' memory as a milestone, unrecognized at the time, marking the end of an era.

'Thank Heaven it's fine,' piously breathed Barbara at the window in the morning. 'I shall wear my white piqué.'

Alex shrugged her shoulders.

Neither she nor Barbara would have dreamed of inaugurating a new form of toilette without previous reference to Lady Isabel, and Barbara's small piece of self-assertion was merely designed to emphasize the butterfly rôle which she was embracing with so much determination.

'Of course, you'll wear your piqué. Mother said so,' Alex retorted, conscious of childishness. 'You've worn a piqué at every tennis party you've been to.'

'Well, this is a new piqué,' said Barbara, who invariably found a last word for any discussion, and she went downstairs singing in a small, tuneful chirp made carefully careless.

'Who is coming?' Alex inquired, having taken no part whatever in the lengthy discussions as to partners and handicaps which had engrossed Cedric and Barbara for the past ten days.

Cedric looked up, frowning, from the list on which he was still engaged. He did not speak, however; but Barbara said very sweetly, and with an emphasis so nearly imperceptible that only her sister could appreciate it:

'Oh, nobody in whom you're at all specially interested, I'm afraid.'

Alex did not miss the implication, and coloured angrily.

'I'm going to play with that artist, the one staying with the Russells. He isn't at all a good player,' said Barbara smoothly.

'Then why are you playing with him?'

Barbara smiled rather self-consciously. 'It would hardly do to annex the best partners for ourselves, would it?' she inquired. 'And we're trying to equalize the setts as far as possible. Cedric has to play with the youngest Russell girl, who's too utterly hopeless.'

'I shall take all her balls,' said Cedric calmly, 'so it'll be all right. She doesn't mind any amount of poaching. We shall lose on her serves, of course, but that may be just as well.'

'Why, dear?' innocently inquired Lady Isabel.

'I don't think it looks well to carry off a prize at one's own show,' Cedric said candidly.

'I should rather love the Indian bangles,' owned Barbara, glancing enviously at the array of silver trifles that constituted the prizes.

'You won't get them, my child – not with McAllister as your partner. You'll see, Lady Essie Cameron will get them, or one of the Nottinghams, if they're in good form.'

'Peter Nottingham is playing with you, Alex,' Barbara informed her.

'That boy!'

'Nottingham is nearly eighteen, let me tell you,' said Cedric in tones of offence, 'and plays an extraordinarily good game of tennis. In fact, he'll be about the best man there probably, which is why I've had to give him to you for a partner. As you've not taken the trouble to practise a single stroke the whole summer, I should advise you to keep out of his way, and let him stand up to the net and take every blessed thing he can get. It'll be a nice thing for me,' said Cedric bitterly, 'to have to apologize to Nottingham for making him play with the worst girl there, and that my sister.'

'Cedric,' said his mother gently, 'I'm sure I've seen Alex play very nicely.'

Alex was grateful, but she wished that, like Barbara, she had practised her strokes under Cedric's tuition.

It was characteristic of her that when the occasion for excelling had actually come, she should passionately desire to excel, whereas during previous weeks of supine indifference, it had never seemed to her worthwhile to exert herself in the attainment of proficiency.

After breakfast she went out to the tennis-court, freshly marked and rolled, and wondered if it would be worthwhile to make Archie send her over some balls, but Cedric hurried up in a business-like way and ordered everybody off the ground while he instructed the garden boy in the science of putting up a new net.

Alex moved disconsolately away, and tried to tell herself that none of these trivial, useless enthusiasms which they regarded so earnestly were of any real importance.

She wandered down to the chapel and sat there, for the most part pondering over her own infinitesimal chances of success in the coming tournament, and thinking how much she would like to astonish and disconcert Barbara and Cedric by a sudden display of skill.

It was true that she had not practised, and was at no time a strong player, but she had sometimes shown an erratic brilliance in a sudden, back-handed stroke, and, like all weak people, she had an irrational belief in sudden and improbable accessions of luck.

Needless to say, this belief was not justified.

Peter Nottingham, a tall, shy boy with a smashing service and tremendous length of reach, was intent on nothing but victory, and though he muttered politely, 'Not at all, 'm sure,' at Alex' preliminary, faltering announcement of her own bad play, the very sense of his keenness made her nervous.

She missed every stroke, gave an aimless dash that just succeeded in stopping a ball that would obviously have been 'out,' and felt her nerve going.

Just as success always led her on to excel, so failure reduced her capabilities to a minimum. Her heart sank.

They lost the first game.

'Will you serve?' inquired Peter Nottingham politely.

'I'd rather you did.'

Alex was infinitely relieved that responsibility should momentarily be off her own shoulders, but young Nottingham's swift service was as swiftly returned by Lady Essie Cameron, an excellent player, and one who had no hesitation in smashing the ball on to the farthest corner of the court, where Alex stood, obviously nervous and unready.

She failed to reach it, and could have cried with mortification.

Thanks to Nottingham, however, they won the game.

It was their solitary victory.

Alex served one fault after another, and at last ceased even to murmur perfunctory apologies as she and her partner, whose boyish face expressed scarlet vexation, crossed over the court. She was not clear as to the system on which Cedric had arranged the tournament, but presently she saw that the losing couples would drop out one by one until the champions, having won the greatest number of setts, would finally challenge any remaining couples whom they had not yet encountered.

'I say, I'm afraid this is pretty rotten for you, old chap,' she heard Cedric, full of concern, say to her partner.

'Perhaps we may get another look in at the finals,' said Peter Nottingham, with gloomy civility.

He and Alex, with several others, sat and watched the progress of the games. It gave Alex a shock of rather unpleasant surprise to see the improvement in Barbara's play.

Her service, an overhand one in which very few girl players were then proficient, gave rise to several compliments. Her partner was the good-looking artist, Ralph McAllister.

'Well played!' he shouted enthusiastically, again and again.

Once or twice, when Barbara missed a stroke, Alex heard him exclaim softly, 'Oh, hard luck! Well tried, partner.'

Alex, tired and mortified, almost angry, wondered why Fate should have assigned to her as a partner a mannerless young cub like Nottingham, who thought of nothing but the horrid game. It did not occur to her that perhaps McAllister would not have been moved to the same enthusiasm had she, instead of Barbara, been playing with him.

The combination, however, was beaten by Cedric and the youngest of the Russell girls, a pretty, roundabout child, who left all the play to her partner and screamed with excitement and admiration almost every time he hit the ball.

It was quite evident that the final contest lay between them and Lady Essie Cameron, a strapping, muscular Scotch girl, whose partner kept discreetly to the background, and allowed her to stand up to the net and volley every possible ball that came over.

When she and her partner had emerged victorious from every contest, nothing remained but for Cedric and Miss Russell to make good their claim to the second place by conquering the remaining couples.

Alex played worse than ever, and the sett was six games to love. As she left the court, Cedric muttered to her low and viciously:

'Are you doing it *on purpose*?'

She knew that he was angry and mortified at his friend Nottingham's disappointment, but his words struck her like a blow.

She stood with her back to everyone, gulping hard. 'You didn't have a chance, old man,' said a sympathetic youth behind her. 'They might have arranged the setts better.'

Peter Nottingham growled in reply.

'Who was the girl you were playing with?'

Alex realized that her white frock and plain straw hat were indistinguishable from all the other white frocks and straw hats present, seen from the back.

'Hush,' said young Nottingham more cautiously. 'That was one of the girls of the house, a Miss Clare.'

'Can't play a bit, can she? The other one wasn't bad. Didn't one of them give poor Cardew the chuck or something?'

'Oh, shut up,' Nottingham rebuked the indiscreet one. 'Much more likely *he* chucked *her*, if you ask me.'

Alex could bear the risk of their discovering her proximity no longer, and hastened into the house.

It was the first afternoon since her arrival at Windsor that she had not looked eagerly for the afternoon post.

The letter, a square, bluish envelope of cheap glazed paper, caught her eye almost accidentally on the table in the hall.

She recognized it instantly, and snatching it up, opened and read it standing there, with the scent of a huge bowl of late roses pervading the whole hall, and the distant sound of cries and laughter faintly penetrating to her ears from the tennis-court and garden outside.

Mother Gertrude's writing showed all the disciplined regularity characteristic of a convent, with the conventional French slope and long-tailed letters, the careful making of which Alex herself had had instilled into her in Belgium.

The phraseology of the Superior's letter was conventional, too, and even her most earnest exhortations, when delivered in writing, bore the marks of restraint.

But this letter was different.

Alex knew it at once, even before she had read it to the end of the four closely-covered sheets.

'Sept. 30, 1897.

'My Dearest Child,

'There are many letters from you waiting to be answered, and I thank you for them all, and for the confidence you bestow upon me, which touches me very deeply.

'Now at last I am able to sit down and feel that I shall have a quiet half-hour in which to talk to my child, although I dare not hope that it will be an uninterrupted one!

'So the life you are leading does not satisfy you, Alex? You tell me that you come in from the gaieties and amusements and little parties, which, after all, are natural to your age and to the position in which God has placed you, full of dissatisfaction and restlessness of mind.

'Alex, my dear child, I am not surprised. You will never find that what the world can offer will satisfy you. Most of us may have known similar moments of fatigue, of disillusionment, but to a heart and mind like yours, above all, it is inconceivable that anything less than Infinity itself should bring any lasting joy. Let me say what I have so often thought, after our conversations together in my little room – there is only one way of peace for such a nature as yours. *Give up all, and you shall find all.*

'I have thought and prayed over this letter, my little Alex, and am not writing lightly. You will forgive me if I am going too far, but I long to see my child at rest, and for such as you there is only one true rest here.

'Human love has failed you, and you are left alone, with all your impulses of sacrifice and devotion to another thrown back upon yourself. But, Alex, there is One to whom all the love and tenderness of which you know yourself capable can be offered – and He *wants* it. Weak though you are, and all-perfect though He is, He wants you.

'I don't think there has been a day since I first heard His call, when I have not marvelled at the wonder of it – at the infinite honour done to me.

'If I have told you more of the secret story of my vocation than to anyone else, it has been for a reason

245

which I think you have guessed. I have seen for a long while what it was that God asked of you, Alex, and I believe the time has come when you will see it too. Your last letter, with its cry of loneliness, and the bitter sense of being unwanted, has made me almost sure of it.

'You are not unwanted – you need never be lonely again. "*Leave all things and follow Me!*" If you hear that call, which I believe with all my heart to have sounded for you, can you disobey it? Will you not rather, forsaking all things, follow Him, and in so doing, find all things?

'I have written a long while, and cannot go on now. God bless you again and again, and help you to be truly generous with Him.

'Write to me as fully as you will, and count upon my poor prayers and my most earnest religious affection. I need not add, come and see me again on your return to London. My child will always find the warmest of welcomes! It was not for nothing that you came into the convent chapel to find rest and quiet, that summer day, my Alex!

'Your devoted Mother in Christ,
'Gertrude of the Holy Cross.'

Alex stood almost as though transfixed. The letter hardly came as a surprise. She had long since known subconsciously what was in the Superior's mind, and yet the expression of it produced in her a sort of stupefaction.

Could it be true?

Was there really such a refuge for her, somewhere a need

of her, and of that passionate desire for self-devotion that was so essential a part of her?

The thought brought with it a tingling admixture of bitter disappointment and of poignant rapture.

She realized almost despairingly that she could no longer stand in the hall clasping Mother Gertrude's letter unconsciously to her.

Already light, flying feet were approaching from the garden.

'I came to look for you, Alex,' said Barbara breathlessly in the doorway. 'They're going to give the prizes. What are you doing?'

'I'm coming,' said Alex mechanically. She was rather surprised that Barbara should have taken the trouble to come for her. 'Did mother send you?'

'No,' said Barbara simply; 'but I thought it would look very bad if you kept out of the way of it because you happened to play badly and not win a prize.'

So Alex assisted at the prize-giving, and saw Lady Essie accept the jingling, Indian silver bangles that were so much in fashion, with frank pleasure and gratitude, and saw consolation prizes awarded to Cedric and to his partner, who appeared entirely delighted, although she had done nothing at all to deserve distinction.

'You ought to have a prize, you know,' she heard Ralph McAllister tell Barbara. 'If you'd had a better partner you'd have won easily. You play much better than Lady Essie, really!'

It was not in the least true that Barbara played better than Lady Essie, or nearly so well, but she put on a little, gratified, complacent smile, that apparently satisfied Ralph McAllister quite as well as modest disclaimers.

Alex kept out of her partner's way, and avoided his eye. Not much probability that *he* would address flattering speeches to her!

All the time a subconscious emotion was surging through her at the thought of Mother Gertrude's letter and what it contained.

'The life you are leading does not satisfy you. You will never find that what the world can offer will satisfy you.'

It was true enough, Heaven knew, Alex thought drearily, as she addressed perfunctory and obviously absent-minded civilities to her mother's guests.

In the sense of depression engendered by the afternoon's failure, no less than by the sight of McAllister's evident delight in Barbara's demure, patently-artificial, alternate coyness and gaiety, Alex realized both her own eternal dissatisfaction with her surroundings and the subtle allurement of a renunciation that should yet promise her all that she most longed for.

CHAPTER EIGHTEEN

※※※※※※※※※※※

CRISIS

When Alex went back to London in the beginning of October, it was with a sensation as though an enormous gulf of time had been traversed between her visits to the convent in the hot, arid summer days and her return there. For one thing the cold weather had set in early and with unusual severity, and the sight of fires and winter furs seemed to succeed with startling rapidity to the roses and lawn-tennis at Windsor.

In her first greeting with Mother Gertrude, too, Alex was strongly conscious of that indefinable sensation of having made some strange, almost unguessed-at progress in a direction of which she was only now becoming aware. It frightened her when the Superior, gazing at her with those light, steady eyes that now held a depth of undisguised tenderness, spoke firmly, with an implication that could no longer be denied or ignored.

'So the great decision is taken, little Alex. And if peace has not yet come to you, do not feel dismayed. It will come, as surely as I stand here and tell you of it. But there may be – there must be – conflict first.'

Whether she spoke of the conflict which Alex foresaw, half with dread and half with exultation, as inevitable between herself and her surroundings, or of some deeper, inward dissension in Alex' own soul, she could not tell.

But there was both joy and a certain excitement in having her destiny so much taken for granted, and the mystical and devotional works to which the Superior gave her free access worked upon her imagination, and dispelled many of her lingering doubts. Those which lay deepest in her soul, she never examined. She was almost, though not quite, unaware of their existence, and to probe deeper into that faint, under-lying questioning would have seemed a disloyalty equally to that intangible possession which she had begun to think of as her vocation, and to Mother Gertrude. The sense of closer companionship – of a more intimate spiritual union expressed, though never explicitly so in words, in her relation with the Superior, was unutterably precious to Alex. In the joy that it brought her she read merely another manifestation of the consolation to be found in the way of the Spirit.

A feeling of impending crisis, however, hung over the hurrying days of that brief November, when the convent parlour in the afternoons was illuminated by a single gas-jet that cast strange, clean-cut shadows on the white-washed walls.

Just before Christmas Sir Francis spoke:

'What is this violent attraction that takes you out with your maid in the opposite direction to your mother's expeditions with Barbara?' he suddenly inquired of Alex one evening, very stiffly.

She started and coloured, having retained all the childish, uneasy belief that her father lived in an atmosphere far above that into which the sound and sight of his children's daily doings could penetrate to his knowledge without the special intervention of some accredited emissary such as their mother.

As he spoke Lady Isabel looked up, and Barbara left the piano and came slowly down the room.

'*It has come*,' flashed through Alex' mind. She only said very lamely:

'I – I don't know what you mean, father.' There was all the shifting uneasiness in her manner that Sir Francis most disliked.

'Oh, darling, don't prevaricate,' hastily broke in Lady Isabel, with an obvious uneasiness that gave the impression of being rooted in something deeper and of longer standing than the atmosphere of disturbance momentarily created.

'But you did not want me to come with you and Barbara to the Stores this afternoon,' said Alex cravenly. The instinct of evading the direct issue was so strongly implanted in her, that she was prepared to have recourse to the feeblest and least convincing of subterfuges in order to gain time.

'Of course, I don't want you to come *anywhere* when it all so obviously bores you,' plaintively said Lady Isabel. 'I have almost given up tryin' to take you anywhere, Alex, as you very well know. You evidently prefer to go and sit in a little stuffy back-room somewhere with Heaven knows whom, sooner than remain in the company of your mother and sister.'

Alex felt too much dismayed and unwillingly convicted to make any reply, but after a momentary silence Sir Francis spoke ominously.

'Indeed! is that so?'

The suspicion that had laid dormant in Alex for a long time woke to life. Her father's disappointment in her, none the less keenly felt because inarticulate, had become merged into a far greater bitterness: that of his resentment on behalf of his wife. A personal grievance he might overlook, though once perceived he would never forget it, but where Lady Isabel's due was concerned, her husband was capable of implacability.

'And may one inquire whose is the society which you find so preferable to that of your family?' he asked her, with the manifest sarcasm that in him denoted the extreme of anger.

Alex was constitutionally so much terrified of disapproval that it produced in her a veritable physical inability to explain herself. She cast an agonized look around her. Her mother was leaning back, her face strained and tired, and would not meet her eye. Sir Francis, she knew without daring to look at him, was swinging his eye-glasses to and fro, with a measured regularity that indicated his determination to wait inexorably and for any length of time for a reply to his inquiry. Barbara's big, alert eyes moved from one member of the group to another, acute and full of appraisement of them all.

Alex flung a wordless appeal to her sister. Barbara did not fail to receive and understand it, and after a moment she spoke:

'Alex goes to see the Superior of that convent near Bryanston Square. She made friends with her in the summer, didn't you, Alex?'

'Yes,' faltered Alex. Some instinct of trying to palliate what she felt would be looked upon as undesirable made her add in feeble extenuation, 'It is a house of the same Order as the Liège one where I was at school, you know.'

'Your devotion to it was not so marked in those days, if I remember right,' said her father in the same rather elaborately sarcastic strain.

Lady Isabel, no less uneasy under it than was Alex herself, broke in with nervous exasperation in her every intonation:

'Oh, Francis, it is the same old story – one of those foolish infatuations. You know what she has always been like, and how worried I was about that dreadful Torrance girl. It's this nun now, I suppose.'

'Who is this woman?'

'How should I know?' helplessly said Lady Isabel. 'Alex?'

'The Superior – the Head of the house.' Alex stopped. How could one say, 'Mother Gertrude of the Holy Cross?' She did not even know what the Superior's name in the world had been, or where she came from.

'Go on,' said Sir Francis inexorably.

They were all looking at her, and sheer desperation came to her help.

'Why shouldn't I have friends? . . . What is all this about?' Alex asked wildly. 'It's my own life. I don't want to be undutiful, but why can't I live my own life? Everything I ever do is wrong, and I know you and father are disappointed in me, but I don't know how to be different – I wish I did.' She was crying bitterly now. 'You wanted me to marry Noel, and I would have if I could, but I knew that it would all have been wrong, and we should have made each other miserable. Only when I did break it off, it all seemed wrong and heartless, and I don't know *what* to do – ' She felt herself becoming incoherent, and the tension of the atmosphere grew almost unbearable.

Sir Francis Clare spoke, true to the traditions of his day, viewing with something very much like horror the breaking down of those defences of a conventional reserve that should lay bare the undisciplined emotions of the soul.

'You have said enough, Alex. There are certain things that we do not put into words . . . You are unhappy, my child, you have said so yourself, and it has been sufficiently obvious for some time.'

'But what is it that you want, Alex? What would make you happy?' her mother broke in, piteously enough.

In the face of their perplexity, Alex lost the last feeble clue to her own complexity. She did not know what she wanted – to make them happy, to be happy herself, to be adored and admired and radiantly successful, never to know loneliness or misunderstanding again – such thoughts surged chaotically through her mind as she stood there sobbing, and could find no words except the childish, foolish formula, 'I don't know.'

She saw Barbara's eager, protesting gaze flash upon her, and heard her half-stifled exclamation of wondering contempt. Sir Francis turned to his younger daughter, almost as though seeking elucidation from her obvious certainties – her crude assurance with life.

'Oh!' said little Barbara, her hands clenched, 'they ask you what you want, what would make you happy – they are practically offering you anything you want in the world – you could choose anything, and you stand there and cry and say you don't know! Oh, Alex – you – *you idiot!*'

'Hush!' said Sir Francis, shocked, and Lady Isabel put out her white hand with its glittering weight of rings and laid it gently on Barbara's shoulder, and she too said, 'Hush, darling! why are you so vehement? You're happy, aren't you, Barbara?'

'Of course,' said Barbara, wriggling. 'Only if you and father asked me what *I* would like, and I had only to say what I wanted, I could think of such millions of things – for us to have a house in the country, and to give a real, proper big ball next year, and for you to let me go to restaurant dinners sometimes, and not only those dull parties and – heaps of things like that. It's such an *opportunity*, and Alex is wasting it all! The only thing she wants is to sit and talk and talk and talk with some dull old nun at that convent!'

Long afterwards Alex was to remember and ponder over again and again that denunciation of Barbara's. It was all fact – was it all true? Was that what she was fighting for – that the goal of her vehement, inchoate rebellion? Had she sought in Mother Gertrude's society the relief of self-expression only, or was her infatuation for the nun the channel through which she hoped to find those abstract possessions of the spirit which might constitute the happiness she craved?

Nothing of all the questionings that were to come later invaded her mind, as she stood sobbing and self-convicted at the crisis of her relations with her childhood's home.

'Don't cry so, Alex, darlin'.' Lady Isabel sank back into her armchair. 'Don't cry like that – it's so bad for you and I can't bear it. We only want to know how we can make you happier than you are. It's so dreadful, Alex – you've got everything, I should have thought – a home, and parents who love you – it isn't every girl that has a father like yours, some of them care nothing for their daughters – and you're young and pretty and with good health – you might have such a perfect time, even if you *have* made a mistake, poor little thing, there'll be other people, Alex – you'll know better another time . . . only I can't bear it if you lose all your looks by frettin' and refusin' to go anywhere, and everyone asks me where my eldest daughter is and why she doesn't make more friends, and enjoy things – ' Lady Isabel's voice trailed away. She looked unutterably tired. They had none of them heard so emotional a ring in her voice ever before.

Sir Francis looked down at his wife in silence, and his gaze was as tender as his voice was stern when he finally spoke.

'This cannot go on. You have done everything to please Alex – to try and make her happy, and it has all been of no use. Let her take her own way! We have failed.'

'No!' almost shrieked Alex.

'What do you mean? We have your own word for it and your sister's that you are not happy at home, and infinitely prefer the society of some woman of whom we know nothing, in surroundings which I should have thought would have proved highly uncongenial to one of my daughters, brought up among well-bred people. But apparently I am mistaken.

'It is the modern way, I am told. A young girl uses her father's house to shelter and feed her, and seeks her own friends and her own interests the while, with no reference to her parents' wishes.

'But not in this case, Alex. I have your mother and your sisters to consider. Your folly is embittering the home life that might be so happy and pleasant for all of us. Look at your mother!'

Lady Isabel was in tears.

'What shall I do?' said Alex wildly. 'Let me go right away and not spoil things any more.'

'You have said it,' replied Sir Francis gravely, and inclined his head.

'Francis, what are you tellin' her? How can she go away from us? It's her home, until she marries.'

Lady Isabel's voice was full of distressed perplexity.

'My dear love, don't – don't agitate yourself. This is her home, as you say, and is always open to her. But until she has learnt to be happy there, let her seek these new friends, whom she so infinitely prefers. Let her go to this nun.'

Alex, at his words, felt a rush of longing for the tenderness, the grave understanding of Mother Gertrude, the atmosphere of the quiet convent parlour where she had never heard reproach or accusation.

'Oh yes, let me go there,' she sobbed childishly. 'I'll try and be good there. I'll come back good, indeed I will.'

Barbara's little, cool voice cut across her sobs:

'How can you go there? Will they let you stay? What will everyone think?'

'So many girls take up slummin' and good works nowadays,' said Lady Isabel wearily. 'Everyone knows she's been upset and unhappy for a long while. It may be the best plan. My poor darling, when you're tired of it, you can come back, and we'll try again.'

There was no reproach at all in her voice now, only exhaustion, and a sort of relief at having reached a conclusion.

'You hear what your mother says. If her angelic love and patience do not touch you, Alex, you must indeed be heartless. Make your arrangements, and remember, my poor child, that as long as her arms remain open to you, I will receive you home again with love and patience and without one word of reproach.'

He opened the door for Lady Isabel and followed slowly from the room, his iron-grey head shaking a little.

Alex flung herself down, and Barbara laid her hand half timidly on her sister's, in one of her rare caresses.

'Don't cry, Alex. Are you really going? It's much the best idea, of course, and by the time you come back they may have something else to think about.'

She giggled a little, self-consciously, and waited, as though to be questioned.

'I might be engaged to be married or something like that, and then you'd come back to be my bridesmaid, and no one would think of anything unhappy.'

Alex made no answer. Her tears had exhausted her, and she felt weak and tired.

'How are you going to settle it all?' pursued Barbara tirelessly. 'Hadn't you better write to them and see if they'll have you? Supposing Mother Gertrude said you couldn't go there?'

A pang of terror shot through Alex at the thought.

'Oh no, no! She won't say she couldn't have me.'

She went blindly to the carved writing-table with its heavy gilt and cut-glass appointments, and drew a sheet of paper towards her.

Barbara stood watching her curiously. Feeling as though the power of consecutive thought had almost left her, Alex scrawled a few words and addressed them to the Superior.

'We can send it round by hand,' said Barbara coolly. 'Then you'll know tonight.'

Alex looked utterly bewildered.

'It's quite early – Holland can go in a cab.'

Barbara rang the bell importantly and gave her instructions in a small, hard voice.

'It's no use just waiting about for days and days,' she said to Alex. 'It makes the whole house feel horrid, and father is so grave and sarcastic at meals, and it makes mother ill. You'd much rather be there than here, wouldn't you, Alex?'

Alex thought again of the Superior's welcome, which had never failed her – the Superior who knew nothing of her wicked ingratitude and undutifulness at home, and repeated miserably:

'Yes, yes, I'd much rather be there than here.'

The answer to the note came much more quickly than they had expected it. Barbara heard the cab in the square outside, and ran down into the hall. She came back in a moment with a small, twisted note.

'What does it say, Alex?'

Alex read the tiny missive, and a great throb of purest relief and comfort went through her.

'I may go at once. She is waiting for me now, this minute, if I like.'

'What did I tell you?' cried Barbara triumphantly.

She looked sharply at her sister, who was unconsciously clasping the little note as though she derived positive consolation from the contact. She went to the door.

'Holland! is the cab still there?'

'Yes, Miss Barbara.'

'Why don't you go back in it now, Alex?'

'Tonight?'

'Why not? She says she's waiting for you, and it would all be much easier than a lot of good-byes and things, with father and mother.'

'I couldn't go without telling them.'

'I'll tell them.'

Alex felt no strength, only a longing for quiet and for Mother Gertrude.

'Ask if I may,' she said faintly.

Barbara darted out of the room.

When she came back, Alex heard her giving orders to Holland to pack a dressing-bag with things for the night.

Then she hurried into the room again.

'They said yes,' she announced. 'I think they agree with me that it's much the best thing to do it at once. After all, you're only going for a little visit. Mother said I was to give you her love. She's lying down.'

'Shall I go in to her?'

'You'd better not. Father's there too. I've told Holland to pack your bag. We can send the other things tomorrow.'

'But I shan't want much. It's only for a little while.'

'Yes, that's all, isn't it?' said Barbara quickly. 'It's only for a little while. Shall I fetch your things, Alex?'

Alex was relieved to be spared the ascent to the top of the house, for which her limbs felt far too weary. She sat and looked round her at the big, double drawing-room, crowded with heavy Victorian furniture, and upholstered in yellow, brocaded satin. She had always thought it a beautiful room, and the recollection of its splendour and of the big, gilt-framed pictures and mirrors that hung round its wall, was mingled with the earliest memories of her nursery days.

'Here you are,' said Barbara. 'I've brought your fur boa too, because it's sure to be cold. Holland has got your bag.'

Without a word Alex rose, and they went down the broad staircase.

'I hope it'll be nice,' said Barbara cheerfully. 'It's very brave of you to go, I think, Alex, and you'll write and tell me all about it, and how you like poor people, and all that sort of thing.'

Alex realized that her sister was talking for the benefit of the servants.

There was a rush of icy, sleet-laden wind as the front door was opened.

'Gracious, what a night!'

Barbara retreated to the stairs again.

'Good-bye, Alex. Let me know what things you want sent on.'

'Good-bye,' said Alex, apathetic from fatigue.

She turned and waved her hand once to Barbara, a slim, alert little figure clinging to the great, carved foot of the balustrade, the lamp-light casting a radiance over her light, puffed-out hair, and gleaming fitfully over the shining steel buckles on her pointed shoes.

Alex hurried through the cold evening to the shelter of the cab.

It jolted slowly through the lighted streets, and she leant back, her eyes closed.

A wave of sick apprehension surged over her every now and then, and she shivered spasmodically under her fur.

'Here we are, Miss. Shall I get out and ring, so that you won't have to wait in this cold?' said the maid compassionately.

From the dark corner of the cab Alex watched the trim, black-clad figure mount the steps.

There was always a long wait before the convent door was opened.

But tonight it was flung back and warm light streamed out.

Alex, cold and frightened, stumbled up the steps in her turn.

It was not the old portress who had thrown back the open door.

The Superior was waiting, her hands outstretched.

'My child, my child, come in! Welcome home.'

BOOK II

CHAPTER NINETEEN

BELGIUM

'Sister Alexandra, I have put a letter in your cell. And will you go to Mother Gertrude's room after Vespers?'

'Thank you, Sister. I wonder if Mother Gertrude remembers that I have to go down to the children at five o'clock, though?'

'Oh, I dare say not. Perhaps you could get someone to replace you there. Shall I see if Sister Agnes is free?'

'Thank you, I will speak to Mother Gertrude first.'

The nuns separated, the lay-sister returning to her eternal task of polishing up the brasses and gilt candlesticks of the chapel perpetually dimmed by the rain and mists of the Belgian climate, and Alexandra Clare, professed religious, wearily mounting the steep, narrow stairs to the tiny cubicle in the large dormitory, designated a 'cell'. There would just be time to fetch the letter and put it into the deep pocket of her habit before the bell rang for Vespers, otherwise they would have to wait till next morning, for she knew there would be no spare instant for even a momentary return to the cell until she went to bed that night, far too tired for anything but such rest as her pallet-bed could afford. She felt little or no curiosity as to her correspondence.

Nobody wrote to her except Barbara, who had kept her posted in all the general family news with fair regularity for the past nine years.

She recognized without elation the narrow envelope with the thin black edge affected by Barbara ever since she had become the widow of Ralph McAllister, during the course of the war in South Africa. It all seemed to her very remote. The fact that Mother Gertrude had sent for her after Vespers was of far more importance than any news that Barbara might have to give of the outside world that seemed so far away, and unreal.

Sister Alexandra had not been very greatly moved by any echoes from without, since the sudden shock of hearing of her mother's death, while she herself was still a novice preparing to take final vows.

Alex still remembered the bewilderment of seeing a black-clad, sobbing, schoolgirl Pamela in the parlour, and the frozen rigidity of grief which had masked her father's anguish.

Barbara and Ralph McAllister had been recalled from their honeymoon – he still rapturous at a marriage which had been deferred for nearly two years owing to Sir Francis' objection to his profession, and Barbara drowned in decorous tears, through which shone all the self-conscious glory of her wedding-ring and her new position as a married woman. Alex had been thankful when those trying interviews had come to an end – she had been sent to Liège just before her religious profession. It had mitigated the wrench of a separation from her Superior, although the first months spent away from

Mother Gertrude had seemed to her unutterably long and dreary. But less than a year later Mother Gertrude had come to the Mother-house as Assistant Superior, and the intercourse between them had been as unbroken as the rule permitted.

It was eight years since Alex had left England, but, except for the extreme cold of the winter, which told upon her health yearly, she had grown to be quite unaware of the surroundings outside. The wave of rather febrile patriotism that rolled over England at the time of the Boer War, left her quite untouched, and no description of Barbara's conveyed anything to her mind of the astoundingly wholesale demolition of old ideals that fell with the death of Victoria, and the succession of Edward VII to the English throne.

For Alex there was no change, except the unseen progress of time itself. She only realized how far apart she had grown from the old life when the news of her father's death reached her in the winter of 1902, and woke in her only a plaintive pity and self-reproachful wonder at her own absence of any acute emotion.

No one came to see her in the parlour after Sir Francis' death. For one thing, she was in Belgium, and too far away to be easily visited, and the South African casualties, amongst whom had numbered Barbara's young husband, had familiarized them all with the ideas of death and parting, so that there was little of the consternation and shock that Lady Isabel's death had brought to her children. The house in Clevedon Square knew no more big receptions and elaborate At Home days, but Cedric, already of age, had taken over the headship of the household, and Alex had been conscious of a vague relief that she could still picture the surroundings she remembered as home for the boys and Pamela. Even that picture had become dim and strangely elusive, three years later, at the thought of Cedric's marriage.

Alex had accepted it, however, as she accepted most things now, with a passivity that carried no conviction to her mind. What her outer knowledge told her was true, failed to impress itself in any way upon her imagination, and consequently left her feelings quite untouched. To her inner vision, the life outside remained exactly as she had last seen it, in that summer that she still thought of as 'Diamond Jubilee year.'

Inside the convent, things had not changed. Looking back, she could remember a faint feeling of amusement when she had returned to the house at Liège at twenty-two years old, believing herself to be immeasurably advanced in years and experience since her schooldays, and had found that scarcely any alteration or modification in the rule-bound convent had taken place. She now sat among the other nuns at the monthly *réclame* and watched the girls rise one by one in their places, their hands concealed under the ugly black-stuff pélerine, their hair tightly and unbecomingly strained back, their young faces demurely made heavy and impassive, as they listened to the record read aloud just as unrelentingly as ever by old Mère Alphonsine.

Sister Alexandra very rarely contributed any words of praise or blame to the judgment. At first she had been young, and therefore not expected to raise her voice amongst the many dignitaries present, but even now, when by convent standards she had attained to the maturity of middle age, her opinion would have been of little value.

She was seldom sent among the children, although she gave an English lesson to the *moyennes* on two evenings a week. In her first year at Liège, there had been an American girl of fourteen, who had taken a sudden rapturous liking to her, which had never proceeded beyond the initial stages, since Alex, without explanation, had merely been told to hand over the charge of the child's English and French lessons hitherto in her hands, and had herself been transferred to other duties. Since then, she had been kept on the Community side of the house, and employed principally by Mother Gertrude to assist with the enormous task of correspondence that fell to the share of the Assistant Superior. She was taught to sew, and a large amount of mending passed through her hands and was badly accomplished, for Lady Isabel Clare's daughter had learned little that could be of use to her in the life she had selected. She was not even sufficiently musical to give lessons in piano or organ playing, nor had she any of the artistic talent that might be utilized for the perpetration of the various pious *objets d'art* that adorned the walls of the parlours or the classrooms.

Nevertheless, Sister Alexandra was hard-worked. No one was ever anything else at the convent, where the chanting of the daily Office alone was a very considerable physical strain, both in the raw cold of the early morning and at the close of the ceaselessly occupied day. Many of the nuns said the Office apart, owing to the numerous duties that called them from the chapel during the hours of praise and supplication, but

Sister Alexandra had so few outside calls upon her time that she was one of the most regular in attendance.

At first her health had appeared to improve under the extreme regularity of the life, and later, when her final vows had been made, it was no longer a subject for speculation. She was not ill; and therefore need never reproach herself with being a burden to her Community. Anything else did not matter – one was tired, no doubt – but one had made the sacrifice of one's life. . . . Thus the conventual creed.

Time had sped by, with strange, monotonous, unperceived rapidity. It was all a matter of waiting for the next thing. At first, Alex Clare had waited eagerly and nervously to be taught some mysterious secret that would enable her to become miraculously happy and good at home in Clevedon Square. Then she had gradually come to see that there would be no return – that her home thenceforward would be with Mother Gertrude, and in the convent. Her novitiate days had come next – strange, trying apprenticeship, that had been lightened and comforted by the woman whose powerful and magnetic personality had never failed to assert itself and its strength.

Belgium, and the anguished waiting and hoping for orders to return to London, and the growing certainty that those orders would not come, had culminated in the rush of relief and joy that heralded Mother Gertrude's unexpected transfer to the Mother-house. After that, her first vows, taken for a term of two years, had inaugurated the long pro-bationary period at the end of which a final and irrevocable pledge would bind her for ever to the way of the chosen few.

Those perpetual vows were held out to her as the goal and crown of life itself, and her mind had speculated not at all on what should follow.

She was twenty-six before she was allowed to become a professed religious – according to conventual standards, no longer a very young woman. The delay had inflamed her ardour very much. It was characteristic of Alex to believe implicitly in an overwhelming transformation which should take place within her by virtue of one definite act, so long anticipated as to have acquired the proportions of a miracle.

It sometimes seemed to her that ever since the embracing of those perpetual vows, she had lived on, waiting for the transformation to operate. There was nothing else to wait for. The supreme act in the life of a religious, to the accomplishment of which her whole being had hitherto been tending, impelled at once by precept and by example, had taken place.

The next initiation could only be obtained through death itself, yet Alex was still waiting.

She would tell herself that she was waiting for the children's summer holidays, for the beginning of the new term, then for the season of Advent and the Christmas festival, for the long stretch of Lenten weeks, with their additional fastings and fatigue, and still as each year slipped by the sense of unfulfilment remained with her, dormant but occasionally stirring.

In the last four years she had become additionally sensible of a growing exhaustion; that seemed to sap her spirit no less than the strength of her body. She had waited for her weariness to culminate in a breakdown of strength that should send her to the convent infirmary, when the rest that her body craved would be imposed upon her as an obligation, but no such relief came to her.

It sometimes struck her with a feeling of wonder that such utter lassitude of flesh and spirit alike could continue with no apparent and drastic effect upon her powers of following the daily rule. But she had no time in which to think, for the most part, and the example of Mother Gertrude's unflagging energy could always shame her into uncomplaint. Her devotion to the elder nun had inevitably increased by the very restrictions that the convent rules placed upon their intercourse.

Even now, after so many years spent beneath the same roof, the thought that she was summoned to a private interview with Mother Gertrude could still make her heart beat faster. Since the days of her novitiate, there had been few such opportunities, and those for the most part hurried and interrupted.

Sister Alexandra went downstairs with a lightened heart.

The bell from the chapel rang out its daily summons, and she mechanically took off her black-stuff apron, folded and put it away, and turned her steps down the long passage.

Her hands were folded under her long sleeves and her head bent beneath her veil, in the attitude prescribed.

Barbara's letter lay in the depths of her pocket, already forgotten.

Her thoughts had flown ahead, and she was hoping that the Superior would allow her to send Sister Agnes in her stead to the children at five o'clock,

In the chapel, she raised her eyes furtively to the big, carved stall on a raised daïs where the Assistant Superior had her place during the frequent absence of the Superior-General.

Mother Gertrude was very often claimed in the parlour or elsewhere, even during the hours of recital of the Office, and Alex was always aware of a faint but perceptible pang of jealousy when this was the case.

Tonight, however, the stately, black-robed figure was present. She was always upright and immovable, and her eyes were always downcast to her book.

Alex went through the Psalms, chanted on the accustomed single high note, and was hardly conscious of a word she uttered. Long repetition had very soon dulled her appreciation of the words, and her understanding of even Church Latin had never been more than superficial.

She had come to regard it as part of that pervading and overwhelming fatigue, that she should bring nothing but a faint distaste to her compulsory religious exercises.

Towards the close of Vespers she saw a lay-sister come on tiptoe into the chapel, and, kneeling down beside Mother Gertrude's daïs, begin a whispered communication.

Immediately a feverish agony of impatience invaded her.

No doubt some imperative summons to an interview with the parents of a nun or a child, or consultation in the infirmary, where two or three little girls lay with some lingering childish ailment, had come to rob the Superior of her anticipated free time.

Alex, in nervous despair, saw her bend her head in acquiescence.

The lay-sister retired as noiselessly as she had come, and Mother Gertrude closed her book.

The concluding versicles and prayers were spoken kneeling, and Alex was compelled to turn towards the High Altar.

She was quivering from head to foot, and gripped the arms of her stall in order to restrain herself from turning her head. Every nerve was strained in her attempt to hear any movement at the back of the chapel, but she could distinguish nothing.

The few minutes that elapsed before the bell sounded for rising, seemed to her interminable.

She had grown accustomed lately to the grip of these nervous agonies, to which she became a prey for the most trivial of causes.

The modern exploitation of hysteria, however, was still in its embryo stage, half-way between the genteel hysterics of the 'sixties and the suppressed neuroticism of the new century. She did not diagnose her complaint. With the sensation, familiar to her, of blood pumping from her heart to her head, making her face burn, while her hands and feet remained dead and cold, she rose from her knees.

Although she had expected nothing else, a feeling of sick disappointment invaded her as she saw that the Superior's place had been noiselessly vacated.

With leaden feet, she moved out of the chapel and slowly resumed the black apron and the stuff sleeves that protected her habit.

In the absence of any direct order to the contrary, she knew that she must take her accustomed place in the class-room of the *moyennes*, and that the English lesson must proceed as usual.

'A vos places.'

She had long ago learnt to speak French fluently, but never without an unmistakable British accent and intonation.

Subconsciously she was always rather relieved, on that account, when the preliminaries were done with, and the lesson could be given, according to the rules, in the English tongue.

'Simone! Begin, please.'

Sister Alexandra, seated at the desk, held the book open in front of her, and her eyes rested upon the page, but her mind took in neither the meaning of the printed words nor the sense conveyed by Simone's droning, inexpressive voice.

She wondered whether someone would come to take her place at the desk and tell her that Mother Gertrude was waiting for her downstairs.

A sudden, stealthy opening of the class-room door made her look up with a flash of hope, but it was only a little girl late for her lesson and sidling in, hoping to escape notice.

Alex did not even trouble to give her the accustomed bad mark.

It would have meant opening her desk, and pulling out the mistress's note-book, and looking for a pencil, and she felt too tired. In her earlier days at the convent she would have felt ashamed at the thought of yielding to such slothful unconcern, and would have magnified the omission into a sin, to be confessed with shame to Mother Gertrude.

Now, she was too tired to care, and besides, she never saw Mother Gertrude. Even the poor little half-hour that had been held out to her was not to be hers, after all. She brooded in resentment over the thought.

A titter going round the room roused her.

'What are you saying, Simone?'

Simone stared back at her stupidly, but another keen-faced girl in the front row of desks spoke eagerly:

'She's said nearly all through the lesson, there's nothing left for anyone else to say.'

'You can repeat it afterwards,' said Alex coldly.

She was vexed that her inattention should have been betrayed to the class, and presently she gave her full attention to the recital.

Just as it was over, the young novice, Sister Agnes, came into the room and, approaching the desk, spoke to Alex in a lowered voice:

'Mother Gertrude sent me, Sister. Will you go down to her and wait in her room? She will come in a moment. I am to take the children back to the study-room for you.'

'Thank you,' said Alex, trembling. The revulsion of feeling was so strong: that she felt the chords tightening in her throat, which denoted approaching tears such as she often shed for no adequate reason. She left the room.

The Assistant Superior's room on the ground floor was vacant.

Alex sat down on the low, rush-bottomed chair drawn close to the Superior's table and closed her eyes. Now that her agony of suspense was ended, she became even more overwhelmingly conscious of fatigue, and began to wonder, almost against her will, whether Mother Gertrude would not notice it, and perhaps tell her that she was to go to bed after supper and not come to the recital of Office in the chapel.

She wondered whether she looked tired. There were no looking-glasses in the convent, but sometimes she had seen her own reflection in the big, full-length mirror of the sacristy, and she knew that she had lost her colour, and that her face had grown thin, with heavy, black circles underneath her eyes. She knew, too, that her step had lost any elasticity, and that she stooped far more than in the days when Lady Isabel had implored her to 'hold up' so that her pretty frocks might be seen to advantage.

Waiting in the small room, with its carefully-closed window, and the big writing-table stacked with papers, and a great crucifix standing upright in the midst of them, she began for the first time to speculate as to the reason of her summons.

It occurred to her, with a slight sense of shock, that such a summons, in the case of nun or novice, had very often been the prelude to an announcement of bad news, such as the death of a relative at home.

Hastily she pulled out Barbara's letter and glanced through it.

There was no hint of approaching disaster in the rather set little phrases, and the four small sheets were mostly concerned with the fact that Barbara was finding it necessary to move into a still smaller house than the one that she and Ralph had taken at Hampstead after their improvident marriage.

Pamela was at Clevedon Square with Cedric and his wife. She was going to heaps of parties, and everyone thought her very pretty and amusing.

There was no mention of Archie, and Alex hastily ransacked her memory as to his whereabouts.

Since the first year of her novitiate in London she had never seen her youngest brother, and although she felt a fleeting sorrow at the thought of harm having befallen him, her tenderness was for the little, curly-haired boy in a sailor suit with whom she had played and quarrelled in the Clevedon Square nursery, and not for the unknown youth of later years.

As she speculated, the well-known tread of the Assistant Superior sounded down the corridors – a hasty, decisive footstep. Alex sprang to her feet as the door opened.

'Oh, what is it?' she cried, at the first sight of the Superior's face.

The strong, lined countenance, suffused with agitation, bore every mark of violent disturbance.

Her deep voice, however, was as well under control as ever, although strong emotion underlay its vibrant quality.

'My little Sister, you have a big sacrifice before you. I cannot pretend to think that it will not cost you dear, as it will me. But we know Who asks it of us.'

'What?' gasped Alex again, utterly at a loss, but feeling the blood ebb from her face.

'Our Mother-General has appointed me as Superior to the new house in South America. The boat sails at the end of this week.'

CHAPTER TWENTY

AFTERMATH

Alex could not believe the extent of the calamity that had befallen her, nor did she realize at first that the very mainspring of her life in the convent was attacked.

It astounded her to perceive that to the rest of the community the news brought no overwhelming shock.

Such sudden uprootings and transfers were not uncommon, and the notice given was generally a twenty-four hour one. Mother Gertrude had nearly a week in which to make her few preparations for an exile that almost certainly was for life, and to prepare herself as far as possible for new and heavy responsibilities.

The Superior-General was herself proceeding to South America with the little band of chosen pioneers, representative of almost every European house of the Order, and after inaugurating the establishment of the new venture, was to return to Liège, with one lay-sister only as companion.

In the general concern for her welfare, and admiration of her courage in undertaking such a journey on the eve of her sixty-third birthday, it seemed to Alex that all other considerations were overlooked or ignored entirely.

She was aware that the convent spirit of detachment, so much advocated, and the consciousness of that vow of obedience made freely and fully, would alike preclude the possibility of any spoken protest or lamentation over the separation.

The severing of human ties was part and parcel of a nun's sacrifice, and her life was in the hands of her spiritual superiors.

There was no discussion possible.

Mother Gertrude, although the look of strain was deepening round her eyes and mouth, went steadily about her duties and spared herself in nothing.

Her place was to be taken temporarily by a French nun who had been for many years at Liège, and the charge was handed over with the least possible dislocation.

It was on a Monday night that Mother Gertrude had been told of the destiny in store for her, and on the following Saturday she was to proceed with her Superior to Paris, and thence to Marseilles to the boat.

Wednesday and Thursday Alex never saw her.

She had expected it, and was, moreover, far too much stunned to realize anything beyond the immediate necessity for taking her habitual place in the Community life without betraying the sense of utter despair that was hovering over her.

On Friday afternoon Mother Gertrude said to her:

'I have not had one spare moment to give you, my poor child. But I think you know everything that I would say to you? Be very, very faithful, Sister, and remember that these separations may be for life, but all Eternity is before us.'

Alex could capture nothing of the rapt assurance that lay in the upraised eyes and vibrant voice.

'What shall I do without you?' she asked despairingly, feeling how inadequate the words were to voice her sense of utter deprivation.

The light, watchful eyes of the Superior seemed to pierce through her.

'Don't say that, dear child. You do not depend in any sense upon another creature. I have been nothing to you but a means to an end. It was given to me to help you a little, years ago, to find your holy vocation. You know that human friendships in themselves mean nothing.'

Something in Alex seemed to be crying and protesting aloud in heart-broken repudiation of the formula to which her lips had so often subscribed, but her own tacit acquiescence of years rose to rebuke her, and the dread of vexing and alienating the Superior at this eleventh hour.

Dumbly she knelt down on the floor beside the Superior's chair.

Mother Gertrude looked at her compassionately enough, but with the strange remoteness induced by the long cultivation of an absolutely impersonal relation towards humanity.

'My poor little Sister, sometimes lately I have wondered whether I have been altogether wise in my treatment of you, and whether I have not allowed you to give way to natural affection too much. Perhaps this break has come in time. You must remember that you have renounced *all* earthly ties, even the holiest and most sacred ones, and therefore you must be ready to make any sacrifice for the sake of your one, supreme Love. There is so much I should like to say to you, but time is getting short now, and there is a great deal to be done. God bless you, my child.'

The Superior laid her hand on Sister Alexandra's bent head.

Alex clasped it desperately.

'I shall still be your child, always?' she almost wailed, with a weight of things unspoken on her heart, and in a last frantic attempt to carry away one definite assurance.

The slightest possible severity mingled in Mother Gertrude's clear gaze, bent downwards as she rose to her full height, her carriage as upright and as dignified as it had been ten years before.

'No, Sister,' she said very distinctly. 'You will be the child of whatever Superior God may send you in my place.

'You know that we in the convent have no human ties, only spiritual ones. You will see your Divine Master, and Him only, in the person of your Superior in religion. Remember that, little Sister. You must learn detachment if you are to be truly faithful. That is my last and most earnest counsel to you. I shall pray daily that you may be given strength to follow it.'

'Don't go!' gasped Alex, hardly knowing what she said, as she saw the Superior's hand upon the door. 'Don't go away like that. Oh, Mother, Mother, how shall I bear it? I've only got you and now you're going away for ever.'

She broke into tearless sobs.

'Sister Alexandra! Has it come to this? I am indeed to blame if you are still so undisciplined and so weak as to cling to a mere creature – you that have been chosen by God to love

Him, and Him only! I could not have believed it.' Mother Gertrude's tone held bitter remorse and shame.

Alex' old, pitiful instinct of propitiating the being she loved best sprang to life within her.

'No, no, I didn't really mean it. I know I mustn't.'

The nun gazed at her in compassionate perplexity.

'You are overstrung, and tired; you don't know what you are saying. When you come to yourself, my poor child, you will hardly believe that you could have proved so disloyal, even for a moment. Now calm yourself, and do not attempt to join the recreation tonight. You are not fit for it. I will tell our Mother-General that I have told you to go to your cell as soon as supper is over. Good-night, and again good-bye.'

Sheer terror at the bare thought of being left there alone forced Alex to her feet, although she could scarcely stand, and was trembling violently. 'You won't forget me?' she entreated almost inaudibly.

'I shall always remember you in my prayers, as I do all those who have been under my direction. Indeed, you will have a special place in them,' said the Superior gravely, 'since I can never forget that, by the grace of God, I was instrumental in bringing you into His holy house. But never forget that *no* human relation, however precious it may be, can have any completeness in itself. It all has to lead on to the one supreme thing, Sister, the "one thing necessary". Now you must detain me no longer.' She freed herself from the convulsive grasp that Alex had unconsciously fastened on to the folds of her habit and moved unhesitatingly to the door.

Alex followed her with eyes that stared blankly from a blanched face. She felt as though she was under a spell and could neither move nor speak. She could not believe that Mother Gertrude would really leave her in that way. The Superior opened the door and passed out, closing it behind her without pausing or looking back.

Alex heard her steps receding, rapid and measured, along the uncarpeted corridor outside.

She stayed on and on in the little cold room, the winter dusk deepening rapidly outside, the silence only broken by the occasional clanging of a bell, to the sound of which she was so much inured that it hardly struck upon her senses. She thought that Mother Gertrude would come back to her.

There must be some other last words between them than those few impersonal counsels of perfection, that repudiated any more intimate link such as Alex' exclusive jealousy, stifled, but never stronger than after those ten years of repression, now claimed with such frantic yearning.

She waited, scarcely moving. She grew colder and colder, but she was unconscious of her icy feet and leaden hands. She was not even aware of consecutive thought.

Her whole body was absorbed in the supreme act of awaiting the Superior's return for the word, the look, that should at least break the dreadful darkness that encompassed her soul at the sudden deprivation of that one outlet which had, unaware, served as a safety-valve for the whole craving dependence of her spirit.

Mother Gertrude did not come back.

Dusk turned rapidly to night, and the distant cries and

laughter of the children's evening recreation fell into a quiet that was only shattered by the single note of the deep-toned bell that proclaimed the hour of silence and the final gathering of the Community for the last recital of the Office in the chapel.

There was the flicker of a light along the passage outside, and the door opened at last.

Alex did not move.

She turned anguished eyes, that held scarcely any comprehension in the immensity of their fatigue, towards the entering figure.

It was that of the old Infirmarian, who put down the lighted candle and threw up her hands in dismay as her gaze met that of the younger nun. Mindful of the hour of silence, she asked no question, but she took Alex away to the convent infirmary, and placed her in a bed of which the mattress seemed strangely and wonderfully soft after the *paillasse* in her cell, and gave her a hot, sweet, strongly-scented *tisane* and bade her sleep.

'Mais demain?' whispered Alex.

She was thinking of the early departure in the raw morning cold, when the convoy that was leaving for South America would be driven away from the convent. But the Infirmarian shook her head and shuffled slowly away, leaving the room in darkness.

She was old and very tired, and for her there was no *demain*, except the glorious dawn that should herald the day of Eternity.

Alex lay awake in the merciful darkness and envisaged the

culmination of long years of stifled repression and self-deception.

She knew now, as she had never let herself know before, what had sustained her through the dragging years after the final objective of her vows had been left behind.

She knew that she had thought herself to be answering to a call of God, when she had been hearing only the voice of Mother Gertrude, and had been craving only for Mother Gertrude's tenderness and approbation.

Physical pangs of terror shot through her and shook her from head to foot as she realized to what she had bound herself, which now presented itself to her overstrung perceptions only in the crudest terms.

To live without earthly affection, to relinquish love as she understood it, in terms of human sympathy, for an ideal to which she knew, with tardy and unerring certainty, that nothing within her would ever conform.

She knew now, with that appalling clear-sightedness to which humanity is mercifully a stranger until or unless the last outposts of sanity are almost reached, that the vocation of which they all spoke so glibly had never been hers.

She had entered a life for which her every instinct declared her to be utterly unfitted, in search of that which her few short years in the outside world had denied her. The convent instinct, engrained in her at last, added to the anguish of startled horror at the wickedness of her own state of mind.

God is not mocked, she thought. Alex had tried to cheat God, and for ten years He had stayed His hand and had allowed her deception to go on.

And now it had all fallen on her – shame and punishment and despair, and nowhere any human help or consolation to turn to. She prayed frenziedly in the darkness, but no comfort came to her. She stifled in the pillow the imploring crying aloud of Mother Gertrude's name that sprang to her lips, but with a pang that sickened her, she recalled the Superior's parting from her that evening, her undeviating fidelity to an austere ideal which should also have been Alex'.

There was nothing, anywhere.

And with that final certainty of negation came a rigidity of despair that no terms of time or space could measure.

Alex fell into exhaustion, then into a state of coma that became heavy, dreamless sleep enduring far into the next day. She woke to instant, stabbing recollection. It was a grey, leaden day, with rain lashing the window-panes, and at first Alex thought that it might be still early morning, but there was all the far-away, indescribable stir that tells of a household when the day's work is in full swing, and presently she realized that it must be the middle of the morning.

'They have gone,' she thought, but the words conveyed no meaning to her. The Infirmarian came in to her and spoke, and asked whether she felt fit to get up, and although on the day before Alex had so craved for rest, she heard her own voice replying indifferently that she thought she was quite well, and that she was ready to rise at once.

'You are sure you have taken no chill? You must have been there in Mother Gertrude's room for a long time after you were taken faint. . . . Can you remember?' The nun looked at her, puzzled and anxious.

'Did I faint?'

'I think so, surely. You were almost unconscious when I came in, quite by chance, and found you there, almost frozen, poor little Sister! Now tell me – ?' The old Infirmarian put a few stereotyped questions such as she addressed to all those of her patients whose ailments could not be immediately diagnosed at sight.

Alex' matter-of-fact replies, for the most part denials of the suggested ills, left her no wiser. Finally she decided on a *refroidissement*. 'Put a piece of flannel over your chest,' she said gravely, 'and you had, perhaps, better spend recreation indoors until the spell of cold is over.'

'Thank you,' said Sister Alexandra lifelessly. 'What time is it?'

'Nearly eleven. Have you any duties for which you should be replaced this morning?'

'There are a lot of things, I think,' said Alex vaguely, 'but I can get up.'

'Very well,' the Infirmarian acquiesced unemotionally. 'There is much work to be done, as you say, and we nuns cannot afford to be ill for long.'

Alex did not think that she was ill – she was quite able to get up and to dress herself, although her head was aching and her hands shook oddly.

She reflected with dull surprise that all the poignant misery of the days that had gone before seemed to have left her. Evidently this was what people meant by 'getting over things'. One suffered until one could bear no more, and then it was all numbness and inertia.

She felt a sort of surprised gratitude to God at the cessation of pain, as one who had undergone torture might feel towards the torturers for some brief respite.

Her thankfulness made tears come into her eyes, and she forced them back with a sort of wonder at herself, but that odd disposition to weep still remained with her.

As she went downstairs, rather slowly and cautiously, because her knees were shaking so strangely, she met a very little girl, the pet and baby of the whole establishment, climbing upwards. She was holding up the corners of her diminutive black apron with both hands, and after looking at the nun silently for a moment, she showed her that it contained two tiny, struggling kittens. 'Les petits enfants de Minet,' she announced gravely, and went on climbing, clasping her burden tenderly.

Alex could never have told what it was that struck her with so unbearable a sense of pathos in the sight of the little childish figure.

Quite suddenly the tears began to pour down her face, and she could neither have checked them nor have assigned any reason for them.

She went on downstairs, wiping the blinding tears from her sight, and amazed at the violence of the uncontrollable sobs that were noiselessly shaking her.

Something had suddenly given way within her and passed far beyond her own control.

It was as though she could never stop crying again.

CHAPTER TWENTY-ONE

FATHER FARRELL

For what seemed a long while afterwards – a period which, indeed, covered three or four weeks – Alex learnt to be intensely and humbly grateful for the convent law that would not allow any form of personalities in intercourse.

She was utterly unable to cease from crying, and in spite of her shame and almost her terror, the tears continued to stream down her face in the chapel, in the refectory, even at the hour of recreation.

Nobody asked her any questions. One or two of the nuns looked at her compassionately, or made some kindly, little, friendly remark; a lay-sister now and then offered her an unexpected piece of help in her work, and the Infirmarian occasionally sent her a cup of *bouillon* for dinner, but it was nobody's business to offer inquiries, and had anyone done so, the rule would have compelled Sister Alexandra to reply by a generality and to change the conversation without delay.

Only the Superior was entitled to probe deeper, and at first the Frenchwoman who was temporarily succeeding Mother Gertrude was too much occupied by her new cares to see much of her community individually.

Alex was relieved when the Christmas holidays began, and she had no longer to fear the notice of the sharp-eyed children, but in the reduction of work surrounding the festive season, it became impossible that her breakdown should continue to pass unnoticed. She did not herself know what was the matter, and could scarcely have given a cause for those incessant tears, except that she was unutterably weary and miserable, and that they had passed far beyond her own control.

The idea that that continuous weeping could have any connection with a physical nervous breakdown never occurred to her.

It was with surprise, and very little thought of cause and effect, that she one night noticed her own extraordinary loss of flesh. She had never been anything but thin and slightly built, but now she quite suddenly perceived that her arms and legs in the last two months had taken on an astounding and literal resemblance to long sticks of white wood. All the way up from wrist to armpit, her left hand, with thumb and middle finger joined, could span the circumference of her right arm.

It seemed incredible.

Her mind went back ten years, and she thought of Lady Isabel, and how much she had lamented her daughter's youthful angularity.

'If she could have seen this!' thought Alex. 'But, of course, it only mattered for evening dress – she wouldn't have thought it mattered for a nun.'

Instantly she began to cry again, although her head

throbbed and her eyes burned and smarted. There was no need now to wonder if she looked tired. Accidentally one day, her hand to her face, she had felt the sort of deeply-hollowed pit that now lay underneath each eye, worn into a groove.

She had ceased to wonder whether life would ever offer anything but this mechanical round of blurred pain and misery, these incessant tears, when the Superior sent for her.

'What is the matter with you, Sister? They tell me you are always in tears. Are you ill?'

Alex shook her head dumbly.

'Sister, control yourself. You will be ill if you cry like that. Don't kneel, sit down.'

The Superior's tone was very kind, and the note of sympathy shook Alex afresh.

'Tell me what it is. Don't be afraid.'

'I want to leave the convent – I want to be released from my vows.'

She had never meant to say it – she had never known that such a thought was in her mind, but the moment that the words were uttered, the first sense of relief that she had felt surged within her.

It was the remembrance of that rush of relief that enabled her, sobbing, to repeat the shameful recantation, in the face of the Superior's grave, pitiful urgings and assurance that she did not know what she was saying.

After that – an appalling crisis that left her utterly exhausted and with no vestige of belief left in her own ultimate salvation – everything was changed.

She was treated as an invalid, and sent to lie down instead

of joining the Community at the hour of recreation, the Superior herself devoted almost an hour to her every day, and nearly all her work was taken away, so that she could walk alone round the big *verger* and the enclosed garden, and read the carefully-selected Lives and Treatises that the Superior chose for her.

Gradually some sort of poise returned to her. She could control her tears, and drink the soups and *tisanes* that were specially prepared and put before her, and as the year advanced, she could feel the first hint of Spring stirring in her exhaustion. She was devoid alike of apprehension and of hope.

No solution appeared to her conceivable, save possibly that of her own death, and she knew that none would be attempted until the return of the Superior-General from South America.

As this delayed, she became more and more convinced, in despite of all reason, of the immutable eternity of the present state of affairs.

It shocked her when one day the Superior said to her:

'You are to go to the Superior of the Jesuits' College in the parlour this afternoon. Do you remember, he preached the sermon for your Profession, and I think he has been here once or twice in the last year or two? He is a very wise and clever and holy man, and ought to help you. Besides, he is of your own nationality.'

Alex remembered the tall, good-looking Irishman very well. He had once or twice visited the convent, and had always told amusing stories at recreation, and preached vigorous, inspiring sermons in the chapel, with more than a spice of originality to colour them.

The children adored him.

Alex wondered.

Perhaps Father Farrell, the clever and educated priest, would really see in some new aspect the problem that left her baffled and sick of soul and body.

She went into the parlour that afternoon trembling with mingled dread, and the first faint stirrings of hope that understanding and release from herself and her wickedness might yet be in store for her.

Father Farrell, big and broad-shouldered, with iron-grey, wavy hair and a strong, handsome face, turned from the window as she entered the room.

'Come in, Sister, come in. Sit down, won't you? They tell me ye've not been well – ye don't look it, ye don't look it!'

His voice, too, was big and bluff and hearty, full of decision, the voice of a man accustomed to the command of men.

He pushed a chair forward and motioned her, with a quick, imperious gesture that yet held kindness, to sit down.

He himself stood, towering over her, by the window.

'Well, now, what's all the trouble, Sister?'

There was the suspicion of a brogue in his cultivated tones.

Alex made a tremendous effort. She told herself that he could not help her unless she told him the truth.

She said, as she had said to the French Superior:

'I am very unhappy – I want to be released from my vows as a nun.'

The priest gave her one very quick, penetrating look, and his thick eyebrows went up into his hair for an instant, but he did not speak.

'I don't think I have ever had any – any real vocation,' said Alex, whitening from the effort of an admission that she knew he must regard as degrading.

'And how long have ye thought ye had no real vocation?'

There was the slightest possible discernible tinge of kindly derision in the inquiry.

It gave the final touch to her disconcertment.

'I don't know.'

She felt the folly of her reply even before the priest's laugh, tinged with a sort of vexed contempt, rang through the room.

'Now, me dear child, this is perfect nonsense, let me tell ye. Did ye ever hear the like of such folly? No real vocation, and here ye've been a professed religious for – how long is it?'

'Nearly four years since I was finally professed, but –'

'There's no *but* about it, Sister. A vow made to Our Blessed Lord, I'd have ye know, is not like an old glove, to be thrown away when ye think ye're tired of it. No, no, Sister, that'll not be the way of it. Ye'll get over this, me dear child, with a little faith and perseverance. It's just a temptation, that ye've perhaps been giving way to, owing to fatigue and ill health. Ye feel it's all too hard for ye, is that it?'

'No,' said Alex frantically, 'that's not it. It's nothing like that. It's that I can't bear this way of living any longer. I want a home, and to be allowed to care for people, and to have friends again – I *can't* live by myself.'

She knew that she had voiced the truth as she knew it, and covered her face with her hands in dread lest it might fail to reach his perceptions.

She heard a change in Father Farrell's voice when next he spoke.

'Ye'd better tell me the whole tale, Sister. Who is it ye want to go back to in the world?'

She looked up, bewildered.

'Anyone – home. Where I can just be myself again – '

'And how much home have ye got left, after being a nun ten years? Is your mother alive?'

'No.'

'Your father?

'No,' faltered Alex.

'They died after ye left home, I daresay?'

'Yes.'

'Then, in the name of goodness, who do ye expect is going to make a home for ye? Have ye sisters and brothers?'

'Yes.' Alex hesitated, seeing at last whither his inquiries were tending.

'Yes, and I'm thinking they're married and with homes of their own by this time,' said the priest shrewdly. 'Let me tell ye, ten years sees a good many changes in the world, and it isn't much of a welcome ye'd get by breaking your holy vows and making a great scandal in the Church, and then planting yourself on relations who've lost touch with ye, more or less, and have homes of their own, and a husband or wife, as the case may be, and perhaps little children to care for. A maiden aunt isn't so very much thought of, in the best of circumstances, let me tell ye.

'Now isn't there reason in what I'm saying, Sister?'

Sick conviction shot through her.

'Yes, Father.'

'Well, then, ye'll just give up that foolish notion, now.'

He looked at her white, desperate face, and began to take long strides up and down the room.

'Have ye confidence in your Superior? Do ye get on with her?' he asked suddenly.

'Our present Superior has only been here a little while – the one before that – '

'I know, I know,' he interrupted impatiently. 'It's the Superior-General I mean, of course – everything must come to her in the long run, naturally. Have ye full confidence in her, now?'

Alex felt as incapable of a negative reply as of an affirmative one. She knew that she did not understand the term 'full confidence' as he did, and she temporized weakly.

'But our Mother-General is away in South America – she keeps delaying, and that's one reason why nothing has been settled about me. She hasn't even left America yet.'

'I'm well aware of that. Don't waste time playing with me that way, Sister, ye'll get no further. Ye know very well what I mean. Now, tell me now, will it do for ye if I arrange for your transfer to another house – maybe to the one in London, or somewhere in your own country?'

The instinct of the imprisoned creature that sees another form of the same trap offered it under the guise of freedom, made her revolt.

'No,' she cried. 'No! I want to get right away – I want to stop being a nun.'

The priest suddenly hit the table with his clenched fist, making it rock, and making his auditor start painfully.

'That's what you'll never do, not if ye got release from the holy vows ten times over. Once a nun always a nun, Sister, although ye may be false and faithless and go back into the very midst of the world ye've renounced. But ye'll find no comfort there, no blessing, and God'll remember it against ye, Sister. A soul that spurns His choicest graces need expect no mercy, either here or hereafter. I tell ye straight, Sister, that ye'll be deliberately jeopardizing your immortal soul, if ye give in to this wicked folly. Ye've to choose between God and the Devil – between a little while of suffering here, maybe, and then Eternity in which to enjoy the reward of the faithful, or a hideous mockery of freedom here, followed by Hell and its torments for ever and ever. Which is it to be?'

Alex was terrified, but it was the priest's anger that terrified her, not the threats that he uttered. At the back of her mind lay the dim conviction that no Hell could surpass in intensity of bitterness that which her spirit was traversing on earth.

Father Farrell looked at her frightened, distorted face, and his voice sank into persuasiveness.

'This'll pass, me dear child. Many a poor soul before ye has known what it is to falter by the wayside. But courage, Sister, ye can conquer this weakness with God's help. You're in no trouble about your faith, now, are ye?'

Had Alex been able to formulate her thoughts clearly, she might have told him that it had long since become a matter of supreme unimportance to her whether or no she still possessed that which he termed her faith. As a fact, the beliefs which could alone have made the convent life endurable to her, had never struck more than the most shallow of roots into her consciousness. Perhaps the only belief which had any real hold upon her was the one that she had gradually formed upon her experience of the living – that God was a Supreme Being who must be propitiated by the sacrifice of all that one held dear, lest He strike it from one.

She looked dimly at Father Farrell, and shook her head, because she was afraid of his anger if she owned to the utter insecurity of her hold upon any religious convictions.

'That's right, that's right,' he said hastily. 'I felt sure ye were a good child at bottom. Now would ye like to make a good general Confession, and I'll give ye absolution, and ye can start again?'

Some hint of inflexibility in the last words roused Alex to a final, frantic bid for liberty.

'It's no use – it won't do for me to begin again. I can't stay on. If I can't get released from my vows I'll – I'll run away.'

Then there was a long silence.

When the priest spoke again, however, his voice held more of meditative speculation than of the anger which she feared.

'Supposing I could arrange it for ye – I don't say I could, mind, but it might be done, if good reasons were shown – what would ye say to another religious order altogether? It may be that this life is unsuited to ye – there have been such cases. I know a holy Carmelite nun who was in quite another Order for nearly fifteen years, before she found out where the Lord really wanted her. Are ye one of those, maybe?'

'No,' spoke Alex, almost sullenly. The conflict was wearing her out, and she was conscious only of a blind, unreasoning instinct that if she once gave ground, she would find herself for ever bound to the life which had become unendurable to her.

'What d'ye mean, *No*?'

'I want to go away. I want to be released from my vows.'

The formula had become almost mechanical now. The Jesuit for the first time dropped the brusqueness of manner habitual to him.

Pacing the length of the big parlour with measured, even strides, his hands clasped behind his shabby cassock, he let his deep, naturally rhetorical voice boom out in full, rolling periods through the room.

'Why did ye come to me at all, Sister? It wasn't for advice, and it wasn't for help. I've offered both, and ye'll take neither. Having put your hand to the plough, you've looked back. Ye say that sooner than remain faithful ye'll run away – ye'll make a scandal and a disgrace for the Community that's sheltered ye, and bring shame and sorrow to the good Mothers here. What did ye expect me to answer to that? If your whole will is turned to evil, it was a farce and a mockery to come to me – I can do nothing.

'But one thing I'll tell ye, Sister. If ye do this thing – if it goes up to Rome, and the vows ye took in full consciousness and free will on the day ye were professed, are dissolved – so far as they ever can be, that is, and let me tell ye that it's neither a quick nor an easy business – if it comes to that, Sister, *there'll be no going back*. No cringing round to the convent afterwards, when ye find there's no place and no welcome for ye in the world, asking to be taken back. They'll not have ye, Sister, and they'll be right. If ye go, it's for ever.'

It seemed to Alex that he was purposely seeking to frighten her – that he wanted to add fresh miseries and apprehensions to those already piled upon her, and a faint resentment flickered in her unquestioning acceptance of such an assumption.

The shadow of spirit thus restored to her, just enabled her to endure the seemingly endless exposition hurled at her in the priest's powerful voice.

When it was all over, she crawled out of the room like a creature that had been beaten.

Stunned, she only knew that yet another fellow-creature had entered the league of those who were angered against her.

CHAPTER TWENTY-TWO

ROME

The crisis passed, as all such must pass, and Alex found herself in the position openly recognized as that of waiting for the dissolution of her religious vows.

It was as Father Farrell had said, neither a short nor an easy business, nor was she allowed to pass the months of her waiting at the Liège Mother-house.

They sent her to a small house of the Order in Rome, thinking, with the curious convent instinct for misplaced economy, to save the petty cost of incessant passing to and fro of correspondence and documents, between the convent in Belgium and the Papal Secretariat at the Vatican.

Alex went to Italy in a dream. It struck her with a faint sense of irony that she and Barbara, long ago, had entertained an ambition to visit Italy, standing for all that was romantic and picturesque in the South. After all, she was to be the first to realize that girlish dream, the fulfilment of which brought no elation.

At first she lived amongst the nuns, and led their life, but when it became evident beyond question that she was eventually to obtain release from her vows, the Community held no place for her any longer.

Her religious habit was taken away, and a thick, voluminous, black-stuff dress substituted, which the nuns thought light and cool in comparison with their own weighty garments, but of which the hard, stiff cuffs and high collar, unrelieved by any softening of white, made Alex suffer greatly.

The house was too small to admit of a *pensionnat*, but the nuns took in an inconsiderable number of lady boarders, and an occasional pupil. Alex, however, was not suffered to hold any intercourse with these. After her six months spent in Community life a final appeal was made to her, and when it failed of its effect she passed into a kind of moral ostracism.

She had a small bedroom, where her meals were served by the lay-sister who waited on the lady-boarders, and a little *prie-dieu* was put in a remote corner of the chapel for her use, neither to be confounded with the choir-stalls, nor the benches for visitors, nor the seats reserved for the ladies living in the house. The librarian Sister, in charge of the well-filled book-case of the Community-rooms, had instructions to provide her with literature. Beyond that, her existence remained unrecognized.

She often spent hours doing nothing, gazing from the window at the *Corso* far below, so curiously instinct with life after the solitude of the Liège grounds, encompassed by high walls on every side.

She did not read very much.

The books they gave her were all designed to one end – that of making her realize that she was turning her back upon the way of salvation. When she thought about it, Alex believed that this was, in truth, what she was doing, but it hardly seemed to matter.

Her room was fireless, and the old-fashioned house, as most Roman ones, had no form of central heating. She shivered and shivered, and in the early days of February fell ill. One abscess after another formed inside her throat, an unspeakably painful manifestation of general weakness.

One evening she was so ill that there was talk of sending for the chaplain – the doctor had never been suggested – but that same night the worst abscess of all broke inside her throat, and Alex saw that there was no hope of her being about to die.

The bright winter cold seemed to change with incredible rapidity into glowing summer heat, and a modicum of well-being gradually returned to her.

She even crept slowly and listlessly about in the shade of the great Borghese gardens, in the comparative freshness of the Pincio height, and wondered piteously at this strange realization of her girlhood's dream of seeing Italy. She never dared to go into the streets alone, nor would the nuns have permitted it.

Her difficult letters to England had been written.

Cedric had replied with courteous brevity, a letter so much what Sir Francis might have written that Alex was almost startled, and her father's man of business had written her a short, kind little note, rejoicing that the world was again to have the benefit of Miss Clare's society after her temporary retirement.

The only long letter she received was from Barbara.

'Dearest Alex,

'Your letter from Rome was, of course, a great surprise. I had been wondering when I should hear from you again, but I did not at all guess what your news would be when it came, as we had all quite grown to think of you as completely settled in the convent.

'I am afraid that, as you say, there may be complications and difficulties about your vows, as I suppose they are binding to a certain extent, and they are sure not to let you off without a fuss.

'Your letters aren't very explicit, my dear, so I'm still somewhat in the dark as to what you are doing and when you mean to come to London, as I suppose you will eventually do. And why Italy? If you're going to get out of the whole thing altogether, it seems funny that the convent people should trouble to send you to Italy, when you might just as well have come straight to England. However, no doubt you know your own affairs best, Alex dear, and perhaps you're wise to take advantage of an opportunity that may not come again!

'Travelling has always been my dream, as you know, but except for that time I had at Neuilly, when you came out – Heavens, what ages ago – and then our honeymoon in Paris, which was so terribly broken into when dear Mother died, I've never had any chance at all, and I suppose now I never shall have. Everything is so expensive, and I'm really not a very good traveller unless I can afford to do the thing *comfortably*, otherwise I should simply love to have run over to Rome for Easter and got you to show me all the sights.

'I suppose your time is quite your own now? Of course, when you really do leave the Sisters, I hope you'll come straight to my wee cottage here – at any rate while you look about you and think over future plans.

'Cedric has written to you, I know, and if you feel you'd rather go to Clevedon Square, needless to say, my dear, I shall more than understand. Please yourself *absolutely*.

'But, of course, one's always rather chary of unknown sisters-in-law, and Violet quite rules the roost nowadays. She and Cedric are a most devoted couple, and all that sort of thing, but as she's got all the money, one rather feels as if it was *her* house. I daresay you know the kind of thing I mean.

'She's quite a dear, in many ways, but I don't go there tremendously.

'Pamela adores her, and lives in her pocket. Pam tells me she hasn't seen you since she was about fifteen – I could hardly believe it. My dear, I don't know what you'll think of her! She's quite appallingly modern, to my mind, and makes me feel about a hundred years old.

'When I think of the way *we* were chaperoned, and sent about everywhere with a maid, and only allowed the dullest of dinner-parties and tea-parties, and then those stiff, solemn balls! Pamela is for ever being asked to boy-

and-girl affairs, and dinner dances and theatre-parties – I must say she's a huge success. Everyone raves about her, and she goes in for being tremendously natural and jolly and full of vitality – and she's had simply heaps of chances already, though I daresay some of it has to do with being seen about everywhere with Violet, who simply splashes money out like water. She paid all Archie's debts, poor boy – I will say that for her. The result is that he's quite good and steady now, and everyone says he'll make a first-rate Guardsman.

'I'm writing a long screed, Alex, but I really feel you ought to be posted up in all the family news, if you're really going to come and join forces with us again, after all these years. It seems quite funny to think of, so many things have happened since you left home for good – as we thought it was going to be. Do write again and tell me what you think of doing and when you're coming over. My tiny spare-room will be quite ready for you, any time you like.

'Your loving sister,
'Barbara McAllister.'

Barbara's letter was astounding.

Even Alex, too jaded for any great poignancy of emotion, felt amazement at her sister's matter-of-fact acceptance of a state of affairs that had been brought about by such moral and physical upheaval.

Had Barbara realized none of it, or was she merely utterly incurious? Alex could only feel thankful that no long, explanatory letter need be written. Perhaps when she got back to England it would be easier to make her explanation to Barbara.

She could hardly imagine that return.

The affair of the release from her vows dragged on with wearisome indefiniteness. Documents and papers were sent for her signature, and there were one or two interviews, painful and humiliating enough.

None of them, however, hurt her as that interview in the parlour at Liège with Father Farrell had done, for to none of them did she bring that faint shred of hope that had underlain her last attempt to make clear the truth as she knew it.

She knew that money had been paid, and Cedric had written a grave and short note, bidding her leave that side of the question to his care, and to that of her father's lawyers.

Then, with dramatic unexpectedness, came the end.

She was told that all the necessary formalities had been complied with, and that her vows were now annulled. It was carefully explained to her that this did not include freedom to marry. The Church would sanction no union of hers.

Alex could have laughed.

She felt as though marriage had been spoken of, for the first time, to an old, old woman, who had never known love, and to whom passion and desire alike had long been as strangers. Why should that which had never come to her eager, questing youth, be spoken of in connection with the strange, remote self which was all that was left of her now?

She reflected how transitory had been the relations into which she had entered, how little any intimacy of spirit had ever bound her to another human being.

Her first love – Marie-Angèle:

'I love you for your few caresses,
I love you for my many tears.'

Where was Marie-Angèle now? Alex knew nothing of her. No doubt she had married, had borne children, and somewhere in her native Soissons was gay and prosperous still.

Alex dimly hoped so.

Queenie Torrance.

Her thoughts even now dwelt tenderly for a moment on that fair, irresponsive object of so much devotion. On Queenie as a pale, demure schoolgirl, her fair curls rolled back from her white, open brow, in her black-stuff dress and apron. On Queenie, the blue ribbon for good conduct lying across her gently-curving breast, serenely telling fibs or surreptitiously carrying off the forbidden sweets and dainties procured for her by Alex, or gazing with cold vexation on some extravagant demonstration of affection that had failed to win her approval.

In retrospect Alex could see Queenie again, the white, voluminous ball dresses she had worn, the tiny wreath of blue forget-me-nots once condemned as 'bad form' by Lady Isabel.

On Queenie Goldstein her thoughts dwelt little. She had heard long ago from Barbara of Queenie's divorce, in an action brought by her husband which had afforded the chief scandal of the year 1899, and then no one had heard or even seen anything of Queenie for a long while, and Barbara had said that she was reported to be abroad with her father.

Five years later Barbara had written excitedly:

'You remember that awful Queenie Goldstein? and how full the papers were of her pictures, when that dreadful divorce case of hers was on, and the five co-respondents and everything? You'll hardly believe it, but she's in London again, having succeeded in marrying an American whom everyone says is *the* coming millionaire. I saw her at the theatre myself, in a box, absolutely slung with diamonds. She's taken to making up her face tremendously, but she hasn't altered much, and she's received everywhere. They say her husband simply adores her.'

Alex still remembered the rebuke with which Mother Gertrude had handed her that letter, bidding her remind her sister that things of the world, worldly, had no place in the life of a nun.

Nevertheless, although she had put the thought from her, she knew that in her heart she had felt a certain gladness that her erstwhile playmate, given over though she might be to the world, the flesh and the Devil, had yet not found those things that she coveted to have failed her.

Queenie, at least, had known what she wanted, and Alex' thoughts of her held no condemnation.

From Queenie, her mind went to the memory of Noel Cardew, and she was faintly surprised at the unvivid presentment of him which was all that she could evoke.

Noel had held no real place in her life at all.

Nothing that would endure had ever passed between him and her. It was years since she had thought of their ill-starred engagement, and then it had always been in connection with Sir Francis and Lady Isabel – their brief pride and pleasure in it, and the sudden downfall of their hopes.

Of Noel himself she had scarcely a recollection. Perhaps her clearest one was that of the earnest young egoist, only made attractive by a certain simplicity, who had taken her to sit in a disused ice-house one hot summer day, and had talked about photography. Of the later Noel, Alex was astounded to find that she retained no impression at all.

She could not even remember whether it was he or his brother Eric who had married red-haired Marie Munroe in the same year that she herself had taken her first vows as a nun.

Perhaps it was Noel.

At all events, he had probably married long ago, and Alex could believe that some corner of land in Devonshire was the better for the earnest supervision that he would accord to it, both in his own person and in that of the generation that would doubtless succeed him.

Mother Gertrude.

At the last and most worshipped of the shrines before which Alex had offered the sad, futile, unmeasured burnt-offerings of her life, her thoughts lingered least.

It had all been a mistake.

She had given recklessly, foolishly, squandering her all because life had cheated her of any outlet for a force of the strength of which she had had no measure given her, and now she had to pay the bitter penalty for a folly which had not even been met by answering human affection.

She wrote no letter to Mother Gertrude, and received no word from her.

As the days crept on, Alex, without volition of her own, found that her journey to England had been arranged for – that money was to be advanced to her for her expenses, that she was expected to supplement with it her utter penury of worldly possessions. One day she went out, frightened and at a loss, and entered some of the first shops she saw, in a street that led down from the Pincio Gates.

They were not large shops, and she had difficulty in making herself understood, but she purchased a ready-made blue-serge skirt, with a coat that she called a jacket, and an ugly black toque, that most resembled in shape those that she remembered seeing in London ten years earlier. She wore these clothes, with a white cotton blouse that fastened at the back and came high up under her chin, for some days before she left Rome, so as to grow accustomed to them, and to lose the sense of awkwardness that they produced in her.

The heavy boots and a pair of black-cotton gloves that she had brought from Belgium, still served her. The day of her departure was fixed, and she wrote to Barbara, but she knew neither by what route she was going nor how long the journey would take.

Her companions, selected by the Superior of the convent, proved to be an old lady and her daughter who were going to Paris. Evidently they knew her story, for they looked at her with scared, curious faces and spoke to her very little. Both were experienced travellers, and on the long, hot journey in the train, when it seemed as though the seats of the railway carriage were made of molten iron, they extended themselves with cushions and little paper fans, and slept most of the way. At Genoa the daughter, timidly, but with kindness, pressed Alex to eat and drink, and after that she spoke to her once or twice, and gave her a friendly invitation to join them at the small *pension* in Paris to which they were bound, for a night's halt before she proceeded to Boulogne and thence to England. Alex accepted with bewildered thankfulness.

She was weak and exhausted, and the old lady and her daughter were pitiful enough, and saw her into the train next day, and gave her the provision of sandwiches which she had not thought to make for herself.

The train sped through flat, green country, with tall poplars shading the small, narrow French houses that dotted the line on either side. Her eyes dilated as she gazed on the sea, when at last Boulogne was reached.

She remembered the same grey expanse of rolling waves tipped with foam on the morning, nearly ten years ago, when the girl Alex Clare had crossed to Belgium, tearful, indeed, and frightened, but believing herself to be making that new beginning which should lead to the eventual goal which life must surely hold in store for her.

Only ten years, and the bitterness of a lifetime's failure encompassed her spirit.

CHAPTER TWENTY-THREE

N.W.

Alex got off the boat at Folkestone, dazed and bewildered. She had been ill all through the crossing, and her head was still swimming. She grasped her heavy, clumsy suit-case and was thankful to have no luggage, when she saw the seething crowd of passengers, running after uniformed porters in search of heavy baggage that was being flung on to trucks to an accompaniment of noise and shouting that frightened her.

She made her way to the train and into a third-class carriage, too much afraid of its starting without her to dare to go in search of the hot tea which she saw the passengers drinking thankfully. It was a raw, grey day, and Alex, in her thin serge coat and skirt, that had been so much too hot in Italy, shivered violently. Her gloves were nearly threadbare and her hands felt clammy and stiff. She took off her little black-straw toque and leant her head against the back of the seat, wishing that she could sleep.

It seemed to her that the other people in the carriage were looking at her suspiciously, and she closed her eyes so as not to see them.

After a long while the train started.

Alex tried to make plans. In the shabby purse which she had clasped in her hand all the way, for fear of its being stolen, was a piece of paper with Barbara's address. She would not go to Clevedon Square, for fear of Cedric's unknown wife. Cedric with a wife and child! Alex marvelled, and could not believe that she might soon make the acquaintance of these beings who seemed to her so nearly mythical.

The thought of Barbara as a widow, living in a little house of her own in Hampstead, seemed far less unfamiliar. Barbara had always written regularly to Alex, and had twice been to see her when she was in the English house and once in her early days in Belgium.

Barbara had often said in her letters that she was very lonely, and that it was terrible having to live so far out of town because of expenses. Ralph, poor dear, had left her very, very badly off, and there had been very little more for her on the death of Sir Francis. Alex supposed that Downshire Hill must be a very unfashionable address, but she did not connect 'N.W.' with any particular locality.

She was always very stupid at finding her way about, and, anyhow, her bag was heavy. She decided that she would take a cab.

At Charing Cross it was raining, and the noise was deafening. Alex had meant to send Barbara a telegram from Folkestone, but had not known where to find the telegraph office, and she now realized with a pang of dismay that her sister would not be expecting her.

'How stupid I am, and how badly I manage things,' she thought. 'I hope she won't be out.'

The number of taxis at the station bewildered Alex, who had only seen one or two crawling about the streets in Rome, and had heard of them, besides, as ruinously expensive. She found a four-wheeled cab and put her bag on the floor. The man did not get down from his box to open the door for her, as she expected. He leant down and asked hoarsely:

'Where d'you want to go, Miss?'

'Downshire Hill,' said Alex. 'No. 101.'

'Downshire 'Ill? Where's that?'

'I don't know,' said Alex, frightened. She wondered if the man was drunk, and prepared to pull her bag out of the cab again.

''Alf a minute.'

He called out something unintelligible to another driver, and received an answer.

'Downshire 'Ill's N.W.,' he then informed her. 'Out 'Ampstead w'y.'

'Yes,' said Alex. 'Can't you take me there?'

He looked at her shabby clothes and white, frightened face.

'I'd like to see my fare, first, if *you* please,' he said insolently.

Alex was too much afraid of his making a scene to refuse.

'How much will it be?'

'Seven and sixpence, Miss.'

She pulled two half-crowns out of her purse. It was all she had left.

'This is all the change I have,' she told him in a shaking voice. 'They will pay the rest when I get there.'

He muttered something dissatisfied, but put the coins into his pocket.

Alex climbed into the cab.

It jolted away very slowly.

The rain was falling fast, and dashing against the windows of the cab. Alex glanced out, but the streets through which they were driving were all unfamiliar to her. It seemed a very long way to Downshire Hill.

She began to wonder very much how Barbara would receive her, and how she could make clear to her the long, restless agony that had led her to obtain release from her vows. Would Barbara understand?

Letters had been very inadequate, and although Barbara had written that Alex had better come to her for a while if she meant to return to England, she had given no hint of any deeper comprehension.

'We must make plans when we meet,' she had written at the end of the letter.

Alex wondered with a sense of apprehension what those plans would be. She had for so long become accustomed to being treated as a chattel, without volition of her own, that it did not occur to her that she would have any hand in forming her future life.

Presently she became conscious that the rain had stopped, and that the atmosphere was lighter. She let down the glass of the window nearest her, and saw, with surprise, that there was a rolling expanse of green, with a number of willow-trees, on one side of the road. It did not look like London.

Then the cab turned a corner, and Alex saw 'Downshire Hill' on a small board against the wall.

This was where Barbara lived, then.

The little houses were small and compact, but of agreeably varying height and shape, with a tiny enclosure of green in front of each, protected by railings and a little gate. No. 101, before which the cab drew up, had a bush that Alex thought must be lilac, and was covered with ivy. There were red blinds to the windows.

She got out, pulling her heavy bag after her, and timidly pushed open the little gate, glancing up at the windows as she did so.

There was no one to be seen.

Still clutching at her suit-case, Alex pulled the bell faintly.

'There's half my fare owing yet,' said the cabman gruffly.

Thus reminded, Alex rang again.

An elderly parlour-maid with iron-grey hair and a hard face opened the door.

'Is – is Mrs. McAllister at home?' faltered Alex.

'I'll inquire,' said the maid, with a lightning glance at the suit-case.

She left the door open, and Alex saw a little flight of stairs. A murmured colloquy took place at the top, and then Barbara, slight and severely black-clad, came down.

'Alex, that's not you?'

'Yes. Oh, Barbara!'

'My dear – I've been expecting to hear from you every day! I've been imagining all sorts of awful things. Why didn't you wire? Do come in – you must be dead, and have you been carrying that huge bag?'

'I came from the station in a cab.'

'A cab!' echoed Barbara in rather a dismayed voice. 'What a long way to come, when you could have done it so easily by the underground railway – but I suppose you didn't know?'

'No,' repeated Alex blankly. 'I didn't know.'

'What's he waiting for? Will he carry your trunk upstairs?'

'That is all the luggage I have, and I can carry it up quite well, and it isn't heavy. But I hadn't quite enough money for the fare – he ought to have another half-crown.'

'Oh, dear,' said Barbara. 'Wait a minute, then, Alex.'

She disappeared up the stairs, leaving Alex alone with the severe parlour-maid, who still held open the front door.

She leant against the wall in the tiny passage, wondering what she had expected of her actual arrival, that the reality should give her such a sense of misery.

If only she had telegraphed to Barbara from Folkestone!

'Here's two shillings. Ada, have you got a six-pence, by any chance?'

'There's sixpence in the kitchen, 'm,' said Ada, and fetched it.

'There!' said Barbara. 'Pay him then, please, Ada. Now, Alex, come upstairs and sit down. You look dreadfully ill and worn-out, my dear.'

Alex lifted the suit-case again.

'Oh, Ada will see to that. Your room is all ready, Alex. It's very small, but then the house is a perfect doll's house, as you see. This is my tiny drawing-room.'

'It's very pretty,' said Alex, sinking into a chair.

'It's not bad – the things are nice enough. Ralph had some exquisite things – but, of course, the house is too hateful, and

I hate living all the way out here. No one ever comes near me. Cedric's wife can't get her chauffeur to bring her – he pretends he doesn't know where it is. The only person who ever comes is Pamela.'

'I thought she was to live with you?'

'Pam! Oh, she wouldn't bury herself out here, for long. Pam's very much in request, my dear. She's been paying visits all over the place, and can go on indefinitely, I believe. She makes her head-quarters with Cedric and Violet in Clevedon Square, you know, but of course she'll marry. Pam's all right.'

'Last time I saw Pam she was in short frocks and a pig-tail.'

'She's come out in the most extraordinary way. Everyone says so. Not exactly pretty, but frightfully taking, and most awfully attractive to men. They say she's so full of life. I must say, when *we* came out, Alex, we didn't have nearly such a good time as she has. Men seem to go down like ninepins before her. She's always bringing them out here to tea, and to look at the view of London from the Heath. One always used to look on Hampstead Heath as a sort of joke – Phil May's drawings, and that kind of thing. I certainly never expected to live here – but lots of artists do, and Ralph had a big studio here. And it's very inexpensive. Besides, if you know your way about, it's quite easy to come in and out from town. Pamela always brings her young men on the top of a 'bus. Girls can do anything nowadays, of course. Fancy father, if one of *us* had done such a thing!'

'Who looks after her?' asked Alex, rather awe-struck.

'She looks after herself, my dear, and does it uncommonly effectively. She could marry tomorrow if she liked – and marry well, too. Of course, Cedric is her guardian in a sort of way, I suppose, but he lets her do anything she likes – only laughs.'

'Cedric!' spoke Alex wistfully. 'Do you know, I haven't seen Cedric since – I left Clevedon Square.'

'My dear, that's ten years, isn't it? Cedric's grown exactly like father. He's got just his way of standing in front of the fire and shaking his spectacles up and down in his hand – you remember father's way? Of course, he's done extraordinarily well – everyone says so – and his marriage was an excellent thing, too.'

'Is – Violet – nice?'

Barbara laughed rather drily.

'She's got a lot of money, and – yes, I suppose she is nice. Between ourselves, Alex, she's the sort of person who rather aggravates me. She's always so prosperous and happy, as though nothing had ever gone wrong with her, or ever could. She's very generous, I will say that for her – and extraordinarily good-natured. Most people adore her – she's the sort of woman that other women rave about, but I must say most men like her, too. Her people were rather inclined to think she could have done better for herself than Cedric. Of course, he isn't well off, and she's two years older than he is. But it's answered all right, and they were tremendously in love with one another.'

'Is she very pretty?'

'She's inclined to be fat, but, of course, she is pretty, in her own style – very. And the little girl is a perfect darling – little Rosemary.

'But, Alex, here am I talking you to death when you must be dying for tea. What sort of a crossing did you have?'

'Not very bad, but I was ill all the way.'

'Oh, no wonder you look so washed out,' said Barbara, as though relieved, but she went on eyeing her sister uneasily through the rapidly increasing dusk.

When Ada came in with the tea appointments, Barbara told her to bring the lamp.

'Yes 'm. And your bag, 'm – may I have the key?'

Alex looked bewildered, then recollected that the maid was offering to unpack for her, and pulled out the key from her purse.

'Isn't there your trunk still to come?' asked Barbara.

'No. You see, I hadn't much to bring – only just one or two things that I got in Rome.'

Alex wondered if Barbara understood that until a few months ago she had been a nun, living the life of a nun. She thought of the apprehension with which she had viewed making an explanation to Barbara, and almost smiled. It appeared that no explanation would be required of her.

But presently Barbara said uneasily:

'It seems extraordinary, your having no luggage like this, Alex. I don't know what Ada will think, I'm sure. I told her that you'd been living abroad for a good many years – I thought that was the best thing to say. But I never thought of your having no luggage.'

'I hadn't got anything to bring, you see. I must get some things,' repeated Alex forlornly.

'You see,' said her sister half apologetically, 'Ada's been

with me ever since I married. She was Ralph's mother's maid, and perfectly devoted to him. I couldn't ever get that sort of servant to live out here, if it wasn't for that – she waits at meals, and maids me, and does everything, except the actual cooking. I know she's rather disagreeable in her manner, but she's a perfect treasure to me.'

When Ada had brought in the lamps and filled the little room with cheerful light, drawing the blinds and curtains, Barbara looked again hard at her sister.

'Good heavens, Alex, how thin you are! and you look as though you hadn't slept for a month.'

'Oh, but I have,' said Alex eagerly, and then stopped.

She did not feel able to explain to Barbara the insatiable powers of sleep which seemed as though they could never be satisfied, after those ten years of unvarying obedience to a merciless five-o'clock bell.

'I am glad to hear it,' Barbara replied in a dissatisfied voice. 'But I never saw anyone so changed. Have you been ill?'

'Rather run down,' Alex said hurriedly, with the convent instinct of denying physical ills. 'I had two or three very troublesome abscesses in my throat, just before Easter, and that left me rather weak.'

'My dear, how awful! You never told me. Did you have an operation? Are you scarred?'

'No. They broke of themselves – *inside* my throat, luckily.'

'Oh – don't!' cried Barbara, and shuddered.

The sisters were very silent during tea. Alex saw her sister looking hard at her hands, and became conscious of contrast.

Barbara was thin, but her hands were slender and exceedingly white. She wore, besides her wedding-ring, a sapphire one, which Alex thought must have been her engagement-ring. On her wrist was a tiny gold watch, and a gold curb-chain bracelet. Her own hands, Alex now saw, were more than thin. They were almost emaciated, with knuckles that shone white, and a sharp prominence at each wrist-bone. They were not white, but rough and mottled, with broken skin round each finger-nail. She wondered if her whole person was in as striking a contrast to her sister's. When she had put on the serge skirt and white muslin blouse, the sensation had overwhelmed her, accustomed to the heavy religious habit, of being lightly, almost indecently clad. But Barbara's dress was of soft, silky material, with a low, turned-down collar, such as was just beginning to come into fashion. Her hair was piled into a shining knot of little, sausage-shaped curls, and parted in front. Though she was only twenty-eight, the grey in Barbara's hair was plentiful, but her small face looked youthful enough, and had none of the hard lines and shadows that Alex knew to lie round her own eyes and lips. Her little, slight figure was very erect, and she wore black suède shoes with sparkling buckles. Alex looked down at her own clumsy, ill-made boots, which had already begun to hurt her feet, and instinctively put up her hands to the cheap black toque, that felt heavy on her head.

'Why don't you take off your hat?' Barbara asked her kindly. 'I am sure it would rest you.'

She was too much used to obedience not to comply instantly, pushing back with both hands the weight of untidy hair that instantly fell over her eyes.

'Oh, Alex ! Your hair!'

'It's growing very fast. I – I've not been cutting it lately. There's just enough to put it up, Barbara.'

'It's much darker than it used to be, isn't it?'

'Yes, it's nearly black now. Do you remember how light the ends used to be? But I think it lost its colour from being always under the veil, you know. The worst of it is that it's not growing evenly, it's all short lengths.'

'Yes. That's very awkward,' said Barbara dispassionately. 'Especially when it's so straight.'

Alex reflected that her sister was just as self-contained as ever.

'Wouldn't you like to come to your room and rest till dinner, Alex?'

Alex got up at once.

'You ought to take Plasmon, or something of that sort, and try to get a little fatter. There's simply nothing of you, Alex – you're all eyes, with rings like saucers round them.'

After Barbara had left her in the tiny, pretty bedroom, that Alex thought looked wonderfully luxurious, she went straight to her looking-glass.

'Good heavens, how ugly I am!' she said to herself involuntarily.

Her face was sallow, with sunken cheeks, and the Roman sun had powdered her skin all over with little, pale freckles. Her eyes, as Barbara had said, had rings like saucers round them, and looked oddly large and prominent, from the slight puffiness of the under-lids.

Her teeth had, perhaps, suffered most of all. She had had one or two taken out, and the gaps were visible and unsightly.

They had never been very good teeth, and she remembered still all that she had suffered at the hands of an unskilled Brussels dentist in Belgium. For the last few years she had endured intermittent toothache, sooner than submit to further torture, and she saw now that a small black patch was spreading between the two front teeth. Barbara, with the grey mingled freely in her light hair, and her severe widow's weeds, might look more than twenty-eight – but Alex, at thirty-one, bore the semblance of a woman of forty.

She hid her face in her disfigured hands.

Presently she saw that there was hot water in a little brass can on the washing-stand, and she thankfully made use of it.

Ada had unpacked everything, and Alex saw the brush and comb that she had hastily purchased, on the dressing-table. Beside them was the packet of hair-pins that she had remembered to get at the last moment, and that was all.

'There ought to be something else, but I've forgotten,' thought Alex.

She wondered if Barbara would expect her to dress for dinner. The idea had not occurred to her. She had one other blouse, a much better one, made of black net, so transparent as to show glimpses of her coarse, white cotton underwear, with its high yoke and long sleeves.

Her hair, of course, was impossible. Even if it had not been so short and of such an intractable, limp straightness, Alex had forgotten how to do it. She remembered with dim surprise that at Clevedon Square Lady Isabel's maid had always done her hair for her.

She brushed it away from her face, and made a small coil on

the top of her head, after the fashion which she remembered best, and tried to fasten back the untidy lengths that fell over her ears and forehead.

The hair-pins that she had bought were very long and thick. She wished that they did not show so obviously.

'Alex?' said Barbara's cool voice at her door.

Alex came out, and they went downstairs together, Alex a few steps behind her sister, since the stairs were not broad enough for two to walk abreast. She tried awkwardly not to step on the tail of Barbara's black lace tea-gown. Ada waited upon them, and although the helpings of food seemed infinitesimal to Alex, everything tasted delicious, and she wondered if Barbara always had three courses as well as a dessert of fruit and coffee, even when she was by herself.

'You don't smoke, I suppose?' Barbara said. 'No, of course not – how stupid of me! Let's go up to the drawing-room again.'

'Barbara, do you smoke?'

'No. Ralph hated women to smoke, and I don't like to see it myself, though pretty nearly everyone does it now. Violet smokes *far* too much. I wonder Cedric lets her. But, as a matter of fact, he lets her do anything she likes.'

'I can't realize Cedric married.'

'I know. Look here, Alex, he'll want to see you – and you'll be wanting to talk over plans, won't you?'

'Yes,' said Alex nervously. 'I – I don't want to have a lot of fuss, you know. Of course, I know it's upsetting for everybody – my coming out of the convent after everyone thought I was settled. But, oh, Barbara! I *had* to leave!'

'Personally, I can't think why you ever went in,' said Barbara impersonally. 'Or why you took ten years to find out you weren't suited to the life. That sounds unkind, and I don't mean to be – you know I don't. Of course, you were right to come away. Only I'm afraid they've ruined your health – you're so dreadfully thin, and you look much older than you've any right to, Alex. I believe you ought to go into the country somewhere and have a regular rest-cure. Everyone is doing them now. However, we'll see what Cedric and Violet say.'

'When shall I see them?' asked Alex nervously.

'Well,' said her sister, hesitating, 'what about tomorrow? It's better to get it over at once, isn't it? I thought I'd ring them up this evening – I know they're dining at home.' She glanced at the clock.

'Look here, Alex, why don't you go to bed? I always go early myself – and you're simply dead tired. Do! Then tomorrow we might go into town and do some shopping. You'll want some things at once, won't you?'

Alex saw that Barbara meant her to assent, and said 'Yes' in a dazed way.

She was very glad to go to her room, and the bed seemed extraordinarily comfortable.

Barbara had kissed her and said anxiously, 'I do hope you'll feel more like yourself tomorrow, my dear. I hardly feel I know you.'

Then she had rustled away, and Alex had heard her go downstairs, perhaps to telephone to Clevedon Square.

Lying in bed in the dark, she thought about her sister.

It seemed incredible to Alex that she could ever have bullied and domineered over Barbara. Yet in their common childhood, this had happened. She could remember stamping her foot at Barbara, and compelling her to follow her sister's lead again and again. And there was the time when she had forced a terrified, reluctant Barbara to play at tight-rope dancing on the stairs, and Barbara had obediently clambered on to the newel-post, and fallen backwards into the hall and hurt her back.

Alex remembered still the agonized days and nights of despairing remorse which had followed, and her own sense of being all but a murderess. She had thought then that she could never, never quarrel and be angry with Barbara again. But she had gone away to school, and Barbara had got well, and in the holidays Alex had been more overbearing than ever in the schoolroom.

And now Barbara seemed so infinitely competent – so remote from the failures and emotional disasters that had wrecked Alex. She made Alex feel like a child in the hands of a serious, rather ironical grown-up person, who did not quite know how to dispose of it.

Alex herself wondered what would happen to her, much as a child might have wondered. But she was tired enough to sleep.

And the next morning Barbara, more competent than ever, came in and suggested that she should have her breakfast in bed, so as to feel rested enough for a morning's shopping in town.

'Though I must say,' said Barbara in a dissatisfied voice, 'that you don't look any better than you did last night. I hoped you might look more like yourself, after a night's rest. I really don't think the others will know you.'

'Am I going to see them?'

'Oh, I talked to Violet last night on the telephone, and she said I was to give you her love, and she hoped we'd both lunch there tomorrow.'

'At Clevedon Square?' asked Alex, beginning to tremble.

'Yes. You don't mind, do you?'

'No, I don't mind.'

It was very strange to be in the remembered London streets again, stranger still to be taken to shops by Barbara and authoritatively guided in the choice of a coat and skirt, a hat that should conceal as much as possible of the disastrous *coiffure* underneath, and a pair of black suède walking-shoes, that felt oddly light and soft to her feet.

'There's no hurry about the other things, is there?' said Barbara, more as though stating a fact than asking a question. 'Now we'd better take a taxi to Clevedon Square, or we shall be late.'

A few minutes later, as the taxi turned into the square, she said, with what Alex recognized in surprise as a kind of nervousness in her voice:

'We thought you'd rather get it all over at once, you know, Alex. Seeing the family, I mean. Pam is staying there anyway, and Violet said Archie was coming to lunch. There'll be nobody else, except, perhaps, one of Violet's brothers. She's always got one or other of them there.'

Alex felt sick with dismay. Then some remnant of courage came back to her, and she clenched her hands unseen, and vowed that she would go through with it.

The cab stopped before the familiar steps, and Barbara said, as to a stranger:

'Here we are.'

CHAPTER TWENTY-FOUR

ALL OF THEM

The well-remembered hall and broad staircase swam before Alex' eyes as she followed Barbara upstairs and heard them announced as:

'Mrs. McAllister – and Miss Clare!'

In a dream she entered the room, and was conscious of a dream-like feeling of relief at its totally unfamiliar aspect. All the furniture was different, and there was chintz instead of brocade, everywhere. She would not have known it.

Then she saw, with growing bewilderment, that the room was full of people.

'Alex?' said a soft, unknown voice.

Barbara hovered uneasily beside her, and Alex dimly heard her speaking half-reassuringly and half-apologetically. But Violet Clare had taken her hand, and was guiding her into the inner half of the room, which was empty.

'Don't bother about the others for a minute – Barbara, go and look after them, like a dear – let's make acquaintance in peace, Alex. Do you know who I am?'

'Cedric's wife?'

'Yes, that's it.' Then as Barbara left them, Violet noiselessly stamped her foot. 'You poor dear! I don't believe she ever told you there was to be a whole crowd of family here. That's just like poor, dear Barbara! I'm sure she never had one atom of imagination in her life, now had she? The idea of dragging you here the very day after you got back from such a journey.' The soft, fluent voice went on, giving her time to recover herself, Alex hardly hearing what was said to her, but with a sensation of adoring gratitude gradually invading her, for this warm, unhesitating welcome and unquestioning sympathy.

She looked dumbly at her sister-in-law.

In Violet she saw the soft, generous contours and opulent prettiness of which she had caught glimpses in the South. The numerous Marchesas who had come to the convent parlour in Rome had had just such brown, liquid eyes, with dark lashes throwing into relief an opaque ivory skin, just such dazzling teeth and such ready, dimpling smiles, and had worn the same wealth of falling laces at *décolleté* throat and white, rounded wrists. Violet was in white, with a double string of wonderful pearls round her soft neck, and her brilliant brown hair was arranged in elaborate waves, with occasional little escaping rings and tendrils.

Alex thought her beautiful, and wondered why Barbara had spoken in deprecation of such sleepy, prosperous prettiness.

She noticed that Violet did not look at her with rather wondering dismay, as her sister had done, and only once said:

'You do look tired, you poor darling! It's that hateful journey. I'm a fearfully bad traveller myself. When we were married, Cedric wanted to go to the south of France for our honeymoon, but I told him nothing would induce me to risk being seasick, and he had to take me to Cornwall instead. Cedric will be here in a minute, and we'll make him come and talk to you quietly out here. You don't want to go in amongst all that rabble, do you?'

'Who is there?' asked Alex faintly.

'Pam and the boys – that's my two brothers, you know, whom you needn't bother about the very least bit in the world, and here's Archie,' she added, as the door opened again.

Alex would have known Archie in a moment, anywhere, he was so like their mother. Even the first inflection of his voice, as he came towards Violet, reminded her of Lady Isabel.

She had not seen him since his schooldays, and wondered if he would have recognized her without Violet's ready explanation.

'Alex has come, Archie. That goose Barbara went and brought her here without explaining that she's only just got back to England, and is naturally tired to death. I'll leave you to talk, while I see what's happened to Cedric.'

'I say!' exclaimed Archie, and stood looking desperately embarrassed. 'How are you, Alex, old girl? We meet as strangers, what?'

'I should have known you anywhere, Archie. You're so like Barbara – so like mother.'

'They say Pam's exactly like what mother was. Have you seen her?'

'No, not yet. She – Violet – brought me in here.'

'I say, she's a ripper, isn't she? Cedric didn't do badly for himself – trust him. Wonder what the beggar'll be up to next? He's done jolly well, all along the line – retrieved the family fortunes, what? It only remains for me to wed an American, and Pamela to bring off her South African millionaire. She's got one after her, did you know?'

He spoke with a certain boyish eagerness that was rather attractive, but his rapid speech and restless manner made Alex wonder if he was nervous.

'Couldn't you ask Pamela to come to me here, so that I could see her without all those people?'

'What people? It's only old Jack Temple, and Carol. Harmless as kittens, what? But I'll get Pam for you in two twos. You watch.'

He put his fingers into his mouth and emitted a peculiar low whistle on two prolonged notes. The signal was instantly answered from the other room, but quaveringly, as though the whistler were laughing.

Then in a minute she appeared, very slim and tall, in the opening between the two rooms.

'I like your cheek, Archie!'

'I say, Pam, Alex is here.'

'Oh, Alex!'

Pamela, too, looked and sounded rather embarrassed as she came forward and laid a fresh, glowing cheek against her sister's.

'Barbara telephoned last night that you'd come, and seemed awfully seedy,' she said in a quick, confused way. 'She ought to have made you rest today.'

'Oh no, I'm all right,' said Alex awkwardly. 'How you've changed, Pamela! I haven't seen you since you were at school.'

Looking at her sister, she secretly rather wondered at what Barbara had said of the girl's attractiveness.

Pamela's round face was glowing with health and colour, and she held herself very upright, but Alex thought that her hair looked ugly, plastered exaggeratedly low on her forehead, and she could not see the resemblance to their mother of which Archie had spoken, except in the fairness of colouring which Pamela shared with Barbara and with Archie himself.

'You've changed too, Alex. You look so frightfully thin, and you've lost all your colour. Have you been ill?'

'No, I've not been ill. Only rather run down. I was ill before Easter – perhaps that's it.'

Alex was embarrassed too, a horrible feeling of failure and inadequacy creeping over her, and seeming to hamper her in every word and movement. Pamela's cold, rather wondering scrutiny made her feel terribly unsure of herself. She had often known the sensation before – at school, in her early days at the novitiate, again in Rome, and ever since her arrival in England. It was the helpless insecurity of one utterly at variance with her surroundings.

She was glad when Violet came back and said: 'Here's Cedric. Go down to lunch, children – we'll follow you.'

Cedric's greeting to his sister was the most affectionate and the least awkward that she had yet received. He kissed her warmly and said, 'Well, my dear – I'm glad we've got you back in England again. You must come to us, if Barbara will spare you.'

'Oh, Cedric!'

She looked at him for a moment, emotionally shaken. That Cedric should have grown into a man! She saw in a moment that he was very good-looking, the best-looking of them all, with Sir Francis' pleasantly serious expression and the merest shade of pomposity in his manner. Only the blinking, short-sighted grey eyes behind his spectacles remained of the solemn little brother she had known.

'Come down and have some lunch, dear. What possessed Barbara to bring you here, if you didn't feel up to coming? We could have gone to Hampstead. Violet says she's been most inconsiderate to you.'

'Yes, *most*,' said Violet herself placidly. 'Dear Barbara is always so unimaginative. Of course, it's fearfully trying for Alex, after being away such ages, to have everyone thrust upon her like this.'

Alex felt a throb of gratitude.

'Barbara thought it had better all be got over at once,' she said timidly.

'That's just like her! Barbara is being completely ruined by that parlour-maid of hers – Ada. I always think Ada is responsible for all Barbara's worst inspirations. She rules her with a rod of iron. Shall you hate coming down to lunch, Alex? Those riotous children will be off directly, they're wild about the skating-rink at Olympia. Then we can talk comfortably.'

She put her hand caressingly through Alex' arm, as they went downstairs. Alex felt that she could have worshipped her sister-in-law for her easy, pitying tenderness.

The consciousness of it helped her all through the long meal, when the noise of laughter and conversation bewildered her, after so many years of convent refectories and silence, and her solitary dinners in Rome.

Violet had placed her between Cedric and Pamela, and the girl chattered to her intermittently, without appearing to require any answer.

'Are you boys ready?' she cried, just as coffee was brought in. 'We can't wait for coffee – come on! My instructor will be engaged.'

'How are you going, Pam?' asked Violet.

'Underground. It's the quickest.'

'Oh no, Pam. Take a taxi. Archie, you must!'

Between laughter and admonition, they were dispatched – Pamela, Archie and the two Temple boys, all laughing and talking, and exchanging allusions and references unintelligible to Alex.

The room seemed much quieter and darker when the hall-door had finally slammed behind them. Alex looked round her.

At the head of his own table, Cedric sat reflective. Violet lounged, smoking a cigarette and laughing, where Lady Isabel's place had always been. Opposite Alex, Barbara, in her prim black, was leaning forward and speaking:

'What's the attraction about this roller-skating? Pamela seems to do nothing else, when she isn't dancing.'

'Everyone's doing it, my dear. I want to take it up myself, so as to reduce my figure, but it's such an impossible place to get at. I've only been to Olympia for the Military

338

Tournaments. But Pam has a perfect passion for getting about by the underground railway. Alex, isn't Pam a refreshing person?'

Alex felt uncertain as to her meaning, and was startled at being addressed. She knew that she coloured and looked confused.

'My dear,' said Barbara impressively, 'your nerves must simply have gone to pieces. Imagine jumping like that when you're spoken to! Don't you think she ought to do a rest-cure, Violet? There's a place in Belgrave Street.'

'No, no,' said Violet's kind, soft voice. 'She's coming to us. You must let us have her, Barbara, for a good long visit. Mustn't she, Cedric?'

'Of course. You must have your old quarters upstairs, Alex.'

The kindness nearly made her cry. She felt as might a child, expecting to be scolded and punished, and unexpectedly met with smiles and reassurance.

'Come up and see Baby,' said Violet. 'She's such a little love, and I want her to know her new Auntie.'

'Violet, we really must talk business some time,' said Barbara, hesitating. 'There are plans to be settled, you know – what Alex is going to do next.'

'She's going to play with Rosemary next. Don't worry, dear – we can talk plans any time. There's really no hurry.'

Alex dimly surmised that the words, and the indolent, *degagée* smile accompanying them, might be characteristic of her new sister-in-law.

Violet took her upstairs.

'The nursery is just the same – we haven't changed a thing,' she told her.

Alex gave a cry of recognition at the top of the stairs. 'Oh, the little gate that fenced off the landing! It was put up when Cedric was a baby, because he would run out and look through the balusters.'

'Was it really?' cried Violet delightedly. 'Cedric didn't know that – he told me that it had always been there. I shall love having you, Alex, you'll be able to tell me such lots of things about Cedric, when he was a little boy, that no one else knows. You see, there's so little difference between him and Barbara, isn't there?'

'I am only three years older than Barbara.'

'Then you're the same age – or a little older than I am. I am twenty-nine – two whole years older than Cedric. Isn't it dreadful?'

She laughed gaily as she turned the handle of the nursery door.

'Baby, precious, where are you?'

Alex followed her into the big, sunny room.

A young nurse, in stiff white piqué sat sewing in the window, and a starched, blue-ribboned baby, with disordered, sunny curls, crawled about the floor at her feet.

When she saw her mother she began to run towards her, with outstretched hands and inarticulate coos of pleasure.

'Come along, then, and see your new Auntie.' Violet caught her up and lifted her into her arms.

'Isn't she rather a love, Alex? Shall we look after her for a little while, while Nurse goes downstairs?'

Alex nodded. She felt as though she hardly dared speak, for fear of frightening the pretty little laughing child. Besides, the constriction was tightening in her throat.

Violet sank down into a low chair, with Rosemary still in her arms.

'I'll stay with her, Nurse, if you like to go downstairs for half-an-hour.'

'Thank you, my lady.'

'Sit down and let's be comfy, Alex. Isn't this much nicer than being downstairs?'

Alex looked round the nursery. As Violet had said, it had not been altered. On the mantelpiece she suddenly saw the big white clock, supported by stout Dresden-china cherubs, that had always stood in the drawing-room in Lady Isabel's day. It was ticking in a sedate, unalterable way.

Something in the sight of the clock, utterly familiar, and yet forgotten altogether during all her years away from Clevedon Square, suddenly caught at Alex. She made an involuntary, choking sound, and to her own dismay, sobs suddenly overpowered her.

'My poor dear!' said Violet compassionately. 'Do cry – it'll do you good, and Baby and I won't mind, or ever tell a soul, will we, my Rosemary? I knew you'd feel much better when you'd had it out, and nobody will disturb us here.'

Alex had sunk on to the floor, and was leaning her head against Violet's chair.

The soft, murmuring voice went on above her:

'I never heard of such a thing in my life as Barbara's bringing you here today – she never explained when she telephoned that you hadn't been in England for goodness knows how many years, let alone to this house. And, of course, I thought she'd settled it all with you, till I saw your face when she brought you into the drawing-room, all full of tiresome people, and brothers and sisters you hadn't set eyes on for *years*. Then I knew, of course, and I could have smacked her. You poor child!'

'No, no,' sobbed Alex incoherently. 'It's only just at first, and coming back and finding them all so changed, and not knowing what I am going to do.'

'Do! Why, you're coming here. Cedric and Rosemary and I want you, and Barbara doesn't deserve to keep you after the way she's begun. I'll settle it all with her.'

'Oh, how *kind* you are to me!' cried Alex.

Violet bent down and kissed her.

'Kind! Why, aren't I your sister, and Rosemary your one and only niece? Look at her, Alex, and see if she's like any one. Cedric sometimes says she's like your father.'

'A little, perhaps. But she's very like you, I think.'

'Oh, I never had those great round grey eyes! Those are Cedric's. And perhaps yours – they're the same colour. Anyway, I believe she's really very like what you must have been as a baby, Alex!'

It was evident that Violet was paying the highest compliment within her power.

Alex put out her hand timidly to little Rosemary. She was not at all shy, and seemed accustomed to being played with and admired, as she sat on her mother's lap. Alex thought how pretty and happy she and Violet looked together. She was emotionally too much worn-out, and had for too many years felt herself to be completely and for ever outside the pale of warm, human happiness, to feel any pang of envy.

Presently Violet reluctantly gave up Rosemary to the nurse again, and said:

'I'm afraid we ought to go down. I don't like to leave Barbara any longer. She never comes up here – or hardly ever. Poor Barbara! I sometimes think it's because she hasn't any babies of her own. Let's come down and find her, Alex.'

They found Barbara in the library, earnestly talking to Cedric, who was leaning back, smoking and looking very much bored.

He sprang up when they entered, and from his relieved manner and from Barbara's abrupt silence, Alex conjectured that they had been discussing her own return.

She stood for a moment, forlorn and awkward, till Violet sank on to the big red-leather sofa, and held out her hand in invitation to her.

'Give me a cigarette, Cedric. What have you and Barbara been plotting – like two conspirators?'

Cedric laughed, looking at her with a sort of indulgent pride, but Barbara said with determined rapidity:

'It's all very well, Violet, to laugh, but we've got to talk business. After all, this unexpected step of Alex' has made a lot of difference. One thought of her as absolutely settled – as father did, when he made his will.'

'You see, Alex,' Cedric told his sister, 'the share which should have been yours was divided by father's will between Barbara and Pamela, and there was no mention of you, except

343

just for the fifty pounds a year which my father thought would pay your actual living expenses in the convent. He never thought of your coming away again.'

'How could he, after all these years?' ejaculated Barbara.

'I know. But I couldn't have stayed on, Cedric, indeed I couldn't. I know I ought to have found out sooner that I wasn't fitted for the life – but if you knew what it's all been like – '

Her voice broke huskily, and despair overwhelmed her at the thought of trying to explain what they would never understand.

'Poor little thing!' said Violet's compassionate voice. 'Of course, you couldn't stay on. They've nearly killed you, as it is – wretched people!'

'No – no. They were kind – '

'The point is, Alex,' Barbara broke in, 'that you've only got the wretched fifty pounds a year. Of course, I'd be more than glad to let you have what would naturally have been yours – but how on earth I'm to manage it, I don't know. Cedric can tell you what a state poor Ralph left his affairs in – you'd never believe how little I have to live on. Of course, the money from father was a godsend, I don't deny it. But if Cedric thinks it's justice to give it back to you – '

She looked terribly anxious, gazing at her brother.

'No, no, Barbara!' said Alex, horrified. 'I don't want the money. Of course, you must keep it – you and Pamela.'

'That's all very well, my dear Alex,' said Cedric sensibly, 'but how do you propose to live? You must look at it from a practical point of view.'

'Then you think – ' broke from Barbara irrepressibly.

'No, my dear, I don't. One knows very well, as things are – as poor Ralph left things – it would be almost out of the question to expect – '

He looked helplessly at his wife.

'Of course, dear,' she said placidly. 'But there's Pamela's share.'

'Pamela will marry, of course. She's sure to marry, but until then – or at least until she comes of age – I don't think – as her guardian – '

Cedric broke off, looking much harassed.

'If Pam married a rich man – which she probably will,' said Violet, with a low laugh.

'We can't take distant possibilities into consideration,' Barbara interposed sharply. 'We're dealing with actual facts.'

Alex looked from one to the other with bewilderment. She hardly understood what they were all discussing. From the natural home of her childhood and girlhood, where she had lived as unthinking of ways and means as every other girl of her class and generation, she had passed into the convent world, where all was communal, and the rights of the individual a thing part shunned, part unknown. She could not, at first, grasp that Cedric and Barbara and Violet, perhaps Pam and Archie, too, were all wondering how she would be able to maintain herself on fifty pounds a year.

'Of course,' Barbara was saying, 'Alex could come to me for a bit – I'd love to have you, dear – but you saw for yourself what a tiny place mine is – and there's only Ada. I don't quite know what she'd say to having two people instead of one, I must say – '

'We want her, too,' Violet exclaimed caressingly. 'Let us have her for a little while, Barbara – while you're preparing Ada's mind for the shock.' She broke into her low, gurgling laugh again.

Barbara looked infinitely relieved.

'What do you think, Alex? It isn't that I wouldn't love to have you – but there's no denying that ways and means *do* count, and in a tiny household like mine, every item adds up.'

'Oh,' said Alex desperately, 'I know what you must feel – the difficulty of – of knowing what to do with me. It's always been like that, ever since I was a little girl. I've made a failure of everything. Don't you remember – Barbara, *you* must – old Nurse saying, "Alex will never stick to anything"? And I never have, I never shall. I can only make dreadful muddles and failures, and upset you all. If only one could wreck one's own life without interfering with other people's!'

There was a silence, which Alex, after her outburst, knew very well was not one of comprehension. Then Cedric said gently:

'You mustn't let yourself exaggerate, my dear. We're very glad to have you with us again, only one can't help wishing it had been rather sooner. But there's no use in crying over spilt milk, and after all, as Violet says, there's no hurry about anything. Come to us and have a good long rest – you look as though you needed it – and get a little flesh on your bones again. We can settle all the rest afterwards.'

Alex saw Barbara looking at her with furtive eagerness. She turned to her, with the utter dependence on another's judgment that had become second nature to her.

'When shall I go?'

'My dear!' protested Barbara. 'Of course, the longer you can stay with me the better I shall be pleased. It's only that Ada – ' She broke off at the sound of Violet's irrepressible laugh.

'You must suit yourself absolutely, of course.'

'Supposing you came to us at the end of the week?' Violet suggested. 'Say Saturday. Pamela is going away then to pay one or two visits – and I shall have you all to myself.'

Alex looked at her wonderingly.

It seemed to her incredible that Violet should actually want her, so engrained was her sense of her own isolation of spirit. That terrible isolation of those who have definitely, and for long past, lost all self-confidence, and which can never be realized or penetrated by those outside.

'That will be delightful,' said Violet, seeming to take her acceptance for granted.

Barbara got up, smoothing her skirt gently. 'We really ought to be going, Alex. I said we'd be in to tea, and it takes such ages to get back.'

Alex rose submissively. She marvelled at the assurance of Barbara, even at the ease of her conventionally affectionate farewells.

'Well, good-bye, my dear. When are you coming out to the wilds to look me up?'

Then, without giving her sister-in-law time to reply, she added gaily, 'You must ring me up and let me know, when you've a spare moment. You know I'm always a fixture. What a blessing the telephone is!'

'Then we'll see you on Saturday, Alex,' said her brother. 'Good! Take care of yourself, my dear.' He looked after her with an expression of concern, as the servant held open the door for her and Barbara and they went into the street. Alex could not believe that this kindly, rather pompous man was her younger brother.

'Cedric has grown very good-looking, but I didn't expect to see him so – so *old*, somehow,' she said.

Barbara laughed.

'Time hasn't stood still with any of us, you know. *I* think Violet looks older than he does – she is, of course. She'll be a mountain in a few years' time, if she doesn't take care.'

'Oh, Barbara! I think she's so pretty – and sweet.'

Barbara shrugged her shoulders very slightly.

'She and I have never made particularly violent friends, though I like her, of course. Pamela adores her – and I must say she's been good to Pam. But her kindness doesn't cost her anything. She's always been rich, and had everything she wanted – she was the only girl, and her people adored her, and now Cedric lets her do everything she likes. She spends any amount of money – look at her clothes, and the way she has little Rosemary always dressed in white.'

'Rosemary is lovely! It's so extraordinary to think of Cedric's child!'

Barbara tightened her lips.

'She ought to have been a boy, of course. Cedric pretended not to care, but it must have been a disappointment – and goodness only knows if Violet will ever – '

She stopped, throwing a quick glance out of the corners of her eyes at her sister.

Alex wondered why she did not finish her sentence, and what she had been about to say.

The constraint in her intercourse with Barbara was becoming more and more evident to her perceptions. It was clear that her sister did not intend to ask any questions as to the crisis through which Alex had passed, and when she had once ascertained that Alex had not 'seen anybody' whilst in Rome, she did not refer to that either.

Alex wondered if Barbara would tell her anything of Ralph and their married life, but the reserve which had always been characteristic of Barbara since her nursery days, had hardened sensibly, and it was obvious that she wished neither to give nor to receive confidences.

She was quite ready, however, to discuss her brother Cedric and his wife, or the prospects of Pamela and Archie, and Alex listened all the evening to Barbara's incisive little clear tones delivering shrewd comments and judgments. She again suggested that Alex should go to bed early, saying as she kissed her good-night:

'It's quite delightful to have someone to talk to, for me. I generally read or sew all the evening.'

'It must be lonely for you, Barbara.'

'Oh, I don't mind quiet,' she laughed, as though edging away from any hint of emotional topic. 'But, of course, it's nice to have someone for a change. Good-night.' She turned towards the door of the bedroom. 'Oh, Alex! there's just one thing – I know you'd rather I said it. If you wouldn't mind some time – any time you think of it – just letting me have the money for those clothes we bought for you today. The bills have come in – I asked for them, as I don't have an account. I knew you'd rather be reminded, knowing what a pauper I am. I only wish I hadn't got to worry you. Good-night, my dear. Sleep well.'

CHAPTER TWENTY-FIVE

※※※※※※※※※

VIOLET

For days and nights to come, the question of the money that Barbara had paid for her clothes weighed upon Alex.

She had no idea how she was to repay her.

The money that had been given her in Rome for her journey to England had only lasted her to Charing Cross, and even her cab fare to Hampstead had been supplemented by Barbara. Alex remembered it with fresh dismay. Even when she had left Downshire Hill and was in Clevedon Square again, the thought lashed her with a secret terror, until one day she said to Cedric:

'What ought I to do, Cedric, to get my fifty pounds a year? Who do I get it from?'

'Don't Pumphrey and Scott send it half-yearly? I thought that was the arrangement. You gave them your change of address, I suppose.'

'Oh no,' said Alex gently. 'I've never written to them, except once, just after father died, to ask them to make the cheques payable to – to the Superior.'

'What on earth made you do that?'

'They thought it was best. You see, I had no banking account, so the money was paid into the Community's account.'

'I see,' Cedric remarked drily. 'Well, the sooner you write and revoke that arrangement, the better. When did they last send you a cheque? In June?'

'I don't know,' Alex was forced to say, feeling all the time that Cedric must be thinking her a helpless, unpractical fool.

'Write and find out. And meanwhile – I say, Alex, have you enough to go on with?'

'I – I haven't any money, Cedric. In Rome they gave me enough for my travelling expenses, but nothing is left of that.'

'But what have you done all this time? I suppose you've wanted clothes and things.'

'I got some with Barbara, but they aren't paid for. And there are some other things I need – you see, I haven't got anything at all – not even stamps,' said Alex forlornly. 'Violet said something about taking me to some shops with her, but I suppose all her places are very expensive.'

'They are – dashed expensive,' Cedric admitted, with a short laugh. 'But look here, Alex, will you let me advance you what you want? It couldn't be helped, of course – but the whole arrangement comes rather hard on you, as things are now. You see, poor Barbara is really as badly off as she can be. Ralph was a most awful ass, between ourselves, and muddled away the little he had, and she gets pretty nearly nothing, except a widow's pension, which is very small, and the money father left. If you'll believe me, Ralph didn't even insure his life, before going to South Africa. Of course, he didn't go to fight, but on the staff of one of the big papers, and it was supposed to be a very good thing, and then what did he do but go and get dysentery before he'd been there a fortnight!'

Cedric's voice held all the pitying scorn of the successful.

'Poor Barbara,' said Alex.

'That's just what she is. Of course, I think myself that Pamela will make your share over to you again when she marries. *She's* not likely to make a rotten bad match like Barbara – far from it. But until then she can't do anything, you know – at least, not until she's of age, if then.'

Cedric stopped, and his right hand tapped with his spectacles on his left hand, in the little, characteristic trick that was so like Sir Francis.

Alex had already heard him make much the same observations, but she realized that Cedric had retained all his old knack of reiteration.

'I see,' she said.

'Well, my dear, the long and the short of it is, that you must let me be your banker for the time being. And – and, Alex,' said Cedric, with a most unwonted touch of embarrassment breaking into his kind, assured manner, 'you needn't mind taking it. There's – there's plenty of money here – there is really – nowadays.'

Alex realized afterwards that it would hardly have occurred to her to *mind* taking the twenty pounds which Cedric offered her with such patent diffidence. She had never known the want of money, either in her Clevedon Square days or during her ten years of convent life. She did not realize its value in the eyes of other people.

The isolation of her point of view on this and other

kindred subjects gradually became evident to her. Her scale of relative values had remained that which had been set before her in the early days of her novitiate. That held by her present surroundings differed from it in almost every particular, and more especially in degree of concentration. All Violet's warm, healthy affection for Rosemary did not prevent her intense preoccupation with her own clothes and her own jewels, or her innocently-assured conviction that no one was ever in London during the month of August, and that to be so would constitute a calamity.

All Cedric's pride in his wife, and love for her, in no way lessened his manifest satisfaction at his own success in life and at the renovated fortunes of the house of Clare.

Both he and Violet found their recreation in playing bridge, Cedric at his club and Violet in her own house, or at the houses of what seemed to Alex an infinite succession of elaborately-gowned friends, with all of whom she seemed to be on exactly the same terms of unintimate affection.

Violet at night, when she dismissed her maid and begged Alex to stay and talk to her until Cedric came upstairs, which he never did until past twelve o'clock, was adorable.

She listened to Alex' incoherent, nervous outpourings, which Alex herself knew to be vain and futile from the very longing which possessed her to make clear, and said no word of condemnation or of questioning.

At first the gentle pressure of Violet's soft hand on her hair, and her low, sympathetic, murmuring voice, soothed Alex to a sort of worn-out, tearful gratitude in which she would nightly cry herself to sleep.

It was only as she grew slowly physically stronger that the craving for self-expression, which had tormented her all her life, woke again. Did Violet understand?

She would reiterate her explanations and dissections of her own past misery, with a growing consciousness of morbidity and a positive terror lest Violet should at last repulse, however gently, the endless demand for an understanding that Alex herself perpetually declared to be impossible.

It now seemed to her that nothing mattered so long as Violet understood, and by that understanding restored to Alex in some degree her utterly shattered self-respect and self-confidence. This dependence grew the more intense, as she became more aware how unstable was her foothold in the world of normal life.

With the consciousness of an enormous and grotesque mistake behind her, mingled all the convent tradition of sin and disgrace attached to broken vows and the return to an abjured world. One night she said to Violet:

'I didn't do anything *wrong* in entering the convent. It was a mistake, and I'm bearing the consequence of the mistake. But it seems to me that people find it much easier to overlook a sin than a mistake.'

'Well, I'd rather ask a *divorcée* to lunch than a woman who ate peas off her knife,' Violet admitted candidly.

'That's what I mean. There's really no place for people who've made bad mistakes – anywhere.'

'If you mean yourself, Alex, dear, you know there's always a place for you here. Just as long as you're happy with us. Only I'm sometimes afraid that it's not quite the sort of life – after all you've been through, you poor dear. I know people do come in and out a good deal – and it will be worse than ever when Pam is at home.'

'Violet, you're very good to me. You're the only person who has seemed at all to understand.'

'My dear, I do understand. Really, I think I do. It's just as you say – you made a mistake when you were very young – *much* too young to be allowed to take such a step, in my opinion – and you're suffering the most bitter consequences. But no one in their senses could blame you, either for going in to that wretched place, or – still less – for coming out of it.'

'One is always blamed by someone, I think, for every mistake. People would rather forgive one for murder, than for making a fool of oneself.'

'Forgiveness,' said Violet thoughtfully. 'It's rather an over-rated virtue, in my opinion. I don't think it ought to be very hard to forgive anyone one loved, anything.'

'Would *you* forgive anything, Violet?'

'I think so,' said Violet, looking rather surprised. 'Unless I were deliberately deceived by someone whom I trusted. That's different. Of course, one might perhaps forgive even then in a way – but it wouldn't be the same thing again, ever.'

'No,' said Alex. 'No, of course not. Everyone feels the same about deceit.'

In the depths of her own consciousness, Alex was groping dimly after some other standard – some elusive certainty, that continually evaded her. Were not those things which were hardest to forgive, the most in need of forgiveness?

Alex, with the self-distrust ingrained in the unstable, wondered if that question were not born of the fundamental weakness in her own character, which had led her all her life to evade or pervert the truth in a passionate fear lest it should alienate from her the love and confidence that she craved for from others.

Sometimes she thought, 'Violet will find me out, and then she will stop being fond of me.'

And, knowing that her claim on Violet's compassion was the strongest link that she could forge between them, she would dilate upon the mental and physical misery of the last two years, telling herself all the time that she was trading on her sister-in-law's pity.

Her days in Clevedon Square were singularly empty, after Violet had tried the experiment of taking Alex about with her to the houses of one or two old friends, and Alex had come back trembling and nearly crying, and begging never to go again.

Her nerves were still utterly undependable, and her health had suffered no less than her appearance. Violet would have taken her to see a doctor, but Alex dreaded the questions that he would, of necessity, put to her, and Cedric, who distrusted inherently the practice of any science of which he himself knew nothing, declared that rest and good food would be her best physicians.

Sometimes she went to see Barbara at Hampstead, but seldom willingly. One of her visits there was the occasion for a stupid, childish lie, of which the remembrance made her miserable.

Alex, amongst other unpractical disabilities, was as entirely devoid as it is possible to be of any sense of direction. She had never known how to find her way about, and would turn as blindly and instinctively in the wrong direction as a Dartmoor pony turns tail to the wind.

For ten years she had never been outside the walls of the convent alone, and when she had lived in London as a girl, she could not remember ever having been out-of-doors by herself.

Violet, always driven everywhere in her own motor, and accustomed to Pamela's modern resourcefulness and independence, never took so childish an inability into serious consideration.

'Alex, dear, Barbara hoped you'd go down to her this afternoon. Will you do that, or come to Ranelagh? The only thing is, if you wouldn't mind going to Hampstead in a taxi? I shall have to use the Mercédès, and the little car is being cleaned.'

'Of course, I shouldn't mind. I'll go to Barbara, I think.'

'Just whichever you like best. And you'll be back early, won't you? because we're dining at seven, and you know how ridiculous Cedric is about punctuality and the servants, and all that sort of thing.'

After Violet had gone, in all her soft, elaborate laces and flower-wreathed hat, Alex, with every instinct of her convent training set against the extravagance of a taxi, started out on foot, rejoicing that a sunny July day should give her the opportunity of enjoying Pamela's boasted delight, the top of an omnibus.

She took the wrong one, discovered her mistake too late,

and spent most of the afternoon in bewilderedly retracing her own footsteps. Finally, she found a taxi, and arrived at Downshire Hill very tired and after five o'clock.

Barbara was shocked, as Alex had known she would be, at the taxi.

'Violet is so inconsiderate. Because she can afford taxis as a matter of course herself, she never thinks that other people can't. I know myself how every shilling mounts up. I'll see you into an omnibus when you go, Alex. It takes just under an hour and you need only change once.'

But that change took place at the junction of four roads, all of them seething with traffic.

And again Alex was hopelessly at sea, and boarded at last an omnibus that conveyed her swiftly in the wrong direction.

She was late for dinner, and when Cedric inquired, with his assumption of the householder whose domestic routine has been flung out of gear, what had delayed her, she stammered and said that Barbara had kept her – she hadn't let her start early enough – had mistaken the time.

It was just such a lie as a child might have told in the fear of ridicule or blame, and she told it badly as a child might have told it, stammering, and with a frightened widening of her eyes, so that even easy-going Violet looked momentarily puzzled.

Alex despised and hated herself.

She knew vaguely that her sense of proportion was disorganized. She was a woman of thirty-one, and her faults, her judgments and appreciations, even her mistakes, were those of an ill-regulated, unbalanced child of morbid tendencies.

When Pamela came back to Clevedon Square, Alex was first of all afraid of her, and then became jealous of her.

She was jealous of Pam's self-confidence, of her enormous security in her own popularity and success, jealous even of the innumerable common interests and the mutual love of enjoyment that bound her and Violet together.

She was miserably ashamed of her feelings, and sought to conceal them, none the less, as she became aware of a certain shrewdness of judgment underlying all Pamela's breezy vitality and *joie de vivre*. She and her sister had nothing in common.

To Pamela, Alex evidently appeared far removed from herself as a being of another generation, less of a contemporary than pretty, sought-after Violet, or than little Rosemary in her joyous, healthy play. Pamela could accompany Violet everywhere, always radiantly enjoying herself, and receiving endless congratulations, thinly disguised as raillery, on her universal popularity and the charm that she seemed to radiate at will. She could play whole-heartedly with Rosemary, thoroughly enjoying a romp for its own sake, and making even Cedric laugh at her complete *abandon*.

'Don't you like children?' Pamela asked Alex, looking up from the nursery floor where she was playing with her niece.

'Yes, I like them,' said Alex sombrely.

She had been reflecting bitterly that she would have known how to play with a baby of her own. But with Pamela and the nurse in the room, she was afraid of picking up Rosemary and making a fuss with her as Pam was doing, afraid with the terrible insecurity of the self-conscious.

And she never would have babies of her own now. The thought had tormented her often of late, watching Violet with her child, and Pamela with her own radiantly-secure future that would hold home and happiness as her rights.

But Alex concealed her thoughts, even, as far as possible, from herself.

The married woman who is denied children may lament her deprivation and receive compassion, but the spinster whose lot forbids her the hope, must either conceal her regrets or know herself to be accounted morbid and indelicate.

'I like babies while they're small,' Pam remarked. 'Don't I, you little horror of a niece? Other people's, you know. I don't know that I should want any of my own – they're all very well when they're tiny, but I can't bear them at the tell-me-a-story stage. I make it a rule never to tell the children stories at the houses where I stay. I always say, the very first evening, that I don't know any. Then they know what to expect. Some girls let themselves be regularly victimized, if they want to please the children's mother, and get asked again. I must say I do hate that sort of thing myself, and I don't believe it really does any good. Men are generally frightfully bored by the sort of girl who's "perfectly wonderful with children". They'd much rather have one who can play tennis, or who's good at bridge.'

Pamela laughed comfortably at her own cynicism. 'I must say I do think it pays one to be honest in the long run. I always say exactly what I feel myself, and don't care what anyone thinks of me.'

Alex felt a dull anger at her sister's self-complacent statement of what she knew to be the truth. Pamela could afford to be frank, and her boast seemed to Alex to cast an oblique reflection on herself. She gazed at her without speaking, wretchedly conscious of her own unreason.

'Look at Aunt Alex, Baby!' mischievously exclaimed Pam in a loud whisper. 'We're rather afraid of her when she pulls a long face like that, aren't we? Have we been naughty, do you think?'

Alex tried to laugh, contorting her lips stiffly. Pamela jumped up from the floor.

'Really and truly, you know, Alex,' she gravely told her sister, 'you ought to try and take things less *au grand sérieux*. I think you'd be much happier, if you'd only cultivate a sense of humour – we all think so.'

Then she ran out of the room.

Alex sat still.

So they all thought that she ought to cultivate a sense of humour. She felt herself to be ridiculous in their eyes, with her eternal air of tragedy, her sombre despair in the midst of their gay, good-humoured conventions, that admitted of everything except of weighty, unseasonable gloom.

Pamela's spontaneous and unwearied high spirits seemed to her to throw her own dejection into greater relief; her own utter social incompetence.

She began to long for the end of July, when the household in Clevedon Square would be dispersed for the remainder of the summer.

Pamela talked incessantly of a yachting invitation which she had received for August, and spoke of the difficulty of 'sandwiching in' country-house visits for autumn shooting-parties, and Alex knew that Violet's people were taking a house in Scotland, and wanted her and Cedric and the baby to make it their headquarters. She wondered, with a sense of impending crisis, what would happen to her.

At last Cedric said to her:

'Have you any particular plans for August, Alex? I want to get Violet up north as soon as possible, she's done so much rushing about lately. I wish you could come with us, my dear, but we're going to the Temples – that's the worst of not having a place of one's own in the country – '

'Oh,' said Alex faintly, 'don't bother about me, Cedric. I shall find somewhere.'

He looked dissatisfied, but said only:

'Well, you'll talk it over with Violet. I know she's been vexed at seeing so little of you lately, but Pamela's an exacting young woman, and chaperoning her is no joke. I wish she'd hurry up and get settled – all this rushing about is too much for Violet.'

'I thought she liked it.'

'So she does. Anyhow,' said Cedric, with an odd, shy laugh, 'she'd like anything that pleased somebody else. She's made like that. I've never known her anything but happy – like sunshine.' Then he flung a half-smoked cigarette into the fireplace, looked awkward at his own unusual expression of feeling, and abruptly asked Alex if she'd seen the newspaper.

Alex crept away, wondering why happiness should be accounted a virtue. She loved Violet with a jealous, exclusive affection and admiration, but she thought enviously that she, too, could have been like sunshine if she had received all that Violet received. She, too, would have liked to be always happy.

She had her talk with Violet.

There was the slightest shade of wistfulness in Violet's gentleness.

'I wish we'd made you happier, but I really believe quiet is what you want most, and things aren't ever very quiet here – especially with Pam. I simply love having her, but I'm not sure she is the best person for you just now.'

'I don't feel I know her very well. I mean, I'm not at all at home with her. She makes me realize what a stranger I am to the younger ones, after all these years.'

'Poor Alex!'

'You're much more like my sister than she is, and yet a year ago I didn't know you.'

'Alex, dear, I'm so glad if I'm a comfort to you – but I wish you wouldn't speak in that bitter way about poor little Pamela. It seems so unnatural.'

Violet's whole healthy instinct was always, Alex had already discovered, to tend towards the normal – the outlook of well-balanced sanity. She was instinctively distressed by abnormality of any kind.

'I didn't really mean it,' said Alex hurriedly, with the old fatal instinct of propitiation, and read dissent into the silence that received her announcement.

It was the subconscious hope of rectifying herself in Violet's eyes that made her add a moment later:

'Couldn't Barbara have me for a little while when you go up to Scotland? I think she would be quite glad.'

'Of course she would. She's often lonely, isn't she? And you think you'd be happy with her?'

'Oh yes,' said Alex eagerly, bent on showing Violet that she had no unnatural aversion from being with her own sister.

But Violet still looked rather troubled.

'You remember that you found it rather difficult there, when you first got back. You said then that Barbara and you had never understood one another even as children.'

'Oh, but that will all be different now,' said Alex, confused, and knowing that her manner was giving an impression of shiftiness from her very consciousness that she was contradicting herself.

As Pamela's claims and her own ceaseless fear of inadequacy made her increasingly unsure of Violet, Alex became less and less at ease with her.

The old, familiar fear of being disbelieved gave uncertainty to every word she uttered, and she could not afford to laugh at Pam's merciless amusement in pointing out the number of times that she contradicted herself. Violet always hushed Pamela, but she looked puzzled and rather distressed, and her manner towards Alex was more compassionate than ever.

Alex, with the impetuous unwisdom of the weak, one day forced an issue.

'Violet, do you trust me?'

'My dear child, what *do* you mean? Why shouldn't I trust you? Are you thinking of stealing my pearls?'

But Alex could not smile.

'Do you believe everything that I say?'

Violet looked at her and asked very gently:

'What makes you ask, Alex? You're not unhappy about the nonsense that child Pamela sometimes talks, are you?'

'No, not exactly. It's – it's just everything. . . .' Alex looked miserable, tongue-tied.

'Oh, Alex, do try and take things more lightly. You make yourself so unhappy, poor child, with all this self-torment. Can't you take things as they come, more?'

The counsel found unavailing echo in Alex' own mind. She knew that her mental outlook was wrenched out of all gear, and she knew also, in some dim, undefined way, that a worn-out physical frame was responsible for much of her self-inflicted torment of mind. Sometimes she wondered whether the impending solution to her whole destiny, still hanging over her, would find her on the far side of the abyss which separates the normal from the insane.

The days slipped by, and then, just before the general dispersal, Pamela suddenly announced her engagement to Lord Richard Gunvale, the youngest and by far the wealthiest of her many suitors.

'Oh, Pam, Pam!' cried Violet, laughing, 'why couldn't you wait till after we'd left town?'

But everyone was delighted, and congratulations and letters and presents and telegrams poured in.

Pamela declared that she would not be married until the winter, and refused to break her yachting engagement. She was more popular than ever now, and everyone laughed at her delightful originality, and gazed at the magnificence of the emerald and diamond ring on her left hand.

And Alex began to hope faintly that perhaps when Pamela was married, things might be different at Clevedon Square.

Then one night, just before she was to go to Hampstead, she overheard a conversation between Cedric and his wife.

She was on the stairs in the dark, and they were in the lighted hall below, and from the first instant that Cedric spoke, Alex lost all sense of what she was doing, and listened.

'. . . they're wearing you out, Pam and Alex between them. I won't have any more of it, I tell you.'

'No, no, my dear old goose. Of course they're not.' Violet's soft laughter came up to Alex' ears with a muffled sound, as though her head were resting against Cedric's shoulder. 'Anyhow, it isn't Pam – I'm delighted about her, of course. Only Alex – I wish she was happier!'

'And why isn't she? You're a perfect angel to her,' said Cedric resentfully.

'I'm so sorry for her – only it's difficult sometimes – a feeling like shifting sands. One doesn't know what to be *at* with her. If only she said what she wanted or didn't want, right out, but it's that awful anxiety to please – poor darling.'

'She always was like that, from our nursery days. You never could get the rights of a matter out of her – plain black or white – she'd say one thing one day and another the next, always.'

'That's what I find so difficult! It's impossible to do anything for a person like that – it's the one thing I *can't* understand.'

'Pack her off to Hampstead tomorrow,' Cedric observed gruffly. 'I *will* not have you bothered.'

'Oh, Cedric! I'm not bothered – how can you? She'll be going next week, anyway, poor dear, and it may be easier for her to be herself with Barbara, who's her own sister, after all. But I don't know what about afterwards – when we get back.'

'You'll have quite enough to think about with Pam's wedding, without Alex on your hands as well. Violet,' said Cedric, with a note in his voice that Alex had never heard there, 'when I think of the way you've behaved to all my wretched family –'

Alex did not hear Violet's answer, which was very softly spoken.

She had turned and gone away upstairs in the dark.

CHAPTER TWENTY-SIX

罗罗罗罗罗罗罗罗罗罗

AUGUST

Was it, after all, only for Cedric's sake that Violet had kept her at Clevedon Square – had shown her such heavenly kindness and gentleness?

Alex asked herself the question all night long in utter misery of spirit. She had craved all her life for an exclusive, personal affection, and had been mocked with counterfeit again and again. She knew now that it was only in despair at such cheating of fate that she had flung herself rashly to the opposite end of the scale, and sought to embrace a life that purported detachment from all earthly ties.

'*I will have all or none,*' had been the inward cry of her bruised spirit.

Fate had taken her at her word, this time, and she had not been strong enough to endure, and had fled, cowering, from the consequence of her own act.

Tortured, distraught, with self-confidence shattered to the earth, she had turned once again, with hands that trembled as they pleaded, to ask comfort of human love and companionship. Violet had not condemned her, had pitied her, and had shown her untiring sympathy and affection – for love of Cedric.

Alex rose haggard in the morning. She wanted to be alone. The thought of going to Barbara in Hampstead had become unendurable to her.

It was with a curious sense of inevitability that she found a letter from Barbara asking her if she could put off her visit for the present. The admirable Ada had developed measles.

'Good Lord, can't they send her to a hospital?' exclaimed Cedric with the irritability of a practical man who finds his well-ordered and practical plans thrown out of gear by some eminently unpractical intervention on the part of Providence.

'I'm sure Barbara never would,' said Violet, laughing. 'Poor dear, I hope she won't catch it herself. It'll mean having the house disinfected, too – what a nuisance for her. But, Alex, dear, you must come with us! I'll send a wire today – mother will be perfectly delighted.'

'Couldn't I stay here?' asked Alex.

Cedric explained that the house would be partially shut up, with only two of the servants left.

'I shouldn't give any trouble – I'd so much rather,' Alex urged, unusually persistent.

'My dear, it's out of the question. Not a soul in London – you forget it's August.'

'But, Cedric,' said Violet, 'I don't see why she shouldn't do as she likes. It will be only till Barbara can have her, after all – I suppose Ada will be moved as soon as she's better, and the disinfecting can't take so very long. If she wants to stay here?'

'I do,' said Alex, with sudden boldness.

'You don't think you'll be lonely?'

'No, no.'

'After all,' Violet considered, 'it will be very good for Ellen and the tweeny to have somebody to wait upon. I never do like leaving them here on enormous board wages, to do nothing at all – though Cedric *will* think it's the proper thing to do, because his father did it.'

She laughed, and Cedric said with an air of concession:

'Well, just till Barbara can take you in, perhaps – if you think London won't be unbearable. But mind you, Alex, the minute you get tired of it, or feel the heat too much for you, you're to make other arrangements.'

Alex wondered dully what other arrangements Cedric supposed that she could make. She had no money, and had never even roused herself to write the letter he had recommended, asking to have her half-yearly allowance sent to her own address and not to that of the Superior of the convent.

But on the day before Cedric and Violet, with Violet's maid, and Rosemary, and her nurse, and her pram, all took their departure, Cedric called Alex into the study.

She went to him feeling oddly as though she was the little girl again, who had, on rare occasions, been sent for by Sir Francis, and had found him standing just so, his back to the fireplace, spectacles in hand, speaking in just the same measured, rather regretful tones of kindliness.

'Alex, I've made out two cheques – one to cover the servants' board wages, which I thought you would be good enough to give them at the end of the month, and one for your own living expenses. You'd better cash that at once, in case you want any ready money. Have you anywhere to keep it under lock and key?'

Cedric, no more than Sir Francis, trusted to a woman's discretion in matters of money.

'Yes, there's the drawer of the writing-table in my bedroom.'

'That will be all right, then. The servants are perfectly trustworthy, no doubt, but loose cash should never be left about in any case – if you want more, write to me. And, Alex, I've seen old Pumphrey – father's man of business. He will see that you get your fifty pounds. Here is the first instalment.'

Cedric gravely handed her a third cheque.

'Have you a banking account?'

'I don't think so.'

'Then I'll arrange to open one for you at my bank today. You'd better deposit this at once, hadn't you – unless you want anything?'

'No,' faltered Alex, not altogether understanding.

'You will have no expenses while you're here, of course,' said Cedric, rather embarrassed. Alex looked bewildered. It had never occurred to her to suggest paying for her own keep while she remained alone at Clevedon Square. She gave back to her brother the cheque for twenty-five pounds, and received his assurance that it would be banked in her name that afternoon.

'They will send you a cheque-book, and you can draw out any small sum you may need later on.'

'I don't think I shall need any,' said Alex, looking at the other two cheques he had given her, made payable to herself, and thinking what a lot of money they represented.

'You will have a thorough rest and change with Barbara,' Cedric said, still looking at her rather uneasily. 'Then, when we meet again in October, it will be time enough – '

He did not say what for, and Alex remembered the conversation that she had overheard on the stair. With a feeling of cunning, she was conscious of her own determination to take the initiative out of his hands, without his knowledge.

They did not want her, and they would want her less than ever, with all the approaching business connected with Pamela's wedding in December. Barbara did not want her, self-absorbed, and unwearyingly considering how to cut down more and yet more expenses.

Alex had made up her mind to go and live alone. She would prove to them that she could do it, though they thought fifty pounds a year was so little money. She thought vaguely that perhaps she could earn something.

But she gave no hint of her plans to anyone, knowing that Violet would be remonstrant and Cedric derisive.

Obsessed by this new idea, she said good-bye to them with a sort of furtive eagerness, and found herself alone in the house in Clevedon Square.

At first the quiet and the solitude were pleasant to her. She crept round the big, empty house like a spirit, feeling as though it presented a more familiar aspect with its shrouded furniture and carefully shaded windows, and the absence of most of Violet's expensive silver and china ornaments. The library which was always kept open for her, was one of the least changed rooms in the house, and she spent hours crouched upon the sofa there, only rousing herself to go to the solitary meals which were punctiliously laid out for her in the big dining-room.

Presently she began to wonder if the elderly upper-housemaid, Ellen, left in charge, resented her being there. She supposed that the presence of someone who never went out, for whom meals had to be provided, who must be called in the morning and supplied with hot water four times a day, would interfere with the liberty of Ellen and the unseen tweeny who, no doubt, cooked for her. They would be glad when she went away. Never mind, she would go very soon. Alex felt that she was, only waiting for something to happen which should give her the necessary impetus to carry out her vague design of finding a new, independent foothold for herself.

A drowsy week of very hot weather slipped by, and then one morning Alex received three letters.

Cedric's, short but affectionate, told her that Violet had reached Scotland tired out, and had been ordered by the doctor to undergo something as nearly approaching a rest-cure as possible. She was to stay in bed all the morning, sit in the garden when it was fine, and do nothing. She was to write no letters, but she sent Alex her love and looked forward to hearing from her. Cedric added briefly that Alex was not to be at all anxious. Violet only needed quiet and country air, and no worries. She was looking better already.

Alex put the letter down reflectively. Evidently Cedric did not want his wife disturbed by depressing correspondence, and she did not mean to write to Violet of her new resolution. She even thought that perhaps she would continue to let Violet believe her at Clevedon Square or with Barbara.

Her second letter was from Barbara. It was quite a long letter, and said that Barbara had decided to leave Ada at a convalescent home and take her own much-needed summer holiday abroad. Would Alex join her in a week's time?

'What do you think of some little, cheap seaside hole in Brittany, which we could do for very little? I wish I could have you as my guest, dear, but you'll understand that all the disinfecting of the house has cost money, besides forcing me to go away, which I hadn't meant to do. However, I'm sure I need the change, and I dare say it won't do you any harm either. We ought to do the whole thing for about fifteen pounds each, I think, which, I suppose, will be all right for you? Do ring me up tonight, and let's exchange views. I shan't be free of a suspicion as to these wretched measles till next week, but I don't think really there's much danger, as I've had them already and am not in the least nervous. Ring up between seven and eight tonight. I suppose Violet, as usual, has kept on the telephone, even though they're away themselves?'

Alex knew that she did not want to go abroad with Barbara. She nervously picked up her third letter, which bore a foreign post-mark. When she had read the sheet of thin paper which was all the envelope contained, she sat for a long while staring at it.

The nuns in Rome, with whom she had spent the few weeks previous to her return to England, had sent in their account for her board and lodging, for the few clothes she had purchased, and for the advance made her for her travelling expenses. The sum total, in francs, looked enormous.

At last Alex, trembling, managed to arrive at the approximate amount in English money.

Twenty pounds.

It seemed to her exorbitant, and she realized, with fresh dismay, that she had never taken such a debt into consideration at all. How could she tell Cedric?

She thought how angry he would be at her strange omission in never mentioning it to him before, and how impossible it would be to explain to him that she had, as usual, left all practical issues out of account. Suddenly Alex remembered with enormous relief that twenty-five pounds lay to her credit at the bank. She had received her new cheque-book only two days ago. She would go to the bank today and make them show her how she could send the money to Italy.

Then Cedric and Violet need never know. They need never blame her.

Full of relief, Alex took the cheque-book that morning to the bank. She did not like having to display her ignorance, but she showed the bill to the clerk, who was civil and helpful, and showed her how very simple a matter it was to draw a cheque for twenty pounds odd. When it was done, and safely posted, Alex trembled with thankfulness. It seemed to her that it would have been a terrible thing for Cedric to know of the expenses she had so ignorantly incurred, and of her incredible simplicity in never having realized them before, and she was glad that he need never know how almost the whole of her half-year's allowance of money had vanished so soon after she had received it.

She telephoned to Barbara that night, and said that she could not go abroad with her.

'Oh, very well, my dear, if you think it wiser not. Of course, if you don't *mind* London at this time of year, it's a tremendous economy to stay where you are. . . . Are the servants looking after you properly?'

'Oh yes.'

'Well, do just as you like, of course. I think I shall get hold of some friend to join forces with me, if you're sure you won't come. . . .'

'Quite sure, Barbara,' said Alex tremulously. She felt less afraid of her sister at the other end of the telephone.

She went and saw Barbara off the following week, and Barbara said carelessly:

'Good-bye, Alex. You look a shade better, I think. On the whole you're wiser to stay where you are – I'm sure you need quiet, and when once the rush begins for Pam's wedding, you'll never get a minute's peace. Are you staying on when they get back?'

'I'm not sure,' faltered Alex.

'You may be wise. Well, come down to my part of the world if you want economy – and to feel as though you were out of London. Good-bye, dear.'

Alex was surprised, and rather consoled, to hear Barbara alluding so lightly to the possibility of her seeking fresh quarters for herself. Perhaps, after all, they all thought it would be the best thing for her to do. Perhaps there was no need to feel guilty and as though her intentions must be concealed.

But Alex, dreading blame or disapproval, or even assurances that the scheme was unpractical and foolish, continued to conceal it.

She wrote and told Violet that she had decided that it would be too expensive to go abroad with Barbara. Might she stay on in Clevedon Square for a little while?

But she had secretly made up her mind to go and look for rooms or a boarding-house in Hampstead, as Barbara had suggested. As usual, it was only by chance that Alex realized the practical difficulties blocking her way.

She had now only five pounds.

On the following Saturday afternoon she found her way out by omnibus to Hampstead. She alighted before the terminus was reached, from a nervous dread of being taken on too far, although the streets in which she found herself were not prepossessing.

For the first time Alex reflected that she had no definite idea as to where she wanted to go in her search for lodgings. She walked timidly along the road, which appeared to be interminably long and full of second-hand furniture shops. Bamboo tables, and armchairs with defective castors, were put out on the pavement in many instances, and there was often a small crowd in front of the window gazing at the cheaply-framed coloured supplements hung up within. The pavements and the road, even the tram-lines, swarmed with untidy, clamouring children.

Alex supposed that she must be in the region vaguely known to her as the slums.

Surely she could not live here?

Then the recollection of her solitary five pounds came to her with a pang of alarm.

Of course, she must live wherever she could do so most cheaply. She had no idea of what it would cost.

It was very hot, and the pavement began to burn her feet. She did not dare to leave the main road, fearing that she should never find her way to the 'bus route again, if once she left it, but she peeped down one or two side-streets. They seemed quieter than Malden Road, but the unpretentious little grey houses did not look as though lodgers were expected in any of them. Alex wondered desperately how she was to find out.

Presently she saw a policeman on the further side of the street.

She went up to him and asked:

'Can you tell me of anywhere near here where they let rooms – somewhere cheap?'

The man looked down at her white, exhausted face, and at the well-cut coat and skirt chosen by Barbara, which yet hung loosely and badly on her stooping, shrunken figure.

'Somebody's poor relation,' was his unspoken comment.

'Is it for yourself, Miss? You'd hardly care to be in this neighbourhood, would you?'

'I want to be somewhere near Hampstead – and somewhere very, very cheap,' Alex faltered, thinking of her five pounds, which lay at that moment in the purse she was clasping.

'Well, you'll find as cheap here as anywhere, if you don't mind the noise.'

'Oh no,' said Alex – who had never slept within the sound of traffic – surprised.

'Then if I was you, Miss, I'd try No. 252 Malden Road – just beyond the *Gipsy Queen*, that is, or else two doors further up. I saw cards up in both windows with "apartments" inside the last week.'

'Thank you,' said Alex.

She wished that Malden Road had looked more like Downshire Hill, which had trees and little tiny gardens in front of the houses, which almost all resembled country cottages. But no doubt houses in Downshire Hill did not let rooms, or if so they must be too expensive. Besides, Alex felt almost sure that Barbara would not want her as a very near neighbour.

She was very tired when she reached No. 252, and almost felt that she would take the rooms whatever they were like, to save herself further search. After all, she could change later on, if she did not like them.

Like all weak people, Alex felt the urgent necessity of acting as quickly as possible on her own impulses.

She looked distastefully at the dingy house, with its paint cracking into hard flakes, and raised the knocker slowly. A jagged end of protruding wire at the side of the door proclaimed that the bell was broken.

Her timid knock was answered by a slatternly-looking young woman wearing an apron, whom Alex took to be the servant.

'Can I see the – the landlady?'

'Is it about a room? I'm Mrs. 'Oxton.' She spoke in the harshest possible Cockney, but quite pleasantly.

'Oh,' said Alex, still uncertain. 'Yes, I want rooms, please.'

The woman looked her swiftly up and down. 'Only one bed-sittin'-room vacant, Miss, and that's at the top of the 'ouse. Would you care to see that?'

'Yes, please.'

Mrs. Hoxton slammed the door and preceded Alex up a narrow staircase, carpeted with oil-cloth. On the third floor she threw open the door of a room considerably smaller than the bath-room at Clevedon Square, containing a low iron bed, and an iron tripod bearing an enamel basin, a chipped pitcher and a very small towel-rail. A looking-glass framed in mottled yellow plush was hung crookedly on the wall, and beneath it stood a wooden kitchen chair. There was a little table with two drawers in it behind the door.

Alex looked round her with bewilderment. A convent cell was no smaller than this, and presented a greater aspect of space from its bareness.

'Is there a sitting-room?' she inquired.

'Not separate to this – no, Miss. Bed-sitting-room, this is called. Small, but then I suppose you'd be out all day.'

For a moment Alex wondered why.

'But meals?' she asked feebly.

'Would it be more than just the breakfast and supper, and three meals on Sunday?'

Alex did not know what to answer, and Mrs. Hoxton surveyed her.

'Where are you working, Miss? Anywhere near?'

'I'm not working anywhere – yet.'

Mrs. Hoxton's manner changed a little.

'If you want two rooms, Miss, and full board, I could accommodate you downstairs. The price is according, of course – a week in advance, and pay by the week.'

Alex followed the woman downstairs again. She was sure that this was not the kind of place where she wanted to live.

Mrs. Hoxton showed her into a larger bedroom on the first floor, just opening the door and giving Alex a glimpse of extreme untidiness and an unmade bed.

'My gentleman got up late today – he don't go to 'is job Saturdays, so I 'avent put the room to rights yet. But it's a nice room, Miss, and will be vacant on Monday. It goes with the downstairs sitting-room in the front, as a rule, but that's 'ad to be turned into a bedroom just lately. I've been so crowded.'

'Will that be empty on Monday, too?' asked Alex, for the sake of asking something.

'Tonight, Miss. I let a coloured gentleman 'ave it – a student, you know; a thing I've never done before, either. Other people don't like it, and it gives a name, like, for not being particular who one takes. So he's going, and I shan't be sorry. I don't 'old with making talk, and it isn't as though the room wouldn't let easy. It's a beautiful room, Miss.'

The coloured gentleman's room was tidier than the one upstairs, but a haze of stale tobacco fumes hung round it and obscured Alex' view of a short leather sofa with horse-hair breaking from it in patches, a small round table in the middle of the room, and a tightly-closed window looking on to the traffic of Malden Road.

'About terms, Miss,' Mrs. Hoxton began suggestively in the passage.

'Oh, I couldn't afford much,' Alex began, thinking that it was more difficult than she had supposed to walk out again saying that she did not, after all, want the rooms.

'I'd let you 'ave those two rooms, and full board, for two-ten a week!' cried the landlady.

'Oh, I don't think – '

Mrs. Hoxton shrugged her shoulders, looked at the ceiling and said resignedly:

'Then I suppose we must call it two guineas, though I ought to ask double. But you can come in right away on Monday, Miss, and I think you'll find it all comfortable.'

'But – ' said Alex faintly.

She felt very tired, and the thought of a further search for lodgings wearied her and almost frightened her. Besides, the policeman had told her that this was a cheap neighbourhood. Perhaps anywhere else they would charge much more. Finally she temporized feebly with the reflection that it need only be for a week – once the step of leaving Clevedon Square had been definitely taken, she could feel herself free to find a more congenial habitation at her leisure, and when she might feel less desperately tired. She sighed, as she followed the line of least resistance.

'Well, I'll come on Monday, then.'

'Yes, Miss,' the landlady answered promptly. 'May I have your name, Miss ? – and the first week in advance my rule, as I think I mentioned.'

'My name is Miss Clare.'

Alex took two sovereigns and two shillings, fumbling, out of her purse and handed them to the woman. It did not occur to her to ask for any form of receipt.

'Will you be wanting anything on Monday, Miss?'

Alex looked uncomprehending, and the woman eyed her with scarcely veiled contempt and added, 'Supper, or anything?'

'Oh – yes. I'd better come in time for dinner – for supper, I mean.'

'Yes, Miss. Seven o'clock will do you, I suppose?' Alex thought it sounded very early, but she did not feel that she cared at all, and said that seven would do quite well.

She wondered if there were any questions which she ought to ask, but could think of none, and she was rather afraid of the strident-voiced, hard-faced woman.

But Mrs. Hoxton seemed to be quite satisfied, and pulled open the door as though it was obvious that the interview had come to an end.

'Good afternoon,' said Alex.

'Afternoon,' answered the landlady, as she slammed the door again, almost before Alex was on the pavement of Malden Road. She went away with a strangely sinking heart. To what had she committed herself?

All the arguments which Alex had been brooding over seemed to crumble away from her now that she had taken definite action.

She repeated to herself again that Violet and Cedric did not want her, that Barbara did not want her, that there was no place for her anywhere, and that it was best for her to make her own arrangements and spare them all the necessity of viewing her in the light of a problem.

But what would Cedric say to Malden Road? Inwardly Alex resolved that he must never come there. If she said 'Hampstead' he would think that she was somewhere close to Barbara's pretty little house.

But Barbara?

Alex sank, utterly jaded, into the vacant space in a crowded omnibus. It was full outside, and the atmosphere of heat and humanity inside made her feel giddy. Arguments, self-justification and sick apprehensions, surged in chaotic bewilderment through her mind.

CHAPTER TWENTY-SEVEN

THE EMBEZZLEMENT

Alex, full of unreasoning panic, made her move to Malden Road.

She was afraid of the two remaining servants in Clevedon Square, both of them new since she had left England, and only told Ellen, with ill-concealed confusion, that she was leaving London for the present. She was unaccountably relieved when Ellen only said impassively, 'Very good, Miss,' and packed her slender belongings without comment or question.

Suddenly she remembered the cheque which Cedric had given her for the servants. She looked at it doubtfully. Her own money was already almost exhausted, thanks to that unexpected claim from the convent in Rome, and Alex supposed that the sum still in her purse, amounting to rather less than three pounds, would only last her for about a fortnight in Malden Road. She decided, with no sense of doubt, that she had better keep Cedric's cheque. It was only a little sum to him, and he would send money for the servants. He had said that he was ready to advance money to his sister.

Characteristically, Alex dismissed the matter from her mind as unimportant. She had never learnt any accepted code in dealings with money, and her own instinct led her to believe it an unessential question. She judged only from her own feelings, which would have remained quite unstirred by any emotions but those the most matter-of-fact at any claim, direct or indirect, justifiable or not, upon her purse.

She had never learnt the rudiments of pride, or of straight-dealing in questions of finance. But in Malden Road Alex was, after all, to learn many things.

There were material considerations equally unknown to Clevedon Square and to the austere but systematic doling-out of convent necessities, which were brought home to her with a startled sense of dismay from her first evening at 252. She had never thought of bringing soap with her, or boxes of matches, yet these commodities did not appear as a matter of course, as they had always done elsewhere. There was gas in both the rooms, but there were no candles. There was no hot water.

'You can boil your own kettle on the gas-ring on the landing,' Mrs. Hoxton said indifferently, and left her new lodger to the realization that the purchase of a kettle had never occurred to her at all.

Buying the kettle, and a supply of candles and matches and soap, left her with only just enough money in hand for her second week's rent, and when she wanted notepaper and ink and stamps to write to Barbara, Alex decided that she must appropriate Cedric's cheque for the servants' wages to her own uses. She felt hardly any qualms.

This wasn't like that bill from Rome, which she would have

been afraid to let him see. He would have talked about the dishonesty of convents, and asked why she had not told him sooner of their charges against her, and have looked at her with that almost incredulous expression of amazed disgust had she admitted her entire oblivion of the whole consideration.

But this cheque for the servants.

It would enable her to pay her own expenses until she could get the work which she still vaguely anticipated, and the sum meant nothing to Cedric. She would write and tell him that she had cashed the cheque, sure that he would not mind, in fulfilment of his many requests to her to look upon him as her banker.

But she did not write, though she cashed the cheque. The days slipped by in a sort of monotonous discomfort, but it was very hot, and she learnt to find her way to Hampstead Heath, where she could sit for hours, not reading, for she had no books, but brooding in a sort of despairing resignation over the past and the nightmare-seeming present. The conviction remained with her ineradicably that the whole thing was a dream – that she would wake up again to the London of the middle 'nineties and find herself a young girl again, healthy and eager, and troubling Lady Isabel, and, more remotely, Sir Francis, with her modern exigencies and demands to live her own life, the war-cry of those clamorous 'eighties and 'nineties, of which the young new century had so easily reaped the harvest. She could not bring herself to believe that her own life had been lived, and that only this was left.

Alex sometimes felt that she was not alive at all – that she was only a shade moving amongst the living, unable to get into real communication with any of them.

She did not think of the future. There was no future for her. There was only an irrevocable past and a sordid, yet dream-like present, that clung round her spirit as a damp mist might have clung round her person, intangible and yet penetrating and all-pervading, hampering and stifling her.

The modicum of physical strength which she had regained in Clevedon Square was ebbing imperceptibly from her. It was difficult to sleep very well in Malden Road, where the trams and the omnibuses passed in incessant, jerking succession, and the children screamed in the road late at nights and incredibly early in the mornings. The food was neither good nor well prepared, but Alex ate little in the heat, and reflected that it was an economy not to be hungry.

The need for economy was being gradually borne in upon her, as her small stock of money diminished and there came nothing to replace it. Presently she exerted herself to find a registry office, where she gave her name and address, and was contemptuously and suspiciously eyed by an old lady with dyed red hair who sat at a writing-table, and asked her a fee of half-a-crown for entering her name in a ledger.

'No diplomas and no certificate won't take you far in teaching nowadays,' she said unpleasantly. 'Languages?'

'French quite well and a little Italian. Enough to give conversation lessons,' Alex faltered.

'No demand for 'em whatever. I'll let you know, but don't

expect anything to turn up, especially at this time of year, with everyone out of town.'

But by a miraculous stroke of fortune something did turn up. The woman from the registry office sent Alex a laconic postcard, giving her the address of 'a lady singer in Camden Town' who was willing to pay two shillings an hour in return for sufficient instruction in Italian to enable her to sing Italian songs.

Elated, Alex looked out the conversation manual of her convent days, and at three o'clock set out to find the address in Camden Town.

She discovered it with difficulty, and arrived late. The appointed hour had been half-past three.

Shown into a small sitting-room, crowded with furniture and plastered with signed photographs, she sank, breathless and heated, into a chair, and waited.

The lady singer, when she came, was irate at the delay. Her manner frightened Alex, who acquiesced in bewildered humiliation to a stipulation that only half-fees must be charged for the curtailed hour. She gave her lesson badly, imparting information with a hesitation that even to her own ears sounded as though she were uncertain of her facts. However, her pupil ungraciously drew out a shilling from a small chain-purse and gave it to Alex when she left, and she bade her come again in three days' time.

The lessons went on for three weeks. They tired Alex strangely, but she felt glad that she could earn money, however little; and although the shillings went almost at once in small necessities which she had somehow never foreseen, it was not until the middle of September that she began once more to reach the end of her resources.

Just as she had decided that it would be necessary for her to write to Cedric, she received a letter from him, forwarded from her bank.

Alex turned white as she read it.

'My dear Alex,

'I am altogether at a loss to understand why Ellen (the upper-housemaid at home) writes to Violet on Friday last, Sept. 12, that you have left Clevedon Square, and that she and the other servant have not yet received the money for their board and wages. This last I take to be an oversight on your part, but you will doubtless put it right at once, since you will remember that I handed you a cheque for that purpose just before leaving London. As to your own movements, I need hardly say, my dear Alex, that I do not claim to have any sort of authority over them of whatever kind, but both Violet and I cannot help feeling that it would have been more friendly, to say the least of it, had you given us some hint as to your intentions. Knowing that Barbara is already abroad, and Pamela with her friends yachting, I can only hope that you have received some unforeseen invitation which appealed to you more than the prospect of solitude in Clevedon Square. It would have been desirable had you left your address with the servants, but I presume the matter escaped your memory, as they appear to be completely in the dark as to your movements.

'Violet is looking quite herself again, and sends many affectionate messages. She will doubtless write to you on receipt of a few lines giving her your address. I am compelled to send this letter through the care of Messrs. Williams, which you will agree with me is an unnecessarily elaborate method of communication.

'Your affectionate brother,
'Cedric Clare.'

Alex was carried back through the years to the sense of remorse and bewilderment with which she had listened to the measured, irrefutable condemnations, expressed with the same unerring precision, of Sir Francis Clare. She realized herself again, sick with crying and cold with terror, standing shaking before his relentless justice, knowing herself to be again, for ever and hopelessly, in the wrong. She would never be anything else.

She knew it now.

Her sense of honour, of truth and justice, was perverted – in direct disaccord with that of her world. What would her brother say to her misuse of the money that he had entrusted to her? Alex knew now, with sudden, terrifying certainty, how he would view the transaction which had seemed to her so simple an expedient. She knew that even were she able to make the almost incredible plea of a sudden temptation, a desperate need of money, that had led her voluntarily to commit an act of dishonesty, it would stand her in better stead than a mere statement of the terrible truth – that no voice within her had told her of dishonour, that she had –

outrageous paradox! – committed an act of dishonesty in good faith.

To Cedric, the lack in her would seem so utterly perverted, so incomprehensible, that there would appear to be no possibility of that forgiveness which, as a Christian, he could consciously have extended to any wilful breaking of the law. But there would be no question of forgiveness for this. It was not the money, Alex knew that. It was her own extraordinary moral deficiency that put her outside the pale.

Perhaps, thought Alex drearily, this was how criminals always felt. They did the things for which they were punished because of some flaw in their mental outlook – they didn't see that the things mattered, until it was too late. They had to be saved from themselves by punishment or removal, or sometimes by death; and for the protection of the rest of the community, too, it was necessary to penalize those who could not or would not conform to the standard. Alex saw it all.

But dimly, involuntarily almost, an echo from her childhood's days came back to her, vaguely formulated into words:

'*Always take the part of the people in the wrong – they need it most.*'

The only conviction to which she could lay claim was somehow embodied in that sentiment.

CHAPTER TWENTY-EIGHT

CEDRIC

She wrote to Cedric, the sense of having put herself irrevocably in the wrong by her own act making her explanation into an utterly bald, lifeless statement of fact. She felt entirely unable to enter into any analysis of her folly, and besides, it would have been of no use. Facts were facts. She had taken Cedric's money, which he had given her for one purpose, and used it for another. There had not even been any violent struggle with temptation to palliate the act.

Alex felt a sort of dazed stupefaction at herself.

She was bad, she told herself, bad all through, and this was how bad people felt. Sick with disappointment and utterly unavailing remorse, knowing all the time that there was no strength in them ever to resist any temptation, however, base.

She wondered if there was a hell, as the convent teachers had so definitely told her. If so, Alex shudderingly contemplated her doom. But she prayed desperately that there might be nothing after death but utter oblivion. It was then that the thought of death first came to her, not with the wild, impotent longing of her days of struggle, but with an insidious suggestion of rest and escape.

She played with the idea, but for the most part her faculties were absorbed in the increasing strain of waiting for Cedric's reply to her confession.

It came in the shape of a telegram:

'Shall be in London Wednesday 24th will you lunch Clevedon Square 1.30 Reply paid.'

Alex felt an unreasonable relief, both at the postponement of an immediate crisis, and at the reflection that, at all events, Cedric did not mean to come to Malden Road. She did not want him to see those strange, sordid surroundings to which she had fled from the shelter of her old home.

Alex telegraphed an affirmative reply to her brother, and waited in growing apathy for the interview, which she could now only dread in theory. Her sense of feeling seemed numbed at last.

Something of the old terror, however, revived when she confronted Cedric again in the library. He greeted her with a sort of kindly seriousness, under which she wonderingly detected a certain nervousness. During lunch they spoke of Violet, of the shooting that Cedric had been enjoying in Scotland. The slight shade of pomposity which recalled Sir Francis was always discernible in all Cedric's kindly courtesy as host. After lunch he rather ceremoniously ushered his sister into the library again.

'Sit down, my dear – you look tired. You don't smoke, I know. D'you mind if I – ?'

He drew at his pipe once or twice, then carefully rammed

the tobacco more tightly into the bowl with a nicotine-stained finger. Still gazing at the wedged black mass, he said in a voice of careful unconcern:

'About this move of yours, Alex. Violet and I couldn't altogether understand – That's really what brought me down, and the question of that cheque I gave you for the servants. I couldn't quite make out your letter – '

He paused, as though to give her an opportunity for speech, still looking away from her. But Alex remained silent, in a sort of paralysis.

'Suppose we take one question at a time,' suggested Cedric pleasantly. 'The cheque affair is, of course, a very small one, and quite easily cleared up. One only has to be scrupulous in money matters because they are money matters – you know father's way of thinking, and I must say I entirely share it.'

There was no need to tell Alex so.

'Have you got the cheque with you, Alex?'

'No,' said Alex at last. 'Didn't you understand my letter, then?'

Cedric's spectacles began to tap slowly against the back of his left hand, held in the loose grasp of his right.

'You – er – cashed that cheque?'

'Yes.'

Alex felt as though she were being put to the torture of the Inquisition, but was utterly unable to do more than reply in monosyllables to Cedric's level, judicial questions.

'May I ask to what purpose you applied the money?'

'Cedric, it's not fair!' broke from Alex. 'I've written and

told you what I did – I needed money, and I – I thought you wouldn't mind. I used it for myself – and I meant to write and tell you – '

'You thought I wouldn't mind!' repeated Cedric in tones of stupefaction.

'You said you would advance me money – I knew you could write another cheque for the servants' wages. I – I didn't think of your minding.'

'*Mind!*' said Cedric again, with reiteration worthy of his nursery days. 'My dear girl, you don't suppose it's the money I mind, do you?'

'No, no – I ought to have asked you first – but I didn't think – it seemed a natural thing to do – '

'Good Lord, Alex!' cried Cedric, more moved than she had ever seen him. 'Do you understand what you're saying? A natural thing to do to *embezzle money?*'

Tears of terror and of utter bewilderment seized on Alex' enfeebled powers and deprived her of utterance.

Cedric began to pace the library, speaking rapidly and without looking at her.

'If you'd only written and told me what you'd done at once – though Heaven knows that would have been bad enough – but to do a thing like that and then let it rest! Didn't you know that it *must* be found out sooner or later?'

He cast a fleeting glance at Alex, who sat with the tears pouring down her quivering face, but she said nothing. It was of no use to explain to Cedric that she had never thought of not being found out. She had meant no concealment. She had thought her action so simple a one that it had hardly needed explanation or justification. It had merely been not worthwhile to write.

Cedric's voice went on, gradually gaining in power as the agitation that had shaken him subsided under his own fluency.

'You know that it's a prosecutable offence, Alex? Of course, there's no question of such a thing, but to trade on that certainty – '

Alex made an inarticulate sound.

'Violet says of course you didn't know what you were doing. That wretched place – that convent – has played havoc with you altogether. When I think of those people – ' Cedric's face darkened. 'But hang it, Alex, you were brought up like the rest of us. And on a question of honour – think of father!'

Alex had stopped crying. She was about to make her last stand, with the last strength that in her lay.

'Cedric – listen to me. You must! You don't understand. I didn't look at it from your point of view – I didn't see it like that. There's something wrong with me – there must be – but it didn't seem to me to matter. I know you won't believe me – but I thought the money was quite a little, unimportant thing, and that you'd understand, and say I'd done right to take it for granted that I might have it.'

'But it's *not* the money!' groaned Cedric. 'Though what on earth you wanted it for, when you had no expenses and your allowance just paid in – But that's not the point. Can't you see, Alex? It's not this wretched cheque in itself; it's the principle of the thing.'

Alex gazed at him quite hopelessly. The flickering spark of spirit died out and left her soul in darkness.

Cedric faced her.

'I couldn't believe that your letter really meant what it seemed to mean,' he said slowly; 'but if it does – as on your own showing it does – then I understand your leaving us, needless to say. Where are you living – what is this place, Malden Road?'

Characteristically, he drew out her letter, and referred to the address carefully.

'Where is Malden Road?'

'In Hampstead – near Barbara.'

'Are you in rooms?'

' Yes.'

'How did you find them? Who recommended them?'

She made no answer, and Cedric gazed at her with an expression of half-angry, half-compassionate perplexity.

'You are entitled to keep your own counsel, of course, and to make your own arrangements, but I must say, Alex, that the thought of you disturbs me very much. Your whole position is unusual – and your attitude makes it almost impossible to – ' He broke off. 'Violet begged me – quite unnecessarily, but you know what she is – not to let you feel as though there were any estrangement – to say that whatever arrangement you preferred should be made. Of course, Pamela's marriage will add to your resources – you understand that? She is marrying an extremely wealthy man, and I shall have not the slightest hesitation in allowing her to make over her share of father's money to you as soon as it can be arranged. She wishes it herself.'

He paused, as though for some expression of gratitude from Alex, but she made none. Pam had everything, and now she was to have the credit and pleasure of a generosity which would cost her nothing as well. Alex maintained a bitter silence.

'The obvious course is for you to join Barbara, paying your half of expenses, as you will now be enabled to do.'

'Barbara doesn't want me.'

'It is the natural arrangement,' repeated Cedric inflexibly. 'And I must add, Alex, that you seem to me to be terribly unfitted to manage your own life in any way. If what you have told me is the case, I can only infer that your moral sense is completely perverted. I couldn't have believed it of one of us – of one of my father's children.'

Alex knew that the bed-rock of Cedric's character was reached. She had come to the point where, for Cedric, right and wrong began and ended – honour.

They would never get any nearer to one another now. The fundamental principle which governed life for Cedric was deficient in Alex.

She got up slowly and began to pull on her shabby gloves.

'Will you forgive me, Cedric?' she half sobbed.

'It isn't a question of forgiveness. Of course I will. But if you'd only asked me for that wretched money, Alex! What you did was to embezzle it – neither more nor less. Oh, good Lord!'

He looked at her with fresh despair, and then rang the bell.

'You're going to have a taxi,' he told her authoritatively. 'You're not fit to go any other way. Alex, my dear, I'd give my right hand for this not to have happened – for Heaven's sake come to me if you want anything. How much shall I give you now?'

He unlocked the writing-table drawer agitatedly. Alex thought to herself hysterically, 'He thinks I may *steal* money, perhaps, from somebody else, if I want it, and *perhaps I should.*' And with a sense of degradation that made her feel physically sick, she put into her purse the gold and the pile of silver that he pushed into her hand.

Cedric straightened himself, and taking off his glasses, wiped them carefully.

'Write to me, Alex, and let me know what you want to do. Barbara will be back soon – you *must* go to her – at any rate for a time – till after Pamela's wedding. You know that's fixed for December now? And, my dear, for Heaven's sake let's forget this ghastly business. No one on this earth but you and I and Violet need ever know of it.'

'No,' said Alex.

She looked at him with despair invading her whole being.

'Good-bye, Cedric. You've been very, very kind to me.'

'The taxi is at the door, sir.'

'Thank you.'

Cedric took his sister into the hall, and she gave a curious, fleeting glance round her at the familiar surroundings, and at the broad staircase where the Clare children had run up and down and played and quarrelled together, in that other existence.

'Goodbye, dear. Write your plans, and come and see us as soon as we get back. It won't be more than a week or two now.'

Cedric put her into the waiting taxi, and stood on the steps looking after her as the cab turned out of Clevedon Square. And Alex, crouched into a corner of the swiftly-moving taxi, knew herself capable of any treachery, any moral infamy to which she might be tempted, since Cedric had been right when he said that her sense of honour, of fundamental rectitude, was completely perverted.

CHAPTER TWENTY-NINE

FORGIVENESS

The weather broke suddenly, and it became cold and rainy. For two or three days Alex sat in her sitting-room at Malden Road and heard the trams and the omnibuses clash past, and the children screaming to one another in the street. She could hardly have said when she had first realized that it was impossible for her to go on living. But the determination, now that it was there, full-grown, had brought with it a sense of utter finality.

For two or three days she felt stunned, and yet driven by a desperate feeling that it was necessary for her to think, to make a plan. But she could not think.

Then one evening Mrs. Hoxton, the landlady, said to her curiously:

'Wouldn't you like a fire tonight?' She seldom said 'Miss' in speaking to Alex. 'It's so chilly, all of a sudden, and you look ill, really, now, you do.'

Alex felt rather surprised. Perhaps she was ill, which would account for the impossibility of consecutive thought. A fire would be very nice. She shivered involuntarily, looking at her little empty grate crammed with cut paper. She remembered that there was no need to consider expense any more.

'Yes, I'd like a fire, please,' she said gently. And that evening she sat close to the pleasant blaze flickering on the wall, and dimly recalling to her the nursery at Clevedon Square in the old days, and the power of thought came back to her.

It was as though the warmth and companionship of the flames had suddenly unsealed something frozen up within her, and she became more herself than she had been for many months. With the horrible, pressing dread of an unbearable present and an unimaginable future lifted from her heart, Alex felt a pervading lucidity of thought, to which she had for years been a stranger, take possession of her. She knew suddenly that she was, for a little while, to regain faculties that had been atrophied within her since the far, free days of her girlhood. She began to reflect.

Why had life, to which she had looked forward so eagerly, with such confident anticipation of some wonderful happiness, which should be in proportion to the immense capacity for realizing it which she knew to exist within her, have proved to be only a succession of defeats, of receding hopes and of unfulfilled desires?

Alex did not question that the fault lay with herself. From her baby days, under the unvarnished plain speaking of old Nurse, she had known herself to be the black sheep of every flock. And she had not sinned splendidly, dramatically, either. Her sins had been those of petty meanness, of shirking and evading, of small self-indulgences and childish tyranny at the expense of others, of vulgar lies and half-truths; those sins which find little or no place in the decalogue, and which stand lowest in the scale by which the opinion of others is meted out to us.

Those are the things which are not forgiven. That was it, Alex told herself, with a feeling of having suddenly struck the keynote. Forgiveness.

Forgiveness was the key to everything. Alex, in the sudden surety of vision that had come to her, did not doubt that her own interpretation of the word was the right one. Forgiveness meant understanding – not condemnation and subsequent pardon. It did not mean the bewildered, scandalized, and yet regretful oblivion to which Cedric would consign her memory and that of her many failings; it did not mean Barbara's detached, indifferent kindness, carefully measured in terms of material resources, nor Pamela's and Archie's good-natured patronage, half-stifled in mirth, of which the very object was the gulf that separated them from their sister. It did not even mean Violet's soft pity and unresentful acceptance of facts that amazed her. Looking further back, Alex knew that it did not mean either the serious, perplexed pardon that Sir Francis had tendered to his troublesome daughter, or Lady Isabel's half-complaining, half-affectionate remonstrances.

It did not in any way occur to her to blame them for a lack of which she had all her life been subconsciously aware in all their forbearance. She told herself, with a fresh sense of enlightenment, that they had not understood because it was in none of them to have yielded to those temptations which had beset and mastered her so easily. Measuring her frailty by their own strength, they had only seen her utter failure in resistance, and been shamed and grieved by it. Alex knew that in herself was another standard of forgiveness; she could never condemn, for the simple reason that she herself had failed, in every sense of the word. Unresentfully, she was able to sum it all up, as it were, when she told herself, 'People who would have resisted temptation themselves, can't understand those who fall – so they can't really forgive. But the bad ones, who know that they have given way all along the line, know that any temptation would have been too strong for them – it's only chance whether it comes their way or not – so they can understand.'

She felt oddly contented, as at having reached a solution.

Later on, her thoughts turned to the past again, and to the childish days when she had been the leading spirit in the Clevedon Square nursery. But the memory of that past, incredible, security and assurance, made her begin to cry, and she wiped away blinding tears, and told herself that she must not give way to them. She did not at first quite know why she must reserve the tiny modicum of strength still left her, but presently she realized that the end which had become inevitable could not be reached without decisive action of her own.

Alex' logic was elementary, and its directness left her no loophole for doubt.

She could endure the plane of existence on which she found herself no longer. If she fled in search of other conditions, it was with full certainty that these could not be less tolerable than those from which she was flying, and at the back of her mind was a strange, growing hope that perhaps that forgiveness of which her mind was full, might be found beyond the veil.

'After all,' thought Alex, 'it's even chances. If religion is all true, then I *must* go to hell, whether I kill myself or not, and if it isn't, then perhaps I shall just go out and know nothing more – ever – or perhaps it will be really a new beginning, and there will be somebody or something who will forgive me, and let me start over again.'

She began to feel rather excited, as though she were about to try an experiment that might best be described as a gamble.

Mrs. Hoxton, coming in with the small supper-tray, looked at her sharply two or three times, and when she had gone away again, Alex, turning to the glass, saw that her eyes were shining and looking enormously large and wide-pupilled.

'I believe I am happy tonight,' she thought wonderingly.

While she ate her supper she tried to make a plan, but the excitement within her was growing steadily, and she could only think out eager self-justification for her own decision.

'It won't hurt anyone else – nobody will mind. In fact, when they've got over the first shock, it will be a relief to them all. They've been very kind – Violet and Cedric – Violet most of all – but they haven't understood. They'd have understood better if I'd been a bad woman – lived with wicked men, or things like that. I suppose I should have done that too, if it had come my way – but then I never had the temptation. I had only little, mean, horrible temptations – and I didn't resist any of them. The other sort of sin would have made me happier – it would have meant a sort of success in a way – but I have been a failure at everything – always.'

Her heart hammering against her side, Alex resolved that in this, her last disgrace, she would not fail.

Making no preparations, no written farewells, she rose presently and went to her room, where she put on her thickest coat and tied a woollen scarf over her head.

Then she went out.

It had stopped raining, and the air was soft and moist. It was a starless night, and when Alex got to the Heath and away from the lighted streets, it was very dark. Underneath her sense of adventure she was conscious of terror – sheer physical terror – and also of the deeper dread that her resolution might fail her.

'I mustn't – I mustn't,' she kept on muttering to herself.

Then, as though reassuring somebody else, 'But it's only like going for a journey – to a quite new place where everything may be different and much, much better . . . or else to sleep, and never any waking up to misery again. . . . Just one dreadful minute or two, perhaps, and then it will all be over . . . only a question of a little physical courage . . . not to struggle . . . like taking gas . . . much easier if one doesn't struggle.'

She was struck by a sudden thought, and said aloud triumphantly, as though she were defeating by her inspiration someone who was urging difficulties upon her:

'I won't give myself any chances. I'll put big stones in my pocket and tie my scarf over my mouth. That'll make it quicker, too.'

When she came to the part of the Heath where the water lay, Alex began to stoop down and hunt for stones. She pounced on each one that seemed larger than its fellows with a sense of pride at her own success, and put them into the pockets of her coat. The moon appeared palely through clouds and then disappeared again, but not before she had taken her bearings.

She was on one of the many wide bridges that span the long pools dotted over the Heath – pools shelving at the sides with an effect of shallowness and deepening suddenly in the middle. Alex threw an indifferent glance at the dark water, and only felt annoyance that so few stones should be loose upon the pathway, and none of them very large ones. When her pockets were filled, she did not think the weight very noticeable.

Then came another evanescent gleam of moonlight, and Alex, still with that sharpening of all her perceptions, noticed that there was a man's figure at the far end of the bridge. He appeared to be stationary, leaning on the parapet and gazing down at the almost invisible pond.

She was conscious of vexation. His presence would surely interfere with her scheme.

For a moment she wondered, detachedly enough, whether she should go away and come back the following evening. But the next instant she recoiled from the thought, as though seeing in it the promptings of her own weakness.

'I am not frightened tonight – at least, hardly at all. If I wait I may never feel like this again. I shall make a failure of it all, and that would be worse than anything. I must do it tonight, while I'm not frightened.'

She was not cold. Walking in her heavy coat had warmed her, and the evening was mild as well as damp. So she waited quietly in the shadow, hoping that the man would presently move away.

The thought crossed her mind, with a certain humour, that the situation held possibilities of romance.

'If it were in a book, he would save me at the last minute and fall in love with me, and it would all end happily. Or he would see me now, and perhaps speak to me, and he would understand all I told him, and persuade me not to. Anyhow, it would all come right.'

She smiled in the darkness.

'But that won't happen to *me*. There never was anyone – and nobody would love me now, especially when they knew all about me.' She remembered the haggard, distorted countenance, with its strange, hunted expression that the looking-glass had shown her – the great, starting eyes with discoloured circles beneath them, and the blackened, prominent teeth, more salient than ever from the thinness of her face.

She could almost have laughed, without any conscious bitterness, at the idea of any romance in connection with her present self.

And yet the girl, Alex Clare, could have loved – had looked forward to love and to happiness as her rights, just as Pamela Clare did now.

But Pamela was different. Everyone was different. No.

It was Alex that was different – that had always been different.

She began to feel less warm, and shivered a little as she waited.

It occurred to her, not with any sense of fear, but with vexation, that her purpose would be far more difficult of achievement if she waited until she was physically chilled.

She looked up at the bridge again, and the figure was still there, at the furthest end. Alex measured the length of the bridge with her eyes.

It was doubtful if he would see her from the furthest end of it, but she reflected matter-of-factly:

'If I jump there will be the noise of a splash – and he might do something – he would try to save me, I suppose – or run for help. It wouldn't be safe. If he would *only* go.'

She became irritated. With a sense of despair she determined to circumvent the motionless, watchful figure.

Moving very quietly and almost soundlessly over the soft, muddy ground, Alex made her way from the path to the bank, and further and further down it till only a short declivity of shelving mud lay between her and the water.

She could feel the brambles catching in her thick coat, as though pulling her back, but she went on, cautiously and steadily. Once or twice she pushed at the low, tangled bushes that impeded her progress, and paused aghast at the rustling that ensued. But from the bridge above her there came no sound.

Within a few steps of the dark water, her feet already sinking ankle-deep into the wet, spongy ground, she stopped.

She realized with wondering joy that, after all, she was not very much afraid. It was as though the self-confidence which had for so long deserted her had come back now to carry her through the last need.

She felt proud, because she knew that for this once she was not going to fail.

She talked to herself in a whisper:

'This one time – just a few minutes when it may be very bad – but remember that it can't last long, and then it'll all be over. And perhaps there'll never be anything more afterwards – like being always asleep, and no one need be vexed or disappointed any more. But perhaps – '

She paused on the thought, and her heart began to beat faster with a hopeful excitement such as she had not known for a very long while.

'Perhaps it will be much better than one imagines possible. Perhaps there'll be real forgiveness and understanding – and then my having done this won't matter. Anyway, I shall know very soon, if only I'm brave just for a few minutes.'

She drew a long breath, then, instinctively stretching her arms straight out before her so as to balance herself, she began to move forward.

The first unmistakable touch of the water round her feet made her gasp and stifle a scream, but she waded on, encouraging herself in a low murmur, as though speaking to a child:

'It's only like going into the sea when one's bathing – pretend it's that, then you won't be frightened. Just straight on – it will be over quite soon – '

She was moving, slowly, but without pause, her hands held out in front of her, the ground still beneath her slipping feet, which felt oddly weighted. Once she began to pull the woollen scarf over her mouth, but with the sense of breathlessness came the beginning of panic, and she tore it away again.

'Go on – coward – coward,' she urged herself. 'Remember what it would mean to make another muddle of this, and to fail.'

The cold invaded her body, and her teeth began to chatter.

For an instant she stood, surrounded by the silent water, cold and terror and the weight of her now sodden skirts paralyzing her, so that she could move neither backwards to the shore nor forward into the blackness in front of her.

'I must,' muttered Alex, and wrenched one foot desperately out of the mud below. With the forward movement, she lost her balance, and her hands clutched instinctively at the water's level. Then the clogging bottom of the pond sheered away suddenly from beneath her, and there was only water, dark and icy and rushing, above and below and all round her.

CHAPTER THIRTY

EPITAPH

They sat round, afterwards, in the Clevedon Square drawing-room – all the people who had helped misguided, erring Alex, according to their lights, or, again, according to their limitations, and who had failed her so completely in the ultimate essential.

Pamela and her lover whispered together in the window.

'After all, you know,' hesitated the girl, 'she had nothing much to live for, poor Alex. She'd got out of touch with all of us – and she had no one of her very own.'

'Not like us.'

His hand closed for an instant over hers.

'There was no reason why she should not have come to us if – if she was in money difficulties,' reiterated Cedric uneasily. He consciously refrained from adding 'again.'

Violet was crying softly, lying back in the depths of a great arm-chair.

'Poor Alex! I never guessed Malden Road was like that. Why *did* she go there? Oh, poor Alex!'

'You were nicer to her than any of us, Violet,' said Archie

gruffly. 'She was awfully fond of you, wasn't she, and of the little kid?'

Barbara, hard and self-contained, gazed round the familiar room. For a moment it seemed to her that they were all children again, sent down from the nursery by old Nurse, on Lady Isabel's At Home afternoon.

Her eyes met those of Cedric, who had taken up his stand against the mantelpiece, in his hand his glasses, which he was shaking with little, judicial jerks.

'Oh, Cedric,' said Barbara, with a sudden catch in her voice, 'don't you remember – Alex was such a *pretty* little girl!'

London, 1917
Bristol, 1918

APPENDIX

The Times Literary Supplement 5 June 1919

The title of CONSEQUENCES (Hodder and Stoughton, 6s. net) is derived from the round game of that name, in which the dramatic purpose of one player is systematically but blindly thwarted by his equally self-centred neighbour. Miss E.M. Delafield has written the story of a thwarted life. Alex Clare was a pot marred in the making, some elements – for instance, the glaze that gives protection as well as service-ableness – having been left out of her composition. That in spite of her disabilities and angularities she might have become a happy and useful woman if she had met wih more sympathy, it is, we imagine, the purpose of the story to show.

It is to lack of sympathy that Alex herself would attribute her failure; but she contributed too much to her own undoing to take a high place in the immaculate ranks of the misunderstood. Nor did she , poor soul, even attain eminence as a sinner. Her faults , exasperating though they were, seldom amounted to sins of commission; they sprang from self-consciouness and irresolution – from an inability to say and do the right thing at the right time, that was due partly to egotism and obstinacy, and still more perhaps to mere clumsiness and lack of perception. Nothing went right with her. After being branded as the black sheep of her aristocratic nursery, she alienated her parents by breaking off her engagement with an eligible man whom she found (and could not help finding) too stupid to be tolerable. She then sought from God what had been denied her by man; but failed to find tranquillity in her convent. After ten years, with much humiliation, she demanded and obtained her release from her strict Order. Returning as a religious outcast to a world where there was no place for her, she estranged such friends and relations as were prepared to tolerate a *gauche* and penniless woman by committing embezzlement – an action too imbecile in the circumstances to deserve censure. Every thread that bound her to life being thus cut, she drowned herself.

It will be gathered that in a negative way she did not lack character. Her history was one of innocent but reckless attachments. In her scale of values only the personal element counted. She hung first on one person and then on another; and being incapable of inspiring the romantic fervour for which she craved she suffered disappointment after disappointment. She suffered from the aimlessness of a Victorian education; she suffered from the knowledge that she was a failure in the eyes of her parents if she did not attract young men; most of all, she suffered from the spiritual loneliness of the convent. It was under the influence of a certain Mother Gertrude that she became a nun; and when her prop was removed from her by a turn of the ecclesiastical machine, it was borne in on her that she was without the religious feeling which would have replaced the human intercourse forbidden by convent rules.

The character of Alex is drawn with subtlety and insight, and with the kind of detached comprehension with which one credits Mother Gertrude; but it develops in accordance with a cast-iron scheme in which all things and all persons are too exclusively designed for her discomfiture. No single incident, except the embezzlement, is in the least improbable; no single person but might have behaved to Alex, as represented. But there is an element of exaggeration about the whole. Collectively the incidents suggest a deliberately malignant fate; and the behaviour of the people to Alex is not easily reconcilable with their behaviour to one another. All of us have known an Alex – the name is applicable to both sexes – many of us have tried to help her, and the vast majority have given her up as making too great a demand on energies that could be more profitably employed on more responsive material. Alex is so abnormal, so little adaptable that we accept her fate without thinking the harder of this rough-and-ready world. There was no place for her in its economy. Her hold on the universal – and that is the common ground where readers and characters in fiction meet – is that she displays an emotional egotism frequently met with in less fatal proportions.

Miss Delafield's three previous novels, *Zella Sees Herself*, *The War Workers* and *The Pelicans* have made her well known among lovers of English fiction and seekers after the unusual in this country [America]. As the daughter of Lady Clifford, whose novels, published before her second mariage while she was writing as Mrs Henry De La Pasture, have been widely read in both England and the United States, an immediate interest in her books would have awaited her. But with characteristic English independence she chose to forego all this possible prestige and to win whatever interest and acclaim might be her fortune solely upon her own merits. Accordingly she disguised her name sufficiently to conceal her family connection, and as E.M. Delafield has made her appeal to the reading public. Since her first novel was published, two years ago, her pen has been busy, and critics have noted in each new book an increasing surety of touch and widening of outlook.

This new story goes back for its scene to the England of the middle and late nineties and comes to its tragic end ten years later. The central character, for whose depiction and for the working out of whose destiny the novel seems to have been written, is the eldest daughter of a wealthy and aristocratic family, Alex Clare, who had the misfortune of being a neurotic young girl before science and society had discovered how profoundly interesting and important neurotics are. She has boundless possibilities of emotional life and an ardent desire to worship somebody, almost anybody who will permit her devotion, without the ability to inspire corresponding feeling in return. In consquence, from her childhood until her death she is constantly being hurt, defeated, made to feel that there is no place, no purpose for her in the world. The repression and rigidity that seem to have characterised English life down to the end of the last century are vividly portrayed in the depiction of the childhood and growth of Alex Clare and her brothers and sisters. In common with nearly all English novels that bring in children and their relation to their parents, *Consequences* inspires and nourishes the conviction that English boys and girls must be the most disagreeable brats in the world and their fathers and mothers the most unfeeling, uninterested, unsympathetic and cold-hearted parents to be found anywhere – a conviction that actual acquaintance never bears out.

It is a brilliantly and convincingly painted panorama of the life and growth of one family, with Alex, the oldest child, always in the foreground, that Miss Delafield gives us, but one cannot repress the wondering question if even Victorian days ever produced just such a family. One feels very sceptical also as to the truth to life of the earnest young egotist who wants Alex Clare to marry him and during their engagement of several weeks never more than coldly brushes her cheeks with his lips, and that but once. One strongly suspects him of being thus caricatured for the sake of emphasising Alex's inability to inspire feeling as, in short, a necessity of the scheme of the story. Alex finally tries to find an outlet for her emotional nature in a convent, chiefly because the Mother Superior has won for the moment her wandering and unrequited affections. But there, too, after the lapse of some years, she finds disappointment and defeat.

The book has its social and psychological implications in its suggestion for the thoughtful reader of the tremendous waste of human energy in such a society as that portrayed. One feels that it was largely from such neurotic, defeated womanhood, chafing against its uselessness, as is represented in Alex Clare, that the militant suffragists recruited their explosive forces in the years before the war. It must be said of Miss Delafield that she employs the English language frequently without appreciation of its niceties of meaning, as when, for instance, she uses 'infinitely', that adverb of limitless significance, for all manner of petty and common-place purposes, as 'infinitely better cooked food'.

If you have enjoyed this Persephone book why not telephone or write to us for a free copy of the Persephone Catalogue and the current Persephone Quarterly? All Persephone books ordered from us cost £10 or three for £27 plus £2 postage per book.

PERSEPHONE BOOKS LTD
59 Lamb's Conduit Street
London WC1N 3NB

Telephone: 020 7242 9292
Fax: 020 7242 9272
sales@persephonebooks.co.uk
www.persephonebooks.co.uk

Persephone Books publishes forgotten fiction and non-fiction by unjustly neglected authors. The following titles are available: